Praise for

THE MADNESS OF LORD IAN MACKENZIE

"Ever-versatile Ashley begins her new Victorian Highland Pleasures series with a deliciously dark and delectably sexy story of love and romantic redemption that will captivate readers with its complex characters and suspenseful plot." —*Booklist*

"Ashley's enthralling and poignant romance . . . touches readers on many levels. Brava!" —*Romantic Times*

"Mysterious, heartfelt, sensitive, and sensual . . . Two big thumbs up." —*Publishers Weekly*'s Beyond Her Book

"A story of mystery and intrigue with two wonderful, bright characters you'll love . . . I look forward to more from Jennifer Ashley, an extremely gifted author." —*Fresh Fiction*

"Brimming with mystery, suspense, an intriguing plot, villains, romance, a tormented hero, and a feisty heroine, this book is a winner. I recommend *The Madness of Lord Ian Mackenzie* to anyone looking for a great read." —*Romance Junkies*

"Wow! All I can say is *The Madness of Lord Ian Mackenzie* is one of the best books I have ever read. [It] gets the highest recommendation that I can give. It is a truly wonderful book." —*Once Upon A Romance*

"When you're reading a book that is a step or two—or six or seven—above the norm, you know it almost immediately. Such is the case with *The Madness of Lord Ian Mackenzie*. The characters here are so complex and so real that I was fascinated by their journey . . . [and] this story is as flat-out romantic as any I've read in a while . . . This is a series I am certainly looking forward to following." —*All About Romance*

"A unique twist on the troubled hero . . . Fresh and interesting." —*Night Owl Romance*

"A welcome addition to the genre." —*Dear Author*

"Intriguing . . . Unique . . . Terrific." —*Midwest Book Review*

Lady Isabella's Scandalous Marriage

JENNIFER ASHLEY

BERKLEY SENSATION, NEW YORK

THE BERKLEY PUBLISHING GROUP
Published by the Penguin Group
Penguin Group (USA) Inc.
375 Hudson Street, New York, New York 10014, USA

Penguin Group (Canada), 90 Eglinton Avenue East, Suite 700, Toronto, Ontario M4P 2Y3, Canada
(a division of Pearson Penguin Canada Inc.)
Penguin Books Ltd., 80 Strand, London WC2R 0RL, England
Penguin Group Ireland, 25 St. Stephen's Green, Dublin 2, Ireland (a division of Penguin Books Ltd.)
Penguin Group (Australia), 250 Camberwell Road, Camberwell, Victoria 3124, Australia
(a division of Pearson Australia Group Pty. Ltd.)
Penguin Books India Pvt. Ltd., 11 Community Centre, Panchsheel Park, New Delhi—110 017, India
Penguin Group (NZ), 67 Apollo Drive, Rosedale, North Shore 0632, New Zealand
(a division of Pearson New Zealand Ltd.)
Penguin Books (South Africa) (Pty.) Ltd., 24 Sturdee Avenue, Rosebank, Johannesburg 2196,
South Africa

Penguin Books Ltd., Registered Offices: 80 Strand, London WC2R 0RL, England

This is a work of fiction. Names, characters, places, and incidents either are the product of the author's imagination or are used fictitiously, and any resemblance to actual persons, living or dead, business establishments, events, or locales is entirely coincidental. The publisher does not have any control over and does not assume any responsibility for author or third-party websites or their content.

LADY ISABELLA'S SCANDALOUS MARRIAGE

A Berkley Sensation Book / published by arrangement with the author

PRINTING HISTORY
Berkley Sensation mass-market edition / July 2010

Copyright © 2010 by Jennifer Ashley.
Excerpt from *The Many Sins of Lord Cameron* by Jennifer Ashley copyright © by Jennifer Ashley.
Cover art by Gregg Gulbronson.
Cover design by George Long.
Cover hand lettering by Ron Zinn.
Interior text design by Laura K. Corless.

ISBN: 978-0-425-23545-4

BERKLEY® SENSATION
Berkley Sensation Books are published by The Berkley Publishing Group,
a division of Penguin Group (USA) Inc.,
375 Hudson Street, New York, New York 10014.
BERKLEY® SENSATION and the "B" design are trademarks of Penguin Group (USA) Inc.

PRINTED IN THE UNITED STATES OF AMERICA

10 9 8 7 6 5 4 3 2 1

Thanks go to my editor, Kate Seaver, and editorial assistant, Katherine Pelz, for all their efforts in support of this book. Also to those at Berkley who do so much work "behind the scenes" to take a book from manuscript to printed novel.

And as always, to my husband, Forrest, for being there.

Chapter 1

All of London was amazed to learn of the sudden marriage of
Lady I— S— and Lord M— M—, brother of the Duke of K—, last
evening. The lady in question had her Come-Out and her Wedding the same night, leading debutantes to plead with fathers to
make their coming-out balls just as eventful.

—*From a London society newspaper, February 1875*

SEPTEMBER 1881

Isabella's footman rang the bell at the house of Lord Mac
Mackenzie on Mount Street, while Isabella waited in the
landau, wondering for the dozenth time since she'd set off
whether this were wise.

Perhaps Mac would be out. Maybe the unpredictable
man had gone off to Paris, or to Italy, where summer would
linger for a time. She could investigate the matter she'd
discovered by herself. Yes, that would be best.

As she opened her mouth to call back her footman, the
large black door swung open, and Mac's valet, a former
pugilist, peered out. Isabella's heart sank. Bellamy being
here meant Mac was here, because Bellamy never strayed
far from Mac's side.

Bellamy peered into the landau, and a look of undisguised astonishment crossed his scarred face. Isabella

hadn't approached this house since the day she'd left it three and a half years ago. "M'lady?"

Isabella took Bellamy's beefy hand to steady herself as she descended. The best way to do this, she decided, was simply to do it.

"How is your knee, Bellamy?" she asked. "Are you still using the liniment? Is it too much to hope that my husband is at home?"

As she talked, she breezed into the house, pretending not to notice the parlor maid and a footman popping out to stare.

"The knee's much better, m'lady. Thank you. His lordship is . . ." Bellamy hesitated. "He's painting, m'lady."

"So early? There's a wonder." Isabella started up the stairs at a quick pace, not letting herself think about what she was doing. If she thought about it, she'd run far and fast, perhaps lock herself into her house and not come out. "Is he in his studio? No need to announce me. I'll go up myself."

"But m'lady." Bellamy followed her, but his damaged knee wouldn't let him move quickly, and Isabella reached the landing, three floors up, before Bellamy had mounted the second flight.

"M'lady, he said not to be disturbed," Bellamy called upward.

"I won't be long. I need only ask him a question."

"But, m'lady, he's . . ."

Isabella paused, hand on the white doorknob of the right-hand attic room. "I shall take full blame for invading his lordship's privacy, Bellamy."

She lifted her skirts as she swung open the door and walked into the room. Mac was there, all right, standing in front of a long easel, painting with fervor.

Isabella's skirts slid from her nerveless fingers, the beauty of her estranged husband striking her like a blow. Mac wore a kilt, threadbare and paint-flecked, and he was naked from the waist up. Though it was cool in the studio, Mac's torso gleamed with sweat, his skin tanned from spending the summer on the warmer Continent. He wore a red kerchief on his head, gypsy style, to keep paint out of his hair. He'd always done that, she remembered with a pang. It made his cheekbones more prominent, emphasized the handsomeness of his face. Even the rough boots, much worn and paint-splotched, were familiar and dear.

Mac laid paint on his canvas with energy, obviously not hearing Isabella open the door. He held the palette in his left hand, arm muscles tight, while his right moved the brush in swift, jerking strokes. Mac was a stunning man, made still more attractive when absorbed in doing something he loved.

Isabella used to sit in this very studio on an old sofa strewn with cushions, simply watching him paint. Mac might not say one word to her while he worked, but she had adored watching the play of muscles on his back, the way he'd smear paint on his cheek when he'd absently rub it. After a particularly good session, he'd turn to her with a wide smile and pull her into his arms, never minding that paint now smeared all over *her* skin.

So absorbed in Mac was she that Isabella didn't notice what he painted with such intensity until she forced herself to look away from him and across the room. She barely stifled her dismay.

A young woman lay on a raised platform draped with yellow and red coverings. She was nude, which came as no surprise—Mac generally painted women who wore nothing or very little. But Isabella had never seen him paint anything so blatantly erotic. The model lay on her back with her knees bent, her legs wide apart. Her hand rested on her private place, and she was spreading herself open without shame. Mac scowled at the offering and painted with rapid brushstrokes.

Behind Isabella, Bellamy reached the top landing, puffing from exertion and distress. Mac heard him and growled but didn't look 'round.

"Damn it, Bellamy, I told you I didn't want to be disturbed this morning."

"I'm sorry, sir. I couldn't stop her."

The model raised her head, spied Isabella, and grinned. "Oh, hello, yer ladyship."

Mac glanced behind him once, twice, then his copper gaze riveted to Isabella. Paint dripped, unheeded, from his brush to the floor.

Isabella strove to keep her voice from shaking. "Hello, Molly. How is your little boy? It's all right, Bellamy, you can leave us. This won't take long, Mac. I only came to ask you a question."

Damnation.

What the hell was Bellamy playing at, letting her up here?

Isabella hadn't set foot in the Mount Street house in three and a half years, not since the day she'd left him with nothing but a short letter for explanation. Now she stood in the doorway, in hat and gloves donned for calling. Today of all days, while Mac painted Molly Bates in her spread glory. This wasn't part of his plan, the one that had made him leap onto a train to London after his brother's wedding and follow Isabella down here from Scotland. He'd call this a grievous miscalculation.

Isabella's dark blue jacket hugged her torso and cupped her full bosom, and a gray skirt of complicated ruffles spread over a small bustle. Her hat was a concoction of flowers and ribbons, her gloves a dark gray that wouldn't show London grime. The gloves outlined slender fingers he wanted to kiss, hands he longed to have slide up his back as they lay together in bed.

Isabella had always known how to dress, how to present herself in colors dear to his artist's eye. Mac had loved to help her dress in the mornings, lacing her gowns against her soft, sweet-smelling skin. He'd dismiss her maid and perform the tasks himself, though those mornings it had taken them a long time to descend for breakfast.

Now Mac drank in every inch of her, and *damn it*, grew hard. Would she see, and would she laugh?

Isabella crossed to the dressing gown Molly had left in a heap on the floor. "You'd better wrap up in this, dear," she said to the model. "It's chilly up here. You know Mac never believes in feeding the fire. Why don't you warm up downstairs with a nice cup of tea while I have a chat with my husband?"

Molly leapt to her feet, her grin wide. Molly was a beautiful female in the way many men liked—large-bosomed, round-hipped, doe-eyed. She had a mass of black hair and a perfect face, an artist's dream. But next to the glory of Isabella, Molly faded to nothing.

"Don't mind if I do," Molly said. "It's stiff work posing for naughty pictures. My fingers are that cramped."

"Some teacakes ought to loosen you again," Isabella said as Molly slid on the dressing gown. "Mac's cook always used to keep currant ones in large supply, in case of emergencies. Ask her if she still does."

Molly's dimples showed. "I've missed you, no lie, your ladyship. 'Is lordship forgets we 'ave to eat."

"It's his lordship's way," Isabella said. Molly strolled from the studio without worry, and Mac watched as though from far away as Bellamy followed Molly out and closed the door.

Isabella turned her lush green eyes to him. "You're dripping."

"What?" Mac stared at her then heard a glob of paint hit his board floor. He let out a growl, slammed the palette onto the table, and thrust the brush into a jar of oil of turpentine.

"You've begun early today," Isabella said.

Why did she keep on in that friendly, neutral voice, as though they were acquaintances at a tea party?

"The light was good." His own voice sounded stiff, harsh.

"Yes, it's a sunny morning for a change. Don't worry, I'll let you get back to it soon. I only want your opinion."

Blast her, had she come here to throw him off guard on purpose? When had she gotten so good at the game?

"My opinion on what?" he asked. "Your new hat?"

"Not my hat, although thank you for noticing. No, I want your opinion on this."

Mac found the hat in question right under his nose. Gray and blue ribbons trailed into glossy curls that beckoned to be lifted, smoothed.

The hat tilted back until he was looking into Isabella's eyes, eyes that had snared him across a ballroom so long ago. She hadn't been aware of her power then, the sweet debutante, and she didn't know it now. Her simple look of inquiry, of interest, could pin a man and give him the most erotic dreams imaginable.

"On this, Mac," she said impatiently.

She was lifting a handkerchief toward him. In the middle of its snowy whiteness lay a piece of yellow-covered canvas about an inch long and a quarter inch wide.

"What color would you say this was?" she asked.

"Yellow." Mac quirked a brow. "You drove all the way here from North Audley Street to ask me whether something is yellow?"

"Of course I know it's yellow. What kind of yellow, specifically?"

Mac peered at it. The color was vibrant, almost pulsing. "Cadmium yellow."

"More specific than that?" She wiggled the handkerchief as though the motion would reveal the mystery. "Don't you understand? It's *Mackenzie* yellow. That astonishing yellow you mix for your paintings, the secret formula known only to you."

"Yes, so it is." With Isabella standing so close to him, her heady scent in his nostrils, he didn't give a damn if the paint was Mackenzie yellow or graveyard black. "Have you been amusing yourself slicing up my pictures?"

"Don't be silly. I took this from a painting hanging in Mrs. Leigh-Waters's drawing room in Richmond."

Curiosity trickled through Mac's impatience. "I've never given a painting to Mrs. Leigh-Waters of Richmond."

"I didn't think you had. When I asked her about it, she told me she bought the picture from an art dealer in the Strand. Mr. Crane."

"The devil she did. I don't sell my paintings, especially not through Crane."

"Exactly." Isabella smiled in triumph, the red curve of her lips doing nothing to ease his arousal. "The painting is signed *Mac Mackenzie*, but you didn't paint it."

Mac looked again at the strip of brilliant yellow on the handkerchief. "How do you know I didn't paint it? Maybe some ungrateful blackguard I gave a picture to sold it to raise money to pay a debt."

"It's a scene from a hill, overlooking Rome."

"I've done many scenes overlooking Rome."

"I know that, but this wasn't one of yours. It's your style, your brushwork, your colors, but you didn't paint it."

Mac pushed the handkerchief back at her. "How do you know? Are you intimately acquainted with all my works? I've painted quite a few Rome pictures since you . . ." He couldn't bring himself to say "since you left me." He'd gone to Rome to soothe his broken heart, painting the bloody vista day after day. He'd done too damn many pictures of Rome, until he'd grown sick of the place. Then he'd moved to Venice and painted it until he never wanted to see another gondola as long as he lived.

That was when he'd still been a debauched, drunken sot. Once he'd sobered up, replacing his obsession for single-malt with one of tea, he'd retreated to Scotland and stayed put. The Mackenzies didn't view whiskey as strong drink—they viewed it as essential to life—but Mac's drink of choice had changed to oolong, which Bellamy had learned to brew like a master.

At his words, Isabella flushed, and Mac felt a flash of sudden glee. "Ah, so you *are* intimately acquainted with everything I've painted. Kind of you to take an interest."

Her blush deepened. "I see notices in art journals, is all, and people tell me."

"And you've become so familiar with each of my pictures that you know when I didn't paint one?" Mac gave her a slow smile. "This from a woman who changed her hotel when she knew I was staying in it?"

Mac hadn't thought Isabella could grow any more red. He felt the dynamics in the room change, from Isabella in a bold frontal attack to Isabella in hasty retreat.

"Don't flatter yourself. I happen to notice things, is all."

And yet she'd known straightaway that he hadn't painted what she'd seen in Mrs. Leigh-Waters's drawing room. He grinned, liking her confusion.

"What I'm trying to tell you is that someone out there is forging Mac Mackenzies," Isabella said impatiently.

"Why would anybody be fool enough to forge something by me?"

"For the money, of course. You are very popular."

"I'm popular because I'm scandalous," Mac countered. "When I die, the paintings will be worthless, except as souvenirs." He set the slice of paint and handkerchief on the table. "May I keep this? Or do you plan to restore it to Mrs. Leigh-Waters?"

"Don't be silly. I didn't tell her I was taking it."

"You left the painting on her wall with a bit sliced out, did you? Won't she notice that?"

"The picture is high up, and I did it carefully so it doesn't show." Isabella's gaze moved to the painting on his easel. "That is quite repulsive, you know. She looks like a spider."

Mac didn't give a damn about the painting, but when he glanced at it he wanted to groan. Isabella was right: It was terrible. All of his paintings were terrible these days. He hadn't been able to paint a decent stroke since he'd gone sober, and he had no idea why he'd thought this one would be any better.

He let out a frustrated roar, picked up a paint-soaked rag, and hurled it at the canvas. The rag landed with a splat on Molly's painted abdomen, and brown-black rivulets ran down the rosy skin.

Mac turned from the picture in time to see Isabella swiftly exiting the room. He sprinted after her and caught up to her halfway down the first flight of stairs. Mac stepped around her, slamming one hand to the banister, the other to the wall. Paint smeared on the wallpaper Isabella had picked out when she'd redecorated his house six years ago.

Isabella gave him a cold look. "Do move, Mac. I have half a dozen errands to attend before luncheon, and I'm already late starting."

Mac took long breaths, trying to still his rage. "Wait. *Please.*" He made himself say the word. "Let us go down to the drawing room. I'll have Bellamy bring tea. We can talk about the paintings you think are forged." Anything to keep her here. He knew in his heart that if she walked away from this house again, she'd never return.

"There is nothing more to say about the forged paintings. I only thought you'd want to know."

Mac was aware that his entire household lurked below, listening. They wouldn't do anything so gauche as peer up the staircase, but they'd be in doorways and in the shadows, waiting to see what happened. They adored Isabella and had mourned the day she'd left them.

"Isabella," he said, pitching his voice low. "Stay."

The tightness around her eyes softened the slightest bit. Mac had hurt her, he knew it. He'd hurt her over and over again. The first step in winning her back was to stop the hurting.

Her lips parted, red and lush. Because he was two steps below her, Isabella's face was on level with his. He could close the few inches between them and kiss her if he chose, feel her mouth on his, taste her warm moisture on his tongue.

"Please," he whispered. *I need you so much.*

Molly chose that moment to climb toward them up the stairs. "Are you ready for me again, yer lordship? You still want me sticking me fingers in me Mary Jane?"

Isabella closed her eyes, her lips thinning into a long, immobile line. Mac's temper splintered.

"Bellamy!" he shouted over the banisters. "What the devil is she doing out of the kitchen?"

Molly came closer, her smile good-natured. "Oh, her ladyship don't mind me. Do you, yer ladyship?" Molly sidled around first Mac, then Isabella, her dressing gown rustling as she headed back up to the studio.

"No, Molly," Isabella said in a cool voice. "I don't mind *you.*"

Isabella lifted her skirt in her gloved hand and prepared to start around Mac. Mac reached for her.

Isabella shrank away. Not in loathing, he realized after

the first frozen heartbeat, but because the hand he stretched toward her was covered in brown and black paint.

Mac slammed himself back against the stair railing. He wouldn't trap her. At least not now, with all his servants watching and listening, and Isabella looking at him in that way.

Isabella moved down the stairs around him, very carefully not touching him.

Mac strode after her. "I'll send Molly home. Stay and have luncheon. My staff can run your errands for you."

"I very much doubt that. Some of my errands are quite personal." Isabella reached the ground floor and took up the parasol she'd left on the hall tree.

Bellamy, don't you dare open that door.

Bellamy swung the door wide, letting in a wash of London's fetid air. Isabella's landau stood outside, her footman ready with the door open.

"Thank you, Bellamy," she said in a serene voice. "Good morning."

She walked out.

Mac wanted to rush after her, grab her around the waist, drag her back into the house. He could have Bellamy lock and bolt the doors so she couldn't leave again. She'd hate him at first, but she'd gradually understand that she still belonged with him. Here.

Mac made himself let Bellamy close the door. Tactics that worked for his barbaric Highland ancestors would be useless on Isabella. She'd give him that cool look from her beautiful eyes and have him on his knees. He had prostrated himself for her often enough in the past. The feeling of carpet on his knees had been worth her sudden laughter, the cool tinge leaving her voice as she said, "Oh, Mac, don't be so absurd." He'd pull her down to the carpet with him, and the forgiveness would take an interesting turn.

Mac sat down heavily on the bottom stair and put his head in his paint-stained hands. Today had been a misstep. Isabella had caught him off guard, and he'd ruined the beautiful opportunity she'd handed him.

"Oh, the painting's all spoiled." Molly hurried from the floors above in a flurry of silk. "Mind you, I think I look a bit funny in it."

"Go on home, Molly," Mac said, his voice hollow. "I'll pay you for the full day."

He expected Molly to squeal in pleasure and hurry off, but instead she sank down next to him. "Oh, poor lamb. Want me to make you feel better?"

Mac's arousal had died, and he didn't want it to rise again for anyone but Isabella. "No," he said. "Thank you."

"Suit yourself." Molly stroked slender fingers through his hair. "It's the absolute worst when they don't love you back, ain't it, me lord?"

"Yes." Mac closed his eyes, his rage and need swirling around him until he was sick with it. "You're right, it is the absolute worst."

Lord and Lady Abercrombie's hunt ball in Surrey the following night was stuffed to the rafters with fashionable people. Isabella entered the ballroom with some trepidation, expecting at any moment to see her husband, who, her maid Evans had informed her, had also received an invitation. Evans had obtained the information directly from her old crony, Bellamy.

Seeing Mac in his studio like a half-naked god yesterday had sent Isabella straight home to fling herself on her bed in tears. Her errands had never got done, because she'd spent the rest of the afternoon curled into a ball feeling sorry for herself.

Isabella had risen the next morning and made herself

face facts. She had two choices—she could completely
avoid Mac as she had in the past, or resign herself to
encountering him about London as they lived their lives.
They could be civil. They could be friends. What she ought
to do was become *so* used to seeing him that his presence
no longer plagued her. Grow inured to him so that her heart
no longer leapt into her throat at one glimpse of his strong
face or the flash of his wicked smile.

The second choice was the more unnerving, but Isabella
berated herself until she stepped up to the task. She would
not hide at home like a frightened rabbit. Hence, her acceptance of Lord Abercrombie's invitation, even though she
knew the odds were high that Mac would attend.

Isabella bade Evans dress her in a new ball gown of blue
satin moiré with yellow silk roses across her bodice and
train. Maude Evans, who could boast having been a dresser
to famous actresses, several opera singers, a duchess, and
a courtesan, had been dressing Isabella since the morning
after Isabella's scandalous elopement with Mac. Evans had
arrived at Mac's house on Mount Street, where Isabella,
Mac's ring heavy on her finger, had stood in her ball gown
from the previous night, having no other clothes at hand.
Evans had taken one look at Isabella's innocent face and
become her fierce protector.

*I look quite acceptable for a matron of nearly five and
twenty.* Isabella surveyed herself in the mirror as Evans
draped diamonds across Isabella's bosom. *I have nothing
to be ashamed of.*

Even so, her heart froze when she entered Lord Abercrombie's ballroom and spied a tall Mackenzie male in the
supper room beyond. Broad shoulders stretched a formal
black coat as he rested an elbow on the fireplace mantel,
his kilt Mackenzie plaid.

Isabella realized in the next heartbeat that the man was
not Mac, but his older brother Cameron. Touched by relief

and delight, she broke from the friends she'd arrived with, caught up her satin skirts, and sped through the crowd to him.

"Cam, what on earth are you doing here? I thought you'd be up north, frantically preparing for the St. Leger."

Cameron tossed the cigar he'd been smoking into the fire, took Isabella's hands, and leaned to kiss her cheek. He smelled of smoke and malt whiskey; he always did, though those were sometimes accompanied by the scent of horses. Cameron kept a stable full of the best racehorses in England.

The second-oldest brother, Cameron was a little larger than Mac, a little broader of shoulder and taller of stature, and a deep scar cut across his left cheekbone. Cam's unruly red-brown hair was the darkest of the four brothers', his eyes more deeply golden. He was known as the black sheep, a daunting task in a family whose exploits filled the scandal sheets. It was common knowledge that Cameron, a widower with a fifteen-year-old son, took a new mistress every six months, having his pick of famous actresses, courtesans, and highborn widows. Isabella had stopped trying to keep track of them long ago.

Cameron shrugged in answer to her question. "Not much more to do. The trainers have my instructions, and I'll meet them there before the first race."

"You're a bad liar, Cameron Mackenzie. Hart sent you, didn't he?"

Cameron didn't bother to look embarrassed. "Hart was worried when Mac raced after you following Ian's wedding. Is he making a nuisance of himself?"

"No," Isabella said quickly. She loved Mac's brothers, but they did tend to stick their noses into each other's business. Not that she wasn't grateful to them—they could have shut her out when she'd decided to leave Mac three and a half years ago, but instead they'd rallied to her side.

Hart, Cameron, and Ian had made it known that they still considered Isabella part of the family. And as she was part of the family, they tended to watch over her like protective older brothers.

"So Hart sent you down to play nanny?" she asked.

"He did," Cameron drawled, straight-faced. "You should see me in my cap and pinafore."

Isabella laughed, and Cam joined her. He had a gravelly laugh, sounding as though something had scratched away at his voice.

"Is Beth well?" she asked. "She and Ian are all right?"

"Fine when I left them. Ian is extremely pleased at the prospect of becoming a father. He mentions it only about once every five minutes."

Isabella smiled in true delight. Ian and Beth, his new wife, were so happy, and Isabella looked forward to holding their little one in her arms. The thought gave her a pang as well, which she quickly suppressed.

"And Daniel?" Isabella went on, keeping the conversation light. "Did he come with you?"

Cameron shook his head. "Daniel is lodging with an old don of mine who is to stuff his head with knowledge before Michaelmas term. I want to give Danny's tutors less cause to beat his lessons into him."

"Lessons instead of horses? I'm certain that rankles our Danny."

"Aye, but if he keeps getting poor marks, he'll never get into university."

He sounded so like a concerned father, this tall man with the dark reputation, that Isabella laughed again. "He tries to emulate you, Cam."

"Aye, he does. That's wh't worries me."

Behind Isabella, the strains of a waltz began, and couples in the ballroom glided into place. Cameron held out his broad arm. "Dance, Isabella?"

"I'd be most happy to—"

Isabella's polite acceptance was cut off when strong fingers closed over her elbow. She smelled Mac's soap and masculine scent overlaid with the faint odor of turpentine.

"This waltz is mine," Mac said in her ear. "And don't bother to tell me your card is full, my wife, because you know I'll make short work of that."

Chapter 2

The Mount Street residence of a famous Scottish Lord and his new Lady has undergone a complete transformation. Privileged guests have reported wallpaper, carpets, and objects d'art of exquisite *taste* and *refinement*, which speaks of the Lady's most gracious upbringing. The guests range from quite a *Parisian* crowd to foreign princes to the lofty ladies who grace our London stages.

—*April 1875*

Isabella was never certain how she reached the ballroom floor without stumbling over her rose-studded train or high-heeled slippers. She heard the music begin, felt Mac's hand cup her waist, felt herself pulled into the sway of the dance. Her ploy of making herself blasé about Mac seemed suddenly ridiculous.

She'd always loved the waltz and had loved best to dance it with Mac. He'd guide her unerringly until she'd forget about the steps and simply flow with the music. She'd float as though she danced on air, safe in the arms of the man she loved.

Tonight, her slippers pinched and her heart banged against too-tight boning. Mac's hand on her waist burned through bodice, corset, and chemise, as though his fingers branded bare skin. His strong legs moving against her skirt heated her body still more.

"You were rude, you know," she said, as though every

step didn't unnerve her. "I was enjoying speaking with Cameron."

"Cameron knows when he's gooseberry."

The picture of Cameron the womanizer as a gooseberry should have been amusing, but Isabella was too distracted by Mac for laughter. She wished she didn't like feeling the play of his shoulder under her hand, the way her fingers were lost in his firm grip. They both wore several layers of clothing, fashion being what it was, but in her opinion, the number of layers wasn't nearly enough.

"I suppose you are pleased with yourself," she said, trying to keep her voice light. "You know I couldn't refuse to dance with you without the scene being repeated all over London. Everyone loves to gossip about us."

"London's insatiable need for gossip is one weapon in my arsenal," Mac said, his voice as smooth as fine wine. "Though not always a reliable one."

Isabella couldn't bring herself to look straight into his eyes. She had enough trouble balancing without letting herself become fixated on those copper irises. Instead, she focused on his chin, which was brushed with red gold whiskers. Remembering she knew what they tasted like did not help.

"Interesting, and a bit insulting, that you talk of what is between us in terms of weapons of war," she said.

"It's an apt metaphor. This ballroom is a battlefield, this dance the engagement, *your* weapon that decadent gown that hugs you so well."

Mac's gaze swept over her off-the-shoulder bodice and rested on the yellow roses at her décolletage. Isabella had favored yellow roses since he'd painted her with them the second day they were married. His eyes darkened, and her exposed skin burned.

"Then another of your weapons is dancing me until my feet hurt," Isabella said. "That and your kilt."

He looked nonplussed. "My kilt?"

"You look particularly fine in a kilt."

Mac's gaze flickered. "Yes, I remember, you always liked looking at my legs. And other parts of my anatomy. Rumor has it that a Scotsman wears nothing at all under his kilt."

Isabella remembered mornings when he'd wear nothing *but* a kilt draped carelessly around his hips, his feet up at the table in their bedroom while he perused the morning paper. Mac was heady enough in formal dress, but in undress, he was devastating.

"You read too much into my statement," Isabella said, voice unsteady.

"Do I? Would you like to come out to the terrace and satisfy your curiosity about the other part?"

"I want to go nowhere near a terrace with *you*, thank you very much." On the terrace at her father's house, after he'd walked into her debut ball without invitation, Mac had kissed her for the first time.

Mac's eyes glinted, a sinful smile touching his mouth. "You fear it a more dangerous battleground?"

"If you must keep on with the war metaphor, then yes, I feel that the terrace would give me a tactical disadvantage."

Mac pulled her the slightest bit closer. "You always have the advantage of me, Isabella."

"I hardly think so. Why should I?"

He tugged her closer still. "Because you can unman me by simply walking into a room—as you did yesterday in my studio. I've lived like a monk for three and a half years, and to see you so close, to smell you, to touch you . . . Have pity on a poor celibate."

"Not pursuing others was your choice."

Mac caught and held her gaze, and finally she looked into his eyes. Behind the teasing sparkle, she saw a quietness she'd never noted before in him.

"Yes," he said. "It was."

Isabella believed him. She could easily name half a dozen women who would leap into bed with Mac Mackenzie the moment he indicated they were welcome. Isabella knew he hadn't pursued women, either before or after she'd left him, because plenty of people would have delighted to tell her so if he had. Even their more spiteful acquaintances had to admit that Mac had remained faithful to his wife, even after their separation.

"Perhaps I should change my perfume," Isabella said.

"It has nothing to do with the perfume." Mac leaned to her, his breath touching the curve between her neck and shoulder. "I like that you still wear attar of roses."

"I am fond of roses," she said faintly.

"I know. Yellow ones."

Isabella tripped again. Mac straightened, his hand tightening on her waist. "Careful."

"I'm clumsy tonight," she said. "These slippers are wretched. May we please sit down?"

"I told you, not until the waltz is over. This dance is my price, and I can't very well let you go when you've only half-paid, can I?"

"Your price for what?"

"For not kissing you senseless in front of all these people. Not to mention yesterday on the stairs."

Isabella's fingers shook. "You would have kissed me yesterday, even though I did not wish it?"

"But you did wish it, my wife. I know you so very well."

Isabella didn't answer, because he had the truth of it. When they'd stood face-to-face on the stairs, in the house they used to share, she'd almost let him kiss her. If Molly hadn't interrupted them, Isabella would have let him take her into his arms and press his paint-stained face to hers, to touch her as much as he liked. But Mac had let her go, his choice.

"Please, may we stop now, Mac? I really am quite warm."

"You do look flushed. There's only one remedy for that."

"A seat and a cool drink?"

"No." A smile spread over his face, the same wicked smile that had destroyed Isabella the debutante more than six years ago. He swung her out of the dance, tucked her arm through his, and led her swiftly across the ballroom and out of the French windows. "A stroll on the terrace."

"Mac."

Mac ignored her protest and propelled them along the length of the chill and dimly lit terrace. He stopped at the end of it, in the shadows beyond the lit windows.

"Now then," he said.

Isabella found herself against the wall, Mac's strong hands on either side of her.

⁓

Isabella's breath was sweet, her body a warm length in the cool air. Her bosom rose against her décolletage, diamonds sparkling on her skin.

They'd stood like this on her father's terrace the night they'd met, Isabella against the wall, Mac's hand splayed on the bricks beside her. Isabella had been eighteen then, her dress virgin white, her only adornment a necklace of pearls. A pure, untouchable maiden with glorious hair, a ripe plum ready to be plucked.

The temptation to touch her had been irresistible. The wager Mac had agreed to that night had been simple—enter the overly priggish Earl Scranton's house without invitation, dance with the prim and proper debutante in whose honor the ball was being held, and entice her to kiss him.

Mac had expected to find a stick-thin maiden with a prissy mouth and irritating mannerisms. Instead, he'd found Isabella.

It had been like discovering a butterfly among colorless moths. The instant Mac had seen Isabella, he'd wanted to know her, to talk to her, to learn everything about her. He remembered how she'd watched him push through the crowded ballroom toward her, her chin lifted, her green eyes daring him to do his worst. Her friends had whispered behind her, no doubt warning her who he was, hoping to watch her rebuff the scandalous Lord Roland "Mac" Mackenzie. Isabella, Mac had come to know, was quite good at the rebuff.

He'd stopped before her, and without saying a word, Isabella had taken his breath away. Her hair spilled over her shoulder in a river of red, her eyes glinted with cool intelligence, and he'd wanted her. To dance with her, to paint her, to make love to her. *Come, sweetheart. Sin with me.*

Mac had grabbed the nearest male acquaintance and forced the man to introduce them, knowing that this perfectly raised young lady would refuse to speak to him at all until then. When Mac had held out his hand and asked the conventional question, "My lady, may I have this waltz?" she'd given him a cool look and lifted her wrist to show him her dance card dangling from it.

"What a pity," she'd said. "My card is full." Of course it was. She was a well-protected debutante, the oldest daughter of Earl Scranton, an advantageous catch. One of her father's handpicked gentlemen would even now be pushing his way through to her, hurrying to claim his waltz.

Mac had caught the card in his hand, removed a pencil from his pocket, and slashed a heavy diagonal line through all the names. Across this line he wrote in his careless scrawl—*Mac Mackenzie.*

He dropped the card and held out his hand. "Come dance with me, Lady Isabella," he'd said. *I dare you . . .*

He had expected her to freeze him with a cutting dismissal. She'd walk away, her nose in the air, seek her father's footmen, and instruct them to throw the blackguard out.

Instead, she'd placed her hand in his. They'd eloped that very night.

Tonight, in the semidarkness of Lord Abercrombie's terrace, Isabella's hair stood out like fire, but her eyes were shadowed. She hadn't screamed and fled from him the night they'd met, and she didn't scream and flee now.

On the terrace at her father's house, she'd regarded him with courage, her eyes unafraid. Mac had touched his lips to hers, a touch only, not a kiss. When he'd eased back, Isabella had stared up at him in shock.

Mac had been equally shocked. He'd intended to laugh at her fluttering modesty and leave her. Debutante kissed, wager won. But after the first touch of lips, he couldn't have dragged himself away if he'd been tied to one of Cameron's swiftest racehorses.

At the next touch of mouths, Isabella had parted her lips, trying to kiss him back. Mac had laughed softly in triumph, told her she was impossibly sweet, and claimed her mouth. He'd wanted her in his bed that very night, needed it, craved it. But he'd ruin her utterly if he didn't marry her, and Mac didn't want to hurt a hair on this lady's head.

Ergo, he'd married her.

That night, after the kiss, Isabella had opened her lips and whispered his name. Tonight, those same red lips parted, and she said, "Have you looked into the forgery I told you about yesterday morning?"

The present returned to Mac like a cold slap. "I told you, Isabella, I don't give a damn if some fool wants to copy my paintings and sign my name to them."

"And sell them?"

"He's welcome to the money." Whoever it was could have it and enjoy it.

Isabella regarded him in earnest, her eyes wide. "It is not only the money. He—or she—is stealing a part of you."

"Is he?" Mac couldn't imagine what part. Isabella had

taken most of him when she'd left, leaving a hole where Mac had been.

"He is. Painting is your life."

No, painting *had been* his life. Attempting the picture of Molly yesterday had been a complete disaster. The pictures he'd started in Paris this summer had been equally disastrous and had ended up on the scrap heap. Mac had accepted it—that part of his life was over.

"You know I took up painting only to annoy my father," he said, his tone light. "That was a long time ago, and the old bastard is out of reach of my annoying hobbies now."

"But you fell in love with art. You told me that. You've produced some wonderful work, you know you have. You might be dismissive of it, but your paintings are astonishing."

Astonishing, yes. That was what hurt so much. "I've rather lost the taste for it."

"I saw you painting with great energy when I barged in yesterday morning."

"On a picture which, as you rightly pointed out, was bloody awful. I paid Molly for a full sitting and told Bellamy to destroy it."

"Good heavens, it wasn't that bad. A bit odd for your style, I admit."

He shrugged. "I painted it to win a wager. Before I went to Paris, a few fellows egged me to do some erotic pictures, betting that I wouldn't. They said I'd become far too prudish to paint anything naughty."

Isabella laughed out loud, her breath warm in the cool air. It reminded him of how she used to laugh into his skin while they lay together on cold winter nights.

"You?" Isabella said. "Prudish?"

"I took the wager to save my honor, thank you very much, but I will forfeit." Forfeiting rankled, but not because of his pride. Mac had realized yesterday that he wouldn't be able to paint the wretched pictures no matter how he tried. He simply couldn't paint anything at all.

"What happens if you lose?" Isabella asked.

"I don't remember the details. I think I'll have to sing tunes with the Salvation Army band or something equally ridiculous."

Isabella laughed again, the sound silken. "What utter cheek."

"Wagers are wagers, my dear. The wager is all."

"I suppose this is a male ritual I'll never understand. Although at Miss Pringle's Select Academy, we could get up to some fine dares."

Mac leaned his arm on the wall, putting himself even closer to her. "I'm certain Miss Pringle was shocked."

"Not shocked, only cross. She always seemed to know what we were up to."

"The very perceptive Miss Pringle."

"She is highly intelligent. Don't make fun of her."

"Never. I'm rather fond of her. If *you* are the product of her academy, all young ladies ought to attend."

"She wouldn't have room for them," Isabella said. "That is why it's called Miss Pringle's *Select* Academy."

This was how it used to be with Isabella, the two of them chattering nonsense while he let the silk of her hair trickle through his fingers. They'd lounge in bed, talking, laughing, arguing about nothing, everything.

Damn it to hell, I want that back.

He'd missed her with his entire body since the moment Ian had handed him the letter. *What's this?* Mac had asked, not in the best temper—his head aching from a night of drunken debauchery. *Does Isabella have you passing billets-doux now?*

Ian's golden gaze had slid to Mac's right shoulder, Ian uncomfortable with looking into anyone's eyes. *Isabella is gone. The letter explains why.*

Gone? What do you mean, gone? Mac had broken the seal and read the fateful words: *Dearest Mac. I love you. I will always love you. But I can live with you no longer.*

Ian had watched while Mac swept the contents of his painting table to the floor in rage. Once he'd cooled down, Mac had stared bleakly at the letter again, and Ian, a man who didn't like to be touched, had laid his hand on his brother's shoulder. *She was right to go.*

The weeping came much later, when Mac had drunk himself into a stupor, the letter crumpled on the table next to him.

Isabella shivered suddenly, breaking his thoughts.

"You're cold," Mac said. The temperature had dropped, and Isabella's low-cut gown was no defense against an autumn evening. Mac slid off his coat and draped it around her shoulders.

He kept hold of the edges of the coat while his need for her plucked at him. They were relatively alone and unseen, she was his wife, and he needed so much to touch her. Dancing with her had been a mistake. It had given him a taste of her, and he hungered for much, much more. He wanted to unravel her complicated curls, have her long hair spill over his naked body. He wanted her to look up at him with languid eyes and smile at him, wanted her to lift to his hand as he pleasured her.

Mac had painted her the morning after their hasty wedding, Isabella sitting on the edge of the bed, nude, the sheets tangled around her. She'd been winding her flame-colored hair into a knot, her firm breasts lifting with her movements. She'd taken that painting with her when she'd gone, and Mac had never asked for it back. He wished he had now, because at least he could look at her, and remember.

"Isabella." The word came out half whisper, half moan. "I've missed you so much."

"I've missed you." She touched his face, her hand cool and soft. "I do miss you, Mac."

Then why did you leave me?

He bit back the words that rose in his mouth. Remonstrations would only anger her, and there had already been too much anger.

You aren't trying hard enough to get her back, Ian had told him not long ago. *I never thought you were this bloody stupid.*

But Mac knew he had to go slowly. If he pushed Isabella too quickly, she'd slip out of his reach, like a sunbeam he tried to capture in his hands.

"Actually, if you'll allow me a few precious moments," Mac said, clearing his throat, "I brought you out here for a reason."

She smiled. "To let me cool from our rather arduous dance?"

"No." *Damn it, let me do this.* "To ask you for your help."

Chapter 3

The lofty Lord of Mount Street, so recently a Groom, has not, we have been assured, ceased his hobby of painting in the manner of the *Parisians*, and in fact, has been painting with renewed vigor since his marriage.

—May 1875

Isabella's eyes flickered in genuine surprise. "My help? What on earth could I do for a lofty lord like you?"

"Nothing very difficult," Mac said. "I simply need some advice."

A faint smile touched her mouth, and his blood started to burn. "Good heavens, Mac Mackenzie seeking advice?"

"Not for me. For a friend." This suddenly seemed like a bloody stupid idea, but Mac hadn't been able to think of a better one. "I know a gentleman who wishes to court a lady," he said in a rush. "I've come to ask you how to go about it."

Isabella's brows climbed high, her eyes so close in the darkness. "Truly? Why should you need my advice about that?"

"Because I don't know much about courting, do I? Our own courtship lasted, what was it, about an hour and a half? Besides, this is a delicate matter. The lady in question

loathes him. Once, years ago, this man hurt her. Deeply."
Mac shifted, every muscle aching. "She will need coaxing.
A vast amount of coaxing."

"But ladies do not like to be coaxed," Isabella said,
that half smile hovering. "They like to be admired and
respected."

Like hell. They wanted to be adored, wanted men pant-
ing in anticipation at the merest crook of a finger. A smile
from the lady would cost even more.

"Very well," Mac said in a tight voice. "What is your
view about gifts?"

"Ladies do like gifts. Tokens of affection. But appropri-
ate gifts, nothing wildly extravagant."

"But he's bloody rich, this friend. He likes to be
extravagant."

"That doesn't necessarily impress a lady."

Like hell, again. Women cooed over strands of diamonds, glittering blue sapphires, emeralds as green as their
eyes. Mac had once bought Isabella a strand of emeralds to
drape softly across her breasts. The first night she'd worn
them they'd been alone, her very lovely breasts bared for
him. He still remembered the taste of the emeralds against
her skin.

"Then I will teach him the difference between appropri-
ate and extravagant," Mac said, his voice thick. "Anything
else?"

"Yes. Time. The lady will need time to think and not be
rushed. To decide whether the gentleman will be appropri-
ate for her."

Time. There'd been too damn much of that. Wasted
weeks and months and years, when Mac could have been
curled against her in bed, tasting her and smelling her, feeling her warmth against the length of his body.

"You mean time for the fellow to prove his devotion?"

Mac couldn't keep the impatient edge out of his voice. "Or time for the lady to drive him completely mad?"

"Time for the lady to decide whether his devotion is true or all his imagination."

"The lady decides that, does she?"

"She does. Always."

Mac growled. "Bloody hard luck on the gentleman isn't it, when a lady knows his mind better than he does?"

"That is how things are in courtship," Isabella said coolly. "You *did* ask for the advice."

"What if the damned fellow is in love and he knows it?"

"In that case, he would never have hurt the lady in the past."

The sudden flare of pain in her eyes cut him, and Mac had to look away. Yes, he'd hurt her. Mac had hurt her and kept hurting her, and he knew it. She'd hurt him back, the two of them thrusting and parrying and trying desperately to keep their footing. What a bloody stupid way to conduct a marriage.

He drew an uneven breath. "What I propose is for you to teach me what my friend should do. Give me the lessons in courting. I will then teach what I learn to my friend."

Mac waited while she pursed her lips. She always did that while she thought, and he'd always loved leaning closer, closer, until he brushed his mouth across that gentle pucker. Then she'd laugh and say something like, *Darling Mac, you are so silly.*

"I suppose I could be persuaded," Isabella said now with her soft, red mouth. "Though this is not what's meant by courting, you know."

Mac pulled back a hairsbreadth. "What isn't?"

She wet her lips, making his longing spike. "You have started badly, I am afraid. You do not ask a lady to dance by tearing her away from the partner she's just accepted, and when she's overheated, you walk her to a chair and fetch her an ice. You don't whisk her out to the terrace and into the shadows."

"Why not?"

"That is seduction, not courting. You could ruin the lady."

"Ah." Mac returned his hand to the wall beside her, noticing that it was shaking. "Then you consider that I've failed that lesson."

"Almost." She smiled, and his heart turned over. "You are very flattering, which is always a point in a gentleman's favor."

"I can be more flattering than that. I can tell you that your hair is a trail of fire, your lips sweeter than the finest wines, that your voice flows inside me and stirs all my desires."

A swallow moved down her throat. "A proper lady might be taken aback by such comparisons."

"I remember a proper lady who didn't mind me talking about the pillows of her breasts and the glory that lay between her legs."

"Then she couldn't have been a proper lady," Isabella said softly.

Mac leaned to her. "Would the proper young lady be shocked to learn I'm in danger of taking her right here, uncaring of who might wander to our end of the terrace?"

Her lashes swept down. "I don't think such a thing would be practical in this gown."

"Don't tease, Isabella. I'm perfectly serious."

"I've never been able to resist teasing you." She gave him her coy little smile, and his limbs hurt. "But I have been thinking about this rather a lot, Mac. We have both closed in on ourselves, barely able to speak to one another, which has caused great strain. Perhaps if we grow more used to seeing each other, stop avoiding events where we both might attend—like tonight—perhaps we would become comfortable with each other."

Mac's bubble of hope dissipated. "Comfortable? What the devil does that mean? As though we were in our dotage, nodding to each other in our Bath chairs?"

"No, no. I meant that if we become used to each other's company, perhaps your wanting would decrease. We would be more civil to each other. As it is we are nervous. About everything."

Mac wanted to burst into laughter, and then again, he wanted to rage. "Bloody hell, Isabella, do you think that the strain between us is all to do with me *wanting* you? Oh, my darling girl."

"Of course I do not believe it is so simple. But perhaps, if we agree to become more, well, easy with each other, perhaps we could catch sight of each other without simmering."

"I very much doubt that." Mac slanted her a hot smile. "I've been simmering for you since the night we met. I've never stopped, and I never will, no matter how many times I have the pleasure of taking you to bed."

Isabella's lips parted in surprise. Had she thought the solution to their unhappiness so simple? That if they grew bored with each other's company, Mac would cease wanting her and let her be? Some men—utter fools—did lose interest in a woman once they'd bedded her, but Mac couldn't imagine ever, ever losing interest in Isabella.

He let his smile grow predatory. "My dear Isabella, I will take your suggestion and show you what happens when you play with fire. I will make certain we see each other quite, quite often. And there will be no growing jaded with each other. Because you see, my dear, when I at last take you home again, it will be forever. No regrets, no games, no being 'comfortable.' We will be man and wife, in all ways, and it will be final."

Isabella gave him a haughty look. That was his Isabella. A firecracker, no whimpering miss. "I see. So the games we play must be ones of *your* choosing."

He touched her lips with his fingertip. "Exactly, my sweet. And when I win, Isabella, it will be for good. I promise you that."

Isabella opened her mouth to retort, but Mac silenced her with one hot, swift kiss. The taste of her was enough to crumble him to dust, but he made himself, just as swiftly, release her.

He ran his finger down her neck to the shadow of her cleavage. "Good night, my darling," he said. "Keep the coat."

Walking away from her, so delectable in that low-cut dress, his own coat draped over her shoulders, was one of the most difficult things Mac had ever done. At every step, he expected her to call after him, to beg him to come back, even to curse him.

Isabella never said a word. Mac's need berated him soundly as he kept walking the length of the terrace and stepped back into the overly stuffy house.

Mac's arousal hadn't died by the time he reached home and climbed the four flights to his studio. He stood in the middle of the room, absorbing the ruined picture still propped on the easel, the table strewn with jars and palettes, his brushes fastidiously washed and sorted. Even when Mac lost his temper and threw things about, he always took care of his brushes. They were an extension of the painter's fingers, the mad old artist who'd first trained him had told him. They needed to be treated with care.

The labored breathing of Bellamy sounded behind Mac as the valet puffed up the attic stairs. Mac absently pulled off his cravat and waistcoat and handed them over to the disapproving Bellamy when the man entered the room. Mac had conducted wild painting sessions in evening dress before, and Bellamy had said flatly in his East End accent that he wouldn't be held responsible for his lordship's clothes if his lordship insisted on mucking them up with oil paints.

Mac didn't much care, but Bellamy did, so Mac piled the man's arms high with his garments and told him to go. Once Bellamy closed the door, Mac pulled on the old kilt he kept up there to paint in along with his paint-streaked boots.

He tossed the ruined canvas facedown on the floor and propped a blank one in its place. His charcoal pencil nestled into his palm, and with the ease of long practice, Mac began to sketch.

It took only a few lines to draw what he wanted—the eyes of a woman, another few lines to fill in her face, more to depict the spill of brilliant hair down her shoulder. The beauty and simplicity of the drawing caught at his heart as he finished.

He took up his palette, globbed on colors, and started to paint. Muted tones, many shades of white, the paint for the shadows mixed from green and umber and darkest red. Her green eyes toned down with black, the shine of them caught exactly right.

Dawn filtered through the skylights before Mac finished. In the end, he dropped his palette to the table, shoved his brushes into the cleaning solution, and contemplated the painting.

Something in him rejoiced. After so long—*so long*— the brilliance Mac's mentor had seen in him finally broke through once more.

A woman looked out of the canvas: her chin a bit pointed, her lips parted in a half smile. Red hair trickled down her shoulder, and her eyes regarded him with a haughty yet seductive look. Yellow rosebuds, painted the vibrant yellow of Mac's signature color, drooped from her curls as though she'd danced the night away and come home tired. He hadn't painted the gown she'd worn tonight, just suggested it with dashes of deep-shadowed blue that blended into the background.

It was the most beautiful thing he'd painted in years. The picture sang out of the canvas, the colors and lines flowing with effortless grace.

Mac let his blunt, paint-stained fingers hover above the woman for a few seconds. Then he resolutely turned his back on the picture and left the room.

Isabella settled the gloves on her fingers the next morning with quick jerks and checked the angle of her hat in the hall mirror. Her heart was thumping, but she was determined. If Mac wouldn't do anything about the forged paintings, Isabella would.

She nodded to her butler as he opened the front door for her. "Thank you, Morton. Please make certain his lordship's coat is cleaned and returned to him by this afternoon."

Isabella took her footman's hand and settled herself in her landau. Not until the vehicle had rolled into morning traffic did she droop against the cushions and let out her breath.

She'd slept very little after she'd returned from Lord Abercrombie's ball the night before. When Mac had walked away from her down the terrace, the pain of his leaving had struck her to the heart. She'd wanted to rush after him, to make him turn back to her, to beg him with everything she had to stay.

As it was, she'd had to make do with his coat. She'd laid it next to her when she'd gone to bed, where she could touch it and smell his scent on it. She'd remained awake and restless, craving him, until she finally drifted into dreams of his smile and that sinfully hot kiss.

In the morning, she'd tossed the coat carelessly at Evans, instructing her to tell Morton to look after it.

She directed her coachman to take her to the Strand, where Messrs. Crane and Longman, purveyors of fine art, kept a shop. There was no longer a Mr. Longman, he having died and left Mr. Crane the entire business, but Mr. Crane had never removed Longman's name from the sign.

Mr. Crane, a smallish man with soft palms and well-manicured nails, shook Isabella's hand when she entered, then began spewing forth praise of Mac Mackenzie.

"Mr. Crane, Mac is precisely who I've come to see you about," Isabella said when he'd wound down. "Please tell me about the painting you sold to Mrs. Leigh-Waters."

Crane pressed his hands together and tilted his head, which made him look like a small, plump bird. "Ah, yes, *Rome from the Capitoline Hill*. An excellent work. One of his best."

"You do know that Mac doesn't sell his paintings? He gives them away to whoever wants them. Did it not strike you as odd when this one came up for sale?"

"Indeed, I was quite surprised when his lordship instructed us to sell it," Mr. Crane said.

"*Mac* instructed it? Who told you that?"

Mr. Crane blinked. "I beg your pardon?"

"Who brought in the painting and told you his lordship wanted it sold?"

"Why, his lordship himself."

Now Isabella blinked. "Are you certain? Mac carried the painting in here and handed it to you himself?"

"Well, not to me, as a point of fact. I was out. My assistant received it and cataloged it. Said his lordship told him he didn't care what price he got."

Isabella's thoughts whirled. She had assumed her errand

would be simple—point out to Mr. Crane that he'd sold a forgery and demand to know what he would do about it. Now she wondered. Had Mac actually painted it himself and sold it? And why?

"Does your assistant know Mac by sight?" she asked. "He didn't assume that the gentleman was Mac without asking?"

"My lady, I was as surprised as you are, but my assistant described his lordship precisely. Even that careless way he has of talking, as though nothing about his art very much matters. So charming, when he has such talent. Mind you, his lordship hasn't done much lately, so I was happy I could obtain something at all from him."

Isabella had no idea what to say next. She'd pictured herself interrogating Mr. Crane on who had brought in the painting, to scold him for letting forgeries pass through his hands. Now she did not know how to continue. She'd been so certain that Mac hadn't painted the scene, although come to think of it, Mac had neither confirmed nor denied it when she'd asked him.

"Ah, your lordship," Crane said brightly. "How propitious of you. We were just speaking of you and that lovely picture you did of Rome. Welcome to my humble shop."

Isabella whirled. Mac himself stood in the doorway, blotting out the weak sunlight outside.

He stepped across the threshold, swept off his hat, sent a smile to Isabella that weakened her knees, and said, "Now then, Crane. What have you been up to, selling forgeries of my blasted paintings?"

Chapter 4

The smitten Groom of Mount Street has purchased his Lady a country Cottage in Buckinghamshire where she hosts charity Garden Fetes now that the weather has grown warm and Town swelters. The great and the good attend these parties and speak of nothing else.

—July 1875

Crane spluttered, but Mac couldn't summon up much anger for the little man. Mac's entire awareness centered on Isabella standing near him as resplendently beautiful in a brown-and-cream day dress as she had been in her elegant satin ball gown and diamonds.

If Mac were to paint her in this costume he'd use the palest of yellows for the trim, cream and umber for the bodice, darker brown for the shadows. For her skin, tints of cream and pink. Darkened red for her lips, which would be the only color on her face, rippling red orange for the curls under her hat. Eyes a suggestion of black and green, in shadow.

"Mac, I was just explaining . . ."

Mac didn't hear her. Or rather, he couldn't hear Isabella's words—he heard only her voice, low, musical, designed to make his heart dance.

"Your lordship." Crane rubbed his hands together in

that irritating manner he had. "You brought me the paintings yourself."

"Paint*ings*?" Mac's brows rose. "You mean, there's been more than one?"

"Of course. I have another here." Crane minced his way into a back room and came out with a framed canvas almost as tall as himself. Mac laid his walking stick and hat on a table helped Crane lift the painting to a hook on the wall.

It was a Venice picture. Two men worked a gondola in the foreground, with the buildings of the Grand Canal fading into the mist, the merest suggestion of reflections of them in the murky water.

"One of your best, your lordship," Crane said. "From your Venetian Period."

The painting was damned good, Mac had to say that. The composition was finely balanced, the colors just right, light and shadow precise without being dull. Mac had painted quite few a pictures of canals while he'd been wallowing in self-pity after Isabella's departure. But he hadn't painted this one.

Isabella rolled her lower lip under her teeth, rendering it red and kissable. She shot Mac a worried look. "It *is* a forgery, isn't it?"

"I didn't paint that, Crane. Someone's having you on."

Mr. Crane pointed at the corner of the painting. "But you signed it."

Mac leaned close to see the words *Mac Mackenzie* scrawled in the corner in his usual lazy style. "That does look like my signature." He stepped back and regarded the picture fully. "Mind you, it isn't bad."

"Isn't bad?" Isabella burst forth like a fury. "Mac, it's a *forgery*."

"Yes, and a damned good one. The fellow paints better than I do."

Crane looked horrified. He glanced over his shoulder as though the police might come flooding in any moment to drag him away to a dank, dark dungeon. "But, your lordship, my assistant swore you brought it in yourself."

"Mr. Crane," Isabella began.

Mac cut her off. "Don't blame him, love. If I didn't know better, I couldn't tell the difference myself."

"Well, *I* could."

"Because you have an eye for it. How many of these did you take, Crane?"

"Just the two," Crane said in a small voice. "But I'm afraid I asked for more."

Mac burst out laughing. Isabella looked indignant, but Mac couldn't help himself. It was too idiotic. He hadn't been able to paint anything decent in years, and this upstart not only painted better than Mac did, he gave Mac the credit for it.

"Out of curiosity, how much did Mrs. Leigh-Waters pay you?" Mac asked.

"A thousand guineas, my lord," Crane whispered.

Mac whistled then laughed harder.

Isabella glared at him. "That's criminal."

Mac wiped his eyes. "Good Lord, Crane, I'm sure you were happy with *that* commission. What became of her payment, by the way? I'm sure this 'Mac Mackenzie' didn't let go of his share."

Crane looked troubled. "Funny thing, my lord. He's never come for it. And he left no address or name of a bank where we could send it on. That was three months ago."

"Hmm," Mac said. "Well, if ever he does come 'round—"

"You must contact his lordship at once," Isabella said.

"I was going to say, let the fellow have the cash. He's obviously desperate for money."

"Mac . . ."

"He did the work, after all."

Mac wasn't sure whether Isabella was more beautiful when she smiled or when she was bloody furious. Her cheeks were red, her eyes shone with green fire, and her breasts rose delightfully inside her tight bodice.

"What about Mrs. Leigh-Waters?" Crane's face was ashen. "I should tell her what I've done."

Mac shrugged. "Why? She likes the painting—praised it to the skies, my wife tells me. If Mrs. Leigh-Waters is happy, why spoil it for her?" He took up his stick and hat. "But if any more Mac Mackenzies turn up to sell you paintings, be warned. I never sell mine. I see no reason to charge people for my worthless drivel."

"Drivel?" Crane cast him an indignant look. "Your lordship, they call you the English Manet."

"Do they? Well, you know my opinion of 'them.'"

"Yes, my lord, you've said."

"Utter idiots, I believe is the term I prefer. Good morning to you, Crane. My dear?" Mac offered his arm to Isabella. "Shall we go?"

To his surprise, Isabella took his arm without rebuff and let him escort her out of the shop into the now-falling rain.

Isabella tried to remain angry as Mac assisted her into her landau, but the strength of his hands as he lifted her dissolved all thought.

She dropped into her seat and settled her skirts, expecting to hear the door shut and Mac say his farewells. Instead, the carriage listed as Mac climbed in and sat down beside her.

Isabella tried not to shrink away. "Do you not have your own coach?"

"Yours will suit my needs for now."

Isabella started to give him a heated answer, but just then droplets poured from her hat brim to stain her tight jacket. "Oh bother, the rain. My new hat will be ruined."

"Take it off."

Mac flipped his own hat to the opposite seat as the landau jerked forward. Rain drummed on the canvas roof, a hurried thrumming that matched the beating of Isabella's heart.

She snatched out hat pins, removed the hat, and dabbed at the straw with her handkerchief. The ostrich feathers were already soaked, but perhaps Evans could save them. She leaned forward to drop the hat on the seat next to Mac's, and when she sat back again, Mac had extended his arm across the seatback behind her.

Isabella stilled. Being a large man, Mac liked to spread out, usually crowding Isabella to do it. She used to love to snuggle into him when they rode in a carriage, as though he were a great bear rug. She'd felt so protected and warm.

Mac regarded her with a lazy smile, knowing damn well why she remained upright on the seat, back rigid.

"What about your coachman?" she asked stiffly.

"He knows his way home. He's lived there for years."

"Very amusing." Isabella tried a different tack. "Why on earth did you spew that nonsense to Mr. Crane about letting this other man keep the money? He is forging your paintings and selling them. Why should he profit?"

Mac's arm brushed her as he shrugged. "But he hasn't returned for the money, has he? Perhaps his game is different. Perhaps he knew he couldn't sell his things under his own name, so he used mine."

"Your name, your style, and your colors. How do you suppose he came up with the formula for your yellow? You keep it a secret."

Mac shrugged again, his body moving in a most distracting manner. "Trial and error? And you're rather assuming the forger is a man. It could be a woman."

"Crane said a man calling himself Mac left the paintings."

"The woman could have a male accomplice, someone who resembles me."

He sprawled so comfortably, as though there were no tension at all between them. Mac wore trousers instead of a kilt today, a trifle disappointing.

"You are being most maddening about this," she said.

"I told you, I don't care."

"Whyever not?"

Mac sighed and rubbed his eyes with the heel of his hand. "Must we go over it again, sweeting? That part of my life is in the past."

"Which is absolute nonsense."

"Perhaps we should change the subject." Mac's face settled into firm lines. "How are you this morning, love? Had any interesting correspondence?"

He wore that stubborn Mackenzie look, which said if he didn't want to talk about a thing, an iron bar couldn't pry his mouth open to do it. Well, she could pretend as well.

"I had a letter from Beth, as a matter of fact. She and Ian are settling in nicely. I miss her."

Isabella couldn't keep the sigh from her voice. Beth was a delightful young woman, and Isabella was excited that she had a new sister. Isabella hadn't seen her own younger sister, Louisa, since the night she'd married Mac. Isabella's family had disowned her, the upright Earl Scranton appalled that his daughter had eloped with a *Mackenzie*. The Mackenzies might be rich and powerful, but they were also decadent, immodest, profligate, promiscuous, and worst of all, Scots. Louisa was seventeen now, nearing her own come-out. The thought made Isabella's heart ache.

"You'll see Beth in Doncaster," Mac was saying. "That is, if you can tear yourself away from London to go."

"Of course I will be at the St. Leger. I haven't missed it in years. Do you think Beth will come? I mean, with the baby."

"Since the baby isn't born yet, I imagine it will accompany her."

"Very droll. I meant, do you think Beth will want to travel? Even on a train? She needs to be careful, you know."

"Ian will keep an eagle eye on her, my love. I have every confidence in him."

True, Ian kept Beth in his sight at all times. Ever since Beth had broken the news that she was due to deliver a baby sometime in the spring, Ian's protectiveness had doubled. Beth sometimes rolled her eyes about it, but she exuded joy at the same time. Beth was very well loved, and she knew it.

"It is a delicate time for a woman, even one as hearty as Beth," Isabella said, words tumbling from her. "Even with Ian constantly watching over her. She will need to rest and take care, and not try to do too much." The last word ended on a sob, and Isabella pressed the backs of her fingers to her mouth.

She wished she weren't so exhausted from her sleepless night and early morning. Then she could sit here in no danger of breaking down. She wouldn't weep in front of Mac; she'd promised herself that she wouldn't.

"Love." His voice caressed her. "Please don't."

Isabella angrily brushed away her tears. "I am happy for Beth. I want her to be happy."

"Hush, now." His arms came around her, Mac shutting her away from anything that wanted to hurt her.

"Stop," she said. "I can't fight you now."

"I know." Mac rested his cheek on her hair. "I know."

She heard the break in his own voice, turned her head to see his copper-colored eyes swimming with tears. It was his tragedy too, she knew. Their shared grief.

"Oh, Mac, no." Isabella rubbed a drop from his cheek. "It was so long ago. I don't know why I'm crying."

"I do."

"Let's not talk of it. Please. I can't."

"I won't make you. Don't worry."

His eyes were still wet. Isabella slid her arms around his neck, rubbing under his hair, knowing he found that soothing. A tear trickled to his upper lip, and Isabella instinctively kissed it away.

Their mouths met, touched, warmth on warmth, clung. Mac's lips parted, and she tasted the sharp sweep of his tongue, the salt of his tears. This was no seduction; he kissed for comfort, hers and his own.

Even after more than three years apart, everything about Mac was familiar. The rough-silken feel of his hair, the texture of his tongue, the burn of whiskers on her lips, all were the same.

But there was one difference. Instead of being overlaid with the bite of single-malt, Mac's mouth tasted only of Mac.

Mac eased away, but his lips lingered on hers like mist on glass. Another light brush of mouths, and Mac sat back, tracing her cheek. "Isabella." It was a whisper, filled with sadness.

"Please don't."

He knew what she meant. "This will not be a weapon in our game," Mac said. "I'd never, ever do that to you."

"Thank you."

Their breaths mixed as she gratefully exhaled. Mac smiled a little and touched another kiss to her lips.

"My coat, on the other hand . . ."

"Morton is having it cleaned," Isabella said quickly as she accepted the handkerchief Mac handed her. "You'll soon have it back."

Mac leaned on his elbow on the back of the seat. "I meant the story that you kept my coat in your bed with you all night. Lucky garment. You forget how swiftly gossip runs between our houses. Our servants have a messaging system that Prussian generals would envy."

"Nonsense." Isabella's heart thumped. "I put the coat down on the bed last night, is all, then I forgot about it and fell asleep."

"I see." Mac's eyes glinted with his knowing smile, despite the tears that hadn't yet dried on his cheeks.

Isabella gave him a haughty look. "You know what staff can be like when they get an idea into their heads. The story grows with each retelling."

"Servants can be quite perceptive, my sweet. Far more intelligent than their masters."

"I only mean that you shouldn't take everything they say as absolute."

"Of course not. May I beg a glove from you so I can lay it on my pillow tonight? You can refuse my request, of course."

"I do refuse. Most emphatically."

"I wish only to entertain the servants," he said.

"Then send them to a music hall."

Mac's smile widened. "I like that idea. I'd have the house to myself for an evening." He ran one finger down her arm. "Perhaps I could invite someone to call."

Isabella strove not to jump. "I am certain that your chums would enjoy a night of billiards and a generous amount of Mackenzie whiskey."

"Billiards. Hmm." Mac's look turned thoughtful. "I might take pleasure in a game of billiards, with the right companion." He took her hand, traced a design on her palm through her tight kid glove. "I could think of a few interesting wagers we could have. Not to mention the double entendres I could make about thrusting cues and balls and pockets."

Isabella snatched her hand away. "You do like to hear yourself talk, Mac. Now, I must insist you tell me why you have no interest in the forged paintings."

Mac lost his smile. "Drop the topic, Isabella. I banish it from our game."

"This isn't a game. It is our lives—your life. Your art. And I'd be a bloody fool to play any game *you* invented."

Mac leaned to her as the carriage slowed. Isabella had no idea where they were, and she didn't have the energy to lift the curtain to find out.

"It is a game, my love." He held her gaze. "It is the most serious game I've ever engaged in. And I intend to win it. I will have you back, Isabella—in my life, in my house, and in my bed."

Isabella couldn't breathe. Breathing meant she'd inhale his scent and his warmth.

His eyes were hard, the copper irises still and cool. When he looked at her like this, she could believe that his ancestors had ruled the Highlands and swept nearly all the way through England in attempt to wrest it back for the Stuarts. Mac was a decadent man who went to parties in the finest houses, but the gentlemen who hosted the parties would quickly back down from the look in his eyes at present. Mac was determined, and when he was determined, 'ware all those who stood in his way.

Isabella lifted her chin. Betraying weakness to him would be fatal.

"Very well, then," she said. "I intend to pursue the forger. If I play your game, I must make up my own rules."

He didn't like that, but Isabella had learned enough about Mac to know she should never let him have it all his way. She'd go down swiftly if she did that.

To her surprise, he made a conceding gesture. "If you must. Do your worst."

"I said that about you after you left me at the ball."

By Mac's sudden, blazing smile Isabella realized she'd miscalculated. She hadn't meant to say the words—they had slipped out before she could stop them. But she'd hugged herself on the cold terrace as she huddled there in Mac's coat, angry, unnerved, lonely, scared, and angry again. "Do your worst, Mac Mackenzie," she'd breathed in frustrated rage. "Do your absolute worst."

"A fine invitation." Mac cupped her face between his hands. He was strong; she'd never forgotten what natural power Mac had.

He kissed her, not tenderly this time. It was a hard, rough, hungry kiss, one that mastered her and bruised her lips. She realized with dismay that she kissed him just as hungrily back.

Mac pulled away, leaving her lips parted and raw. "I promise you," he said. "This is nothing compared to my worst."

Isabella tried to answer with a cutting remark, but her voice no longer worked. Mac gave her a feral smile, snatched up his hat and stick, and flung open the door of the now-still landau.

Isabella saw that they had halted in a snarl of traffic on Piccadilly, the landau perilously close to the posts that separated road from buildings and people. Mac leapt to the ground without bothering with the step.

"Until next time." He clapped on his hat. "I look forward to another engagement on whatever battlefield you choose."

Whistling, Mac strolled away. Isabella followed his broad

back as he moved smoothly through the crowd until the
footman slammed the door, cutting off her view. She peered
through the rain-streaked window, but the familiar form of
her husband was lost to the mist and crowd.

Feeling bereft, Isabella fell back against the seat as the
landau jerked to roll on through Piccadilly.

Mac thoroughly disliked formal musicales, but he made an
exception and dressed to attend the one at Isabella's house
two nights later. Two nights of restless sleep, twitching as
he relived the kisses in the landau. In his fevered visions
he would continue, loosening her bodice and licking her
creamy breasts as they welled over the top of her corset.

He mused that lusting after one's own wife was far more
frustrating than lusting after a stranger. Mac knew exactly
what Isabella looked like under her clothes, exactly what
he was missing. He had many times undressed her during
their marriage, liking to dismiss Evans and take over the
servant's duties to prepare Isabella for bed. As Mac lay
awake alone, sweating, and randy, he remembered peel-
ing each layer from her body—bodice, skirts, petticoats,
bustle, corset, stockings, chemise.

Firelight would brush her skin and dance in her red hair.
Then Mac would kiss every part of her. He would savor the
touch of Isabella's lips, each swirl of her tongue, the taste
of her skin beneath his mouth. He'd move his hands to cup
her buttocks, or slide his fingers between her thighs to find
liquid heat there.

The hair between Isabella's legs was not as bright red
as that on her head; it was more the color of brandy. Mac
would lay her on the floor or on the bed, or better still, have
her sit in an armchair, while he'd lick his way from her
breasts, over the flat of her stomach, to the fiery pleasure
that awaited him between her parted thighs.

The night after their meeting in Crane's shop followed by the delicious fencing match in the landau, Mac had thrown back his bedcovers, climbed to the attic, and spent the next several hours painting.

This time, he portrayed Isabella lying in his bed, on her side, asleep. He painted from memory, showing her body relaxed, one breast soft against the sheet. One leg was bent as she sought a comfortable position, her arms stretched across the pillow. Her fingers were loose, untroubled. Her face was turned downward, half hidden by her hair, and another tuft peeked coyly from between her thighs.

As in the picture of Isabella in her ball gown, Mac left the background vague, splotches of paint that suggested shadows. The bedding was cream-colored, Isabella's hair, lips, and areolas being the only splashes of vivid color. Those and a yellow bud in a slim vase—Mac painted yellow roses into all pictures of Isabella. He signed the painting with his scrawl and left it to dry beside the other.

As Bellamy buttoned Mac into a black suit with Mackenzie kilt, Mac wondered if he'd be able to be in the same room with Isabella without tenting out the tartan. He hadn't received an invitation to her musicale, but he didn't intend to let that stop him.

"Let me in, Morton," Mac told Isabella's butler upon arriving at North Audley Street.

Morton had worked for Mac once upon a time, but the butler had become smitten with Isabella and her knack for household management. Even at age eighteen, Isabella had recognized that Mac had no idea how to run a houseful of servants and had begun making changes the morning after her arrival. Mac had cheerfully handed her the reins and told her to get on with it. When Isabella had left Mac, Morton had followed her.

Morton looked down his haughty nose at Mac. Being a

foot shorter, Morton had to crank his head back to do so, but he managed it. "Her ladyship stipulated that tonight's entertainment is by invitation only, my lord."

"I know she did, Morton. However, please keep in mind that I pay your wages."

Morton didn't like the vulgar mention of money. His nose rose even more. "Invitation *only*, my lord."

Mac glared, but Morton was made of stern stuff. He refused to move aside, though he knew quite well that Mac could simply pick him up and haul him out of the way if he wanted to.

"Never mind," Mac said. "Tell her ladyship she keeps a fine guard dog."

He tipped his hat to a large woman with enormous ostrich plumes on her head, who was stepping up to enter the house. He sensed the woman's delight that she'd just witnessed Morton turn Isabella's untamed husband away.

Whistling a music-hall ditty, Mac swung himself onto the scullery steps, clattered down the stairs, and entered the kitchen through the back door. The staff looked up through the steam-filled kitchen and froze in surprise. The cook stopped in the act of icing a row of teacakes, and a lump of icing fell from her spoon. The scullery maid squeaked and dropped a greasy cloth to the flagstone floor.

Mac removed his hat and gloves and shoved them at a footman. "Look after those for me, Matthew, there's a good lad. Don't mind if I snatch a seedcake, do you Mrs. Harper? I never had any tea today. Thank you, you're a good woman."

So saying, Mac snatched up a sliver of seedcake and popped it into his mouth. He winked at Mrs. Harper, who had once been an undercook at Kilmorgan. She blushed like a schoolgirl and said, "Go on with you, your lordship."

Mac ate the cake on the way up the stairs and licked his fingers as he pushed open the green baize door at the top. He emerged into the hall to nearly run into the woman with the ostrich plumes again. Mac bowed to her while she stared with pale eyes, then he gestured for her to precede him into the drawing room.

Chapter 5

Signs of strain have issued from home of our Scottish Lord and his Lady. The gentleman has disappeared, rumored to have fled to Paris weeks ago, while the lady remains entertaining marchionesses and actresses alike. All is seeming delight at the big house, the absence of its Lord glibly explained away by his madness for painting in Montmartre.

—*October 1875*

Isabella's only sign of exasperation when she caught sight of Mac was a tightening around her eyes. But Isabella had been trained by a series of governesses and Miss Pringle's Select Academy to be a gracious hostess no matter what disasters might ensue.

Isabella continued chatting with her guests, never once looking directly at Mac. Mac envied the lady and gentleman she spoke to as she leaned to them with a smile and a little flick of her hand. He'd always loved being the focus of her green gaze, loved watching her lips purse as she listened to him and formed her next answer.

She wore burgundy tonight, a satin shoulder-baring dress that rippled like water when she moved. Her bosom swelled over the décolletage, inviting his gaze and the gaze of all other gentlemen present. Mac stifled a growl. He might have to start killing people soon.

The double drawing room was packed, Isabella's evenings

always popular. Mac greeted major and minor nobility, ambassadors, foreign princesses, old friends, mere acquaintances. Artists presented by Isabella always had successful come-outs. She'd gained a reputation for excellent taste, and although her own family would not speak to her, the rest of society had seen no reason to shun her. Even Isabella's separation from her husband had alienated only a few. The Mackenzies were so very rich after all. Hart was the second-highest duke in the land behind the royal dukes, and the ambitious wanted to cultivate his support and patronage. If that meant they attended salons and musicales hosted by Hart's sister-in-law, so be it.

Mac had never understood Isabella's liking for so many damned people in the house, but he had to admit that he'd never really tried to understand her likes and dislikes. He'd simply drunk her in like fine wine, not questioning, letting her fill and inspire him. He never thought to ask how the wine felt.

He didn't have to turn to know that Isabella had stopped at his elbow. He would recognize her presence were he blind and deaf in the middle of the barren sands of Egypt.

"Odd," she said in her musical voice. "I do not recall your name on my guest list."

Mac turned, and his breath caught. Isabella stood beside him like living flame. She'd threaded her red hair with yellow rosebuds, and as she had at Lord Abercrombie's ball, she wore a diamond necklace on her bosom. She was beauty incarnate, even when her eyes sparkled in annoyance—at him.

"Why would I not attend one of my own wife's famous musicales?" he asked.

"Because I never sent you an invitation. I would have remembered. I write them all myself."

"Don't blame Morton. He did his best to keep me out."

"Oh, I know precisely where the blame lies."

Mac shrugged, trying for carelessness. Never mind that his hands were sweating and that he was in danger of dropping the glass of water Morton had grudgingly fetched for him. "Now that I am here, I might as well be useful. Who would you like me to woo?"

The lines around Isabella's eyes tightened even more, but she would never make a scene. Not in public. She was too finely bred for that.

"The princess of Brandenburg and her husband. They haven't much wealth, but they are fashionable and have great influence. Scotland fascinates them. You are wearing your kilt, so you can give them your full Highland charm."

"As you wish, my love. I will prepare to be very Scottish."

Isabella laid her fingers on his arm and smiled, and Mac's heartbeat rose to dangerous levels. He told himself that the smile was not for him; she was aware they'd become the center of the room's attention and wanted to make a good show of it. She'd smile until her lips fell off to keep people from reporting an entertaining argument between Mac Mackenzie and his estranged wife.

"Don't overdo it, Mac," she said. "It is Mrs. Monroe's night, and I don't wish the spotlight taken from her."

"Mrs. Who?"

"The soprano. Whose name you would have known if you'd received an invitation."

"I did come here for a reason tonight, my lovely—other than to drive you mad, of course. I came to tell you that I have not been idle about the forger."

Isabella's smile became more genuine. Mac's gaze shifted to the curl that lay against her right shoulder, and he fought the temptation to lean down and take the red lock between his lips.

"Truly?" she asked. "What progress have you made?"

"I talked to Inspector Fellows. Told him the problem and that I wanted it kept quiet. No official complaint, no official investigation."

"I see." She sounded skeptical, and her attention wandered to a knot of guests who'd gathered around the nervous-looking soprano.

"And here I imagined you'd be pleased that I'm taking the problem seriously."

She saw right through him, as usual. "You are not taking it seriously. You are passing it off to Mr. Fellows, at the same time telling him not to barge around and ask questions."

"These Scotland Yard men have an amazing knack for ferreting out information. You know that."

"And you have an amazing knack for not doing things that don't interest you." Isabella turned away. "Do escort the princess to her seat. We're about to start."

She glided off. Mac's fingers slid from her water-smooth gown, his whole body longing for the feel of the warm woman beneath the satin.

~~~

Mrs. Monroe sang to a silent, enraptured room, which exploded into applause and cries of "Brava!" as she finished. Isabella saw that even Mac was entranced, his usual sardonic expression replaced by one of appreciation.

Oh, why couldn't she keep her eyes off the blasted man? She didn't believe for one minute his glib explanation that he'd come to report that he'd spoken to the police. A note informing her would have sufficed. No, Mac had come to torment her, to demonstrate that she could shut him out of her life only when he chose to let her. He'd proved that even her devoted butler couldn't bar him from the house.

Mrs. Monroe's performance ended, and the audience descended upon her. The plump young soprano would now be a success. Isabella handed her off to her admirers and glanced at the seat Mac had occupied. He'd disappeared.

Botheration. Knowing Mac roamed the house but not where was rather like having a wasp loose in the place. Keeping an eye on it before the servants could arrive to chase it out was essential.

"You have a gift for discovering rare talent, Isabella."

Isabella dragged her gaze from the crowd and focused with difficulty on Ainsley Douglas, an old school friend from Miss Pringle's. Ainsley still wore black for her husband dead these five years, but the beauty of her fair hair, pink cheeks, and gray eyes hadn't dimmed.

"She will do well, I think," Isabella answered distractedly, still looking for Mac.

"I thought you might like to know, Isabella. I spoke to your mother yesterday in the Burlington Arcade."

Isabella snapped her attention back to her. Ainsley regarded her with a neutral look, aware that too many guests hovered near, but then Ainsley had always been excellent at subterfuge. Whenever Miss Pringle's cook had demanded to know who had raided the buttery the night before, no one could look more innocently surprised than Ainsley. She was one of Queen Victoria's ladies now, but her eyes still hinted at the mischievous tomboy she'd been.

"My mother?" Isabella asked, trying to keep her voice steady.

"Yes. And your sister, Louisa."

Ainsley's gray eyes were sympathetic, and Isabella swallowed a lump in her throat. Isabella hadn't been allowed to see or speak to her mother and younger sister since the night of her debut ball and subsequent elopement. For more than six long years, her father had forbidden her all communication with the family, even after she'd stopped living with Mac.

"How are they?" she managed.

"Quite well," Ainsley said. "They are looking forward to Louisa's come-out in the spring."

An ache burrowed into Isabella's heart. "Yes, I'd heard Louisa is due to make her bow. She is seventeen now, time enough."

"Eighteen, your mother said."

Isabella's breath caught on a sob. Eighteen already. Isabella had lost track, which hurt her all the more.

She remembered with clarity the afternoon of her fateful coming-out ball. Louisa had helped Isabella dress, spinning dreams of what she'd do at her own debut ball, crying because she was too young to attend Isabella's.

Louisa would be the girl in white now, with pearls around her throat. Gentlemen would scrutinize her, deciding her worth as their bride.

"I'm sure she'll be a success, Isabella," Ainsley said. "Louisa is so very lovely."

On impulse, Isabella reached for Ainsley's hands. She had no idea how to ask without sounding desperate, so she took a breath and simply asked. "When you see Louisa again, will you tell her how proud I am of her? Not within my mother's hearing, of course."

Ainsley smiled. "Of course I will." She squeezed Isabella's hands. "And I will bring you any message she wishes to send. Your mama doesn't need to know a thing."

Isabella breathed a sigh. "Thank you, Ainsley. You were always good-hearted."

"Despite what the others said?" Ainsley's smile turned wicked, and she wound her fingers through Isabella's in a complicated pattern they'd come up with at the academy. Isabella started to laugh. "Miss Pringle's ladies are ever loyal," Ainsley said.

They shared another laugh, and Ainsley flowed back into the crowd toward where her brother and his wife stood with the press of Mrs. Monroe's admirers.

Isabella suddenly could stand the crush no longer. She hurried to the door at the rear of the drawing room and plunged into the shadowed back hall. She had ordered the lights to be left off there and on the upper staircase, to discourage the guests from wandering the house. The quiet here was soothing, and she drew a breath of relief.

A movement caught her eye at the top of the stairs, followed by a whiff of cigar smoke. Isabella pressed her lips together, gathered her skirts, and mounted the stairs.

She moved around the landing to the man lounging against the railings, but as she neared, she realized that two figures stood there. Two cigar ends glowed with light, illuminating not only Mac but his tall and spare nephew, Daniel.

Isabella's skirts swished as she released them. "Good heavens, Daniel, how did you get here? What are you even doing in London?"

"I asked him the same question," Mac said, his voice deceptively mild.

"Before or after you gave him the cheroot?"

Mac raised his hands. "Not guilty. *He* gave a cheroot to *me*."

Isabella ignored him. "Daniel, you are supposed to be with Cam's professor, taking extra study."

"I know, but I couldn't stick it." Of all the Mackenzies, Daniel had least let English public schools dim his Scots accent. "The man is daft, and it's bloody unfair that I'm imprisoned in Cambridge while Da' does th' St. Leger."

"Your Da' is here in London," Isabella said.

A furious puff on the cigar. "I know. Uncle Mac just told me. Why's he here? He's no business traipsing to London when the races are about to start."

Isabella frowned at his cheroot. "You are too young for that."

"I'm fifteen. Besides, Da' gives them to me. He says I

need to learn the bad habits of gentleman right away so I won't seem prudish when I'm older."

"Perhaps Uncle Mac should have a word with your Da'."

Mac backed away in surrender, the cigar held between two fingers. "Uncle Mac should stay the hell out of Cameron's business. If my brother wants to spoil his son rotten, who am I to stop him?"

"But he don't spoil me rotten," Daniel protested. "He locks me up with an old man who can barely speak and who makes me read dull books in Latin all day. It's not fair. Da' was bad as bad could be when he was a lad. They still talk about wha' he got up to at Harrow. Why can't I be like him?"

"Perhaps Cameron has realized that being bad didn't pay," Isabella said.

Daniel snorted. "Not bloody likely. He's still as bad, and now there's no one to stop him." His look turned pleading. "Can I stay here with you, Auntie? Please? Just until the races? If I stay with Uncle Mac, Da' will find me and give me a thrashing. You won't tell on me, will you?"

Though it was practiced, Daniel's pleading touched Isabella's heart. Cameron carelessly shuttled the lad between school and the Mackenzie brothers' houses, not always having time for his son. Daniel was a lonely young man. But that did not mean that Daniel should be allowed to run wild, that Isabella should condone him disobeying his father. "I ought to say no."

"That's all right," Daniel said cheerfully. "If ye turn me out, I can always sleep in the gutter, or in a bawdy house."

Mac chuckled softly, and Isabella threw him a glare. "You'll sleep in my back bedroom at the top of these stairs," she said severely. "Go on up, and I'll have one of the footmen make up the bed for you." As Daniel started a happy jig, she went on. "Only until we go to Doncaster, mind, where I will turn you over to your father. And only if you behave. Any mischief, and I'll send for him right away."

"I'll be good, Auntie. I don't care if Da' locks me up with monks afterward as long as I don't miss the St. Leger."

"And no cigars."

Daniel removed the cigar from his mouth and dropped it into an antique porcelain bowl on a side table. "Say, Aunt Isabella, can a pretty maid come up and make my bed rather than a footman?"

"No," Mac said at the same time as Isabella.

Isabella continued, "I'll give my maids permission to slap you if you pester them. They work too hard to be annoyed by you."

"Aw, I was only teasing." Daniel seized Isabella's hands and kissed her cheek. "Good night, Auntie. You're my favorite aunt, you know."

"I heard you say the same to Beth not more than a week ago."

"Her too." Daniel laughed as he charged up the stairs and into the room at the top. He slammed the door behind him so hard the stairs trembled.

Isabella let out a sigh. "He runs more wild each year."

Mac fished the cheroot from her priceless antique bowl and laid the two cigars on the edge of the table, positioned so they wouldn't burn the wood. "You're good for the lad."

"I'm too soft on him. He needs a firm hand."

"He needs a gentle one as well," Mac pointed out.

"I remember the morning after you married me, Daniel came charging into our house in Mount Street and mistook me for one of your models."

"Aye, I remember boxing his ears for his impertinence."

"The poor mite. He didn't know." Isabella turned to the railing, watching her guests talking and laughing below, wondering why she didn't want to go back down to them. "He was all of nine years old, seeking refuge because he'd been sent home from school again and was afraid to tell Cam."

"Spare him your sympathy. The 'poor mite' dropped a mouse down my coat to get back at me for the ear boxing."

"I think perhaps none of you ever grew up."

"Oh, but we did."

Mac's hands came around Isabella's waist. His warmth covered her back, her bustle bent under his weight, and his lips burned the curve of her neck.

Chapter 6

A most lavish soiree held by the Lady of Mount Street Saturday last was marred somewhat by the failure of her Lord to make an appearance. The Lady assured her guests that his Lordship would be only a little late, but it was discovered in the small hours of the morning that he had gone to Rome instead. Perhaps he took a wrong turning?

—February 1876

Isabella closed her eyes, gripping the railing until her fingers ached. "I should go down."

Mac's teeth grazed her skin. "They are enjoying themselves on their own. Your task is finished."

He was right. The crowd had a new focus point—the soprano. Isabella's mission had been to draw notice to the singer's talent, and she'd done it. She was the director who could now retire to the wings. An excellent excuse to linger.

As Mac's hands glided along the satin of her bodice, Isabella's thoughts fled back through years, to the night she and Mac had hosted their first grand soiree at his Mount Street house. They'd stood like this on the landing while their guests roamed below, eager to see what effect Mac's marriage had wrought on his bachelor's abode. Isabella had felt wild and wicked and reckless. All those people, many well-respected members of society, had no idea that she stood in the shadows above, letting her rakish husband put love bites on her neck.

"You still wear yellow roses for me," he said into her skin.

"Not necessarily for you," she said faintly. "Redheads can't wear pink ones."

"You wear what you please and damn your detractors." Mac nibbled her earlobe, her earring trickling into his mouth.

It would be easy to give in to him. Easy to let him touch her until she forgot pain and grief, despair and anger, and her burning loneliness.

She'd done it before. She'd smiled at him and welcomed him back after each one of his disappearances, and all would be sunshine between them again. More than sunshine—it had been happiness words couldn't express, an expanse of joy that tore at her until she'd thought she'd come apart.

Then it would start again. Mac's nearly obsessive attentiveness would give way to irritation, deteriorating tempers on both their parts. Their quarrels would start small and then escalate into blazing rows. Then more hurting, more sorrow, Mac retreating into drunkenness and wild behavior until Isabella would wake to find him gone again.

Mac pressed a kiss behind her ear, and the memory of the bad times dissolved into pure feeling. His mouth was hot, his clever tongue touching places that he knew aroused her. Below them, guests chattered and talked, unaware of the two in the shadows above. Mac moved his hand to her décolletage, slid fingers inside her bodice.

Isabella leaned back into him, letting him take her weight in his arms while his hard fingertips played with her breast. She turned her head, and Mac caught her lips with his.

Mac had taught Isabella to kiss, taking his time and showing her every technique. He'd begun the lessons on her father's chill terrace, continued them in the carriage on the way to the bishop's house. More still on the way back to his own house, while his ring, which he'd slipped on her finger during the makeshift ceremony, had weighed heavily on her hand.

He'd carried her up the stairs to his bedroom and then taught her that her preconceptions of what husband and wife did in bed were all wrong. No lying quietly while her husband took his pleasure with her body, as was her "duty." No praying it would be over soon. No pain, no fear.

Mac had touched her as though she were an exquisite piece of art, learning her body while he encouraged her to learn his. He'd been so incredibly gentle and loving, and at the same time, wicked. He'd teased her and made her blush, taught her naughty words, and let her explore the hard planes of his interesting body. He'd taken her virginity slowly, never rushing, never hurting her.

He'd had oils that let him slide gently into her, easing her tightness so she could take him without pain. He'd done other things with the oils—used them to glide his hands across her skin, showed her how to use them on *his* body to bring him to arousal. He'd taught her that he could find exquisite pleasure with her even when he didn't enter her, and then Mac proved that he could give Isabella the same kind of pleasure in turn.

Isabella had fallen in love with his tenderness as well as his strength, his playfulness as well as the way his smiles died just before his climax came. She'd loved Mac's laughter, his growls, even his irritation, which could become laughter again in an instant.

Isabella's gaze strayed to her bedroom door, not five feet from where they stood. Below her, people talked and laughed, oblivious, as Mac's tongue caught and tangled hers. She craved Mac with everything she had. And the bedchamber was so close.

Mac broke the kiss and stepped back, removing his wonderful warmth. "No," he said. He drew a shaking breath. "I don't want this."

Isabella blinked, the sudden cold on her skin like a slap. "You certainly do want this. Do you wish me to kiss you or kick you away? Please be consistent."

Mac ran a hand through his hair, his eyes tight in the darkness. "What I want is everything. I refuse to take crumbs."

Isabella shook her head. "I can't give you everything. Not now."

"I know you can't. But understand this: I want to take you to bed and have you wake up with me, unashamed, no regrets, no tossing me out before anyone catches us. I want your trust, whole and unblemished. I will keep fighting until I have that."

Confusion made her voice sharp. "And what assurance do I have that you won't make me deliriously happy and then tear me apart again? Like you did every single time you left and turned up again weeks later, expecting forgiveness?"

Mac stepped to her again, took her face between his hands. "I know what I did to you. And I have punished myself over and over for it, believe me. If it makes you feel better, the months after I'd ceased drinking were hell on earth. I wanted to die, and probably would have expired if not for Bellamy."

"That does not make me feel better," she said, anguished. "I hate to think of you like that."

"Never worry—I learned to drink tea instead of whiskey. I've become rather obsessed with tea, in fact. Bellamy finds and brews the best exotic blends. He's a master." Mac traced her cheekbone, his thumb a point of warmth. "But I will tell you what makes *me* feel better. That in the years we've been apart, neither of us has turned to another for comfort. That tells me a great deal."

"It tells me I was too crushed to trust a man with my heart ever again."

He gave her his breath-stopping smile, and Isabella quailed. Mac always managed to gain the upper hand; how, she did not know.

Yes, she did know: Mac Mackenzie was master at the art of seduction.

"It tells me I still have a chance," he said. "One day you'll ask me to stay, Isabella. One day. And I'll be there for you. I promise."

Mac released her, and Isabella slammed her arms over her chest. "No. I don't want to see you again. Do not come back into my house. It's not fair."

He laughed. "I'm not interested in being fair. I'm fighting for our marriage and our life. Fair doesn't come into it." Mac cupped her cheek again. "But tonight, I'll leave you to your guests and not scandalize you."

Isabella drew a sharp breath, not certain whether to be pleased by the development. "Thank you."

"We'd better go back down before someone happens to notice we've both disappeared. Speculation will run rampant. London likes to talk." Mac adjusted the edge of her décolletage that he'd mussed, the brush of his fingers sending fires across her skin.

He touched her lips again, his eyes full of heat, but he turned her around and let her precede him down the stairs.

When she reached the bottom, the guests in the hall surged around her, and Isabella had to turn and greet them. She saw Mac out of the corner of her eye make his way down the stairs and through the crowd, talking, smiling, shaking hands as though he were still the master of the house. She heard his laughter, and then she was pulled into the drawing room, and Mac was lost to sight. When she emerged much later, to see her guests off, Mac was gone.

~~~~

The wee hours of the morning found Mac back in his studio. He'd yielded to Bellamy's annoyed look and stripped out of his evening suit for his kilt again. He tied his red gypsy scarf over his head and started piling colors onto his palette.

Painting was the only thing that relieved his craving for Isabella. No, *relieved* was too tame. *Kept it at bay for a few brief moments* was a better description.

The painting he'd done of her sleeping on her side was still wet, and Mac set it carefully on a rack stretched between two tables to dry before he propped another canvas on the easel. For this one he began with charcoal, outlining the picture that came to him in crystal clarity.

Isabella was nude in this one as well. She sat with her legs stretched in front of her, knees slightly bent. She leaned her elbows on her knees, rendering her back a long, bare curve. Her hair partly obscured her face and fell in red rivulets over her skin.

Mac kept the colors completely pale for this one: whites, yellows, and light browns; even her hair was more brown than red, as though she sat in shadow. Mac lovingly stroked the paint across her long legs, her arms, down the length of her back. Curls straggled over her shoulders, hiding all but one firm curve of breast. She was contemplating something on the floor next to her, and Mac painted it in, a half-blown yellow rose.

He was sweating by the time he'd finished, though the room was cold. Mac stood back, breathing hard, and studied what he'd created. The painting sang with life, the simple lines of Isabella's body exuding beauty, serenity, and sensuality.

Kissing her tonight, feeling her skin under his fingers, breathing her warmth, had ramped up Mac's desires until he thought he'd die. He'd seen her glance at the door near them on the landing, had guessed that her bedroom lay behind it. It had been all he could do to stop himself snatching her up and running inside it with her, tossing her on the bed and tearing off that beautiful satin gown. He'd done such a thing before, and those times, she'd surrendered to him with laughter.

Mac jammed a brush into dark brown paint and scrawled "Mackenzie" across the bottom. Chasing Isabella to London suddenly seemed very foolish, the way in which Mac was sure to lose the rest of his sanity.

He tossed the brush onto the table just as he smelled the first heavy odor of fire.

Mac opened the studio door to see a black wedge of smoke issuing from the door opposite. Snatching up a heavy drop cloth, Mac hurried across the landing and opened the door.

He looked into a cave of flames. Fire crawled from a pile of broken furniture in the middle of the room, eating the dry board floor and the stack of discarded drapes from the last redecoration Isabella had done. The flames had already caught the furniture that remained whole—a heavily carved chest of drawers, an old chaise, a cradle.

Mac rushed inside. He knew it was hopeless even as he unfurled the drop cloth and beat at the fire. He'd taken too long to notice, been too absorbed in his painting, and now the flames were out of control.

"My lord!"

At Bellamy's shout, Mac ran out, slamming the door, and shoved open the door of the next room, where two maids lay sleeping. "Up!" Mac roared at them. "Get up and out. Hurry!"

The two girls screamed, first at being jerked awake by the master of the house in nothing but a kilt, then again when they saw the smoke.

Mac left them to it and ran back to his studio. Every foul word he'd ever learned poured from his mouth as he gathered up the three paintings he'd finished. He stacked them carefully, using the drying rack he'd designed to separate them. There would be some smearing, but hopefully he could repair the damage. He wrapped the entire bundle in a sheet and carried it out in time to run into Bellamy coming up the stairs.

The hall was thick with smoke, the fire consuming the attic door. Mac coughed, and Bellamy said frantically, "Mary and Sal ain't come down yet."

Mac shoved the wrapped canvases at him. "You get those out. I'll get Mary and Sal."

"No, my lord. *You* come down. Now!"

"Bellamy, those canvases are worth my life. You guard them with yours. *Go.*"

He released the pictures so Bellamy would have to grab for them. Giving Mac a despairing look, Bellamy retreated down the attic stairs, the sheet-wrapped bundled clenched in his big hands.

Mac pushed open the door to the maids' room again. The wall between their bed and the attic was in flames, the smoke thick. Both Sal and Mary were on the floor, Sal coughing—both had lingered to try to dress.

Mac grabbed Sal around the waist. "Come on. Go."

"Mary," Sal sobbed.

Mary lay unmoving on the floor. Mac stooped and lifted her over his shoulder, at the same time shoving Sal out into the hall in front of him.

The landing was bathed in flames. Mac heard a creak and a groan as the stairs to the lower floors gave way.

Sal screamed at the top of her lungs, "We're trapped. We're trapped."

"My lord!" Bellamy stood below, looking up in anguish.

"Damn you, Bellamy. Get those paintings *out*. We'll escape through the roof."

Mac pushed Sal into his studio and slammed the door on smoke. In a matter of seconds, the fire would jump to this room—a room filled to the brim with paints, oil of turpentine, and other things that liked to explode.

He dragged his table to the middle of the room, leapt upon it, and pushed open the skylight. He grabbed Sal first, boosting her up through the opening. Sal bravely grabbed the roof slates and rolled out, pressing a foot against Mac's shoulder to help.

Mac jumped down and lifted Mary, who was starting to come 'round now that she was out of the smoke. Her eyes fluttered open and she gasped at him in stark terror.

Mac gave her an encouraging grin. "No time for screaming, my dear. Up you go."

Sal reached down and helped Mac get Mary through the opening, Sal pulling the girl up and onto the roof. Mac jumped, grabbed the sill, and slithered through the skylight just as the fire burst into the studio.

"What do we do now?" Sal wailed. "We're so high."

"We get away from here before that fire gets to all my paints. Onward."

Mary started to cry, staring across the roofs in sheer terror. Sal was a little more resilient, quietly seizing Mac's offered hand in a desperate grip. Both girls clung to him but allowed him to tow them across the sloping roof to the roof of the house next door.

The house was currently empty, Mac knew, the family

away in the country. The skylight was latched, not yielding to Mac's tugging. He jerked the gypsy scarf from his head, wrapped it around his fist, and punched through the pane. The glass was thick, and it took several tries. He cut his hand badly, but at last he reached through the hole he'd made and released the catch.

The cold, stuffy attic, free of smoke, smelled good as Mac lowered himself into it. He reached up to catch first Mary then Sal as they slithered after him. He led the two maids out of the attic room and down the long staircases to the front door.

The two girls were sobbing in relief when Mac unbolted and threw open the door. People had poured out of nearby houses, neighbors and their servants already forming a bucket chain. Mac joined them until the clanging of bells announced the arrival of the fire brigade with their water pump and hoses. The machinery might not save Mac's house, but it could prevent the fire from spreading down the street.

Mac scowled at an empty-armed Bellamy, who came running toward him. "Where the devil are my paintings?"

"In your coach, my lord. I got it and the horses out of the mews."

Something inside Mac loosened. "I think you need a rise in wages, Bellamy. You didn't happen to bring one of my shirts out as well, did you?"

"In the coach, sir. A complete set of clothing."

Mac clapped Bellamy on his beefy shoulder. "You're a marvel of a man. No wonder you won all your matches."

"Preparation, sir." Bellamy looked up at the house and the smoke above it, the crowded street, the firemen plying the walls with water. "What do we do now, my lord?"

Mac laughed, which ended on a cough. "We climb into the coach you so thoughtfully prepared and find another

place to spend the night. I believe I know just where
to go."

⁓

Isabella leaned over the landing where Mac had kissed her
not six hours ago and drew her wrapper closed over her
chilled body.

"Morton, what on earth is going on?"

The babbling of voices below didn't cease, and Morton
didn't answer. Isabella trotted down the stairs, stopping in
astonishment before she reached the bottom.

Mac's entire household—Bellamy, Mac's cook, footmen, and two maids—were trailing toward the back stairs,
all talking excitedly to Morton and other members of Isabella's staff. "You should have seen 'im, Mr. Morton," the
maid called Mary said. "His lordship was like the hero in
a magazine story, carrying us out and across the rooftops
and all. I'd like to have *swooned*."

Isabella cupped her hands around her mouth. "Morton!"

Mac strolled out of her dining room, arrogant as you
please, and grinned up at her. His shirt was open to the
waist, his kilt pocked with burn-marks, his face soot-
stained, his auburn hair partially singed.

"Beg pardon, yer ladyship," he said in an exaggerated
Cockney accent. "But could you see your way to taking in
meself and me band of gypsies?"

Chapter 7

Mount Street is once more overflowing with *entertainment* as the Titian-haired Lady held an End-of-Season ball lasting *a day and a night*. The Lord and Lady were once more billing and cooing, their guests among the most glittering in the land, including the Lord's oldest brother, the high-placed Duke. Meanwhile the Lady's father, a redoubtable peer, spends his days giving lectures on *temperance* and *modesty*.

—June 1876

Isabella stared down the stairs in shock. "Mac, what the devil happened?"

Mac's grin remained in place as he looked up at her, but his eyes held anger. Down the hall, Morton herded the babbling group, including Daniel, toward the back stairs. The door shut behind them, halving the noise.

"Someone set fire to my attics," Mac said. "The fire brigade managed to quash the blaze before it destroyed the entire house, but the upper floors are pretty much ruined."

Isabella's eyes widened. "Your studio?"

"Gone. Or at least I assume so. The lads from the fire brigade wouldn't let me back in."

"Is everything in the attics burned?" A small dart of pain lanced her heart. "Everything?"

"Yes." Mac's eyes softened. "It's gone. I'm sorry."

Isabella swallowed, her throat burning, and she wiped away a tear that trickled from her eye. How silly, she thought in anger. Why weep over a piece of furniture when Mac and his people were obviously safe?

She cleared her throat. "Your servants may, of course, stay here. I wouldn't turn them out."

"And what about the master, your ladyship?" Mac rested one arm on the newel post, unnerving in his disheveled dress. "Would you turn him out?"

"*You* can afford a hotel."

"No hotel will admit me looking like this, love. I am in desperate need of a bath."

A vision swooped at her of Mac leaning back in the zinc-lined tub in her large bathroom, his voice raised in some Scottish tune. He always sang in the bathtub, and for some absurd reason that memory made her blood heat.

"Cameron is in town," she began.

"Ah, but he's lodging at the Langham Hotel. Same problem."

"I cannot imagine you have no more friends in Mayfair who can put you up."

"Most of my friends are off in the country riding horses or shooting things. Or they're in Paris or Italy painting the view."

"What about Hart's house? It's always staffed."

"It is the middle of the night, and I don't want to wake them." Mac's raffish grin returned. "I'm afraid you are my last hope, my dear."

"You're a poor liar. I do hope that the gossip newspapers do not put about that you started the fire yourself as an excuse to come here. I can imagine them saying so."

Mac lost his smile. "I will strangle them if they do. Sal and Mary almost burned to death."

Isabella shivered, the weight of the situation pressing at her. "I know you'd never be that ruthless."

"Oh, I *can* be ruthless, love. Never doubt that." Mac mounted the stairs toward her, the acrid scent of smoke clinging to him. "Whoever did this couldn't be bothered to care that two girls were snug in their beds not ten feet away. He didn't worry about who else he might hurt." Mac's copper-colored eyes sparked with anger, but he was gentleness itself as he brushed the tear from her face. "Whoever this chap is, he doesn't know the meaning of ruthlessness. But I assure you, my love, he will find out."

Mac did sing in the bathtub.

A bathroom had been added to Isabella's house by the previous owner, the room squeezed between the front and rear bedrooms on the second floor. A door from each led to it. The tub and sink had running water, fortified by a pump and cistern in the basement.

Isabella sat stiffly before her fireplace, hands clenched on the arms of her chair. Half an hour ago she'd heard Mac enter the bathroom, heard his low conversation with Bellamy, then the water filling the tub. Finally, Mac splashed into it, Bellamy departed, and Mac's voice rose in song.

Isabella could not bring herself to go back to bed while Mac bathed himself on the other side of her door. She would sit and wait until he retreated to his own room and all was quiet again.

"*And it is, it is, a glorious thing, to be a pirate kiiiing . . .*"

Mac's baritone cut out, and she heard more splashing. He should be finished by now, drat him. He'd rise from the bath, water dripping down his tall body, slickly wet as he reached for a towel.

Isabella's hands tightened until her nails dug into the fabric of the chair. If Mac hadn't remained such a handsome man in the intervening years, would it have been easier to turn him away tonight? She thought it might have been. Rather unfair of her.

No, she thought as Mac began to hum again. He'd be *Mac* no matter what he looked like. Charming, reckless, smiling, stealing her heart.

The tune was slower this time, his voice low and dark.

In bonny town, where I was born.
There was a fair maid dwellin'.
Made every youth cry, "well-away!"
Her name was Iiiis-a-bella.

Isabella jumped to her feet, stormed to the door, and flung it open.

Mac lay in the bathtub, up to his neck in soapy water, his arms resting carelessly along the sides of the tub. Little red cuts laced his hands and arms from where he'd broken the skylight to save the maids. He gave her a leisurely smile as she halted, hand frozen on the doorknob.

"The fair maid's name was Barbara Allen," Isabella said coldly.

"Was it? I must have forgotten the words."

Isabella clutched the knob, her palm damp. "You're lingering. Finish, dress, and leave my house. You're clean enough now to find a hotel."

"I *am* finished." Mac gripped the sides of the tub and hauled himself to his feet.

Isabella's mouth went dry. Mac Mackenzie had always had the most delectable male body, and nothing had changed. Water slicked his muscles and darkened the red-brown hair on his head and chest, and the thatch between his legs gleamed copper. He was half erect, the crown of his cock pushing toward her as though it sought her touch.

Mac's smile went positively sinful. He was challenging Isabella to behave like a maiden—perhaps the cruel Barbara Allen of the ballad, a standoffish beauty for whom men died. He was waiting for Isabella to scream, to have hysterics, or at least grow angry and slam the door.

Isabella arched her brows, leaned against the doorframe, and deliberately looked her fill.

Red touched Mac's cheekbones as he stepped out of the tub to trickle water all over the floor. He put his hands behind his neck, clasping his fingers to press his arms out and back. The muscles of his body rippled like a symphony.

Isabella made herself stand still even when he began walking toward her. She caught the scent of the soap Bellamy must have brought for him, an odor filled with memories. She'd often slipped into the bathroom at Mount Street to wash Mac's back, sitting on the side of the tub while she lathered his skin. Often these bathing sessions ended up with her being pulled into the water with him, dressing gown and all.

Isabella's heart throbbed in sickening beats as Mac came closer. He was going to kiss her. He was going to take her in his arms and take her in a punishing kiss, claiming her until she could no longer deny her need for him.

At the last minute, Mac reached to the wall beside her and pulled a towel from a hook.

He wrapped the towel around his waist. "Disappointed?" he asked.

Bloody cheek. "Don't be silly."

Isabella knew Mac didn't want this to be easy for her. He wanted her to work at what was between them, to peel back the layers of cool politeness behind which they'd retreated, to admit the raw core of their pain.

"I'm not ready," she whispered.

Mac touched her chin, water dripping from his fingertip to chase down her throat. "I know. Else you'd not have cried about the cradle."

Her throat tightened. "Perhaps it was symbolic."

Mac's voice went gruff. "No, it was not symbolic, or a

message from the other side, or any other occult nonsense. It simply happened to be in the room where a madman started a fire."

"I know."

Isabella hadn't meant that the cradle's destruction was a bad omen, a portent for their future together. She'd meant that perhaps the fire had removed a reminder of their failure; perhaps with that barrier burned to ash they could start afresh.

"That's my girl." Mac stepped back. A towel around his waist did not make him any less mouth-watering; it only made Isabella long to hook her finger around the cloth and pull it away. "Sensible in the face of tribulation," he said. "I've always loved that about you."

Isabella lifted her chin and willed her voice not to shake. "Miss Pringle taught us that practical common sense was much more important than learning how to pour tea."

"Someday I must meet Miss Pringle and congratulate her on her success."

"She'd hardly want to meet you. She has no use for men."

Mac leaned closer, warmth filling the space between them. "Maybe she'll make an exception for me. After all, I'm in love with her best and brightest student."

"I was one of her dullest, not brightest."

"Liar."

Mac slid his hand to the back of her neck, under her hair, and a trickle of water found its way inside her collar. His breath touched her lips, and Isabella closed her eyes, waiting for the soft pressure of his mouth.

It never came. He caressed her neck for a moment or two then released her. As chill disappointment wrapped her heart, Mac kissed his fingertip, slightly wrinkled from the water, and pressed it to her lips.

"I've changed my mind about the hotel," he said. "Your

house is much more comfortable. See you in the morning, love."

He turned from her, made for the other door, and just as he opened it, dropped the towel.

Isabella sagged against the doorframe as her gaze riveted to his tight and beautiful backside. His skin was bronzed above the waist, paler below where his kilt would cover him from country sunshine.

She remembered how she'd loved to watch his naked body as Mac lounged in bed after lovemaking, kicking back the covers when he grew too warm. They'd laugh and talk, tease each other, and return to loving, so comfortable with each other. Those days seemed so long ago, so far away.

Mac grinned over his shoulder at her, and whistling, walked into his bedroom and closed the door behind him.

It was a long time before Isabella could peel herself from the doorway and return to sit rigidly in her chair before the fire. Going to bed for the remaining few hours of the night was out of the question.

~

Isabella entered her dining room in the morning to see two newspapers held by two sets of male hands, one set large and muscular, the other narrower and bonier. The occasional crunch of toast sounded behind the sheets of newsprint.

Isabella seated herself in the chair Bellamy held out for her, while her footman set a plate of steaming eggs and sausage before her. She thanked both servants politely and started sorting through the post that lay to the right of her plate. Down the table, pages turned and more toast crunched.

Haughty society ladies might be surprised to see the wild Mackenzies apparently tamed into such domestic order. *An illusion,* Isabella would have to tell them. Newspapers and breakfasts simply kept them quiet for a time.

And yet, there *had* been many mornings like this. Breakfasts at Kilmorgan Castle when all four brothers were under one roof were happy occasions, filled with loud laughter and male speech. Breakfasts at Mount Street had been cozy and quiet—sometimes Mac would walk down the length of the table to her on some pretense, sit next to her, lift her onto his lap. They'd cuddle together, feeding each other bits of the cooling breakfast. Isabella eyed the barrier of Mac's newspaper and shivered with memories.

Someone thumped on the front door. Bellamy set down a pot of steaming coffee and departed to answer it.

Why was Bellamy answering doors? Isabella wondered. Where the devil was Morton? Mac had been in the house perhaps five hours, and already he was rearranging the staff's schedule.

"Let me in, Bellamy," came a gravelly, male voice. "I know he's in there."

Daniel's newspaper flew high as he exploded out from under it. He gave Isabella one wild, pleading look then raced through the connecting door to the library.

Mac laid down his paper and took up another piece of toast. Cameron strode into the dining room and scowled at Mac, Isabella, the hastily pushed back chair, and the scattered newspaper. Isabella motioned Bellamy to pour her more coffee, and Mac took a bite of toast as Cameron made for the connecting door, flung it open, and stormed inside.

There was the sound of a scuffle, voices raised in protest, and the bang of another door. Cameron entered the dining room through the hall again, dragging a struggling Daniel with him.

"Ow, Da', let me go."

Cameron shoved Daniel back into his chair. "What the devil do ye think ye're doing here?"

"Aunt Isabella said I could stay."

Isabella continued to sort through her letters as though nothing very remarkable had happened. "I thought it best, Cam. He'd only have run away again if I'd sent him back to your professor."

"Aye, that's likely true." Cameron scraped back a chair and sat heavily on it. The big man wore a black evening suit and kilt, presumably leftover from the night before. His cravat was crumpled and his face dark with whiskers, but otherwise, he looked as wide awake as Mac. Isabella, on the other hand, was groggy from lack of sleep. Mac lying in a bed two rooms away had kept her on the chair, eyes open, for the rest of the night.

"Bring me something to eat, Bellamy," Cameron said. "I'm famished. And coffee, lots of it."

Bellamy was already on his way with the coffeepot. The footman opened the dumbwaiter and extracted another tray of covered dishes to place in front of Cameron.

Daniel rubbed his neck. "You're supposed to be in Scotland with the ponies, Da'. How did you know I was here?"

"Dr. Nichols telegraphed to Kilmorgan that you'd gone missing. Hart telegraphed me."

"Dr. Nichols is a daft old man," Daniel grumbled. "I thought he'd be too scared of you to tell on me."

Cameron dissected his eggs and sausage. "That daft old man is one of the most brilliant physicists in the world, ye little beggar. I wanted him to teach you something."

"Not if it means missing the St. Leger."

"Daniel did promise to return to his studies if he was allowed to go to the races," Isabella said. "Didn't you, Daniel?"

"I did," Daniel said in a bright voice. "I promise I'll become a dried-up stick like Dr. Nichols if you let me go to Doncaster w' ye. It's damned unfair for me to have to miss it. I never miss the St. Leger."

"You watch your language around a lady," Cam growled.

"Aunt Isabella don't mind."

"That doesn't make any difference. Apologize."

"Oh, very well. Sorry, Auntie, for m' foul tongue."

Isabella gave Daniel a gracious nod, while Mac turned another page of his newspaper. Cameron gave attention to his coffee and held out the cup for Bellamy to refill.

"What the devil are *you* doing here, Mac? And why is Isabella serving you breakfast instead of dropping you down the cistern?"

"My house burned down," Mac said from behind his paper.

"What?"

Mac folded his newspaper, slid it to Cam, and tapped an article. The banner read: "Conflagration at peer's Mayfair home."

"They've got that wrong," Daniel said. "Uncle Mac's not a peer. Only Uncle Hart is."

"The reading public doesn't care, my boy," Mac said. "They just want to read about a fire at the house of an aristocrat."

"What the hell happened?" Cameron demanded.

Mac explained while Cam listened in growing bafflement and anger. "You think whoever's forging your paintings tried to burn you out? Why? Because you found out he was doing it? How did the bastard get inside your house at all? Beg pardon, Isabella."

Mac shrugged. "My front door stood unlocked much of the day. I have a footman stationed at the door, but I imagine he'd have had to relieve himself at some point."

"Or he let in the culprit himself," Cameron suggested.

"I'd be surprised; he's loyal. I plan to quiz him, but I'm letting my servants sleep this morning. They had a bad night."

"Bellamy isn't sleeping." Isabella looked pointedly at the former pugilist who remained hovering nearby with the coffeepot.

"He refused," Mac said. He shot Bellamy a severe look, which Bellamy blandly returned. "He seems to think I'll be struck down by an assassin if he lets me out of his sight."

"Could be." Cameron shoved his plate away and wiped his mouth on a napkin. He took another long drink of coffee and clattered the cup to the saucer. "You'll be safe enough here, Mac, with Bellamy and Isabella's household looking after you."

Mac slanted a smile down the table at Isabella. "Exactly what I thought."

"I'm certain the Langham will suit your needs much better," Isabella said coolly.

Cameron shook his head. "Hotel's full up. Heard the manager say it this morning."

If Cameron had been back to the hotel that morning, Isabella would eat her silverware. "Hart keeps his house open and ready at all times," she pointed out.

The brothers looked at each other, wordlessly trying to figure out how to refute her argument. Daniel grinned. "*I'll* stay in Hart's house."

"No, you will not," Cameron returned. "Isabella, would you mind if Danny stays on with you? It's only a few days until we go to Doncaster."

Daniel simultaneously brightened at the confirmation he'd get to attend the races and looked crestfallen that he'd have to stay with an auntie who didn't like him smoking. "I can go to the hotel with you, Da'. You already have a room there. I can squeeze in."

Cameron shook his head. "I'm in and out too much to keep a proper eye on you. Isabella's is the best place for you to stay." Cameron rose, came to Isabella, and kissed the top of her head. "Thank you, sister-in-law. Lovely breakfast. See you on the train, Mac."

He shot his son one last scowl and strode out of the room. In the hall he thanked the footman who'd scuttled to open the door for him, and was gone.

The room settled into silence, as though a hurricane had just blown itself out. Cameron Mackenzie was a force of nature.

Daniel stared wordlessly at the table while Isabella and Mac went back to their breakfasts. Daniel's long arms had grown out of his jacket; he'd sprouted up this summer, and now was nearly as tall as his father.

He was a little boy no longer, but he wasn't a man yet, either. His throat worked as he said, "Da' doesn't want me with him."

Isabella's heart squeezed in sympathy. "The hotel is full, that is all. And he's right: I can look after you more properly here."

"Don't patronize me, Auntie. He sent me to Dr. Nichols to get me out of his hair, and he's having me stay with you for the same reason. Da' doesn't give a monkey's ass whether I learn physics or not. He just doesn't want me at the hotel with him. He wants to go about w' women, and he doesn't want a fifteen-year-old son in his way."

"You take it too hard. Cam simply wants what he thinks best for you."

"The boy is right," Mac said. Isabella sent him a glare, but Mac shook his head. "Cam's never been domestic, and you know it. I don't know what woman can make him settle down, but I'd love to meet her."

Daniel brightened, prone to lightning changes of moods. "Settle down like you did, Uncle Mac?"

"Mind your tongue, boy."

"Leave him be." Isabella signaled to Bellamy, who approached with more coffee. "You're perfectly welcome to stay with me, Daniel. We'll play games all day, and you can escort me to the theater at night. I'm certain your Uncle Mac will have far too much to do to pay much attention to us."

"On the contrary." Mac set down his cup. "I have all the time in the world." He winked at Daniel. "Besides, I'm very good at games."

~

Mac spent the next two days busily trying not to go mad. Living in a house with Isabella, knowing she slept in the bedroom just beyond the bathroom, kept him sleepless and randy. But considering that someone had succeeded in burning Mac out of his house, possibly this person forging his paintings, possibly simply a mad arsonist, he wanted to keep a close eye on Isabella. A few of Bellamy's cronies from his pugilist days agreed to help watch Isabella's house, and Mac asked Inspector Fellows to have someone watch Crane's gallery in case the forger returned. The efficient inspector already had done so.

Meanwhile, Mac had to get through the strain of living in close proximity with Isabella without touching her. The worst was when he heard her maid prepare the bath for her, followed by the soft splash as Isabella descended into the water.

He'd groan and rub his face, his body demanding that he fling open the door and fall into the water with her. She'd be soapy and bare, her skin flushed with heat. Even stroking himself for relief didn't do much good. The only hands that could appease him were hers.

Leaving for Doncaster couldn't come quickly enough for him—but then again, Mac was loathe to abandon the cozy setup of the two of them in one house. Daniel was there too, of course, the boy cheerfully escorting Isabella about. Mac would trail along with them, wishing Cameron could take care of his own son, but not having the heart to send Daniel away.

Mac strolled into the drawing room the day before they were to leave, while Daniel was out stocking up on books. That is, Daniel *claimed* that he was off to the book shops, but he was likely holed up somewhere playing cards with his friends.

Isabella sat near the window overlooking the garden behind the house. An open magazine rested in her lap, but she wasn't reading it. She gazed out at the rainy garden, the scarlet glory of her hair bright against her gray and blue frock.

She looked around when she heard him enter, and Mac saw that her eyes were rimmed with red.

He moved to the sofa and sat next to her. "Love, what is it?"

Isabella looked away. "Nothing."

"I know you far too well to believe that. 'Nothing' usually translates to 'something dreadful.'"

Isabella opened her mouth to argue, then closed it again and slid a cream-colored paper out from between the pages of her magazine. Mac took it and read.

My dearest sister,

I am excited beyond all measure at the prospect of communicating with you again. Mrs. Douglas has my deepest gratitude. My debut will commence this spring—dare I hope that I will be able to see you after my coming-out? I will look for you at every soiree and musicale and ball, longing for one glimpse of the beautiful sister I miss with all my heart. I must not linger on this note, or Papa will suspect something. I dare not risk you writing back to me, but if you were to give Mrs. Douglas any little message, or even the promise of a kiss when at last we meet, I would treasure it as the most precious diamond. Ever your loving sister,

Louisa

Familiar anger at Isabella's father rose as Mac read the missive. Earl Scranton was a selfish, priggish bastard. Isabella had cried without consolation when, after writing to her sister and mother immediately after her marriage to Mac, her letters had been returned by her father, cut into shreds. The earl had added a stern note forbidding Isabella further contact with the family. Scranton had never lifted the ban, not even when Isabella had ceased living with Mac.

Mac handed the letter back to Isabella. She slid it into her jacket, nestling it over her heart.

"This Mrs. Douglas is your old school chum?" he asked, striving for something light to say. "The one who could scramble down a trellis in her nightdress?"

Isabella nodded. "She offered to send my love to Louisa for me when she saw her again. Apparently she coaxed a note from Louisa to give me in return."

Mac leaned uncomfortably into the corner of the small sofa, few pieces of furniture able to accommodate his large body. "Good for Mrs. Douglas."

"She's rather sorry for me." Isabella gave him a faint smile. "But I'm grateful for her help."

"I am too." Mac fell silent, and Isabella looked out the window again.

Earl Scranton was the same kind of unforgiving terror Mac's own father had been, though in different ways. Mac's father had been volatile, hot-blooded, and violent, whereas Isabella's father was ice-cold and never raised his voice.

The litany of the many ways in which marriage to Mac had ruined Isabella's life paraded through his head. That she'd stuck with him for three years said much about her fortitude.

"We leave for Doncaster tomorrow," Isabella said without turning from the window. "You will not share a hotel suite with me there, so put the idea out of your head."

Mac stretched his arm across the back of the sofa. "You won't be staying in a hotel, love. Hart has hired a house for all of us, you and your servants included. Ian insists that Beth will be more comfortable in our own accommodations, and I agree with him." He propped his feet on the tea table, still seeking a comfortable position. "Beth will want you with her."

Isabella threw him an exasperated look. "Mac, we are separated. That is the end of it."

"No, it is not."

She frowned at him, green eyes filled with anger. He was glad to see the fury; anything to erase her heartbroken look.

"I left you to save my sanity, Mac," she said. "I'll hardly return to it if you continue to drive me mad."

"You like me driving you mad." Mac let his grin blossom. "Your life is empty when I'm not giving you hell." He broke off as Bellamy pushed open the door to allow Evans to carry in a tea tray. "Tea, excellent. I'm famished."

Isabella regarded the setup of two cups and saucers with annoyance. The servants seemed elated to have Mac in the house and had settled into the habit of preparing all meals for two. Which delighted Mac.

Evans and Bellamy retreated, and Mac brought his feet down. "Now, then, Isabella, a courting couple would take tea together, would they not? A gentleman would call on the lady, and she'd serve him tea."

"Not alone." Isabella reached for the teapot. "Her mama or prim governess or maiden aunt would sit against the wall, keeping a disapproving eye on the young couple."

"Very well, we will pretend that Great-Aunt Hortense lounges behind the potted palms." Mac gave a mock salute to an empty chair on the other side of the room. "Then what?"

"Then nothing. I'd pour out, and you'd drink the tea."

Isabella filled the cups as she spoke. Mac's heart skipped a beat when, without asking, she prepared it the way he liked it—two sugars, no milk. She remembered.

Mac took the cup and set it next to him, waiting politely as she lifted the cloth from a basket and laid a scone on a porcelain plate. He didn't reach for it until she'd prepared her own tea; then he pulled the scone into two pieces, mounding its soft innards with pale yellow cream.

"One of the only things the English do right is scones and clotted cream," he said. "The Scots invented scones of course, but the English do them well."

"I am English," Isabella reminded him.

"I know that, my lovely Sassenach."

Mac took a deep bite of scone. Isabella's gaze fixed on his mouth as clotted cream oozed over his lips. Mac licked them clean, deliberately taking his time.

"This is quite good." He gave her a wicked smile. "Would you like to try it?"

His heart beat faster as Isabella's cheeks stained pink. "Yes, I would, rather."

Mac lifted the piece of slathered scone to her. Isabella took it between her lips, her tongue coming out to lift it inside her mouth. Mac's body grew hot as he watched her chew, her slender throat moving as she swallowed.

Mac held up his thumb, showing her a bit of cream clinging to it. "I have a little here."

He waited for her to push him away, to bathe him in scorn and tell him that the game was over. Instead, she guided his hand to her mouth, closed her lips around the tip of his thumb, and sucked away the cream.

Mac groaned. "You are a cruel, cruel woman."

Isabella released his hand and sat back. "Why?"

"Tempting me with a taste of what I can't have."

"It is you who refuses to be satisfied with only a taste."

He set down his plate and ran a hand through his hair. "I don't want a taste, Isabella. I want all of you. Again and again, for the rest of our lives. That's what marriage means, my wife. Together forever. Bound in love."

"In duty, you mean," Isabella said.

He laughed. "Sassenach, if you believed marriage was for duty alone, you'd never have eloped with me in the first place. When you met me you didn't think, *Ah, here is a dashing rake. Let me run off with him so I can be dutiful.* No, you wanted some entertainment instead of marrying a dried-up stick your father picked out for you."

"Perhaps, but most marriages turn into duty and habit, from what I have witnessed."

Mac fell back against the sofa. "Oh, God, Isabella, you'll slay me with your pessimism. Look at Ian and Beth. They're mad about each other. Are you saying their marriage has changed to duty and habit?"

"Of course not."

"Nor did yours. Don't lie."

"No," she said softly. "It didn't."

Thank the Lord for that. He remembered the nights she'd smiled down at him in his bed, her warm body on his while she rode him. *Duty, my balls.*

"The proof is that when I drove you mad, you ran away," Mac said. "A dutiful woman would have stayed and put up with me."

"Gracious, I pity such a woman."

"I know you do, because you are not that woman. What you ought to have done was smash me over the head, repeatedly, until I came to my senses."

"Perhaps my leaving was meant to do just that."

He hid his dart of pain by reaching for the bowl of

cream. "You certainly got my attention, love." He scooped a glob of cream onto his first two fingers and gave her a sly look. "Now, I dare you, my fine lady from Miss Pringle's Academy: From which part of my anatomy would you like to lick this cream?"

Chapter 8

The Lady of Mount Street has retreated to her Cottage in Buckinghamshire, where her Garden Parties have become legendary. She is all smiles despite the sudden absence of her Lord, and she presented a Poetess who is likely to take London by storm. An unruly baron whom more salacious gossip paired with the Lady was coldly and unmistakably rebuffed, leading this paper to rejoice that the Lady remains a pillar of virtue.

—July 1876

Isabella stared at the mound of cream on Mac's blunt fingers, and her mouth went dry. She kept her gaze on the cream so she wouldn't have to look at his wicked smile and the gleam in his eyes.

Mac didn't think she'd do it. He thought she'd tell him to go away, or burn him with some acerbic witticism. He didn't think she'd dare reach over and gently lift a fold of his kilt. But she did.

"What did you say a Scotsman wore under this?" she asked.

Mac's pupils widened, black swallowing copper. "Isabella."

"If you thought your dare would make me blush like a schoolgirl, then you do not know much about schoolgirls."

Mac laughed. His laughter died as Isabella rose, walked to the drawing room door, and turned the key in the lock.

Mac remained on the sofa, watching her with a stunned look.

"The cream is melting," she said.

Mac snapped his gaze to the dribbles of cream running from his fingers. Isabella came to him, caught his hand, and licked his fingers clean.

Mac always tasted agreeable. Isabella savored the smooth sweetness of the cream overlaid with the tangy salt of his skin.

She sat down, touching the tartan again. "Show me?"

Mac swallowed, his laughter gone. He took the hem of his kilt, drew in a breath, and scooted the fabric up to his stomach.

He was bare beneath, his cock dark and hard as it rested on his tight abdomen. He was breathing rapidly, the cock moving a little with his pulse. Isabella remembered the exact feel of it in her hand, how long it was and how thick, exactly how far she had to pull her hand up to complete one stroke. She also remembered precisely how it tasted and felt in her mouth.

Mac had always enjoyed the way she touched him. He'd sometimes joked that she must have studied cock pleasuring at Miss Pringle's Select Academy, because she did it so well.

You taught me, Mac, she'd whisper.

He'd also never gone bare under his kilt. Isabella knew full well that Mac usually wore drawers beneath, claiming that it was all very well to be traditionally Scots, but he had no intention of freezing his goolies off to satisfy tradition. He'd worn nothing today for her. To tease her.

Time for Isabella to turn the tables. "Stand up," she said.

Mac got to his feet in a comically short time, the kilt still lifted. Isabella reached for the bowl of clotted cream, dipped her fingers into it, and smeared cream on his tip.

"Vixen." Mac's voice was ragged. He liked to call her that whenever she instigated play.

The word slid into a groan as Isabella leaned forward and closed her lips around him. His hands balled to fists over the fabric. Mac didn't reach for her, didn't touch her, just held the tartan out of the way in a white-knuckled grip.

Isabella suckled his tip, letting her tongue trace all the way around the flange. She dipped her tongue to the underside of the shaft to catch the cream that had dribbled there.

Mac rocked a little on his heels, but he didn't try to pump into her; he barely even moved. Not that Isabella didn't react herself. She was hot between her legs, and her breasts were tight, her heart pounding behind her corset.

They used to play games like this with each other—stealing pleasure without removing their clothes, seeing how far they could take each other. Even more enjoyable when they did it in an unusual place, such as in a deserted hall outside a ballroom, a summerhouse, Mac's studio. Isabella remembered how they'd tried to stifle their sounds of pleasure and their laughter.

Mac wasn't laughing now. "Little vixen," he whispered. "Naughty minx. My beautiful, wicked wife."

Isabella reached for more cream. Mac's cheekbones were flushed, his eyes desperate. Isabella focused on his cock again, slathering it lovingly with the cream.

Mac furrowed her hair with one hand. "I can't hold out, love. It's been too long."

Isabella couldn't answer, too busy nibbling and licking and suckling. She swallowed the cream she'd coated on him, and now she enjoyed the hot, velvety taste of Mac himself.

Mac touched the nape of her neck. "Pull back, sweetheart. I'm about to lose myself."

He used to warn her like that in case they were in danger of being caught, or were too near a public place, or in case Isabella didn't want to take the game to its conclusion. The courtesy warmed her, and she responded by sliding one hand to his bare buttocks and staying put.

She felt him move in little pulses, and then his warm seed spilled into her mouth. He bunched her hair, his hips rocking as Isabella took all of him. "I love you," he said brokenly. "I love you, my little Sassenach vixen."

Isabella savored him until he had no more to give. She pulled away and Mac collapsed to the sofa, breathing hard, his kilt draping him modestly once more. Isabella reached for her teacup, but Mac jerked the cup from her hand, clattered it back to the table, and wrapped his arms around her.

They sat together a long time, Mac holding her, Isabella's head on his shoulder. Isabella felt the *thrub-thrub* of his heart under her ear, his warm lips on her hair. If it could only be this way always, the two of them quietly absorbing each other, they could possibly live in peace. But they were both too volatile, too selfish, and Isabella knew it.

"Three and a half years," Mac was saying. "Three and a half years since I've felt that. Since I've felt *you*. Thank you, love."

Isabella looked up past Mac's sandpaper chin to his copper-colored eyes, which were tired but fixed on her. "You seemed to need it."

"That wasn't charity you just gave me, my sweet. You enjoyed that."

She gave him a faint smile. "Perhaps I felt it my duty as a wife."

"Pull the other one. It's got bells on."

She widened her eyes. "Good heavens, it has bells?"

Mac burst out laughing. His breath smelled of strong tea and cream. "Lord, I've missed you. I've missed you so much." He stroked a languid hand through her hair. "If anyone can tame the wild Mac, it's you."

"I think I don't want you tame. I like you wild."

"Do you? That's encouraging."

Isabella pushed away from him and reached for her now-cold tea. It was fine tea, but its taste was lost after the headiness of Mac.

"I won't rush you, Isabella," Mac said. "I won't. Promise."

"But you'll risk freezing your goolies off and move yourself into my house?" She smiled, and he smiled back. It was dangerous, Mac's smile.

"I never promised not to torment you. Or tease you, plague you, or make your life hell."

"That is for certain. Thank heavens we are heading to Doncaster where we'll be surrounded by the rest of the family."

"Yes, I'm looking forward to moving in with my three brothers and nephew, all bent upon invading our privacy and driving me insane."

"I think your family is lovely. Four brothers looking after each other."

"Brothers who can't mind their own damn business." Mac picked up his cup and took a long drink of tea. "I prefer my valet. He keeps his opinions to himself—unless I'm bent on ruining my clothes—and he brews one hell of a pot of tea."

Isabella took a thoughtful sip. "You know, I read a novel as a girl, about four sisters in America. They paired off rather like you do—the oldest sister looked after the youngest, as Hart does with Ian, and the two middle sisters looked after one another, as do you and Cameron."

Mac's eyes widened in mock horror. "Good Lord, are you comparing the wild Mackenzies to four virtuous girls from America? I beg you to never say this in public."

"Don't be silly. It was a sweet story." Isabella clenched her teacup. "Come to think of it, one of the sisters was called Beth, and she died."

Mac's arms came around her, his smiles gone. "Don't even think it, love. Beth is made of stern stuff, and Ian won't let a thing happen to her. Just as I won't let anything happen to you."

"How can you know that?"

"You have my word on it. Mackenzies never go back on their word."

"Unless it's expedient."

Mac chuckled into her ear. "I'm crushed. Although being crushed against you has its compensations. By the way, love, I've not gone down one fraction of an inch. Very uncomfortable for tea drinking."

Isabella sent him a sly look, happy to turn the conversation from her worries. She put her hand on his knee and slid it swiftly under his kilt.

Mac inhaled sharply. "My, my, you're good at that. Is that the sort of thing you learned in finishing school, young lady?"

Isabella gently twisted her hand around his shaft, and perspiration formed on Mac's upper lip. "On the contrary. I learned deportment and how to wear a fine hat."

"Nonsense, you had lessons in this. Miss Pringle must have handed out models of cocks, made of plaster of paris maybe." He took on a high falsetto. "Like this, girls. One, two, one, two. Come along, ladies, don't slack."

Isabella burst out laughing. "Just for that . . ." Isabella sped her attack until Mac was arching back on the small sofa, stroking her hair, crying her name, and moving his hips in time with her rhythm.

When he spilled his seed all over her hand, he gathered her into his arms and kissed her until she couldn't breathe, think, or worry about anything but dissolving into his warmth.

Mac warmed as he watched Isabella rush into Beth's arms when they disembarked the train at Doncaster, the pair of them shrieking as though they hadn't seen each other in years, not weeks.

The journey had been a restless one for Mac. He'd conceded to Isabella's request that she ride alone in her own compartment, but the temptation to leave the one he shared with Cam and Daniel and make his way to Isabella's was overwhelming. Playing with Isabella in the drawing room, ending with her bringing him off in that skilled fashion, had only inflamed Mac's already potent desire for her.

Mac didn't want games or the occasional tickle in the drawing room. He wanted all of Isabella—her love, her friendship, her trust. Passion without love and trust was empty, he thought as he watched Beth and Isabella hug each other. He'd learned that brutal lesson too late.

Hart had hired a house a little outside of Doncaster, the country home of a gentleman whose income had dwindled too drastically for him to keep up such a large abode. The gentleman had decided to rent his house to other aristocrats rather than sell it to be turned into a hotel or hospital. His staff, local people, stayed on to be paid by the guests.

The large boxlike structure contained enough rooms for the four brothers, two wives, one nephew, their personal servants, and the dogs. Hart and Ian always brought the dogs. There were five of them, ranging from huge hound to small terrier. They milled about as the family arrived, tails waving furiously. Isabella petted them and addressed each by name: McNab and Fergus; Ruby and Ben; and Achilles, with his one white foot.

Mac loved that Isabella so unflinchingly embraced his family. When she'd met them shortly after marrying Mac, his sweet little bride had instantly charmed his rather skeptical brothers. Cameron had liked her right away, laughing in his loud way and telling Mac she would lead him a merry life. Ian had regarded Isabella for a time with his sideways look, before offering to show her his collection of Ming bowls. For Ian, this was the equivalent of declaring undying devotion.

Hart had taken slightly longer, having faced Isabella's father in political battles—Hart pro-Scottish; Earl Scranton still annoyed about the Highland uprising a hundred and forty years ago. Isabella had won Hart over by not letting him tread on her. Hart respected strong women, and he'd softened toward Isabella within days. Hart had done much the same with Beth, Mac had heard, Mac still sorry he'd missed *that* encounter.

As soon as they entered the house, Isabella and Beth headed toward the terrace, arms about each other's waists, their nonstop chatter punctuated with much giggling. Mac watched them go with some regret then turned to Ian and clapped his brother on the shoulder. It spoke of how far Ian had relaxed that he didn't immediately pull away. Ian didn't like to be touched—except by Beth. He'd made that abundantly clear.

Ian met Mac's eyes fleetingly, his golden gaze sliding away almost at once. Ian had always had trouble meeting another's eyes, but he was getting better at it. Six months ago, he wouldn't have been able to give Mac even that fleeting glance.

"Have you done it?" Ian asked him.

Mac blinked. "Done what?"

"Is Isabella your wife again?" Ian asked impatiently. His look said, *What else would I be talking about?*

Mac shrugged. "Things are proceeding."

"Does that mean no or yes?"

Ian, always literal. "It means, I am working toward our reconciliation."

"You mean no."

"All right, damn you. No, we're not husband and wife again. Isabella needs time."

"You have had three years and seven months," Ian said. "Tell her you are together again and be done."

"Ah, to live as simple a life as you do," Mac said. "You chased Beth to Paris and cornered her in a pension. A quick wedding, and she devoted herself to you, you lucky sod. What is between Isabella and me is more complicated."

Ian didn't answer, craning to watch Beth through the windows to the terrace. Mac realized that Ian had little idea what Mac was babbling about, and what's more, didn't care.

Mac fell silent while the dogs flowed around them, trying to decide whether to stay with the dullards in the hall or rush into the sunshine with the ladies. Giving up on the dullards, the dogs clattered through the open door after Beth and Isabella.

Ian broke his obsessive gaze and glanced briefly at Mac. "Simple? Of course it's simple. Just get on with it."

Ian strode away and out the doors, pulled by an invisible tether to the woman he loved.

Chapter 9

Clan Mackenzie were seen at Doncaster, their box graced by the radiant beauty of the Lady from Mount Street. The others danced attendance on their lovely Sister, but despite the return of her Lord and their apparent reconciliation, no rumor has yet reached our ears of another impending heir to the Mackenzie throne.

—*September 1876*

Mac remembered Ian's words the next day as they gathered at the Doncaster racetrack to watch the opening races. Cameron and Daniel disappeared to the stables as soon as they reached the track, Cam muttering something about having been away from the horses too long.

Hart also disappeared on whatever business he hoped to accomplish. Hart used any opportunity to push his political agendas, which meant wandering about every social occasion talking to people—*bullying them into seeing things his way,* Mac thought, half in irritation. Hart liked people to dance to his tune.

Hart had been rather short-tempered during the drive to the race, and Mac had sensed tension between him and Ian since arriving at the Doncaster house. Isabella and Beth talking nonstop covered things nicely, but the underlying strain was obvious.

Beth explained the problem as she and Ian, Isabella and Mac settled themselves into the Mackenzie box high above the track. It seemed that Hart had requested Beth to act as hostess for him at upcoming social functions at Kilmorgan Castle. Hart wanted to woo various members of Parliament in his capacity as duke and needed a lovely woman to smile at them and soften them up. Ian had grown protective and annoyed and told Hart to find his own damned wife.

Mac laughed out loud. "I wish I had witnessed that. I love it when you tell Hart to stuff himself, Ian. Though I'm sorry you had to be caught in it, Beth. No one deserves to be squeezed inside a Mackenzie argument."

Isabella rolled her eyes under her ostentatious hat. "That is an understatement."

"I don't mind," Beth said quickly. "I agreed to help a bit, but it's good for Hart learn too that he can't always have things his own way. And Ian is right; Hart does need to marry again. Cameron is worried to death that Hart will fall off a horse and pass the title to him."

An ongoing conundrum. Mac had always felt himself happily removed from the dukedom—he had Cameron and Daniel safely between him and the coronet. If Hart would just pick out a woman and get on with it, Mac could find even more distance between himself and the title. But after the death of Hart's young wife and child, the damn man had stayed stubbornly off the marriage mart. The family had speculated whether he'd again try to win Eleanor Ramsay, who'd previously jilted him but was still unmarried, but Hart had made no move to do so.

Hart entered the box as horses were led out for the first race, his annoyed glance telling Mac he'd guessed what they'd been discussing. He settled in a chair a little way away from them and fixed his opera glasses on the horses below.

Next to Mac, Isabella and Beth chattered about whatever they could think of. Ladies' Day at the races was an invitation for wives and daughters and sisters to show off their best hats and frocks, and Beth and Isabella had entered the fray with enthusiasm. Beth's high-crowned hat was adorned with ostrich feathers that drooped down her back. Isabella's hat was trimmed with a swirl of ostrich feathers and yellow roses. Its precarious angle gave her a coy look, one that made Mac want to pull off the hat and cover her with kisses.

"There's Cam." Isabella peered through her opera glasses, pointing out a large black-coated and kilted man. Daniel, also black-coated and kilted, followed him at a brisk trot. Daniel looked up at the box and waved.

Isabella waved back. "Mac, you must go down and make our wagers for us. On all of Cam's horses, of course."

"All?" Beth asked her. This was Beth's first racing season with the horse-mad Mackenzies, and she looked a bit uncertain.

"Of course, darling. Everyone knows that Cameron raises the best horses in Britain. I think a tenner each way on the first race? We might risk more as the day goes on. It's such fun."

"Cam scratched his filly from the first race," Hart said from beyond Mac. "She came up lame not an hour ago, he told me downstairs."

Isabella lifted her glasses and watched Cameron take the bridle of a horse and lead it away. "Oh, the poor thing."

"She'll live," Hart said. "But she won't race today."

Isabella bit her lip. Unfriendly people might think her fretting about her wagers, but Mac knew that Isabella worried about the horse. The horses were like Cam's children, each one a member of the family, and Isabella had a kind heart.

Beth scanned the racing sheet. "Should we wager on another then?"

Isabella looked over Beth's shoulder. "How about this one? Lady Day. I like that name."

"Wrong color," Ian said.

Isabella threw him a perplexed look. "Ian, the horse won't win the race because she's bay instead of chestnut."

"I mean her jockey. Colors aren't right."

Lady Day's jockey wore blue with green stripes. Mac himself had no clue what Ian was talking about, but when Ian made a pronouncement, Mac knew better than to waste breath arguing with him. Ian was usually correct.

"He's convinced me," Mac said. "Choose another."

"I think you're both mad," Isabella said. "Lady Day to win. Beth?"

Beth shrugged. "Unless my husband has another choice?" She waited for Ian's reaction, but he was staring stoically down at the paddocks, no longer paying attention. Mac grinned, touched his hat to them, and left the box.

"Back again, my lord?" the bookmaker asked him when Mac reached the stand.

"Again? What are you talking about?"

The bookmaker, a little man everyone called Steady Ron, narrowed his eyes. "Didn't you come to place a bet with Gabe over there?" He jerked his chin at the next booth. "Not a half hour ago? I was that hurt. Mackenzies always do business with Steady Ron."

"I've just arrived, and I've been up in my box with my wife. She says she's a firm believer in Lady Day."

"Good choice. Excellent horseflesh, odds seven to two. Win, place, or post?"

"To win, she says." Mac placed the rest of the bets, taking the slips from Ron.

"Could have sworn it was you, me lord," Ron finished.

"Same face, same easy manner. Not much mistaking you."

"Well, you were mistaken this time. Tell you what, if you see me again, make certain it's me before you get your feelings hurt."

Ron grinned. "Right you are, yer lordship. Enjoy the races."

Ron's mistake made Mac uneasy, especially in light of what Crane had told him about the man who'd brought him the paintings to sell, not to mention the fire. Mac's footman had declared that no one but Mac had gone in and out of the house that day, but the man must have gotten in somehow. If the footman had been in the back hall, or down the road a few houses speaking to another footman—or even more distracting, a pretty maid—he might have mistaken the other man for Mac.

Then again, the crowd today was thick. A sea of men in nearly identical black coats and top hats stretched to all corners. Ron could have made a mistake. Gentlemen looked pretty much alike these days, English male fashion being rather monotonous.

Mac's logic tried to comfort him with such thoughts, but Mac felt an itch between his shoulder blades. He didn't like the coincidence.

Back in the box, Isabella and Beth were on their feet, waiting for the race to begin. Ian stood close to Beth, his hand straying to the small of her back. Mac felt a twinge of envy. At one time he'd had the privilege to stand so with Isabella.

A roar rose from the crowd as the horses leapt forward. Beth and Isabella bounced on their toes, peering through opera glasses, growing more and more excited as the horses charged past the stands. The two shouted encouragement to Lady Day, who was running for all she was worth.

"She's going to do it." Isabella turned her laughing face to Mac. "I knew I could pick a winner." She excitedly grabbed Mac's hand, squeezed it, and turned back to the race.

The gesture hadn't been a grand one. Just a little touch, a pressure of the fingers. But the imprint of Isabella's hand lingered, the warmth of it more precious than the most treasured gem. Isabella, un-self-conscious, had touched Mac as she'd done when they'd been friends and lovers. As though nothing terrible had ever happened between them.

Mac savored the moment, memorized it, this small thing even more cherished than what they'd done in the drawing room in London. Satiation couldn't compare to the casual, trusting touch of two people who loved each other.

Well, Mac would prefer *both* kinds of touching, but the fact that Isabella had turned to share her excitement with him made his heart swell.

He was so fixed on Isabella that he didn't notice the horses pulling ahead of Lady Day. Mac only saw the light go out of Isabella's eyes. She'd looked at Mac like that in times past, her vibrancy fading, and Mac, bloody stupid idiot that he'd been, hadn't paused to figure out why.

Lady Day came in sixth. Her jockey patted her as she dropped from gallop to canter to trot, as though reassuring her that he didn't love her less for losing. Mac wanted to lean into Isabella's neck and comfort *her*.

Isabella turned to Ian in exasperation. "All right, Ian. How on earth did you know that Lady Day would lose based on the jockey's colors?"

Ian didn't answer. He was watching the horses trot along the far side of the field, lost in contemplation.

"He means that the horse was recently sold," Hart said from behind Mac. "Lord Powell bought her a few months ago. It's likely she hasn't adjusted to her new surroundings, new routines, new jockey. They shouldn't have put her in the race today. She had no heart for it."

"You couldn't have explained this to me earlier, Hart Mackenzie?" Isabella demanded. Then she softened. "The poor darling. They shouldn't have made her race." If anyone knew about the bewilderment of a young woman ripped from the bosom of her family and deposited among strangers, it was Isabella.

Hart's stern mouth relaxed into a smile. "I didn't want to spoil your fun. And it serves you right for not listening to Ian."

Isabella put her tongue out at Hart then turned back to Ian. "I beg your pardon, Ian. I should know better than to doubt you."

Ian gave her a quick look, and Mac saw Ian's hand tighten on Beth's waist, seeking comfort in her. Ian couldn't always follow the teasing and banter common in his family, words flying about before Ian could catch and understand them. He'd listen with a distracted air before cutting through their gibberish with a pointed remark. It was easy to think Ian simpleminded, but Mac had come to learn that his brother was an amazingly complex man with vast intelligence. Beth had recognized that from the start, and Mac loved her for it.

Cameron's horses did run in the next two races, winning each time. Isabella's excitement returned, and she and Beth cheered on the family's pride. Cameron remained down at the rail, watching like a worried father as his horses galloped to the finish line.

Daniel, on the other hand, capered and danced about, probably rubbing the noses of everyone near in the fact that Mackenzie horses were the very best. Cam would be more interested in the horses' well-being, but Daniel loved to win.

"An excellent showing," Isabella said happily after the third race. "Now then, Beth, let us retire to the tea tent and positively *gorge* ourselves."

"Aren't there more races?" Beth asked.

"We will return and watch later, but part of the St. Leger is to wander about and be seen by everyone. Why else would we have spent so much time on these hats?"

Beth laughed, and the two ladies left the box arm in arm. Ian opened the door for them, falling into step behind them.

Mac prepared to leave after Ian, but Hart's hand on his arm stopped him.

"Not in the mood for a lecture right now, old man," Mac said, impatient as he watched Beth and Isabella disappear down the stairs. "Once I have clasped Isabella to my bosom again—for good—then you can browbeat me. But not just now."

"I *was* going to say, it's good to see you with her again," Hart answered dryly. "It will take you a long time to win back Isabella's trust, but the fact that she is speaking to you at all gives me hope."

Mac turned to him in surprise. Hart and he were the same height, Cameron being the tallest Mackenzie, and Mac could look straight into Hart's golden eyes. Mac saw in them the weight of the dukedom, the responsibility for his brothers, and his own unhappy past, but also a thread of relief. He hadn't realized that the strain between Mac and Isabella worried Hart so much.

"You're getting sentimental in your old age." Mac continued the banter. "What's softened your heart?"

"Loss."

The eagle gaze flickered, and Mac closed his mouth. Hart's mistress of many years had recently passed away in tragic circumstances, and Hart felt it. Hart never said a word about it, but Mac knew he grieved for her.

Hart's expression eased. "If I've gone soft, it comes from seeing Ian happy. I never thought I would witness that."

"Neither did I."

Mac was truly glad for Ian. Mac had alternately pitied and protected his younger brother, who'd spent years locked in an asylum, put there by their devil of a father. But Ian had recently found the contentment and joy that eluded Mac. Ian was the wise man now.

"Don't let go this time," Hart said in clipped tones. "Appreciate what you've got and hold onto it. You never know when it will be taken away."

"Are you speaking from experience?" When Hart had proposed to Eleanor, he'd been so certain of her, and her jilting of him took them all by surprise. But perhaps it was not so surprising. Hart was difficult to endure when he was cocksure.

"Yes, I am. Learn from my mistakes." Hart pinned Mac with a severe look. "And don't make any more."

"Aye-aye, sir," Mac said, and then Hart let him go.

"This is scrumptious." Isabella lifted a spoonful of sweet cream to her mouth, savoring its smooth taste. She didn't like that she immediately remembered licking a similar glob of cream from Mac's erect cock in her drawing room. He'd tasted wonderful. The sight of him hard for her had excited her beyond anything she'd felt in a long while.

"Lovely," Beth agreed. "It's frivolous of me, I know, but I believe I enjoy the lap of luxury."

Sitting on stools in a cramped tea tent was hardly the lap of luxury in Isabella's opinion, but Beth had grown up in poverty. Drinking tea from dainty cups and scooping up spoonfuls of cake and cream while wearing brand new frocks and hats must seem decadent to Beth. Beth was a lady, however, descended from minor gentry, and the manners she'd learned from her long-dead mother were impeccable.

Beth took another dainty bite, eyes dancing. "Our gentlemen look fine, don't they?"

Isabella glanced at Ian and Mac, who stood together not far away. They did indeed look fine, two tall Scotsmen with auburn hair in black coats and kilts. Ian and Mac were close in age, Ian twenty-seven and Mac just thirty. They both wore the Mackenzie plaid, with tartan wool socks emphasizing their muscular calves. As a girl, Isabella had laughed at the thought of men in skirts, but when she'd first seen Mac in his kilt, her opinion had undergone a rapid revision. Mac in a kilt was a glorious sight.

Mac sent Isabella a wicked grin, as though *she* were a spoonful of cream he wanted to eat, and her heart throbbed.

Perhaps, just perhaps, Mac had changed. His words were no longer slurred with drink, his speech no longer erratic or his actions unpredictable. Not that Isabella wanted Mac to be perfectly predictable, but when he spoke with her now she was certain his focus was on *her*. Not on his latest painting or whatever larks he'd been up to with his friends, or his thoughts half-soaked in whiskey. He'd been sober for three years, his brothers had informed her. Many of his friends had deserted him, she'd heard, considering sober, sensible Mac not entertaining enough for them. Selfish sycophants.

But Mac now seemed too subdued, the look in his eyes—behind his teasing—too sad.

Did I do that to him? Isabella's heart squeezed. Her leaving Mac had hurt him badly, she knew. It had hurt her too, but at the time, she'd thought she had no choice. But the knowledge that she'd cause him such pain made her unhappy.

Beth put aside her plate and touched her hand to her stomach. "Mmm. I think I've eaten a bit too much."

Isabella was about to make a jest about her having to eat for two, but one look at Beth's face had Isabella jumping to her feet and calling frantically for Ian.

Ian dropped his plate, his piece of cake landing face-down on the ground. He ran over to the ladies and swept Beth into his arms before she could protest.

"For heaven's sake, Ian," Beth said. "I'm fine. No need for fuss."

Isabella knew quite well that Beth was not fine. Her face was paper white, her lips pale, her pupils enormous.

Ian wasted no time carrying Beth out of the tea tent, scattering startled ladies before him like flocks of birds. Isabella followed, and she sensed Mac on her heels. At one point Mac tried to catch Isabella's arm, but she shook him off and hurried with Ian and Beth toward the gates.

She heard Mac stop someone behind them and instruct him to run for the Mackenzie carriage. Thank God for Mac. He loved his jokes and his escapades, but in a crisis, he knew how to keep his head. Soon Hart's landau careened toward them, the coachman standing on his box.

Ian climbed swiftly in, cradling Beth, and barely waited for Isabella to ascend before he bellowed at the coachman to get them home. They'd traveled to the track with the top down because the day was fine, and the seats were now warm with sunshine. Isabella dropped into one as the coach sprang forward.

Mac got left behind. Isabella looked back and saw him raise his hand to them, and through her panic, she felt grateful to him for knowing what to do.

She felt grateful again when they reached home and a doctor arrived on their heels to look after Beth. Mac had sent a messenger racing through the town to find him, the doctor said, with money for a hansom cab.

The doctor ordered Isabella out of the room. She didn't want to go, but Beth smiled wanly and repeated that she'd be fine. Ian refused to leave, however, and the doctor stopped arguing with him.

Isabella paced the upstairs hall of the long house, barely seeing the grand view the gallery gave to the extensive gardens. The dogs followed her, shooting her worried looks, knowing something was dreadfully wrong. Servants rushed into and out of Beth's room, carrying towels and basins, but no one stopped to speak to Isabella, and she heard nothing from inside the bedroom.

She was still pacing when Mac arrived. All five dogs rushed down the stairs to greet him, then rushed back up the stairs with him.

When he asked, "Any news?" Isabella felt as though she'd burst.

"They won't let me in, they won't tell me. I don't know what is happening." Tears poured from her eyes. "They won't tell me whether Beth's all right."

Mac's strong arms came around her, and the world stopped spinning. He smelled of the outdoors, of smoke and soap, the comforting scents of Mac. He said nothing at all, not wasting time on platitudes or false comfort, and for that she was grateful. Mac knew good and well why Isabella was so worried, and he knew that Isabella's fears weren't groundless. He simply held her like a moor in a safe harbor, and Isabella clung to him without shame.

They stood for a long time, Isabella's head on Mac's shoulder, while sunshine warmed them through the western windows. The dogs quieted, settling down where they could keep an eye them.

The sun was on level with the horizon when the doctor emerged from Beth's room and said quietly to Isabella, "You can see her now."

Isabella tore herself from Mac and rushed to the bedroom, not even waiting to ask the doctor whether all were well.

Chapter 10

The evil rumor that the Scottish Lord has taken up with a lady of Lesser Status has been refuted by all and sundry, and proven to be False. His Lady seems happy to have her Lord returned to her after another sudden absence, and the entertainments once again flow in the Lord and Lady's home.

—*January 1877*

Beth lay under the covers, her face pale above a lace-collared nightgown. Ian, in his kilt and shirtsleeves, stretched out beside her, one large, brown hand splayed across Beth's abdomen.

"Poor Isabella," Beth said as Isabella closed the door. "I didn't mean to give you such a fright."

Isabella crossed to the bed, sank onto the chair beside it, and clasped Beth's fingers between hers. "Are you all right?" she asked shakily. "The baby?"

"Is fine," Beth said, smiling. "And I'm in good hands, as you can see." She looked fondly at Ian, who'd not glanced up at Isabella's entrance.

"Thank God." Isabella bent her head over their clasped hands. The simple prayer poured out of her heart. "Thank God."

"I really am fine, Isabella. I became overheated, that is all, first jumping up and down for the races and then sitting inside the stuffy tent. Also, my lacing was too tight, *and* you saw me gobbling up all those cream cakes."

Her voice was light, ready to make a jest of the whole event. *How silly I am,* she was saying. *And haven't I paid the price?* Isabella closed her eyes and rested her forehead on Beth's hand.

Beth stroked her hair. "Are you crying, Izzy? I truly am all right. What is it, darling?"

"Isabella had a miscarriage," Ian rumbled beside her.

Through a wash of painful memory, Isabella felt Beth start, heard her shocked exclamation.

"Four years ago," Ian went on. "She was at a ball, and I had to take her home. I couldn't find Mac. He was in Paris."

Beth took in Ian's disjointed sentences without question. "I see. Goodness, no wonder you two rushed me here in such alarm."

"The child was a boy, three months gone," Ian went on, reducing the most terrible event of Isabella's life to short, exact phrases. "It took me five days to find Mac and bring him home."

Five days in which Isabella had lain alone in her bed lost in the blackest melancholia she'd ever experienced. She'd thought at one point that she'd die; she hadn't the strength to fight to live. But her body had been young and strong, and she'd recovered physically though not in spirits.

"And for that, I've never forgiven myself," Mac said behind her.

Isabella raised her head to see Mac standing in the doorway, watching her with somber resignation.

"I've told you," Isabella said. "You couldn't have known it would happen."

Mac unfolded his arms and walked into the room with slow, measured steps. "You were the person I most treasured in the world, and I wasn't there to take care of you. You were right to hate me."

"I didn't . . ." Isabella trailed off. She *had* hated him at the time, hated that she'd had to suffer her grief alone. She'd also hated herself because she'd instigated the argument that had made Mac disappear two weeks before the miscarriage. She'd lashed out at him, telling him she was tired of his constant drunkenness and wild escapades with his equally drunken friends. Mac had decided, as usual, that the best thing he could do for her was to leave.

"I don't hate you now," she amended.

Mac sent Beth a faint smile. "Do you see what a very wretched life Isabella led with me? I made her miserable, alternately smothering her and then deserting her. Most of the time my head was fuddled with drink, but that's no excuse."

"That is why you became a teetotaler," Beth said, understanding.

"Partly. Let that be a lesson to those who overindulge. Drink can ruin a life."

Isabella rose with a rustle of skirts. "Don't be so dramatic, Mac. You made a mistake, that is all."

"I made the same mistake repeatedly for three years. Stop excusing me, Isabella. I don't think I can take your pitying forgiveness."

"And I can't take your self-flagellation. It's so unlike you."

"It *used* to be unlike me. I've taken it up as a hobby."

"Stop," Ian growled from the bed. "Beth is tired. Go have your row outside."

"Sorry, old man," Mac said. "I came in here, in fact, to bring something to Beth. To cheer her up."

Isabella watched rigidly. She felt a fool now, panicking over Beth while Mac and Ian had kept their heads. She realized that her fear of watching Beth live out Isabella's remembered ordeal had rendered her unable to think or act.

"I adore presents," Beth said, smiling.

Ian propped himself on his elbow as Mac approached, remaining by Beth's side like a protective dragon. Mac took a large sheaf of banknotes from his pocket and laid them on the blanket.

"Your winnings, madam," he said.

"Oh, heavens, I forgot all about them! Bless you, Mac. What a fine brother-in-law you've turned out to be. You fetch me a carriage and a doctor and my ill-gotten gains—all in one afternoon."

"The least I can do for you for looking after my baby brother."

Beth smiled in delight. Mac looked smug, and Ian . . . Ian had lost the train of the conversation and was tracing patterns on Beth's abdomen.

"What about *my* winnings?" Isabella asked, her voice still shaky.

"I'll distribute those to you outside. Good night, Beth."

Isabella kissed Beth's cheek, and Beth pulled Isabella into a tight hug. "Thank you, Isabella. I'm so sorry I gave you a fright."

"Never mind. You are well. That is the important thing." Isabella kissed her again and left the room through the door that Mac held open for her.

Mac strolled in silence with Isabella down the gallery while the dogs flowed around them, sensing that the crisis was over.

"Well," Isabella said, wishing her cursed voice would stop trembling. "Are you going to give me my money?"

Mac turned her to face him. "Certainly. After I exact my price."

Her heart jumped, and she didn't like that his nearness

made her want to melt to him again. Being held by him had felt too good.

"I am hardly a lady of easy virtue, thank you very much. I won't kiss you for a guinea."

"It's one hundred guineas, and that is not what I had in mind." His eyes glinted. "Though it's an interesting suggestion."

"*Mac.*"

Mac put his hands on her shoulders. Warm, sure hands, which burned through her thin gabardine. "My price is that you promise to stop carrying your grief alone. You accused *me* of self-flagellation, but you've folded in on yourself so tightly you barely let anyone touch you. Promise me you'll cease keeping it to yourself."

Anger rose through her worry. "And who am I to share this painful part of my life with? Who will be willing to listen to me bleat on about my tragedy without feigning an excuse to leave the room?"

"I will."

Isabella stopped. She opened her mouth to answer, but the lump in her throat wouldn't let her.

"It is my tragedy as well as yours," Mac went on in a gentle voice. "When I heard about our baby, I wanted to die. Doubly so, because I was so far away from you. You might have died that night too, and there I was, oblivious and stupid in a Montmartre hotel. Ian never says much, but I know he thought I could do with a few of the tortures he'd endured in the asylum. You thought so too."

Isabella nodded, tears burning her eyes. "But at the same time I needed you so much I didn't care how far Ian had to go to find you."

"Well, he found me," Mac said. He spread his arms. "And here I am again."

"Yes, here you are. What am I going to do with you?"

"I can think of so many things."

The air went still as they regarded each other. The sun warmed Isabella's skin, the last rays shining through the window.

She asked because she didn't know what to do with him springing back into her life. He'd given up drink because of her, and now he was a different Mac—sober, quieter, more cynical, but still with a touch of his old wicked arrogance.

Mac slid his hands around her waist, heating her through her corset. His large body enclosed hers, the strength of his hands both unnerving and comforting. He could easily overwhelm her, take from her what he wanted, and yet he never had. He'd never so much as tried. Not once.

Mac touched her face with gentle fingers. His eyes held no demand, no heat, though she could feel his obvious physical reaction through her skirts.

"I'm here," he said. "You don't have to bear the burden alone anymore."

"For now." Could she have sounded more bitter?

She thought Mac would flinch or grow angry, but he just smoothed her hair. "For always. I'm not leaving you again, Isabella."

"We are separated."

"By legal document. But if you need me—for anything, day or night—you have but to crook your finger, and I'll be there."

She tried a smile. "Mac tied to a woman's apron strings?"

"I'd gladly lash myself to you, love, if you ever wore an apron." He kissed the corner of her mouth, the warmth of his lips burning electricity across her skin. "Especially if you wore nothing *but* an apron."

Mac could still make her laugh, that was certain. He touched another kiss to her lips, but then the house filled with sudden sound as Cam, Daniel, and Hart entered and started up the stairs to check on Beth, followed by all the dogs. Mac smiled at Isabella, kissed her lips, and turned with her to greet them.

~~~~~

Mac wasn't fool enough to assume that Isabella would welcome him back with open arms after one brief kiss in the sunshine. They'd made a bit of progress, but he knew they had a long way to go.

For the next week in the Doncaster house, Cam and Daniel attended the races, Ian stayed with Beth, Isabella stayed home in case Beth needed her, and Mac moved between racetrack and house. He kept an eye out for the man Steady Ron had mistaken for Mac, but neither he, nor Steady Ron, nor the other bookmakers saw the Mac look-alike again. He also heard no word from Fellows in London, but Mac's prickling feeling remained, and he could not relax his guard.

Hart had withdrawn his insistence that Beth act as his hostess in light of her brief illness, and the air between him and Ian thawed. Mac had the feeling that Hart would ask Isabella instead, which made him understand Ian's annoyance. But neither Hart nor Isabella mentioned it. Besides, Hart seemed to vanish quite often from the house these days. He was involved in all kinds of schemes that Mac frankly didn't want to know about. Hart had turned his former propensity for dark, sensual appetites to a ruthlessness for politics. But then, Hart had always had a genius for the game—he'd stood for election at age twenty-two and won by a landslide, years before he'd become the lofty duke and took his seat in the House of Lords. Now he had most of the Lords *and* Commons under his formidable thumb.

Beth and Isabella walked together in the large garden most days, two lovely ladies in colorful dresses, heads bent together. Mac heard much laughter from the two of them and wondered how they found so much to giggle about.

But he liked hearing their voices. Most of all, he liked Isabella's laughter.

While Mac and Ian read newspapers, smoked cigars, or played billiards in companionable silence, Isabella and Beth never ceased talking. They talked about *everything*— from houses and clothes to music to the flora and fauna of far-flung corners of the British Empire. It was domestic and pleasant, and Mac's wild friends would be appalled at him for liking it so much.

At night, Isabella disappeared into her bedroom, and Mac, sleepless, roamed the house. His body was tight with need, and though he and Isabella spoke together more easily these days, he wasn't stupid enough to simply slip off his clothes and slide into her bed. When he finally did gain entrance to that sanctuary, he vowed, he'd do it in such a way that he'd never have to leave it again.

The old house had no bathroom, which meant that when Isabella wanted to bathe, she reclined in a tub the footmen lugged into her bedroom. Mac could hear her in there through the wall between his bedroom and hers, Isabella splashing as she washed her body, her melodious humming arousing him to the point of pain.

One night, Mac couldn't take it anymore. Beth and Ian were ensconced in their own suite, and Cameron and Daniel were out, as was Hart. Isabella's voice drifted through the wall, a lady alone, happily bare in her bathtub.

Mac pushed open her unlocked door and walked inside, not bothering to knock. "Love, are you trying to drive me mad?"

Isabella dropped her sponge into the water with a large splash. She was quite alone, no Evans in sight. She'd piled her hair on top of her head, but a few escaped red ringlets had drifted to her wet shoulders.

Isabella fished up the sponge and regarded him over it

in annoyance. "Not everything I do has to do with you, Mac."

There was no alarm or anger in her voice. She might have been answering him in a drawing room over tea. Mac's thoughts strayed to the last tea they'd taken in her drawing room, and he began to sweat.

He closed the door. "I've always admired your attention to cleanliness. Once a day, Lady Isabella is found in her bath, no matter how far the servants have to haul the water."

"There is a tap at the end of the hall. They do not have to haul it far."

Mac folded his arms so she wouldn't see his shaking fingers. Soap suds and the damned sponge obscured the full view of her body, but the pink arms and the soft knee poking through the water made him ache.

"Did you not tell me that your mother once compared you to a duckling?" Mac asked in a light voice. "Because you like to splash about in whatever water is handy?"

"I suppose I never grew out of it."

She was going to kill him. This was her dastardly plan—to let him glimpse what he couldn't have so that he'd burn into ashes on the carpet. Evans could sweep him up and throw him in the dustbin; no more intruding Mac Mackenzie.

"Ian and Beth are returning to Scotland at the end of the week," he said.

"I know." Isabella ran the sponge up her arm, rivulets of soap and water trickling back into the tub. "Will you be going with them?"

The exact question he wanted to ask *her.* "That depends," he said.

"On what?"

"On how many musicales and little soirees you'll be

putting on in London. It's too cold now for a garden party, so I don't imagine you'll be holding them at the house in Buckinghamshire."

Isabella arched her brows and slid the sponge up her other arm. "My social calendar has been predictable for years. An opening and closing ball for the spring season, garden parties in July and August, the most important races of the circuit through September, shooting season and Christmas at Kilmorgan Castle. I see no reason to alter my plans this year."

"My social calendar seems to be much the same as yours," Mac said. "What a happy coincidence."

"For a change."

Mac went serious. "For a great change."

Isabella regarded him with her beautiful green eyes, and then she lowered her lashes and floated one foot to the edge of the tub. Mac watched the sponge glide from toes to knee, and his hunger grew.

Isabella lifted the sponge. "Mac, will you please wash my back?"

Mac stood still a frozen moment. She looked up at him, and he back at her.

Then he was across the room and shrugging off his coat before the sound of the last syllable had died in the stuffy room.

Chapter 11

The Here-and-Gone habits of the Scottish Lord of Mayfair cause much speculation all around. The Lady appears at balls and operas and hosts soirees with her youngest brother-in-law at her side, her own Lord nowhere in sight.

—April 1877

Isabella held her breath as Mac slid off his coat and dropped it over the nearest chair. She'd been shaking since he'd entered the room. Tonight Mac wore black trousers rather than a kilt, cream waistcoat and white shirt, no different from any other man-about-town; but with Mac, there was always a difference. His presence filled whatever room he entered and pinned her like a flopping fish.

She found herself growing still more nervous as he looked down at her. Would he like what he saw? Mac preferred ladies who were curvaceous, and in the days after Isabella had left Mac's house, she'd lost almost a stone, finding herself unable to eat. She'd regained some of her appetite, but her youthful plumpness had never returned. Mac had remained much the same in looks, although the puffiness that drink settled on his face had vanished, rendering his cheeks square and lean. He was more handsome now than he had ever been.

Mac pulled off his waistcoat and opened the cuffs of his shirt. Isabella's hungry gaze absorbed him as he folded his sleeves to the elbows. His sinewy forearms were covered with dark gold hair that caught the light as he moved.

Once he'd adjusted his sleeves, he smiled at her and leaned to pluck the sponge from her nerveless fingers.

Mac made no pretense of not looking at her. His gaze traveled from her throat to her bosom, down her belly to her lower leg and foot resting on the edge of the tub. He squeezed out the sponge, holding it high so that the water sloshed back into the tub. Mac moved behind her and brushed his hand over the nape of her neck, and she leaned forward, bowing her head.

Isabella closed her eyes at the first touch of the sponge. Warm water flowed down her spine to the cleave of her buttocks; the water and the friction of the sponge made a fine sensation. If Evans had been washing her, the sensation would have remained merely pleasant. But it was Mac, with his hard body so near, his scent and warmth touching her, and *pleasant* became *erotic*.

Isabella laid her cheek on her knees and smiled as Mac continued to wash her back. He rested one hand on the edge of the tub, his skin brown and strong. Bits of paint clung to his fingertips.

The sight of the paint flecks made Isabella's heart constrict. Of all the things she could remember about him, why did those tiny specks fill her with longing? Perhaps because the sight reminded her of what he was—an artist who painted for the love of it, not caring whether others praised him or censured him.

Isabella leaned forward and kissed his fingers.

Mac lifted his hand away, but only so he could snake both arms around her from behind. He pulled her back into his embrace, never mind how much water flowed out of the tub and over his shirt. He slid his hands across her slick skin to cup her breasts, and Isabella closed her eyes.

This was all so familiar, yet distant at the same time. Mac's breath tickled her ear, and his big hands warmed her breasts while his fingers drew her nipples into hot points. He kissed her neck, his mouth a point of fire.

Mac, how I've missed you.

Isabella inhaled as Mac slid one hand down her belly and pressed his fingers between her legs. Isabella's thighs opened at his touch. Her mind warned her to stop him, to modestly push him away, but her body wasn't obeying. It had been too long, and Mac knew how to make her body sing.

Isabella closed her eyes, letting the wanton in her take over. When she lifted her hips so he might stroke her better, he laughed softly.

"That's my wicked lady. You're as smooth and sweet as I recall." Another chuckle. "And as slippery."

"It's the soap."

"No, love." He swirled his fingers around her opening, fingers spreading her petals. "It's you."

"Only because it's been so long."

"I think you're remembering what it's like." Mac nibbled at her earlobe. "Let me remind you, my Isabella, that you made me feel splendid in your parlor. Now let me return the favor."

Isabella's hips rocked as he cupped her, the breathtaking friction driving away all thought but Mac and his beautiful hands. He'd learned to read her well during their marriage, and he put his knowledge to good use. Mac's fingers did their dance, teasing, tickling, making her groan.

As the first of her climax rose, Mac slowed his movements so that she would fade a little and build again. He did this the second time, and the third, until she was growling in frustration. Mac only laughed and brought her almost to climax again.

When she finally went over the top, Isabella nearly slid out of the tub onto him. Mac smiled down at her, his eyes dark. He was soaked, his shirt translucent with water. His hair was wet too, and the floor wasn't much better.

Mac lifted her slippery body and kissed her. The kiss was deep, a lover's kiss. She snaked her hand to the front of his trousers where his cock stood up thick and long.

"Yes, it's hating me," Mac whispered. "I want to gobble you up and not care." He kissed her questing mouth, his lips bruising.

Isabella wanted more. She held onto him, fingers sinking into his wet shirt. "Mac."

"I know what you want." Mac lifted her to the lip of the tub. "Remember how well I know you?"

Isabella nodded. They'd played like this before, and she understood exactly what he needed her to do. She stood up in the water, moving her legs apart, and Mac knelt in front of her on the wet floor.

Her head went back as Mac pressed his mouth to her. If he knew how to use his hands, his skill with his mouth surpassed that. His tongue was a hot pressure that parted her opening and delved straight inside her.

This was heaven. Isabella threaded her fingers through his hair and held on as he drank her. She was going to die. She'd not felt womanly pleasure since they'd parted ways, and she couldn't imagine that any man could have ever pleasured her better than Mac. He knew how to use his tongue and lips, even his teeth, to drive her insane. She found herself rocking back and forth, her incoherent cries ringing to the ceiling.

Mac's unshaven whiskers scratched her skin as his wonderful mouth kept up its torture. He smoothed her back and buttocks, tongue encouraging her to release.

Her next peak was more than she could bear. She wanted to pull him inside her, she wanted him to carry her to bed and never let her leave. This was the Mac who had made her the weakest, the one who could dissolve her into a pliant puddle.

She wanted him so much. She would beg him to take her to bed, just this once. Isabella clutched his shirt, while his mouth drove her on and on. The shirt tore a little under her grip.

"Mac . . ."

Oh, drat it all to hell, she heard Evans's heavy tread in the corridor.

Isabella gasped and pushed him away. Her body cried out with loss as Mac knelt back on his heels and dabbed his mouth with the back of his hand. His eyes had a warm gleam, a man knowing his power.

Isabella plopped back down in the water, feeling a delicious bite where he'd suckled her. "You have to go."

Mac remained on the floor, his smile positively evil. "Why, love? Will you be ruined if you're found here alone with your rake of a husband?"

"No. Just . . ." She made shooing motions, which scattered droplets of water.

"Just what?" Mac stood up, taking his time. His shirt was plastered to his chest, showing his dark hair and the outlines of his aroused nipples. "Hide behind the screen? Or under the bedclothes? Dear, oh dear, what would Lady Priss and Miss Prude say?"

"*Mac.*"

Mac leaned down and gave her another devastating kiss. She tasted herself in his mouth, all mixed up with his spice. "As you wish, my lady. I will leave you. This time."

Isabella breathed a sigh of relief, though she wasn't certain why she should be so worried. Evans had walked in on them plenty of times when they'd been kissing each other, and the maid had always pretended to be oblivious. But for some reason, Isabella did not want Evans to see Mac now. Perhaps the embarrassment came from Isabella having to admit that Mac made her weak?

Mac brushed her face with his fingers and finally headed for the door, opening it just as Evans reached the threshold. Evans gave Mac an even stare over the pile of towels in her arms.

"Good evening, Evans." Mac snatched a towel off the top and started mopping his face and neck with it. "I must warn you. Her ladyship is a bit tetchy tonight."

Isabella screamed in frustration, and her sponge sailed across the room and splatted on the door next to Mac's head. Mac laughed and wiped soapy water from his face. He winked at Evans.

"See what I mean?"

Isabella gave Mac a cool look when he entered the breakfast room the next morning. Mac had to grin when she wasn't looking—Isabella was a master at the cut direct. She didn't make a drama of it or play games, she simply behaved as though the person in question did not exist.

Mac sat back and enjoyed the show. He knew she was furious with him for working her into a frenzy, even though she'd enjoyed every second of it. She'd even enjoyed throwing the sponge at him. But he also knew that it was a good thing Evans had interrupted, because if they'd carried the play to its natural conclusion, Isabella would have pushed Mac away more adamantly than before.

Her anger he could conquer. But if she moved to self-loathing, he wouldn't be able to combat that. Mac could fight Isabella if she didn't trust *him*; he couldn't fight her when she didn't trust herself.

His cock disagreed, the organ only wanting to bury

itself inside her and be happy. Cocks were simpleminded things.

Over breakfast, Isabella declared her plans to accompany the family north to Scotland after the races. That clinched it for Mac. Any other year, Mac would have remained in Doncaster for a time with Cam as he saw to the horses, preferring the company of his fun-loving middle brother and nephew to Hart's unpredictable moods. But when Isabella announced that she would accept Beth's invitation to share a first-class compartment, nothing short of contracting plague would have induced Mac to stay behind.

When they boarded the train a few days later, Ian followed Beth and Isabella into their compartment without apology. Neither he nor Beth seemed surprised when Mac entered and seated himself next to Isabella. Mac leaned back comfortably and crossed his ankles, while Isabella edged close to the window, her face resolutely turned from him.

They changed trains in Edinburgh and again Mac squeezed into the compartment with the other three for the shorter journey to Kilmorgan.

The arrival of the family at the small Kilmorgan station became the major undertaking it always was. The stationmaster came out to welcome Hart home; two landaus and two chaises pulled up; and three valets and two maids each tried to take over directing how the baggage should be moved. The porter, the postmistress, the publican, the publican's wife, and whoever happened to be in the pub at the time also came out to help or just to have a chat.

Hart might be the second-most important peer in the realm, but here in his own demesne, the villagers he'd grown up with talked familiarly to him, giving him advice, laughing when he made a joke. The publican's wife pressed Isabella about the annual harvest festivities that would be held at the "big house" for the villagers and neighboring estates. This would be Beth's first, and Beth asked questions with interest.

The postmistress had no shyness about seizing Mac by the arm and peering into his face through her thick spectacles. Her husband was crippled with rheumatism, and Mrs. McNab looked after him with cheerful spirits. Her routine was to glean information about the lives of her neighbors and relay it all to Mr. McNab.

"Are ye and her ladyship Mr. and Mrs. again?" Mrs. McNab asked, her voice carrying across the platform. "Such a shame ye parted ways, when it was clear to see ye were so much in love, even if she is an English lass."

Mac winked at her. "I am moving things back in that direction, good lady."

"See that ye do. This parting of husbands and wives might be fashionable in the cities, but it's no' but a scandal. What the pair of ye needs is a passel o' bairns. That will make her happy, ye mark my words." Mrs. McNab had six sons, all grown now, towering over their petite mother and terrified to death of her.

Mac saw Isabella's back stiffen, but she gave no other indication she'd heard as she glided out of the station. Mac patted Mrs. McNab's hand, thanked her for her advice, and strode after Isabella.

He wasn't quick enough to get into the coach with her and Ian and Beth, so he rode in the second chaise with Hart. He didn't see Isabella when they reached the house, but Kilmorgan Castle—not really a castle anymore but a sprawling monstrosity of a house—was so gigantic, she could be anywhere. He changed out of his soot-stained suit in his own wing of the house then knocked on the door to the chamber next to his. This room used to be Isabella's, but he found the suite empty, the bed stripped, the grate cold.

"She's staying in a chamber down the hall, milord,"

Evans said, walking by with an armload of dress boxes. "Her ladyship's instructions."

Two weeks ago, Isabella's decision to use a different room might have angered Mac; now it amused him. If she thought moving down the hall would thwart him, she was sorely mistaken.

He continued his search for her and at last found her on the top floor in his studio. She stood with her back to him, studying three canvases propped against the far wall. Mac could see them quite clearly, the three paintings of Isabella that Mac had done in secret before his studio burned down.

⁓

"Bloody hell."

Isabella heard Mac's low exclamation but didn't turn. She *couldn't* turn from the three images of herself that glowed like goddesses from the canvas.

One painting showed her face, neck, and hint of bosom, her hair piled high and laced with yellow roses, as it had been the night of Lord Abercrombie's ball. Another showed her sitting on the floor, bare with her legs stretched out, her hair obscuring her face. The third had her asleep, head on her arm, red hair curling over her naked body.

"I never sat for these," Isabella said without turning around.

"No." Mac closed the door. "I painted from memory."

The pictures were done in muted hues highlighted by Mac's characteristic touches of reds and yellows. The women in these paintings lived and breathed, were *real*. They were her.

"When?" she asked.

"In London, before my house burned."

"Three paintings in a week?"

"I was inspired." Mac's voice was tight. "And they're not really finished."

She finally turned to look at him. Mac remained by the closed door, his hands stuffed into his pockets. Gone was the charming, smiling man who'd determinedly chased her these last few weeks. Here was the somber Mac she'd seen since their separation, the one who'd abandoned drink and his arty set, who'd holed himself up at Kilmorgan or his London house and stayed put.

"These aren't for that wager you made, are they?" she asked. "The one about the erotic paintings?"

He looked outraged. "Good God, no. Do you think I'd allow blackguards like Dunstan and Manning to cast their lust-filled gazes upon my *wife*? If you think that, you don't know me at all, Isabella."

She hadn't really thought that, but Mac had changed so much in the last three years, she could be certain of nothing. "Did I ever really know you?"

"I thought you did. Once." Mac moved to the paintings. "I'll destroy them."

Isabella stepped protectively in front of them. "You will not. These are beautiful."

His brows shot up. "You are happy that your estranged husband painted pictures of your naked body? Perhaps to gaze at what he couldn't have?"

"Is that why you painted them?"

Mac scrubbed his hand through his hair. "No. Or yes. I don't know. I *had* to paint them. They clawed their way out of me. But they're not important now. I'll have Bellamy burn them."

"No."

"Sweetheart, they're the idle indulgences of a frenzied mind. Or do you mean you'd rather rip them apart yourself? I have a knife about somewhere."

"You will not destroy them, because they're the best things you've ever painted."

Mac ran his hand through his hair again. "I agree, they're not bad."

"Not bad? Mac, they're genius. They're the same kind of picture you did the day after I married you. When you first showed me your studio, I was awestruck. Miss Pringle taught us all about great art, and I saw that yours was too."

Mac made a derisive noise. "These are hardly Rubens or Rembrandt, my dear."

"No, more like Degas and Manet, like Mr. Crane said."

"Crane would flatter an ant that tracked paint across a canvas if he could obtain a commission on the sale. Besides, you name highly scandalous and despised men. Respectable society shares your opinion that I'm in the same class as they."

"Will you take this seriously? These are lovely paintings, and I won't let you burn them or cut them up or anything else. In fact, if I have to buy them from you to protect them, I will."

"You know I never sell my paintings. Have them if you like them so much."

Isabella chewed her lip. Mac always brushed off compliments to his talent with carelessness, or so she had thought until she'd realized that it simply didn't matter to him what other people thought. Mac loved painting for its own sake and had no interest in what the world said about what he produced. That was why he gave the canvases away and didn't fight for the approval of the Royal Academy. Mac had no self-pride about his genius. It was simply a part of him, the same way his eyes were the color of copper and his voice retained a slight Scots accent.

"You truly don't care what becomes of them?" Isabella asked.

Mac's gaze went to the paintings with a kind of hunger. "Of course I don't care."

"That is a lie, pure and plain."

"What do you wish me to say? That yes, these are the best things I've ever done, that they come from part of my soul that craves what it can't have? That they scream what I see when I look at you?"

Isabella's face heated. "I only meant you should admit that they are good."

"They are bloody wonderful. They're the only things I've been able to paint in years."

Isabella stared. "In years? What are you talking about?"

Mac turned away, rubbing his head again as though it ached. "Why do you think I've not fussed about this chap who's forging my work?—not until he burned my bloody house down, anyway. I wasn't joking when I said he painted better than I did. You saw that travesty I was doing of Molly. I haven't been able to paint anything since I stopped floating through life on malt whiskey. Everything I attempted after I sobered up was horrible. I conclude that my talent lay in drink, and without it, my ability is nothing."

"Not true—"

"Of course it's true. The last things I painted were Venetian canals until the sight of a gondola made me physically ill. I threw the last painting and my remaining bottles of Mackenzie malt into the Grand Canal the same night. Never tell Hart about the whiskey, by the way—he'd kill me. I headed back to England after that and found that I couldn't paint a stroke. Mind you, in the first months of temperance, my hands were too shaky to let me hold the brush, let alone button my own shirt."

Isabella had a sudden and vivid image of Mac alone in his studio at the top of the Mount Street house, angrily hurling canvases across the room when the paint would no longer form into beautiful pictures. The realization must have broken his heart.

"You never told me," she said.

Mac laughed. "Told you what? That I was a wreck of a man whose dust you should have shaken from your boots long ago? Even when I grew used to being sober, I couldn't paint a shadow that wasn't muddy, a line that wasn't wrong." He blew out his breath. "Then I did *these*."

And they were genius. When Isabella had first entered the room, the paintings had been hidden inside the large wrapped bundle she'd seen Bellamy lug into her London house after Mac's fire. She hadn't paid attention, but today when they'd arrived at Kilmorgan, she'd gotten curious as to what Mac had been working on. She'd found Bellamy up here unpacking things and had urged the man to unwrap the paintings.

Bellamy must not have known what the pictures were, because when they came out, he turned red, mumbled something, and hastened out the door.

At first Isabella had been angry. What business had Mac to paint her without telling her? It was as though he'd peeped through a keyhole and drawn what he'd seen.

Then it had struck her how extraordinary they were. Mac's talent shone in every brushstroke, every color. The Royal Academy had never admitted Mac's work, claiming that his paintings were base and scandalous, but the Royal Academy could go hang as far as Isabella was concerned.

"Is that why you said you'd forfeit that wager?" Isabella asked. "Not because you couldn't paint an erotic picture, but because you couldn't paint *at all*?"

"You saw." Mac met her gaze squarely. "I'd rather forfeit and let them laugh at me than reveal what has happened to my talent."

"You won't forfeit," Isabella said. "You'll win that bloody wager. If all you can paint is me, then you'll paint me."

Mac's neck reddened with sudden anger. "The hell I will. I told you, I will not let my so-called friends look at paintings of you. These weren't meant for anyone's eyes but mine."

"You can paint a body without putting in my face, can't you? You can change the color of my hair. Or hire Molly when you go down to London again and paint her head in for mine. I don't care."

"Paint to order? Choose limbs and heads to suit the viewer? God save us."

"For heaven's sake, Mac, these aren't for a Paris exhibition. They're to win you a wager with a few obnoxious men at your club. Show them the pictures and then rip them up if you like. I'll not have you ridiculed by soft-handed lordlings who have nothing to do all day but think of ways to mock others."

Mac's smile returned, with a flash of his old wickedness. "My, you are protective of your wreck of a husband."

"If I can help you shut Dunstan's and Randolph Manning's jeering mouths, I will."

"I promise you, I care nothing for what those fellows think of me."

"I know *you* don't, but I hate the thought of them laughing at you, saying you're soft and weak and . . . and . . . impotent."

Mac burst out laughing. Still laughing, he laid his arms loosely on her shoulders. "If you want to persuade me to paint erotic pictures of you, my love, I certainly will not argue with you. I'd be mad to argue. But you leave it up to me whether I want to win the blasted wager."

When he looked like this, like the old Mac, charming and smiling and daring her, Isabella wanted to weave her entire life around him and never mind anything else. The knowledge that marriage with Mac hadn't ever been easy faded to nothing in the face of his smile. She'd loved him then, and she loved him now. She had never stopped. But choices—choices were hell.

"Very well," she said. She knew her tone was too capitulating, because Mac's eyes narrowed in suspicion. "It's your wager. Do as you like." She slid out from under his touch as a brassy sound floated up the corridor outside. "Goodness, is that the gong for supper? I haven't even changed my frock."

Mac stepped between her and the door as she tried to leave. His eyes sparkled dangerously. "I'll keep you to your word, my wife. We meet here, tomorrow morning at ten o'clock. Will that be too early? Will her ladyship have had ample time to rise and have breakfast?"

"Nine o'clock. I'll be finished with my morning ride by then."

"Nine it is." Mac cocked a brow. "Don't bother to dress."

Isabella flushed, but she kept her voice cool. "I'll wear my thickest dressing gown. I know you always forget to feed the fire when you're working."

Mac's gaze moved down her throat to her bosom, as though he could see through her gown to what he would paint tomorrow. "As you wish. Until then, my lady."

"Until supper, you mean. Unless you intend to hide in your room and not join us at table."

Mac grinned again. "I wouldn't dream of it."

Isabella gave him a quelling look as she swept by, but his dark gaze had her heart racing. No man could look at a woman like Mac could. He made her feel desired, coveted, wanted. He looked at her as though he imagined her naked and hot on the floor underneath his equally naked and equally hot body. He was a wicked man, and he wanted to do wicked things to her.

Mac laughed behind her, as he always did when she walked away in high dudgeon, because he knew quite well that Isabella wanted to do equally wicked things back to him.

Chapter 12

The coolness between our Lord and Lady in Mount Street has apparently thawed, like welcome spring after a harsh winter. The Lord announced to all and sundry that a small Mackenzie was due to make his debut at the start of the next Season.

—*May 1877*

Mac prepared his canvas and the setting well in advance, wanting to be ready when Isabella arrived so she wouldn't have time to change her mind.

If she came at all. Isabella hadn't spoken directly to him at supper, though she hadn't bathed him in the frosty silences she'd given him in Doncaster. She chattered with Beth, exchanged opinions with Hart, pulled Ian into the conversation.

Mac had watched Ian, marveling at the change in him. His soul-wounded younger brother, who could withdraw into himself until no one could reach him, had been talkative—for Ian—a smile touching his mouth whenever he looked across the table at his wife.

True, Ian still had trouble meeting anyone's gaze but Beth's; true he hung on Beth's words, watching her lips as though he liked the shape of them. But he followed the threads of conversation with the rest of them better than he had before. No withdrawing, no "muddles," as he called them, no sudden tantrums. He gazed at Beth in undisguised love, Ian who'd always had trouble expressing his emotions. Beth had rescued his little brother, and Mac would always be grateful to her for that.

Ian caught Mac watching him as they ate and threw him a triumphant glance. Bloody cheek. After his brothers had struggled to reach Ian for years, two beautiful women had opened the world to him—Isabella with the love of a sister; Beth with the love of a wife. And damn it, wasn't Ian smug about that?

Mac retired to his studio after supper and started preparing for the next morning. He snatched a few hours of sleep on the divan he'd set up there, then rose and dressed in his painting kilt, boots, and kerchief to protect his hair long before Isabella was due to enter.

When, at precisely nine o'clock, Isabella did open the door without knocking, Mac was bent over his worktable mixing paints. He didn't look 'round as she closed the door. Something silken rustled, and his hands started to shake.

"Good heavens, it's actually warm in here," Isabella said in wonder. "I wore my warmest dressing gown, but it seems you stoked the fire."

Mac kept his gaze resolutely on the paint he mixed. "Bellamy did. Can't have her ladyship catching her death, can we? Lock the door, love, unless you want members of my family blundering in to catch you in your altogether."

The lock clicked, and Isabella's dressing gown whispered as she crossed the room. "Am I to sit here?"

Mac busied himself mixing the exact shade of yellow that had made him famous. "Mmm hmm."

"I'll just make myself comfortable until you're ready, then."

Mac worked his palette knife through the paint in hard

strokes. He dribbled in some green—far too much. *Damn*. He threw the batch into a scrap bucket and started again.

"My ride this morning was quite fine, thank you," Isabella said, the blasted dressing gown rustling some more. "Such brisk weather. Refreshing."

A touch more cadmium yellow and it would be perfect. "Mmm hmm."

"Hart rode with me. We had a long conversation. He asked me if I thought it a good idea if he married again."

Mac's muscles worked as he kneaded the large glob of paint to just the right consistency. Anyone who claimed painting wasn't hard work was a bloody fool.

Isabella went on. "We also saw a few pigs flying. Which likely explains what I'm doing up here with you in nothing but a dressing gown."

Mac finally turned.

Isabella was sitting on the edge of the chaise like a debutante at her first tea party. She had her feet primly on the floor, her hands in her lap. Her red hair was pulled into a simple knot, a few tendrils escaping it. The dressing gown was voluminous, but the silk clung to her bare body, and a curve of breast peeked coyly from the opening.

Oh, God.

Mac had set the backless chaise in front of a crimson brocade curtain. One end of the chaise was raised so a lady could recline, half-sitting, half-lying. Mac had piled it with white silk draperies and cushions of brilliant gold. A bowl of bright yellow roses stood on the table next to it. Some of the rose petals had already drooped and fallen.

He drew a sharp breath and made himself turn away. "Lie down and pull the white cloths over your middle. I'll begin in a minute."

He'd barked similar instructions at many a model, feeling nothing as they slid out of their garments and draped themselves over whatever piece of furniture he'd provided. To Mac models were things of light and shadow, lines and colors. The best ones could breathe life into those lines and colors—without talking, wriggling, whining, or trying to flirt with him.

He moved to his easel with his charcoal pencil, keeping his gaze on the canvas. Out of the corner of his eye, he saw Isabella calmly undo the fastenings that held her gown closed. His heartbeat rocketed.

You've painted her before. This is a picture, nothing more.

"Like this?"

He had to look—how was he supposed to paint her without looking at her?

Mac looked. And stifled a groan.

Isabella lay propped on one elbow, her body half-turned toward him, the white sheet trickling across her abdomen. Her creamy breasts were tipped with dusky red, and coppery orange prickled from between her thighs. When they'd first married, Isabella had been eighteen, and her breasts had been high and round, firm little peaches. Six and a half years later, her breasts hung a little lower and her hips were rounder—womanly curves replacing the straight lines of the girl. She was so beautiful he wanted to weep.

"Mac?" Isabella lifted her hand and snapped her fingers. "Are you still here, Mac?"

"Mesmerized." Mac made himself give her a clinical glance, as though she were a bowl of fruit he'd set up to paint. *Fruit. Lord help me.* "This is an erotic picture. Your pose is too tame."

"Well, I don't know much about erotic pictures, do I?"

Mac steadied his voice with effort. "Pretend you've been ravished repeatedly by your lover and then left on your own."

"Ah." Isabella sat up, tucked her feet under her, and mimed writing something on her lap.

Mac stared. "What the devil are you doing?"

"Writing a letter to my solicitor, naming my ravisher in a suit, and outlining the amount I expect to receive in damages."

His heart started thumping again. "Amusing, love. Now lie back down. And sprawl."

Her brows arched. "*Sprawl?* How does one *sprawl?*"

"Do you mean to tell me that the art of sprawling was never taught at Miss Pringle's Select Academy?"

"Neither was taking off one's clothes to be painted," Isabella said. "Nor how one looks after one is ravished. Perhaps I should speak to Miss Pringle about amending the curriculum."

Mac laughed. "I dare you. And please let me be there when you do."

"I imagine that by *ravished*, you mean disheveled." Isabella rubbed her hand through her hair. More tendrils fell from the bun and straggled across her cheek.

She was going to kill him. They were speaking rapidly and lightly, as though none of this truly mattered, but both of them were nervous. Or at least Mac was. Isabella, as always, looked cool and composed.

"More than disheveled," he said. "You have been thoroughly spent by a night of grand passion."

"I will have to use my imagination then. I'm not sure what that is like."

Her sly smile and the sparkle in her eyes snapped Mac's control. He tossed down his pencil and came around the easel to stand over her. "Little devil."

"I said it in jest, Mac. I suppose I've had *one or two* nights of grand passion."

"You, my dear, are coming dangerously near to . . ." He stopped, unable to complete the sentence.

Isabella's lips curved. "Dangerously near to what, my lord?"

A *morning* of grand passion? She was his wife, his other self, and they'd thrown off their clothes and their restraints. Why should he stop himself?

"A tickling," he finished. "You should be tickled until you can no longer make fun of your doddering old husband."

Her glance moved down his body like a lick of flame. "I would never apply the adjectives *doddering* or *old* to you."

Mac found it difficult to breathe. Or talk, or think. He seated himself on the edge of the chaise and yanked the crumpled sheet across her stomach. "I did promise to have these pictures done before Michaelmas. Now, *sprawl*, my dear. Arm overhead like that, leg hanging like this, sheet tangled and pushed aside."

Isabella let him move her arm and leg without a murmur. Mac's hands shook as though he were palsied.

"If a lady were truly sleeping after a grand passion," Isabella said, "she'd bundle up in the sheet so as not to catch her death of cold. After warming herself with a nice cup of tea."

"You are far too exhausted for that. Barely awake at all." Mac patted her hip. "Move that a little off the edge."

"*That?* Are you implying that I am stout, Mac Mackenzie?"

"The word never left my lips, my petite angel."

"Humph. Plump, perhaps? Portly, even?"

He wanted to tell her how much he adored her voluptuousness, her body that had grown even more beautiful since he'd seen it last. She'd actually become a little thinner since her departure, and he'd noticed that her appetite had lessened a bit, which worried him.

But Mac had been painting women since age fifteen, and he knew how sensitive they could be to any even imagined change to their waistline. A wise artist never mentioned it unless he wanted to lose a day's work. He'd always been thankful that Isabella was much more sensible about her body, but even joking as she was, he knew better than to tell her he preferred her curves to the bodies of women who slimmed themselves into sticks.

"My love," Mac said, "you have the finest, as the French say—derriere—imaginable."

"Liar." Isabella hooked her finger on the waistband of his kilt. "Take this off."

Mac froze. "What? Why?"

"You have seen what I have become. Perhaps I would like to see whether your derriere has grown broader with time."

What she would see was a cock that had elongated into a rigid pole. She could hang her St. Leger Ladies' Day hat on it . . . and oh, Lord, why did he just think of that?

"You saw me in the bath, at your house in London," he said. "And I lifted my kilt for you in your drawing room."

"A brief glimpse, both times." Isabella tugged harder on the waistband. "Come now, Mac. Turnabout is fair play."

Mac decided he'd strangle whoever had invented that saying. He drew a deep breath, unpinned and unfastened the kilt, and let the woolen folds drop to the floor.

Isabella's eyes grew round. "Oh. My."

Mac put his knee on the chaise, swung himself on top of her, and lowered his face to hers. "Did you think you could lie here like this without me responding? I've been hard for you, my dear, since you barged into my house and actually spoke to me after three and a half years of silence."

"That was a few weeks ago. You must have found it a bit inconvenient."

"Inconvenient? It's been absolute hell."

Her eyes flickered. "You've borne up well."

"I'm dying for you. I've managed to keep myself from you for all these years. Because *you* wished it. Well, I can't do it any longer."

Isabella's slender throat moved in a swallow. Mac expected her to make another joke, to push him away, to mock him.

She touched his face. "You are with me now," she whispered. "And the door is locked."

Mac growled. "Hell, I wish I were a saint. I'd be able to leave the room if I were a saint."

"If you were a saint, you'd never have married me in the first place." Isabella's voice went soft. "And that would have never done."

"Why not? I made you miserable."

She stroked his skin, her touch feather light. "You saved me from ordinary marriage to an ordinary man who spent his days at his club and his nights with his mistress. I'd have nothing to do but buy new dresses, have teas, and hostess fetes."

"You do buy new dresses, have teas, and hostess fetes."

She shook her head. "I bought gowns I thought you'd like to see me in. I gave tea parties for your friends, so they would be my friends too. I ran fetes to help people who needed help, because I wanted to emulate the way you helped poor artists."

"I left you alone aplenty. Just like an ordinary husband."

"Not to your club or to a mistress, which would have been intolerable."

Her look was tender, her eyes so green. Mac brushed a kiss over her lashes, feeling them lush and full against his lips. "Clubs are rotten places. Gaming hells and cabarets are so much more entertaining. And I mean I'd leave you for weeks at a time. To run off to Paris or Rome or Venice—whatever took my fancy."

"Because you thought I needed to be alone," Isabella said. "Away from you."

Mac swallowed. "Yes."

Marriage to him had been hard on Isabella; Mac had

seen that. After a month or so in his constant company, her eyes would grow strained and her face lined with exhaustion. Their tempers would fray, and they'd quarrel about the most inane and trivial things. Mac had realized early on that the best gift he could give Isabella was peace and quiet. He'd pack a few things and disappear. He'd write to her from wherever he ended up—Paris or Rome or Zurich, telling her gossip about friends and sending her picture postcards. Isabella would never write back, but then, Mac lived a gypsy-like existence, so there wouldn't have been much point. A letter likely wouldn't have reached him.

He'd return after several weeks to her welcoming smile, and all would be honeymoon-like again. Until the next time.

Mac saw in her eyes that Isabella didn't believe that this time would be different. If he were a wise and practical man, he'd leave this room now, indicate that he was ready to take things slowly, to give her a calm, steady, sensible marriage, not one rife with ups and downs.

But he wasn't wise, or practical, and definitely not sensible.

He kissed her.

His entire body came alive. He was aware of his blood boiling through his veins, his muscles tightening, Isabella's mouth softening under his.

"God, you're sweet." Mac licked across her lips, tasting her morning tea laced with sugar. "Sweet little debutante I stole from under Papa's nose."

His sweet little debutante twined her arms around his neck and pulled him down to the chaise, on top of her naked, delectable body.

～～

The feel of her husband on her made Isabella swallow a groan. He smelled of sweat and paint, and his mouth aroused her, promised, taunted. It had been too long, too long.

He pulled back, his eyes dark. "Isabella."

This was different from Mac teasing her in the tub in Doncaster. Then he'd been fully clothed, playing with her, the master of the situation. Now he kissed her, equally naked, their bodies pressed together except where the bunched sheet separated them. Right now, they were man and wife.

"Just kiss me, Mac," she whispered.

"This is not what I want."

Isabella widened her eyes, trying to keep her voice light. "Goodness, you truly *have* embraced abstinence."

His smile could have melted the hardiest ice floe. "Oh, no, my dear, I want you. I want to couple with you for hours on end. Days. Weeks. But I don't want this and nothing more."

Isabella touched his sandpaper whiskers on his chin. He hadn't shaved this morning. "You said that before. But you want everything, all at once. Can we not simply take things as they come?"

"I'm very close to coming at this point."

She laughed, and his brows drew together.

"Don't," he said. "Don't laugh and look so beautiful."

Isabella laughed still more.

"Hell."

Mac stood and lifted her into his arms. "This chaise is a damned bloody nuisance."

Isabella noticed he didn't ask her to go downstairs with him to his bed or hers—she knew that by the time they rose and adjusted their clothing and descended the stairs, they might come to their senses.

Isabella didn't want to come to her senses. Not yet.

Mac laid himself on the backless chaise and pulled

Isabella onto his lap. Holding her in his strong arms, Mac brushed warm kisses to her throat, moving his skilled mouth between her breasts. His hair tickled her chin, and she pressed a kiss to the top of his head.

He held her securely across his thighs, the blunt hardness of his erection pressing her bottom. As he kissed her, Mac slid his fingers between her legs and smiled broadly when his thumb sank into wetness.

"You're ready, Isabella, never doubt that."

"I know."

"I might die on the spot if I don't have you," he said.

Isabella turned in his arms, moving to straddle him, her legs spreading wide over the chaise. "I don't know if I can," she said worriedly. "It's been a long time."

"It is not something you forget, love."

Her sudden panic dismayed her. She'd thought she'd moved beyond this. But Mac hadn't touched her since she'd pushed him away after her miscarriage nearly four years ago now. He'd never insisted, never cajoled, but as the months had drifted by, she'd watched the anger build in his eyes. Isabella had longed to go to him, to comfort both of them, but her fear had not let her.

Now Mac held her gaze. "If you want to stop . . ."

Those were the most generous words he'd ever given her. Isabella knew Mac could barely contain himself, but even now, he was willing to not press her, to walk away if she wanted it.

She lay her hands against his cheeks and gave him a long kiss. "I don't wish to stop," she said. "I want this."

Mac's eyes darkened, black spreading through copper. He kissed her as he pressed fingers to her opening again, and then she felt the hard bluntness of his tip.

"Are you ready?" he asked.

She nodded, still nervous. Mac kissed her as he slowly

eased her onto him, holding her hips as he entered her. Her eyes widened, the feeling of him inside her at once strange and wonderfully familiar.

"You're so tight," Mac whispered. "Why are you so damn tight?"

"Because I've been living like a nun."

"I've been living like a monk. I think we just broke all our vows."

Isabella laughed, then drew in a sharp breath as she settled onto his full length.

It did not hurt at all. Isabella smiled in joy and relief. He was a tight fit, but she was so slippery he slid in without strain. It was beautiful.

So long since they'd joined, and yet Isabella remembered the exact way he felt inside her, as she had from the very first night. He'd imprinted himself on her that long-ago night, and her body had never forgotten.

Mac raked his fingers through her hair, pulling it from the knot until it flowed loose down her back. "I belong here," he murmured.

Yes.

Mac stroked her with gentle hands, and she began to rock on him, the feeling of him inside her blotting out all other thought.

"I love you," Isabella heard herself say.

"I love *you*, my Isabella. I've never stopped loving you, not for one single second."

The room quieted but for the sound of their breathing as they moved against each other, noises of pleasure, the chaise creaking a little.

Mac was right; he belonged inside her. They fit together so well, each having learned the other by heart. Memories of so many nights with him rose in her mind—Mac's firm body pushing her into the mattress, his hands all over her, his hot mouth arousing her again and again. Loving with

Mac could be turbulent and exciting, and then it could be slow and hot, as it was this sunny morning in his studio.

Her skin was warm all over, from the stove and Mac's hands. He studied her with half-closed eyes, his face relaxed in pleasure, a sinful smile on his mouth.

"Scandalous debutante," he said. "With her legs around a wicked lord."

"A loving lord."

"Never doubt that," he said. "But still a wicked lord, very wicked. Wanton minx."

"I was seduced."

"A likely excuse. You were seduced by *this*?" He pushed into her a little harder. Isabella gasped with pleasure. "What about this?" Another thrust, this one harder, as he grasped her hips and expertly drove up into her.

"Yes. Mac, *yes.*"

He broke off, his face twisting. "Ah, damn it, not *yet.*"

He started shuddering, and sweat filmed his skin. Mac thrust his fingers to where they joined, playing, rubbing, teasing her toward climax. Isabella already felt stretched and hot, but his touch sent her into a frenzy. The friction rippled joy through her body, and her voice rang in the big, bright room.

Mac's breathing was hoarse, his arms supporting her with a firm strength. He thrust into her and she arched back, pulling him deeper, deeper.

Her climax swept her into a river of darkness, and when she opened her eyes, Mac was watching her, his face soft, laughing.

"You are beautiful," he rasped. "My love, my joy. You are so beautiful."

Isabella kissed his hot mouth as he pulled her down to him. He lay back on the chaise and gathered her on top of him. They were still joined, Mac as hard as he'd been when they started. And he kept laughing.

They wound down together, the coals in the stove hissing as they burned, warming the room like summer sunshine. It was doubly warm on top of Mac, who was finer than any mattress she'd ever lay on.

Mac drew his finger across her cheekbone. "I've rubbed charcoal pencil all over you. It must have been on my fingers."

Isabella gave him a smile. "I'm used to it."

"I always adored seeing you covered in charcoal pencil."

"Or smeared with paint?" Sometime Mac would turn a wild session of painting into a fury of lovemaking if he and Isabella happened to be alone in the studio.

"I liked that best of all," she said.

She hadn't felt this contented, this eased, in a long, long time. The love was there; it rose up out of him and embraced her.

"We're good together," Mac rumbled beneath her ear. "Every gossip sheet in the country talked about our marriage, but they never knew how truly good it was."

"The newspapers printed such rubbish." Isabella kissed his cheek, loving the taste of his whiskers.

He chuckled. "I especially liked the one that speculated that I took a wrong turn and ended up in Rome instead of at our soiree."

"That was my fault. When I was constantly pestered about where you'd got to that night, I told all and sundry you must have lost your way home. I remember being quite annoyed."

"At me?"

"At them. It was none of their bloody business where you were. Only yours and mine."

"Well, I'm here now," he said softly.

Isabella wriggled her hips, feeling Mac rock-hard inside her. "You certainly are."

A warm sound issued from his throat. "Here to stay. For always."

"That would grow uncomfortable in this position, even for you."

"I don't know." Mac kissed her lips. "I like it here."

Isabella started to answer, but Mac pushed one slow thrust inside her, and Isabella's words died into pleasure. He had always done that, made her pliant and sleepy, then surprised her with a burst of lovemaking so wild they ended up exhausted and sore. He'd leave her breathless, hot, laughing, and well pleasured.

He did it again. By the time they climaxed together a second time, they were on the floor, Isabella still on Mac, the red brocade drape ripped from its hanging and tumbling around them. Mac laughed, his voice low, and then his eyes grew dark, as they did when he was about to release. Mac's hands roved Isabella's sweat-slick body, the odors of lovemaking mingling with that of paint. Oil paint was Mac's smell—she couldn't catch a whiff of it without being plunged into memories of him.

Mac gathered her against him as they quieted, both trying to catch their breath. They lay without talking for a long time, while the sun rose higher outside the long windows.

"Mac," Isabella murmured. "What happened to us?"

Mac smoothed her hair with his palm. "You married a Mackenzie. You must have been mad to do that."

"But I wasn't." Isabella raised her head, looked down at his strong face. "I knew it was the right thing to do. I've never doubted that."

"It was a damn fool thing for me to do. I couldn't resist teasing the little debutante in white, but should have left you the hell alone."

"But I am glad you did not. I knew what sort of man my parents wanted me to marry—my father had picked out three likely gentlemen already. They thought I didn't know, but I did. When you whispered to me on the terrace that you didn't think I'd have the courage to elope with you, I saw my escape, and I took it."

"Escape?" Mac's brows drew together. "I was your escape? Isabella, you wound me."

"I chose *you,* Mac. Not for your riches—Miss Pringle emphasized that money is no reason for a lady to marry; the richest husband can be stingy and make you miserable."

Mac's scowl deepened. "Miss Pringle ought to have been a preacher."

"She did sermonize, rather. But she wasn't wrong."

"Were you thinking of the moral Miss Pringle when you decided to run away from your family and live in scandal with me?"

"We didn't live in scandal; we married." Isabella traced his lips. "If a bit improperly."

"Nothing improper about it. I made damn sure it was a legal marriage, because I knew your father would come sniffing around, trying to annul it."

"Poor Papa. I dashed all his hopes. It made me unhappy to do it, but if I had to choose all over again . . ." She looked straight into Mac's eyes. "I would do the same."

Isabella saw his confusion, his hope, his sadness. "I ruined your life."

"Do not be such a martyr. Do you know why I agreed to marry you, Mac Mackenzie? I'd never met you, but I did know about you—everyone talks about your family. I'd heard all about Ian in that horrid asylum and about Cam and Hart and their unhappy marriages, and about you painting naked women in Paris."

Mac's eyes widened, copper outlined with black. "Gracious, such scandal to touch a maiden's ears."

"I'd have to have been buried in a hole to not hear the gossip, scandalous or no."

"Hart's and Cam's marriages were unfortunate, I grant, but why on earth would that make you want to marry their brother?"

"Because their wives were cared for. Elizabeth was cruel to Cameron, I know she was, but he never says a word against her. And Sarah frustrated Hart by being so timid, but he, too, never said a word. He gave up his longtime mistress to be faithful to her, no matter that Sarah was clearly afraid of him. But he took care of her to the end. Not just to hide the dirty linen, but because he cared. I saw Hart when she and the child died. He was grief-stricken, not relieved as some malicious people put about. Mrs. Palmer's death was the last nail in the coffin. Hart is so lonely."

Mac groaned. "Isabella, if you start making Hart barley tea and knitting him slippers, I will become ill."

"Selfish of you. He needs looking after."

"He is the great Duke of Kilmorgan. *I* need looking after." Mac closed strong arms around her. "I am the man who had all the happiness he could handle before he went and lost it. You need to knit *me* slippers."

"Don't be so ridiculous." Isabella kissed the tip of his nose. He caught her by the back of her neck and pulled her down for a serious, long kiss. The discussion, she realized, was over.

Mac had rolled her over onto the fallen curtain, his body positioned between her legs, when someone thumped on the door. Bellamy's gruff voice sounded through it.

"My lord?"

"Bloody hell," Mac growled. "Go away."

"Ye said if it were urgent . . ."

"Is the building falling down?"

"Not yet, my lord. His Grace wishes to see you."

"Tell His Grace to lose himself, Bellamy. In a land far, far away."

Bellamy paused, clearly unhappy. "I think ye should speak to him, my lord."

"Blast you, man, you work for *me*, not my interfering brother."

"In that case, my lord, I wish to give notice."

Mac heaved an exasperated sigh. The brothers were used to Hart summoning them peremptorily, but Isabella saw that this time, Hart might have gone too far.

"It's all right," she said. She ran her fingertip down Mac's nose to his lips. "It might be important. I won't run away."

Mac gave her a long, intense kiss. The heat of it made her close her arms around him and nestle against him. She somehow knew that when this moment was gone, she'd never have another like it. She wasn't certain how she knew, but the feeling gripped her and made her hold hard to Mac.

Mac himself would have stayed there, she knew, but Bellamy knocked on the door again and coughed.

"This had better be damned important," Mac muttered as he rose from Isabella, snatched up his kilt, and made his way to the door, giving Isabella a fine view of his still-trim derriere.

Chapter 13

The Lady of Mount Street has packed her things and retreated to the seaside after a sudden illness. Mayfair is the lesser for her departure.

—*September 1877*

Urgent, Bellamy had said. *Damned disaster,* Mac thought as he stepped off the stairs.

Hart stood in the ground floor hall with Ian and a woman Mac had never seen before. The grand hall of the Palladian-style house traversed its entire length and was filled with polished wood, oil paintings, and tall windows. The very center of the hall sported a round table with a massive flower arrangement that the staff changed daily. It used to sport a marble statue of an entwined Greek god and goddess by Bernini, but as beautiful as it was, Beth had decided that flowers would be less shocking to ladies who might pay calls there. The Bernini now resided in Hart's private suite upstairs.

Mac doubted that the woman had come to call on Beth or Isabella. She was thin to the point of emaciation and wore a dark brown dress, a battered hat, and a cloak that hung loosely from bony shoulders. Her face was

worn with care, though she did not look to be much
older than Isabella. At her feet, attached to her wrist by a
piece of string, stood a tiny girl with bright red hair and
brown eyes.

Hart spoke to the woman in French. Ian stood next to
them, his hands behind his back, rocking slightly on his
heels as he did when he was distracted or upset.

Mac closed the shirt Bellamy had tossed at him over
his bare torso and approached them. "Hart? What do you
want? Who is *she*?"

The look Hart turned on him could have punched a hole
in a stone wall. Hart's eyes, golden like an eagle's, always
had a predatory bent, and at the moment they were filled
with fury.

"I give you free rein because I'm no saint myself," Hart
said in a tight voice. "But I do not like lies."

"Lies? What lies? What the devil are you talking about?"

Ian cut him off. "She claims the child is yours. She is
wrong."

"Of course she's wrong," Mac said in astonishment.
"I've never seen the woman before in my life."

The young woman watched their conversation with
uncomprehending eyes, looking anxiously from one brother
to the other.

Mac addressed her in impatient French. "You've made
a mistake, Madame."

She gave him an anguished look and started babbling.
Of course she had not mistaken Mac Mackenzie, the great
Scottish lord who had been her lover for years in France.
Mac had left his wife for her, but disappeared a year after
their little girl had been born. She'd waited and waited for
him to return, then she grew ill and too poor to care for
little Aimee. She'd traveled all the way to Scotland to find
Mac and give Aimee to him.

Mac listened in growing amazement. Hart's face was set in anger, and Ian stared at the floor, fist tucked under his chin.

"I swear to you, Hart, I have no idea who she is," Mac said when the woman's speech wound down. "I have never bedded her, and this girl not my child."

"Then why the hell is she saying she is?" Hart demanded.

"How the devil should I know?"

Mac heard a light step behind him and a rustle of silk, and he closed his eyes. *Damnation.*

He opened them again to see Isabella gliding down the last flight of stairs She was fully dressed, every ribbon tied, every button buttoned. The only sign of dishevelment was her hair, which had been brushed into a ponytail that hung down her back. Isabella didn't say a word to the brothers but headed straight for the fragile young woman.

Hart stepped in her way. "Isabella, go back upstairs."

"Do not tell *me* what to do, Hart Mackenzie," she said crisply. "She obviously needs to sit down. Can one of you *men* be prevailed upon to ring for tea?"

"Isabella." Hart tried his stern tone.

"It is not Mac's child," Ian repeated. "Not old enough."

"I heard you," Isabella said. "Come with me, *petite*," she said to the woman in French. "We will sit, and you will rest."

The woman stared at Isabella in astonishment as Isabella put a gentle arm around her shoulders. She let Isabella lead her a few steps before she put her hand to her belly and collapsed to the floor.

Mac shouted at Bellamy, who'd been heading for the servants' hall in response to Isabella's command. "Never mind the blasted tea, Bellamy. Send for a doctor."

He helped Isabella lift the woman and get her to a settee. The woman gazed at Mac in terror, but Isabella spoke quietly to her. "It will be all right, Madame," she said. "A doctor will come. You will rest."

The woman began to weep. "An angel. You are an angel. My poor baby."

The child, watching her mother collapse, hearing the men shout, and being no fool, realized that something dreadful was taking place. She did what all children would do in such a situation—she opened her mouth and started to wail.

The woman's weeping escalated. "My poor baby! What will become of my poor baby?"

Ian turned his back on them all and rushed up the stairs, passing Beth, who was coming down, as though he didn't see her. Beth blinked at Ian's retreating back then paused to debate which way to go—up or down.

She decided on down. Beth went to the little girl and lifted her into her arms.

"Hush now," she said in French. "No one will hurt you. See, here is *Maman*."

Beth carried the child to her mother, but the young woman didn't reach for her baby. She was sitting back against the cushions as though she hadn't sat on something soft in a long time, if ever.

Beth glanced at Mac, meeting his questioning gaze with a grave look. The child had quieted somewhat, but she sniffled into Beth's shoulder.

Isabella held the woman's hand. "The poor thing is exhausted," she said to Beth in English.

"It's more than that." Mac looked at Beth. "Isn't it?"

Beth nodded. "I've seen this before, in the workhouse. A doctor can lessen the pain, but I don't think he can help for long."

"That is why she came." Isabella rubbed the woman's hand and switched to French. "You came here because you are ill."

She nodded. "When the lord did not return, I did not know where else to go."

"We need to get her to bed," Isabella said.

Hart remained in the middle of the hall like a rigid god. "Wait for Bellamy to carry her."

"Good God, I'll do it." Mac scooped the woman into his arms. She was so light he almost overbalanced; it was like carrying a skeleton in clothing. Mac agreed with Beth's assessment. The young woman was dying.

The woman studied Mac's face as he carried her up the stairs, a puzzled pucker between her brows. Beth and Isabella came behind them, Beth still holding the little girl.

"Do you think the child frightened Ian?" Mac heard Beth ask.

"I don't know," Isabella answered. "Don't worry, darling, I'm certain Ian will be fine with your own babies."

Mac could feel Beth's worry, but he didn't know how to comfort her. Ian was by no means a predictable man, and who knew how he'd behave when their child arrived?

Mac carried the woman into a spare bedroom that was kept made up for guests and laid her on the bed. The woman looked around in awe at the elegance, fingering the damask quilt Isabella pulled over her.

Isabella rang for Evans, then took the child from Beth's arms and shoved her at Mac.

"Do look after her, darling. Out you go."

The mite took one look at Mac and started howling again. Isabella ruthlessly led Mac to the door and pushed him into the hall just as Evans hurried in with an armful of clothing. Another maid followed with a basin of water, another with towels.

Little Aimee kept shrieking, and the door slammed in Mac's face.

Ian came toward them down the hall, carrying a stack of boxes. "What are you doing to her?" he asked over Aimee's wails.

"Nothing. I'm holding her. The womenfolk took over and threw me out. I always thought Scottish women were strong-minded, but they are nothing compared to Sassenachs."

Ian looked at Mac as though he had no idea what he was talking about. "I found building bricks. In the attic."

Ian entered the small sitting room across the hall. Mac followed as Ian crouched on the floor and emptied the boxes of building bricks onto the carpet. Aimee looked down at them with interest, and her noise abruptly ceased.

"Set her down," Ian said.

Mac lowered the girl, who stood unsteadily a moment before sitting down on her little rump and reaching for the bricks. Ian stretched out on the floor next to her and showed her how to stack the bricks one on top of the other.

Mac sank into the nearest chair, letting his hands dangle between his kilted knees. "How did you know to find these in the attic?"

"We played with them as children," Ian said.

"I know we did, but that was twenty-five years ago. You remembered they were there, and where, after all this time?" Mac held up his hand. "No, wait, of course you remembered."

Ian wasn't listening. He taught Aimee how to build a low wall, which Aimee gleefully knocked over. Ian waited until she finished then patiently helped her build the wall again.

Mac rubbed his hands through his hair. What an insane morning. One moment he'd had Isabella in his arms, was a happy man. He'd tasted reconciliation in the air, and he could still feel the heat of her body on his. The next, a crazed Frenchwoman had waltzed in to deposit a child in front of them and declare it was Mac's. And Isabella, instead of snatching a pistol from the gunroom and shooting Mac dead, had rushed to help the poor woman.

This had to be a nightmare.

Mac rose. He needed to put something besides his kilt and shirt over his nakedness, and he needed to find out who the devil this woman was.

As soon as he reached the door, Aimee started to keen, a high-pitched sound that dug straight into Mac's skull. She kept up the noise until Mac came back and sat down beside her. Aimee immediately quieted and played with the bricks again.

"What is the matter with her?" Mac asked.

Ian shrugged. "She wants you."

"Why should she?"

Ian didn't answer as he went on building with the bricks. As he'd done when he'd been a boy, Ian tried to stand each block exactly on top of the other, moving it in tiny increments until he was satisfied.

Aimee laughed and knocked them down.

"Ian," Mac said, as Ian began to line up the bricks again. "Why are you the only one who believes me? About the child not being mine, I mean?"

Ian didn't look up from his fascinating task. "You have not been with a woman since Isabella left you, three and a half years ago. This girl is not much more than a baby. Even given the time it takes for a woman to carry a child to term, she is too young to be yours."

Flawlessly logical. That was Ian.

"You know, my brother, I could be lying about the celibacy."

Ian glanced up. "But you are not."

"No, I'm not. Hart thinks me a liar. God knows what Isabella thinks."

"Isabella believes in you."

Mac looked back at his brother and realized that Ian looked directly into his eyes. He warmed. The times Ian managed to do so were precious. And Ian believed Mac, knew in his heart that Mac wasn't lying. Doubly precious.

Ian blinked and became absorbed in the bricks again, the moment gone.

A peculiar odor began to waft through the room. Both men looked at Aimee, who picked up a block and tried to stuff it into her mouth.

Mac grimaced. "Time to find the women, I think."

"Yes," Ian agreed.

The brothers scrambled to their feet. Aimee rocked forward on her hands and boosted herself to her chubby legs, still clutching the block. She held up her arms for Mac.

Ian's glance was evasive, but an amused smile hovered around his mouth. Mac picked up Aimee, who now exuded a sour smell. She happily played with the block as the two men went through the house desperately seeking someone female.

The local doctor came and stayed with the Frenchwoman a long time. Whenever Mac looked into the spare bedroom, he found his wife sitting at the woman's bedside or helping the doctor.

Aimee did not want to let Mac out of her sight. One of the maids, a sunny-faced Scotswoman with five children of her own, cheerfully washed the child and changed her dressing, but Aimee cried when Mac tried to leave the room and only quieted when he picked her up again. For the rest of the day, whenever Mac tried to leave Aimee with Beth, or the housekeeper, or the sunny-faced maid, the little girl would have none of it. Mac fell asleep that night fully clothed on top of his bed with Aimee lying on her stomach next to him.

In the morning, still exhausted, Mac carried Aimee out to the terrace. The wind had turned cold, winter coming early to the Highlands, but the sun was bright in a cloudless sky. The housekeeper brought out a little chair for Aimee and helped Mac bundle her up against the cold. Aimee fell asleep in the sunshine, while Mac perched himself on the low stone balustrade and looked across the gardens to the mountains beyond, their knifelike wall bounding the Highlands.

He heard Isabella's step on the marble terrace behind him but didn't turn. She came to the balustrade and stopped next to him, gazing at the beauty of the landscape.

"She died in her sleep," Isabella said after a time. Tiredness clogged her voice. "The doctor said she had a cancer that spread through her body. He was surprised she'd lived this long. She must have kept herself alive to get her child to safety."

"Did she ever tell you her name?" Mac asked.

"Mirabelle. That's all she would say."

Mac studied the artificially shaped beds of the garden. Soon the fountains would be drained to keep them from freezing, and the beds would be covered with snow.

"I believe you, you know," Isabella said.

Mac turned to look at her. Isabella wore a gown of somber brown this morning, but it shone richly in the sunlight. She stood like a lady in a Renoir painting, regal and still, the light kissing her hair and playing in the folds of the fabric. Her face was pale from her sleepless night but chiseled in beauty.

"Thank you," Mac said.

"I believe you because Mirabelle struck me as being a timid rabbit. She told me she'd done everything she could to keep from coming to find you, that she wouldn't have left Paris at all, but she grew desperate. She was terrified—of me, of you, of this place." Isabella shook her head. "Not your sort of woman at all."

Mac raised his brows. "And if she had been, as you say, my sort of woman?"

"Even if she'd been a plucky young woman ready to put you in your place, you'd never have left her destitute, especially not with a child. That isn't your way."

"In other words, you have no confidence in my fidelity, only in my generosity and taste in females."

Isabella shrugged. "We've lived apart for more than three years. I walked away from you, requested a separation. How can I know whether you sought pleasure elsewhere? Most gentlemen would."

"I am not most gentleman," Mac said. "I did think of it—to make myself feel better or to punish you, I'm not certain which. But you'd broken my heart. I was empty. No feeling left. The thought of touching anyone else . . ."

Mac's friends had viewed his celibacy as a joke, and his brothers had thought he'd been trying to prove himself to Isabella. Proving himself had been part of it, but the truth was that Mac had not wanted another woman. Going to someone else wouldn't have been comfort, or even forgetting. Mac had lost himself when he'd married Isabella, and that was that.

"The father must have been him," Isabella said. "The man who sold those forged paintings to Mr. Crane, I mean."

"I drew the same conclusion. Damn it, who is this bugger?" Mac scowled at the landscape. "When I carried Mirabelle up the stairs, I saw her realize that I wasn't the same man. But she never said a word—did she mention anything to you or Beth?"

"Of course not. Think, Mac. If you were a penniless woman, knowing you were dying, would you rather leave your child with the wealthy brother of a duke or confess your mistake and have said child tossed into the gutter?"

Mac conceded the point. "Aimee won't be tossed into the gutter. She can be fostered with one of the crofters. Our ghillie's wife loves children and has none of her own."

"She won't be fostered at all. I will adopt her."

Mac stared at her. "Isabella."

"Why shouldn't I? It's hardly Aimee's fault that her father abandoned her and her mother fell dead from an incurable illness. I have money, a large house, time to raise her."

Mac pushed himself up from the balustrade. "Her father is obviously a madman. This fellow, whoever he is, paints pictures and signs my name to them, then sells them through reputable art dealers but never collects the money. Steady Ron saw a man he swore was me placing bets at the races, so he's following us about. Not to mention trying to burn down my house."

"All of which is not Aimee's fault."

"I know that. But what happens when he comes for her? And there you are all alone."

"I can protect her," Isabella said stubbornly.

Mac softened his voice. "Sweetheart, I know you want a child."

She turned on him, face flushing with temper. "Of course I want a child. And no one wants Aimee. Why shouldn't I try to help her?"

"And where will you tell the scandal sheets she came from?"

"Why would I tell them anything? Aimee has red hair

like mine. I will claim she's the orphan of a long-lost cousin from America or something."

"My angel, all of London will conclude that she is *my* illegitimate daughter by an unknown woman," Mac said. "They will think exactly what Hart thought."

"I am long past caring what rubbish the scandal sheets print."

Her voice was haughty, but Mac knew she damn well did care. The journalists had used much of his marriage to Isabella to sell newspapers. For some reason, the general public had been fascinated by the details of how Isabella had redecorated the Mount Street house, what happened at their parties, and the subject of every quarrel she had with Mac, real and imagined. As brother to the second most powerful peer in England and Scotland, Mac had long been used to being observed and written about, but Isabella, whose life had been very private, had felt it keenly.

Mac admitted he'd done nothing to keep the news-sheets' attention from them. He'd taken Isabella to gaming hells, had her in his studio while he painted nude models, and traveled with her to Paris where he worked for days without sleep while she shopped and went to parties. The newspapers had loved it.

"But Aimee might care," Mac said. "In time."

Isabella's eyes sparkled with determination. "I will not let that child grow up poor and unwanted. Whoever this man is, he obviously doesn't want Aimee. Mirabelle said she was his model—she thought she was modeling for the great and generous Mac Mackenzie. You were also famous for not betraying your wife—she never would have believed he was you if you and I had still been living together." She drew a breath. "If I hadn't left you."

"Isabella, for God's sake, Aimee's existence is not your fault."

"I should have stayed, Mac. I should have tried to make it work."

She was trembling, her eyes too bright. She hadn't slept all night, the foolish chit, and now she spouted self-recriminations she didn't mean.

"I drove you mad, my love," Mac said. "Remember? I read the letter you wrote me. About a hundred times, each time hoping it would say something different."

"I know. But I ran away. I was a coward."

"Stop." Mac drew her into his arms. She smelled of sunshine, and he wanted to sink into her and stay there the rest of the day. "I've met cowards, Isabella. You aren't one. Good lord, you married *me*. That took courage."

"Don't tease me right now," Isabella said into his shoulder. "Please."

Mac stroked her hair, the brilliant red of it shining in the sunlight. "Hush, my love. You may take care of the baby if you want to."

"Thank you."

Mac fell silent, but he didn't like this. Not Isabella's generosity in wanting to help the poor motherless mite, but he feared she wanted to assuage some imagined guilt by doing so. He also worried about what the madman would do once he found out that Isabella had taken Aimee. Mac needed to find the blackguard.

Aimee woke up, saw Isabella, and cooed for her attention. Right now, the child wanted to be held and fed and made safe. There would be time enough later to sort out complicated adult emotions.

Isabella lifted the girl. Aimee started to cry and reached for Mac. Resigned, Mac held out his arms, trying not to like it when she cuddled under his chin and was quiet.

Isabella smiled, her cheeks still wet. "Whether you like it or not, Mac, she's decided you belong to her."

"Which means if you want to look after her, I'll have to stick close by you."

"Until she gets used to me, certainly. In that case, you'd better have Bellamy buy tickets so we may return to London."

"London? What's wrong with Kilmorgan? She has places to run and play here, and the crofters' children to play with."

Isabella gave him one of those looks that informed Mac that he was hopelessly male. "I must make arrangements for nannies and governesses, there are clothes to be sorted out, a nursery to be prepared. A hundred things to do before the Season starts."

Mac bounced Aimee. "She's not ready to make her debut yet, surely. She's too tiny to waltz."

"Don't be silly. My Seasons are always full, and I'll not send my child packing to the country so I don't have to be bothered with her while I'm entertaining guests."

"As our own dear parents did, you mean?" Aimee enjoyed herself pulling Mac's hair until he swung her high in the air and gently tossed and caught her. She squealed in delight.

"Yes," Isabella said. "I remember what a lonely, unwanted feeling that was. I'll not have Aimee growing up glimpsing us from afar."

Isabella had decided. Mac held Aimee close again but felt a qualm of misgiving. He'd known that losing their baby had hurt Isabella deeply, but he hadn't realized until this moment just how much she longed for children. Enough that she was ready to make Aimee hers? Using a twisted logic that Aimee would never have been born if Isabella hadn't left Mac?

One thing was certain: Whatever Isabella's complicated motivations, she was determined to go to London with

Aimee. Aimee was quiet only around Mac, and Mac was determined not to let Isabella out of his sight.

Ergo, they were off to London. He and Isabella, who'd thus far been two wary satellites circling each other, were now part of a solid threesome.

Chapter 14

London was shocked to hear of the estrangement between the Scottish Lord and his Lady. The Lord has retreated to the Continent, and the Lady lives in Mount Street no longer. There is a saying, that many a bride and groom should heed, which is *Marry in haste, Repent at leisure.*

— *January 1878*

Mac had called Isabella courageous on the terrace, but Isabella saw Mac's true colors on the journey to London. They left the day after giving Mirabelle a proper funeral, her grave sad in the rain-soaked churchyard.

Aimee had taken to Mac with a vengeance and scarcely allowed anyone else to touch her. She'd conceded to letting Isabella hold her, putting together in her tiny brain that Isabella went with Mac. But she also made it clear that she preferred Mac. He cheerfully obliged and let Aimee sit on his lap, play with his watch fob, bounce on his knee, tug his hair, and grab his nose.

Isabella had never thought of Mac as being good with children—when she'd carried his child, she'd been secretly worried that Mac might not be interested in the babe once it was born. Now as she watched from her seat in the compartment, Isabella observed with amusement that Mac might be even better with children than she was. He fed

Aimee milk from a cup, let her tear apart the bread that came with his dinner, and balked only when it was time to change her nappy. There were limits, Mac said as he handed the soiled child to Evans. The servant had softened quite suddenly to Mac after observing him with Aimee, and had taken to giving him indulgent smiles.

As the train rolled on, Mac fell asleep leaning against the compartment wall, and Aimee slept in his arms. The sight of Isabella's large husband in kilt sprawled across the seat with a baby on his chest made her heart warm.

When they reached London the next morning, Mac directed his town coachman to take them to Isabella's house. Isabella was very aware of her neighbors' stares as she descended from the coach in North Audley Street, followed by her estranged husband carrying a baby. She sensed curtains lifting, faces at windows. Mac was right: The gossip would be merciless.

Her household staff, on the other hand, rose to the occasion. Morton had been warned by telegrams from Bellamy to expect them, and he'd cleared the bedroom where Daniel had slept to make a nursery. He'd also taken the liberty of contacting his niece, a nanny who was currently looking for a post. Morton had arranged for Miss Westlock to arrive for an interview that afternoon, if that were convenient for her ladyship, that is.

"This is why I say you stole my best servants," Mac said. "Morton is a god among butlers."

"I endeavor to give satisfaction, my lord," Morton said coolly.

"I know you do, Morton, but I'm aware that you would throw me over in a heartbeat if you had to choose between myself and my wife. Tell Bellamy to fix me a dollop of Darjeeling, there's a good chap."

Isabella did like Miss Westlock when she met her, as she was certain she would if Morton recommended her, and hired her on the spot. A no-nonsense woman of thirty-five, Miss Westlock had taken for granted that she wouldn't be turned away and had her bags with her. She promptly moved in to the upstairs room next to the nursery and assumed her duties.

Isabella planned to spend the rest of the day unpacking and shopping. There were plenty of things to buy—a pram, nappies, baby furniture, baby clothes, toys. Mac left her to it, saying he would return to his own house with Bellamy to look over what the builders were repairing. He ended up taking Aimee and Miss Westlock with him, because Aimee made it clear she wasn't yet ready to let Mac out of her sight.

Isabella felt a twinge amusement but also of sadness as she watched Mac climb into his coach holding the child, Miss Westlock following with a large bag of supplies. Isabella and Mac had been in one another's pockets since leaving London; it seemed strange now to not turn around and trip over him.

Three and a half years I lived without him, she reminded herself. *Three and a half years.* And yet, one afternoon without Mac, and the house seemed empty. She decided that the best recourse was to keep busy, so she ordered the coach and went to Regent Street.

Isabella discovered that she liked shopping for children. She perused the merchandise at so many shops that Evans began growling about shoe leather wearing thin. Isabella shushed her and piled the woman's arms high with picture books, building bricks, a tiny tea service, and a dolly about half Evans's size. The acquaintances Isabella met on this trip were clearly curious, and Isabella told them straight out that she was planning to adopt a child. They'd know sooner or later, she reasoned. She hardly meant to keep Aimee a secret.

When she returned home, the footmen grumbling as

much as Evans as they carried in box after box, Isabella found a letter from Ainsley Douglas waiting on the hall table. Mac had not yet returned, and Isabella hastened to her own chamber to read it.

She read the missive twice through and kissed it. "God bless you, Ainsley, my old mate," she said, and tucked the letter into her bosom.

～

When Mac returned home with a sleeping Aimee in his arms, he found Isabella in the nursery. Miss Westlock had to settle some affairs, so Mac carried Aimee up to put her to bed himself.

Isabella stood at the window in the nursery, staring out at the fading afternoon, stroking the golden hair of a huge doll sitting on the window seat. Mac laid the sleeping Aimee in her cot, covered her with a blanket, and went to Isabella.

Isabella didn't turn. A chance ray of afternoon sunlight touched her face, and the sorrow he saw there broke his heart.

Mac touched her shoulder. "Isabella."

Isabella turned to him, her eyes wet with tears. She opened her mouth as though to excuse her crying, but the words didn't come. Mac opened his arms, and Isabella walked straight into them.

Memories flooded back to Mac as he gathered her against him. *Don't remember. Don't let it hurt.*

But memories were merciless things.

As clear as yesterday, he saw himself walking into Isabella's bedroom in the Mount Street house after she'd miscarried their child. Mac had been falling-down drunk, despite Ian's best efforts to keep him sober.

In the train from Dover to London, Mac had kept a flask of whiskey at his lips in attempt to erase the horrible pain tearing at his insides. He'd never felt anything like it, not even when his mother had died years earlier. He'd never been close to his mother, had barely known her. His father had kept the brothers isolated from the fragile duchess, the old duke's jealousy extending even to his sons. The duchess had died because of that obsessive jealousy.

Mac's grief for his mother was nothing to what he'd felt when Ian finally got it through Mac's head that Isabella had lost their child and was in danger of dying herself. Malt whiskey didn't dampen Mac's guilt and grief a fraction, but he kept pouring it down his throat in desperate attempt.

He'd charged into the house and up the stairs to Isabella's bedroom. He remembered finding Isabella on a chaise drawn up to the fireplace, her red hair hanging loose, her face wan. She'd looked up with red-rimmed eyes as Mac staggered in.

He'd made it to the chaise before collapsing to his knees and burying his face in her lap. "I'm sorry." His voice had come out a croak. "I am so sorry."

He'd expected to feel better at any moment. Any moment now, she'd stroke his hair and whisper that it was all right. That she forgave him.

The touch never came.

Mac had realized in the bleak weeks afterward what a heartless, selfish bastard he'd been. He'd been puzzled and hurt when Isabella hadn't caressed him and relieved his pain. He'd looked up to find her eyes stark and glittering, her face so white it might have been carved from marble. Mac had tried to gather her into his arms, but he'd been so drunk he'd fallen to his hands and knees to be sick on the carpet instead.

Ian, who rarely showed emotion of any kind, had dragged Mac up and out of the room, scowling in fury.

Bellamy had cleaned up Mac while Ian watched in anger. "Isabella cried for you," he said. "So I looked for you. I don't know why she wants you. You are drunk all the time."

Mac had no idea why either. When he felt better, Mac sought out Isabella again, knowing he needed to doubly apologize.

He'd found her in the nursery, her hand on the carved cradle they'd picked out together when they first learned that Isabella was increasing.

Mac came up behind her and slid his arms around her, resting his cheek on her shoulder. "I can't tell you how sorry I am," he said. "That this happened, that I wasn't here, that I'm a drunken lout. I think I'll die if you don't forgive me."

"I imagine I *will* forgive you," Isabella had answered, stroking one finger across the cradle's polished wood. "I generally do."

Tension eased from Mac's shoulders, and he buried his face in her fragrant hair. "We can try again. We can try for another baby."

"It was a boy."

"I know. Ian told me." He kissed the curve of her neck, closing his eyes against a wave of pain. "Maybe the next will be a boy too."

"Not yet." Isabella's answer had been so quiet Mac almost missed it.

Mac thought he understood. She would need time to heal. Mac's knowledge of women's ailments came from his models—he knew they could not pose fully unclothed during their courses, and they sometimes couldn't work for weeks after giving birth or having a miscarriage. They resented the time they couldn't work, because they needed the money. Some of them brought their babies with them to the studio, because they couldn't afford to hire someone to take care of them, and the models often didn't have husbands or even faithful lovers. Mac never minded the little ones, and they seemed to like him.

"When you are ready, tell me," Mac had said to Isabella, caressing her cheek. "Tell me, and we'll start again."

Isabella pulled away from him, her green eyes burning in her white face. "Is it that easy for you? This child didn't live, but that's fine, we will simply try for another?"

Mac blinked at her sudden rage. "That is not what I meant."

"Why did you bother coming back from Paris, Mac? You'd be happier there with your friends, trying to see how much you can drink before you can't walk anymore."

Mac stepped back, stung, more so because she was pretty much right. "I'm not drunk now."

"Not *as* drunk as when you came home to comfort me and vomited on my carpet."

"That was an unfortunate accident."

Isabella clenched her fists. "Damn you, why did you come back at all?"

"Ian said you wanted me."

"Ian said. *Ian* said. Is that the reason you came home? Not because you wanted to be with me? Not because of the horrible thing that happened?"

"Damn *you*, Isabella, stop twisting my words. Do you think I feel nothing? Do you think I haven't torn at my chest trying to stop the hurting inside? Why do you suppose I drink? I'm trying to ease the pain, and I can't."

"You poor, spoiled darling."

If she had slapped him, it wouldn't have stung as much. "What is the matter with you?" he asked. "I've never seen you like this."

"The matter is we lost our child," Isabella nearly shouted. "But you didn't come home to comfort me, Mac. You came so that *I* would comfort *you*."

Mac stared, open-mouthed. "Of course I want your comfort. We should comfort each other."

"I have no comfort left. I have nothing left. I am empty, all the way through. And you weren't here. Damn you, I needed you, and you weren't here!"

She swung away, her arm across her abdomen, the dying light making a flame of her bright hair.

"I know," Mac said, his throat raw. "I know. But love, this was so unexpected. You weren't due for months; neither of us could have known this would happen."

"You would have known if you'd been at that ball with me. If you'd been in London. If you hadn't vanished weeks ago without bothering to tell me where you were going."

"I should be kept on a tether now?" Mac's anger, fed by grief, boiled up. "You know why I left—we were quarrelling almost constantly. You needed a rest from me."

"*You* decided—in the middle of the night, without a word. Perhaps I needed you to stay. Perhaps I'd rather quarrel with you than have the house quiet with you hundreds of miles away. Do you ever ask? No, you just vanish and try to make it up to me by bringing silly presents when you bother to come home at all."

Great God, she drove him madder than had any other woman in his long career of women. No—madder than any other *person*, male or female, end of discussion. "Isabella, my father killed his own wife. Shook her until her neck broke. Why? Because they were arguing, and he was drunk, and he couldn't control his anger. Do you think I want that to happen? Do you think I want to come out of a stupor one day to see that I've hurt you?"

Isabella stared at him in shock. "What are you talking about? You've never laid a finger on me."

"Because I've always gone before it could happen!"

"Good Lord, Mac, are you saying you leave because you want to strike me?"

"No!" Mac had never even imagined doing such a thing, but he'd always been terrified that his father would rise up within him—the father who had beaten and belittled him and his brothers. The old man had sent Ian to an asylum for being the sole witness to the truth of their mother's death, and had whipped Mac for wanting to—needing to—create pictures. "Of course I don't want to strike you, Isabella," he said. "I never have."

"Then why?"

His exasperation returned. "Does a man have to explain his every move to his wife?"

"He does if he's married to me."

Mac suddenly wanted to laugh. "Oh, my little debutante, what claws you have."

"I don't want claws, thank you very much. I also don't want you to tease me or to leave me for my own good. I want a normal marriage. Is that too much to ask?"

"Do you mean a marriage in which I spend all day at my club and grunt behind my newspaper at supper? I would be required to take a mistress to satisfy my lusts, because you would have no interest in the baser pleasures of life. You'd spend all my money shopping for useless things and be relieved that I wasn't underfoot."

He'd run out of breath, hoping to see her smile at this ridiculous scenario, but she only looked angrier.

"That is your usual view—everything or nothing. In your opinion, we must either have a wild and scandalous marriage, or you might as well ignore me completely. Have you ever conceived that we can have something in between?"

"No, because we always do *this*." Mac clenched his hands, trying to calm himself. "You see? We argue about everything. We either make love or shout the house down. I leave because that must be so tiring for you. If you're worried that I run off to other women . . ."

"I don't worry about that. Ian would tell me."

"Ah yes, Ian. Your guardian, my watcher. Dear Ian, who is at your side at all times."

"For heaven's sake, Mac, you aren't jealous of Ian, are you? He'd never in a thousand years dream of betraying you."

"Of course I'm not jealous." Or was he? Not that Ian would try to seduce Isabella, because Ian didn't seduce. His brother satisfied his bodily needs on courtesans but never formed emotional attachments with any woman. Mac wasn't certain whether Ian knew how. But Ian was a good friend to Isabella, perhaps a better friend than Mac ever would be. That rankled. "You seem to prefer him at your side."

"Because he is *here*. You never are, except when it suits you. And then it's to try to shock me, or to show off to your friends that your sweet debutante has the courage to take them as they are. You aren't . . . comfortable."

"Oh Lord, save me from being comfortable. That smacks of doddering old men at clubs and drab slippers. But that is why I leave, my dear. To let you live in comfort."

"It isn't comforting, not in the least. And you weren't here when I needed you most."

Mac had realized halfway through this argument that this time, there would be no easy forgiveness. Isabella wouldn't reach for him, wouldn't smile and tell him she was happy to see him, in spite of the circumstances. There would be no welcoming arms in his bed, no womanly laughter wrapping around him while he reminded himself how good it was to be with his wife.

This time, his reception would be cold.

Mac stepped back, lifting his hands in surrender. "I've apologized, Isabella. I am truly sorry. If there had been a way to know, I would have been at your side. You need to heal—I understand. Send for me again when you want me."

He'd turned on his heel and walked away from her. He'd walked all the way down the stairs, out of the house, and caught the next train to Scotland. There he'd buried himself in Mackenzie single-malt and waited for Isabella's message.

It never came.

Mac's thoughts ran out, and he found himself in the present. He stood in Aimee's nursery, holding Isabella back against him, watching how even weak sunlight glowed in the soft curls above her ear.

"Isabella," he whispered. "I was a selfish, selfish bastard. Do you believe me when I tell you I realize that now?"

Isabella studied the dusting of soot on the windowsill outside. "It was a long time ago."

"And you've forgotten all about it? I doubt it, my love."

Isabella's sigh was so soft he barely caught it. "I am finished with that part of our lives. The anger, the recriminations, the hurt. I don't wish to revisit it."

Mac kissed the warm place behind her ear. "I don't wish to revisit it, either. And I don't want you to forgive me. Do you understand? Never forgive me."

"Mac."

"Hear me out. When I told you that I wanted you in my life again, I meant that I want to give back everything I took from you."

"You took nothing from me," Isabella said.

"Balls. I loved and adored you, but I drained you like a thirsty man at a spring. I loved what you could give me—your admiration, your acceptance, your love, your forgiveness. I forgot to love you for yourself."

"And you've changed?"

He laughed at the skepticism in her tone. "I'd like to think so. I want to make up for all I've done."

Isabella turned in his arms. Her eyes were wet. "May we not talk about it just now, Mac? Please?"

Mac nodded. He was still an idiot—wanting Isabella to admire him for having changed, when she clearly had her mind on other things. Was this his true punishment? To watch the woman he'd treated so rottenly remain indifferent to his efforts to make amends?

"Ainsley wrote me," Isabella was saying. "The letter was waiting when I came home from shopping."

Mac didn't give a damn about anything but Isabella at the moment, but he made himself answer. "How are things progressing?"

"She's planned to let me meet with Louisa. After all these years, I will finally be able to see my sister again."

Mac held her a little tighter, knowing how important this was to her. "Excellent news. Where and when is this meeting to take place?"

"Tomorrow afternoon in Holland Park. And no, you are not invited. This is something I must do alone."

She gave him a stern look, and Mac smiled. "Very well, my dear. I will banish myself." He wouldn't entirely, but she did not need to know that.

"Thank you."

Mac bent his head to kiss her, but just then Aimee awoke. Isabella pushed abruptly from Mac, snatched up the doll, and went to Aimee, giving the girl a wide smile as she showed Aimee her new toy.

~~~

Isabella arrived at the meeting place in Holland Park well before the appointed time of four o'clock. She paced the path, imagining all sorts of reasons that her sister would not be able to come. Perhaps their father would get wind of the scheme and lock Louisa in her bedroom. Perhaps Louisa would change her mind, still angry at Isabella for her elopement.

But no, she could trust Ainsley. Ainsley had charm—she

could get 'round anyone, and the fact that she was a queen's lady would hold much weight with Isabella's mother. Ainsley was also resourceful. If anyone could arrange a secret meeting between Isabella and Louisa, it was Ainsley Douglas.

Still, Isabella clenched and unclenched her hands as she paced. What would she say to Louisa when she saw her? *How have you been the past half-dozen years? My, how you've grown?*

That last time Isabella had spoken to her sister, Louisa had worn her hair in pigtails. Louisa had admired Isabella, asking question after question about clothes, hair, marriage, and men, as though innocent Isabella were an oracle of sorts. Isabella had glimpsed her sister from afar since marrying Mac, noting how she'd sprung up into a lovely young woman, but she'd only been able to watch from a distance with a sore heart.

Isabella heard a rustle behind her, and her pulse raced. She stepped onto the narrow path between thick-standing trees and saw the broad back of a man with dark red hair walking away from her.

"Mac," she said in exasperation, then the man turned.

Not Mac. Isabella whirled and took two steps before he caught her by the waist and pulled her off her feet. He clapped a hand over her mouth as she opened it to scream.

"Isabella," he said, hot spittle touching her ear. "My darling, never leave me again."

Chapter 15

Lady I— M— surprised London by hosting a soiree at her
new abode in North Audley Street, for the express purpose of
introducing Miss Sarah Connelly, a mezzo-soprano lately come
from Ireland, to those of discerning tastes in London. So many
responded to this coveted invitation that the modest house was
quite bursting at the seams.

— March 1878

Isabella bit and fought and kicked, but the man didn't let
her go. He dragged her down the path and through an opening in the tall hedges, cutting her off from the world.

This was madness. She was in the middle of a park, in the
middle of London, in the middle of the afternoon, but this
isolated copse could have been deep in the countryside.

She heard church clocks striking four. Ainsley and
Louisa would be arriving at the appointed spot. But what
would they find? No Isabella. She'd not had the presence of
mind to drop a handkerchief or a brooch as every adven-
turous heroine should. Ainsley might assume that Isabella
had been delayed, or worse, had changed her mind. What
Louisa would think, Isabella couldn't imagine.

The man swung her to him. Isabella clawed at his face,
and he struck her. She tasted blood.

"Don't fight me, my Isabella. We belong together."

He might look like Mac, this tall man with Mac's

coloring, but he sounded nothing like him. Instead of Mac's velvet baritone, his voice was scratchy and thin.

Isabella heard a shout, and without warning, the man let her go. She stumbled and fell, shrubbery scratching her as she went down. Booted feet pounded on the path, and then hands pulled her up again.

She fought blindly until she heard a breathless "Isabella."

Isabella cried out and threw her arms around the real Mac, clinging to him in relief.

Mac pried her from him and examined her face, his eyes bright with rage. "Bloody hell. I'll kill him."

Isabella was too out of breath, too terrified, and too angry to argue. She held on to Mac, absorbing his warmth, his strength, the safety of having him here.

"That was him, wasn't it?" she heard him ask. "My doppelganger?"

She nodded. "He looked so like you from the back."

"And from the front?"

"Like you, and yet not." Mac smelled so good, like male and the scent of outdoors. "No one who knew you well would mistake you after the first moment."

"God damn him. Forging paintings and burning down my house is one thing. Touching my wife is unforgivable."

Isabella closed her eyes. Her heart pounded with fear, not only for herself but at the thought of Mac chasing after a madman. All she wanted to do was relax into the circle of Mac's warmth and go home.

"Stay with me."

Mac held her so close she could feel the agitated beating of his heart, feel his hot, quick breath. "I will, sweetheart. I will."

The strains of clocks chiming the quarter hour made her lift her head. "Louisa," she said miserably.

Mac took her arm and towed her back through the

bushes and down the path to the spot where Isabella was to have met Louisa. No one was there. Across the park, Isabella saw Ainsley and the tall form of Louisa walking away arm in arm. Other people strolled near them, and they were too far away for Isabella to call out without drawing attention.

"Louisa," Isabella whispered.

Mac put his arm around her. "I'm sorry, love. Write to Mrs. Douglas and set up another meeting. In a safer place this time."

Isabella kept her gaze on Louisa, her little sister now so tall, so regal, so elegant in her autumn-colored frock. Louisa never looked back but walked away with Ainsley, her proud head high.

~~~

Not until Isabella was tucked up in the armchair facing a roaring fire with a hot water bottle on her knees did Isabella ask Mac the obvious question.

"How did you come to be at hand for my rescue?"

Isabella looked so pale, so shaken, that Mac's rage wouldn't rest. Today the man, whoever he was, had induced his own death sentence.

"Mac," Isabella prompted.

Mac answered absently, "I was following you, of course."

"Were you? Why?"

"You meeting your sister in an out-of-the-way corner of the park shouldn't worry me? It did. Apparently with good cause."

Isabella took a cup of steaming tea from Evans. "I am grateful for the rescue, of course, but that does not mean I'm happy with you for spying on me."

"Spying? Nothing so dramatic, love. What I truly feared was that your father would find out what you and Ainsley were up to and sail in to stop you. Or that you might attract the attention of a footpad who saw a golden opportunity to gain your jewelry. I never dreamed my nemesis would be lurking in the bushes, waiting to snatch you."

Isabella shivered, and Mac damned the man again.

The sight of Isabella stained with mud and blood on the ground had awoken something primitive in him. Even now the bruise at the corner of her mouth filled him with fury.

Mac held in his anger as he leaned down to kiss her. He caressed Isabella's face, taking care not to touch the bruise. "Will you be all right here for a time? I need to go out."

"Must you?"

This morning, Isabella seizing his hand and begging him to stay would have filled him with joy. At the moment he needed to find this other Mac and break his neck.

"I won't be long," he promised.

"Where are you going?"

"To see a man about a dog." Mac kissed her again, sent a glance at Evans, and left the room.

~

Mac had never been to Scotland Yard and any other time might have found the experience entertaining. He leapt out of his carriage at Whitehall, holding his hat against the gusting wind, and walked into the complex of buildings.

The interior was plain and busy, with men in dark suits or uniforms swarming from room to room. Mac gained someone's attention by yanking him by the shoulder and demanding the way to Inspector Fellows.

"That's C.I.D., guv," the man said. "Top of this staircase."

Mac took the stairs two at a time. He didn't bother asking directions; he simply opened doors until he found the inspector in a room with two other plainclothes detectives.

Mac stormed in and leaned his fists on Fellows's desk.

"So what have you found out?" he demanded. "Any progress?"

Fellows regarded Mac without alarm. "Some."

"Tell me everything. I *want* him."

Fellows's expression changed to one of more interest. He was a good inspector, like a bloodhound on a scent, and liked landing his culprit. "Something new has happened. What?"

"He attacked my wife, that's what happened." Mac slammed his hat and cane to the desk. "He dared lay a hand on Isabella, and he will pay dearly for that."

"Attacked her? When? Where?"

Mac described what had happened while Fellows scribbled on a sheet of paper. He was left-handed, Mac noted.

As Fellows wrote, Mac paced. The other two detectives had their heads bent over papers; one got up and went out, and a uniformed sergeant entered to talk to another. Mac finally grew tired of pacing and dropped into a chair.

"Would it be possible for me to talk to her ladyship?" Fellows asked him. "Whatever she can remember about him will be helpful."

"Not today. She's upset."

"Yes, I imagine she would be. Is she all right? Was she badly hurt?"

"He struck her. He'll pay for that."

Fellows glanced at the other detective and the sergeant, rose from the desk, took Mac by the shoulder, and more or less shoved him out and along the hall to an empty room. Fellows closed the door and faced Mac.

"Now we can talk plainly. What do you intend to do to this man?"

"Killing him came to mind."

"Not something to announce at a police station," Fellows said in a mild voice. "Trust me, I'll get him—for forgery, fraud, arson, and now assault."

"I'll not have Isabella dragged into a witness box at the Old Bailey to describe how a man tried to abduct her. Wouldn't the journalists love that? She doesn't need the humiliation."

"Arson may be enough. If you can prove it."

"That's your job, Fellows," Mac said angrily.

The inspector looked annoyed. "I need evidence, or I'll not get a conviction. It would have been helpful if you'd caught him in your attics. Or seen him running away down the street after the fire was lit."

"Damn it, do you have *anything* for me?"

"I have quite a lot, if you'd stop raving and let me speak."

Mac tried to calm down, but he was too angry, too afraid. The forgery had seemed a good joke—the fake Mac had been able to paint glorious pictures while Mac couldn't manage a brushstroke. The fire had angered him, because the man had endangered the lives of Mac's household, innocents in all this.

But this was different. This man, whoever he was, had dragged Isabella into the equation. He could beat on Mac all he wanted, but he'd die for touching Isabella.

"His name is Samson Payne," Fellows said. "Grew up in Sheffield, came to London to work as a clerk in a solicitor's office about seven years ago. Never gave any trouble, the solicitor says. Quit about two years ago after saving his pennies, keen to see the Continent. Solicitor hasn't heard from him since."

Mac blinked. "You mean you found out who he is? Why the devil haven't you told me?"

"I know his name. Probably. But I don't know *where* he is. And as you pointed out, it's my job to find him and prove he's been doing these things to you."

"All right, fair dues. How the deuce did you find out his name?"

Fellows gave him a cold smile. "I'm a detective. I quizzed Crane and his assistant, went door to door until I put together a description of him, then put out an inquiry for information. I received many replies, and finally found that until a few weeks ago he lived in rooms on Great Queen Street, near Lincoln's Inn Fields. He gave the landlady the name of Samson Payne. More inquiries turned up a gent of the same name who'd worked several years ago for a solicitor in Chancery Lane—stands to reason he'd take rooms again in the area he knew."

"And how do you know this isn't someone who simply happened to look like me walking down the Strand at the wrong time?"

Fellows's smile warmed as he grew enthusiastic about his quarry. "The solicitor had a photograph of him. I showed it to Crane's assistant, who agreed it was the same man. He resembles you greatly, but not exactly. The solicitor told me that his hair was black, but with a little dye, some theatrical makeup to make his cheeks fuller, and he'd be the spitting image of you."

Mac felt a chill. "Please don't tell me he's really a Mackenzie. That my overly promiscuous father is responsible for this monster."

"Fear not. I traced him to Sheffield—mother was a baker's daughter, father was a coachman then retired to run a pub. They're his parents, all right. They said that little Samson always liked to draw, was quite good at it and begged for art lessons, but they couldn't afford to give them to him. They'd had a letter from him when he returned to London not long ago, saying he'd learned painting and would remain in London to seek his fortune."

"And you have no idea where he is now?" Mac asked. "Other than lurking about waiting to accost my wife or set fire to my house?"

"I'm afraid not. Not yet."

"Or why the devil he's pretending to be me?"

Fellows shrugged. "He wanted to be an artist. Perhaps he didn't have the money or connections to sell his work or even be recognized for it. Perhaps one day someone mistook him for you, and he thought he could make some money that way."

"That explains the forgery and tricking Crane to sell the paintings. Not burning me out of my attics and trying to abduct Isabella."

Fellows shrugged again. "People can become fixated. Perhaps he is trying to eliminate you so he can take your place."

"Then why hurt Isabella? She has nothing to do with this—she'd have nothing to do with *me* if I hadn't chased her to London. She left me, washed her hands of me."

Fellows looked uncomfortable, as though not wanting to stray into the territory of Mac's private life. "My sergeant is keeping an eye on the rooms he let, in case he returns, as well as watching the surrounding areas. This is an official inquiry now."

"I want him, Fellows."

Fellows nodded, meeting Mac's gaze with mirrored determination. "We'll get him. Don't you worry."

As soon as Evans stopped clucking around Isabella like a distressed hen and left the bedroom, Isabella was up and at her writing desk. She scribbled a letter to Ainsley, telling her she'd been taken ill suddenly but was recovering. The excuse sounded feeble even as it came out of her pen, but Isabella hardly wanted to distress Louisa with the truth. What Ainsley would make of it, Isabella didn't know, but she trusted her friend to come up with another plan.

Isabella finished the letter, blotted it, tucked it into an envelope, and set it aside to be posted.

Mac still hadn't returned, so Isabella went upstairs to check on Aimee. Miss Westlock examined Isabella's bruised mouth and suggested an herbal poultice, which she then prepared. Isabella admitted that the poultice made her feel better. The swelling had almost completely gone by the time one of the maids brought up tea.

It had been a long time since Isabella had partaken of nursery tea. There was bread and jam, weak tea with sugar and plenty of milk, and a small portion of seedcake. Aimee ate heartily, and Miss Westlock made certain that Isabella ate as well.

Mac still hadn't returned by eight o'clock, and Isabella, weary, climbed into bed.

She woke hours later to find Mac sliding under the sheets with her, wearing, as was his habit, nothing at all.

She sat up. "What are you doing?"

Mac yawned. "Coming to bed. I'm exhausted."

"You have a bedroom of your own."

"Do I? I must have wandered into this one by mistake. Indulge me, my dear, I'm far too tired to get up and move."

"Then I'll go." Isabella was halfway out of bed before Mac's strong arm hauled her back.

"Far too late to be wandering about the house, love. You'll disturb the servants, and they deserve their sleep."

Isabella sank down under the covers, resigned, and Mac lay back and laced his hands behind his head. Isabella had to admit two things—that she was far too comfortable to leave the warm bed, and that Mac lying next to her was a splendid sight.

His broad shoulders stretched across the pillow, his bent arms taking up even more room, a tuft of dark red hair dusting each armpit. A shadow of whiskers the same color lined his jaw, and his eyes gleamed like warm copper from under half-closed lids.

Isabella remembered the night Mac had first brought
her home, how she'd sat on the edge of the bed, entranced,
while he'd shed his clothes. The engrossing wonder of
his body as it emerged, a section at a time, had made her
almost forget her own shyness. She'd never seen a man
unclothed before, had never seen one anything other than
fully dressed, not even her own father. Shirtsleeves were
frowned on in Earl Scranton's house.

And then Isabella had beheld Mac, astonishing and
naked. His body had been hard, his need for her apparent.
He'd put his hands on his hips and laughed at her, not even
embarrassed.

That was when she'd realized, as she sat demurely
on his bed wrapped in his borrowed dressing gown, that
Mac's goal since he'd first seen her had been to bring Isabella here, to his bedchamber. It had not been to flirt, or to
finagle a dance, or to steal a kiss. Even their hasty marriage
had not been his ultimate intent. Mac had wanted all along
to bring her to his bedroom, to smile at her while she sat on
his bed. The flirting, dancing, kissing, and marrying had
simply been the means to get her here.

And, silly girl, Isabella readily succumbed.

Lying next to him now, propped on her elbow so she
could study him, Isabella decided that the silly girl had
never left her. She was still entranced by Mac's body.

Mac brushed her bruised lip with gentle fingers. "That
looks better."

"Miss Westlock made me a poultice."

"The excellent Miss Westlock." Mac's touch lingered on
her face, but his eyes held anger. "I spent all afternoon and
well into the night hunting for the bastard, but he's made
himself scarce."

Isabella pulled back in alarm. "You went looking for
him? Mac, he's obviously dangerous. Be careful."

"*I'm* dangerous, love. I plan to kill him for touching you."

"And then I'll watch you hang for murder. Go to the police, and let them hunt him down."

"I did go to the police. Inspector Fellows knows who the man is and where he's been, but unfortunately not where he is now. He told me he has men working on it, but so far, Mr. Payne has eluded them."

"Payne is the doppelganger's name?"

Mac nodded and told her what he'd learned.

"Do you think he'll return to his rooms?" she asked when he finished.

"With a great clunking police sergeant leaning against the wall outside? He will be smarter than that."

"And does Fellows know why Mr. Payne is pretending to be you?"

"The very question I asked." Mac cradled his head in his hands again and thoughtfully studied the canopy above them. "Only a madman would pretend to be me. I've been wishing for three years that I *wasn't* me."

"That would be a pity."

A pity to have Mac be anything but himself, a large Scottish male stretched out in her bed. He took up most of the room, but on the other hand, she couldn't think of a better bed warmer. Little in her life had been more agreeable than lying against his long body on a winter's night. His voice would soothe her, as would his touch, which could change from gentle to powerfully seductive in an instant.

She expected Mac to make a quip at her statement, but his eyes held wariness. "Do you truly mean that, love?"

"Of course I do."

She'd told Mac once that he never did anything by halves. He tended toward extremes, which made him interesting but highly uncomfortable to live with.

The entire Mackenzie family tended toward extremes. Hart with his focus on politics and his rumored dark appetites; Cameron with his fixation on horses; Ian being able to remember every word of a conversation years after it took place yet unable to understand the subtleties of it, let alone participate in it.

If Mac hadn't been exactly who he was—charming, outrageous, funny, seductive, sensual, and unpredictable—Isabella would never have fallen in love with him. She edged a little closer to him and rested her hand on the warm expanse of his chest.

Mac's eyes darkened. "Isabella, don't play with fire."

Isabella moved closer, leaned down, and kissed him.

Chapter 16

The Marquis of Dunstan showed several pictures in his drawing room on Thursday last, paintings of Venice so vivid that
the viewer was certain to hear the splashing of water and the
songs of the gondoliers. These exquisite paintings are the work
of Lord Mac Mackenzie, although his lordship has retired to the
country in Scotland, and it is assumed that he has finished with
painting pictures of Venetian canals.

—September 1878

Mac's heart beat swiftly as he slid his hand behind Isabella's heavy braid and pulled her into the kiss. *My dearest
darling, don't do this to me.*

Her mouth tasted of sweet tea, and her body was wonderfully bare under her prim-looking nightdress. The little
ruffle at her throat scratched his chin, and he wormed his
fingers in to undo the buttons.

Isabella's kiss was desperate, her lips parting his, her
tongue sweeping into his mouth. The idiot Payne had
scared her out of her senses, although Isabella would never
admit it. She was strong, his beautiful lady, but she felt
things deeply. She was kissing him to seek solace.

Mac wasn't too proud to give her that solace. He gathered her to him, chilled to think how close he'd come to
losing her today. If he hadn't been following her . . .

But he had, and he'd stopped Payne, and now he had

Isabella in his arms. And damned if he would ever let her
out of his sight again.

Isabella started to pull away, as though coming to her
senses.

"Don't," Mac said. "Stay with me."

Isabella's throat moved behind the buttons he'd parted.
"I'm very tired."

"So am I." He broke off, touched the bruise on the side
of her mouth again. "I don't want you to be afraid of me,
Isabella."

She smiled suddenly, the abrasion pulling her mouth
into a crooked line. "Afraid of you? I'll never be afraid of
you, Mac Mackenzie."

Mac didn't laugh. "I meant that I don't want you thinking that I'm anything like him."

"Like this Payne fellow?" Isabella shook her head, the
end of her braid brushing his chest. "Of course I don't."

"He looks like me, and he's decided to try to steal my
life. But I won't let him have it, any part of it." He tightened
his arms around her. "Especially not this part."

Isabella's eyes softened, becoming the shade of a misty
Scottish meadow. "If I do decide to throw you out of my
house, Mac, it will be because *I* want to, not because Payne
has upset me."

"That's my Isabella."

He tugged her to him and swiftly undid the rest of the
buttons on her nightdress.

Warm, supple woman waited for him inside. Mac kissed
her lips, fingered the weight of her breasts, eased her on
top of him. On their wedding night, he'd pulled her under
the covers while she still wore the dressing gown he'd lent
her. He'd wanted to spare her the discomfiture of baring
herself the middle of the room—he suspected she'd never
been naked in front of another human being in her life.

She'd probably been taught to bathe in her undergarments. Prudery at its most ridiculous.

Then, as now, he'd unbuttoned her once she was on top of him under the blankets and tugged off the dressing gown. That night, Isabella had kissed him clumsily; tonight, her kisses held the skill of experience.

Darling, darling Isabella. Men were fools not to make mistresses of their wives. What need did Mac have for courtesans when he had beautiful Isabella? What's more, he could fall asleep with her and wake up with her, spend the day with her, go to bed with her, and begin the wonderful ritual all over again.

His thoughts broke off as she glided one hand around his very aroused cock.

"Don't tease me, sweet," Mac whispered, voice grating. "I need you too much to hold back."

Isabella's answering smile was hot. She stroked him once. "I need *you*, Mac," she said.

All thoughts of his foolish game, of resisting Isabella until their reconciliation was complete, fled his head. To hell with that. Mac caught her hips and half-lifted her to straddle him. She guided Mac to her very wet opening, and closed her eyes as he slid into her.

Oh, yes. Isabella's sheath closed around him like a tight fist. *My beautiful, beautiful darling.* Nothing else mattered when Isabella's scent and lovely slick opening surrounded him, nothing. The first night making love to her had shattered him, and Mac still hadn't found all the pieces.

"It's like heaven inside you," he whispered.

Isabella kissed his lips, the bridge of his nose. "You once said you married me because you thought I was an angel." Her lips curved into the wickedest smile he'd ever seen as she wriggled her hips.

"Little devil," he growled.

She splayed her hot hands on his chest, tilting her head back as she rode him. He was going to die of this. Firelight touched her slim body, her nipples dark against cream-colored skin. Her hair trickled over her body, loose now, like a gossamer cloak of fiery red.

Isabella's face softened, her eyes dark as her moist lips parted. The sight excited him. He thrust high inside her, and they swayed together for a long time, this coupling driving away all fear, all anger, all grief. Nothing mattered but the two of them joining, no longer two but one.

Isabella crooked one arm across her breasts, resting her hand on own shoulder as she lost herself in the pleasure. He knew she was thinking nothing, hearing nothing, only feeling Mac inside her.

He knew when she was drawing to climax, and that excited him even more. He rocked up into her, his own cry of joy ringing with hers as they peaked together.

Isabella collapsed to his chest, her loose hair covering him like a river of red. "It feels so good. I've never felt it like this. It's so . . ." She trailed off, incoherent.

"Good?" Mac wanted to laugh, but his body shuddered with release, and his laughter came out a groan.

They fell silent, Mac burying his fingers in the warmth of her long, silken hair. Mac loved this part, stillness settling between them while his body went heavy, every muscle loose. He'd missed the afterward almost as much as he'd missed being inside her.

"We did this in Scotland," said Isabella after a time, her voice sleepy. "It was glorious then. But this is better. I wonder why."

Mac didn't give a damn why this time seemed even more intense than it had been in his studio, but Isabella wanted an answer. Mac simply wanted to close his eyes and hold her.

"Comfy bed," he murmured. "Difficult day."

"I thought I'd never see you again," Isabella whispered, her breath hot on his cheek. "And then you were there, pulling me out of danger."

"That must be it. I was a hero. I swept you off your feet and made you want me."

"Don't joke." Isabella frowned. "Don't."

"I'm sorry, love. No, it's not a laughing matter."

He kissed the line of her hair. Mac had been in time to prevent the abduction, or whatever Payne had been planning, but it had been a close thing. It made him ill to think how close.

No, he couldn't go on thinking about *what if.* He'd brought her home, safe and sound.

Relatively safe and sound. Mac thought of her bruised lip and rage trickled through him again. Payne would answer for that.

Isabella lifted her head. "Mac."

"Yes, sweet angel?"

"I don't want to sleep yet."

"Fancy a game of cards, do you? Lawn tennis, perhaps?"

"Don't be silly. I want to do some of the things we used to do. You know."

Mac's thoughts scattered as his pulse quickened. "I do know. Wicked lady."

Isabella kissed the tip of his nose. "I was taught by a wicked, wicked lord."

He grinned. "What did you have in mind?"

Isabella showed him. They tried something they'd enjoyed before—Isabella straddling him, facing his legs instead of his face, and then leaning back until she lay full length on him, her back to his chest. Every muscle in Mac's body tightened in pleasure, the arousal incredible.

This position let Mac cup her where they joined. The feel of her wet heat, the sounds of pleasure she made as he stroked her there aroused him all over again. They climaxed together, their shouts mingling in the stillness of the night.

Still hard, Mac rolled Isabella onto the bed and entered her again, face-to-face. A conventional position, but the best, he thought, where he could kiss Isabella's lips and watch her green eyes sparkle with passion. If he could ever capture on canvas her expression as she rose to climax, he would treasure that painting above all others. And show it to no one, of course. It would be his own private, decadent pleasure.

Mac made love to her until both of them were limp with exhaustion. Then he blearily pulled the covers over them and fell asleep in a nest with his beautiful, incredible wife.

When Isabella came down to breakfast the next morning, a bit sore from the night's activities, she was pleased to find a letter from Ainsley lying by her plate.

Mac read the paper at the head of the table, the pages hiding him while he crunched his usual buttered toast. Isabella thanked Morton for the coffee he poured and opened the letter.

She made a faint noise, and Mac's paper came down. "What is it, love?"

Isabella's face heated as she met his gaze. She'd begun her shameless behavior last night because she'd been too restless and anxious to sleep. She'd needed to drop off from exhaustion of the kind that only Mac Mackenzie could provide.

She'd sought oblivion but found pleasure so great it was indescribable. By the glint in Mac's eyes, he understood and was gleeful that he'd been the cause.

"Mrs. Douglas," Isabella answered. "She says she will

try to contrive another meeting between myself and Louisa, but she's not certain yet when she'll be able to."

"When she does, I will accompany you," Mac said.

"You can't. Ainsley is finding it difficult enough to invent excuses to take Louisa out alone, without my mother. Louisa might be too afraid to go through with it if she knew you were involved."

Mac folded his paper and set it aside, his face stern. "Isabella, my lovely, I am not letting you out of my sight. Don't mention to Ainsley that I will be there if she thinks my presence would confound the scheme, but I am going."

"Mac."

"No."

Mac rarely asserted husbandly mastery. He'd told her the first day of their marriage that he thought it nonsense that men presumed to dictate to their wives—what if the husband was a fool? Wouldn't the wife be even more of a fool to obey him? Isabella was to be given complete freedom, because, Mac said, he suspected that Isabella had far better sense than he did.

Isabella saw now that Mac simply had chosen not to assert his rather formidable will. The look in his eyes told her he would not back down, no matter how much she argued.

Isabella tried anyway. "She's my sister."

"And there is a madman lurking in the streets waiting to do who the hell knows what. You go nowhere without me."

Isabella swept her lashes down. "Of course, my dear," she said meekly.

"And don't you dare pretend to capitulate and then sneak away when my back's turned. Your servants agree with me and will tell me if you attempt anything so rash. If you try to leave the house without me, I promise I will drag you back home, chain you up in the cellar, and feed you bread and water with my own hands."

The trouble with Mac making idiotic declarations was that there was a good chance he'd carry them out. Also, he was right. Payne was a danger. Isabella recalled his terribly strong hands on her and suppressed a shiver. She never, ever wanted to feel that helpless again.

"Very well," she said in a cool tone. "Find some way that I can meet with my sister safely, and I will do as you say."

"I will," Mac said. "I am deadly serious, Isabella: Do not leave the house without me. I will escort you wherever you wish to go. I trust no one else to keep you safe."

Isabella smeared jam onto a piece of toast. "Will this not severely limit your own business in town?"

"No. My business in town is you."

"Oh." Isabella went warm with pleasure, but she certainly would not let him see that. "Surely you'll have errands to run."

"And a houseful of servants to run them for me. Anyone I must do business with can come to me here." He lifted his paper again and shook it open. "In fact, I have an important visitor arriving this morning, so don't plan to go out until after that, there's a good wife."

Isabella sent him a glare that could have burned his newspaper to a crisp. But in spite of her irritation at his high-handed arrogance, she couldn't help feeling, deep down, a warm glow at his protectiveness.

~

Her warm glow dimmed an hour and a half later when the Mackenzie family's London solicitor arrived.

Isabella knew Mr. Gordon well. He'd guided her first through the legal ramifications of her marriage to Mac and his settlements on her and then through the morass of issues involved in their separation. Mr. Gordon had advised her against divorce, which he explained was costly and difficult to achieve. It would involve Isabella accusing Mac of heinous behavior, and Mac defending himself in court in front of the world. Separations were less scandalous and less of a headache, and after all, Isabella wanted only to live in peace and comfort on her own. Mac would provide a full income to Isabella, and she could do as she liked. Mr. Gordon had been kind and patient during the turmoil, and Isabella would be forever grateful to him for that.

"Your ladyship." Gordon bowed and shook her hand. Unlike the stereotype of the dried-up, rather elderly solicitor, Mr. Gordon was tall, round, and pink-faced, with an amiable smile. He was married and had five children as round and pink as he was.

"Mr. Gordon, how pleasant to see you. How is your family?"

While Mr. Gordon effused about his growing brood, Isabella led him to the front drawing room. They entered to find Mac on his hands and knees playing horsie with Aimee.

Isabella paused in the doorway to take in the sight. Mac was in shirtsleeves and waistcoat, his coat and watch chain safely out of the way. Aimee had her hands full of Mac's hair, pulling him where she pleased as he galloped over the floor, Aimee squealing in delight.

"This must be the child in question," Mr. Gordon said.

Mac gently tipped Aimee to the ground then lifted her high, making her squeal again. He settled her in the crook of his arm and turned to greet Gordon.

"In question?" Isabella asked. She bade Mr. Gordon sit down and took a seat herself on the sofa.

Mac perched on the sofa's arm, still holding Aimee. "I've asked Gordon to come 'round and make the adoption official. I'll become Aimee's guardian until she's of age."

"You will?" Isabella asked. "I thought I was to be doing the adopting."

"So I told Gordon, but he suggested it would be better for Aimee in the long run if I make her my legal ward, extending her the protection of the Mackenzie family. With you to raise her as you like and make all the crucial decisions of course."

High-handed again, but Isabella warmed with relief. She'd half feared that Mac would view Aimee in a different light this morning—the daughter of the man who'd accosted Isabella—and want nothing more to do with her. Obviously not. Mac could separate the actions of the guilty from the lives of the innocent, which was another reason she loved him.

"Are you certain of all this, my lord?" Mr. Gordon asked. "Taking on guardianship of a child, especially a girl, carries a weight of responsibilities."

Mac gave Gordon his careless shrug. "She'll need someone to pay for her dresses and hats and ribbons and other fripperies. We'll send her to Miss Pringle's for finishing and give her a debut ball the like of which London has never seen." He winked at Isabella. "And we'll sternly forbid her to elope with any stray lordlings."

"Very amusing," Isabella said.

"I mean it. Her mother's dead, poor sprite, and her father has abandoned her. Besides, her father is a villain. She'll be much safer with us."

That seemed to be enough for Gordon, but then, the man had always been fond of Mac and his brothers. He behaved more like a sympathetic uncle than a family lawyer.

"Aimee has obviously adopted you," Isabella said, watching Aimee play contentedly with a button on Mac's waistcoat.

"I did ask her, you know, what she thought about living with Uncle Mac and Aunt Isabella for the rest of her life. She approved."

Isabella narrowed her eyes. "She said that, did she?"

"Well, she doesn't know many words yet, and all of them French, but she *is* of the decided opinion that I have a large nose."

Isabella barely stopped herself from laughing. "Well, anyone can see that."

"My darling, you wound me."

No, he wounded *her*. Mac was one of those people who always looked as though he was about to smile or laugh over some joke, and the laughter on his face made him devastatingly handsome. That only changed when he was very angry, or, as when she'd seen him in Paris, empty.

"There shouldn't be much trouble," Mr. Gordon said. "A few formalities and it's done. The child is essentially an orphan."

And Mac was so very rich, his family so very powerful. No wonder Gordon had suggested that Mac instigate the adoption himself. Payne, a poor solicitor's clerk from Sheffield, would hardly prevail against the might of Hart Mackenzie, Duke of Kilmorgan. Aimee would be theirs.

Miss Westlock entered the room then, the professional nanny in her sensing that the time had come for the child to return to the nursery. Aimee went without fuss, which raised Isabella's opinion of Miss Westlock. Aimee did insist on kissing Mac and Isabella good-bye first, however.

Isabella held Aimee's warm little body briefly as she pressed a sticky kiss to Isabella's cheek. *Mac wants a child,* she realized. He hadn't brought Gordon here to start the adoption only for Isabella's sake. He'd taken to Aimee, that was obvious from the way he'd let her sleep on him in the train and ride so happily on his back through the drawing room. Isabella thought about their exuberant bed games last night and in Mac's studio at Kilmorgan and wondered if a baby would come of them. It was certainly possible. Her heart beat faster as she watched Miss Westlock carry Aimee from the room and close the door.

"And now for the other matter," Gordon said. He lifted a sheaf of legal-looking papers from his case and handed them to Mac. "I believe these are in order."

"What other matter?" Isabella asked.

Mr. Gordon glanced at Mac in surprise. "Did you not mention to her ladyship that I would be coming today?"

Mac busied himself looking at the papers, not answering.

"His lordship must have forgotten," Isabella said in a crisp voice. "We have been quite in turmoil the last few weeks. What is this matter?"

"The reversal of your separation, of course," Mr. Gordon said. He gave her a benevolent smile. "I am pleased to perform this task for you, have looked forward to doing it these many years. It's a happy day for me, your ladyship."

~

Mac sensed Isabella's anger boil up and over. He rose from the arm of the sofa, moved to a chair, and dropped into it, resting his feet on the tea table in front of it. Mac didn't look at Isabella, but he felt her glare scorch the space between them.

"The reversal of our separation?" she asked in a chill voice.

"Yes," Mr. Gordon said. He started to say more then he looked from Isabella to Mac and subsided.

"It only makes sense, my love." Mac rested his gaze on a painting on the opposite wall. It was a soaring landscape by Claude Lorrain that he'd bought Isabella years ago as an apology for one of his sudden departures. The incredible blue of the sky and the gray-green of the land with its Greek ruins never failed to lift joy in him, but right now they didn't calm him much. "I've been living here with you, openly and scandalously," he said. "People talk."

"Oh, do they?"

"Our servants have been gossiping like mad, taking wagers about us, so Bellamy tells me. Your neighbors observe our comings and goings. It's only a matter of time before word of our reconciliation spreads far and wide."

"Reconciliation?" Her voice could have etched glass. "What reconciliation?"

Mac finally forced himself to look at her. Isabella sat on the edge of the sofa, back straight, rigidly haughty, green eyes sparkling. She was stunning even when furious, a dream today in a dress of light and dark blue with hints of cream. Mac's fingers itched for a paintbrush, wanting to capture her just as she was, with that one beam of sunlight spilling into her lap.

"Isabella," he said. "We lived apart and in silence for three and a half years. Now we are speaking to each other, living with each other, even sharing a bed from time to time. The world will assume us no longer separated. There is no reason not to make it legal."

"Except that I wish to remain separate."

Mac's temper stirred. "Even when I'm so willing to make another go of it? A good solicitor would advise you to let me try."

Gordon, the good solicitor, kept himself occupied with his papers and pretended to be elsewhere.

"But I don't want this." Isabella's voice took on a panicked note.

"What other course can we steer, sweetheart? I've given you no grounds for divorce. I don't beat you, I don't keep a fancy lady, I haven't touched a drop of whiskey in years. I haven't abandoned you—in fact, of late I've been quite reliably at your side. We have been living as man and wife. We should become that in truth again."

Isabella was on her feet. "Damn you, Mac Mackenzie. Why can you not leave things alone?"

Mr. Gordon made a discreet cough. "Perhaps I can

return at a later date, my lord, after you have discussed this with her ladyship."

"Please do not bother, Mr. Gordon," Isabella said coldly. "I am so sorry that you were forced to witness this rather sordid scene. Please pass on my regards to Mrs. Gordon." She stormed to the door, skirts swirling like blue froth, and out into the foyer.

Gordon looked distressed, but Mac leapt to his feet and stormed right after her. "And where the devil are you going?"

"Out," Isabella said.

"Not alone, you are not."

"No, of course not. Morton, will you please send for the landau, and have Evans meet me upstairs? Thank you."

She swept up the stairs with her head high, as Gordon discreetly emerged from the drawing room, his case in his hand. Morton handed the solicitor his hat.

"Thank you, Gordon," Mac told him. "I'll write you when I have this sorted."

"Yes, my lord," came Gordon's tactful reply, and he was gone.

Upstairs a door banged. Mac planted a chair by the front door, seated himself on it, and waited.

He had no intention of letting Isabella out of the house without him; he didn't care how furious she was. He knew he'd miscalculated, moved too fast. But, damnation, she'd given him every sign of reconciliation. Last night—sweet God, last night. How he could have stayed away from the beautiful, desirable Isabella all this time, Mac had no idea. She'd become his love again, the woman to whom he'd taught every game of pleasure, the woman who'd learned her lessons well. Isabella had skills that made him hard just thinking about them.

His skilled lady sailed down the stairs the same moment Mac heard the landau pull up outside. She'd exchanged her frilly blue dress for a snug bottle-green jacket over a gray walking dress, and a hat stuck to her curls with colorful beaded hatpins.

She tugged on her gloves on her way to the door. "Please get out of my way."

"As you wish." Mac grabbed his hat from the hall tree, opened the door for her, and followed her out.

At the landau, Isabella ignored Mac's outstretched hand and let her footman help her into the carriage. The lad shot an apologetic glance at Mac, but Mac only winked at him and climbed in after Isabella. The footman slammed the door, and the landau jerked forward as Mac landed on the heavily padded seat facing Isabella.

She shot him an angry look. "Can I not have a moment to myself?"

"Not with a madman assaulting you in parks. I was not joking when I said I wouldn't let you out of my sight."

"My coachman and footmen will let no one near me, and I don't intend to walk through any dark, deserted passages by myself. I'm not a ninny, and this isn't a gothic novel."

"No, I believe we are in a comedy of errors, my love, but that doesn't mean the man isn't damned dangerous."

"Then why not send Bellamy with me? He is plenty dangerous himself."

"Because I need him to guard the house, in case our friend Payne decides to try his trick of wandering in pretending to be me. Even you mistook him for me at first glance."

"Yes, very well, I take your point." Isabella huffed out her breath, which made her bosom move in an agreeable way. "We should be careful. But the separation? Why are *you* allowed to decide when we will end it? Why did you not consult me before sending for Mr. Gordon? The poor man was most embarrassed."

Mac heard the growl emerge from his throat. She was right that he shouldn't have presumed, but bloody hell, he was tired of everything on earth being his fault.

"Did *you* consult *me* when you decided we would have a separation in the first place? Did you consult me when you wanted to leave me? No, you disappeared and sent me a damned note. No, wait. You didn't even send it to me; you sent it to Ian."

Isabella's voice rose. "Because I knew that if I sent it to you, you'd never take it seriously. I trusted Ian to make certain you read it, to make certain you understood. I feared that if I sent it directly to you, you'd simply laugh and toss it on the fire."

"Laugh?" What the hell was she talking about? "Laugh that my beloved wife had decided to leave me? That she told me she couldn't bear living with me? I read that bloody letter over and over until I couldn't see the words anymore. Your idea of what makes me laugh is damned peculiar."

"I tried to tell you myself. Believe me, I tried. But I knew that if I faced you, you would only talk me 'round, convince me to stay with you against my better judgment."

"Of course I would have," Mac shouted. "I love you. I'd have done anything to get you to stay, if you'd only given me the chance."

Chapter 17

Both the Scottish Lord and his Lady appeared at the opera house in Covent Garden this past evening, but they might have been in *two different* opera houses altogether. The Lord lounged in the box of the Marquis of Dunstan while the Lady appeared across the house with the Duke of K—, the Lord's brother. Observers say the Lord and Lady passed each other in the mezzanine but never spoke to, or even seemed to notice, one another.

—*February 1879*

Isabella's green eyes snapped in fury. Even raging, she managed to be beautiful. "I gave you three *years* of chances, Mac. Very well, perhaps you would have talked me into staying, but what then? You'd have downed a bottle of champagne to celebrate, and I'd have woken the next morning to find you gone off somewhere in the world, with a note—*maybe*—to tell me not to worry. I decided to give you a taste of what you had given me for the three years of our marriage."

"I know. I know. I was an idiot. But damn it, I'm trying to make it right, *now*. I'm willing to try, but you are determined not to let me."

"Because I am tired of being a fool about you. Look at us—I give you an inch, and you jump a mile. I go to you for comfort, and you decide we are reconciled and send for our solicitor."

Mac's chest burned. "Comfort? Is that what last night was?"

"Yes."

"I don't believe you."

"Believe what you like. You have a lofty opinion of yourself."

"A lofty opinion, is it?" As happened when he got angry enough, Mac's Scots accent banished years of English veneer. "I believe you were the one cryin' out in climax four or five times last night. I remember. I was quite close to ye at the time."

"One's bodily reactions are not always under one's control. That is a medical fact."

"I did no' couple with 'one.' I was with you, Isabella."

Isabella's face flamed. "You know you were taking advantage of my loneliness. I should have kept my door locked."

Mac hauled himself across the landau into the seat next to her. She didn't cringe away; Isabella would never show fear, especially not to him. "If ye say ye came to me for comfort, then *you* were taking advantage of *me*. I'm not blameless in this."

"You've been following me about. You admitted it. Somehow you finagled yourself into my house and back into my life. I think I should have a say in that."

"If ye think it through, ye live in *my* house. 'Tis my money that pays for the house and servants and pretty frocks. Because ye are still my *wife*."

Isabella rounded on him. "Do you think I am not aware of that every day of my life? Do you know how weak it makes me feel that I live entirely on your charity? I could beg Miss Pringle to give me a job teaching younger students, but I have no experience, and I'd be living on *her* charity. So my pride remains in tatters while you pay all my bills."

"Bloody hell." Mac cast a glance out the window, but

he found no help in the clogged traffic of Oxford Street. "I don't give ye charity. Paying for your living is the least I can do for anyone fool enough to marry me."

"Ah, so now I am foolish as well as weak."

"You enjoy putting words in my mouth, do ye? Your method of arguing is to decide what *I* say as well as what you say. I might as well go fishing while you finish. Send me word when the argument is over."

"And you try to win by shouting about everything but what it is you've done to make me angry in the first place! You decided to revoke our separation without bothering to tell me. Remember?"

Mac couldn't deny the charge. He had hoped to put the revocation through so fast she wouldn't have time to object. No, to be honest, he'd hoped Isabella would give him a big, warm smile and tell him she was glad he'd done it. She would be happy that they were truly together again.

Too fast. He'd rushed in before she was ready.

"Can you blame me for wanting this to be real?" The Scots started to fade as Mac tried to rein in his temper. "Haven't we had enough time apart, Isabella?"

"I don't know."

She was so elegantly beautiful sitting there next to him, her red hair in perfect curls, her jacket hugging her lovely torso. How could any man not want her?

Mac could have divorced her for abandoning him, but he'd decided, even before Gordon advised him, that he'd be damned if he would give the world more food for vicious gossip. Divorce would have made Isabella a ruined woman, vulnerable to any unscrupulous man. And Mac would die before he let any man touch his Isabella. As much as she'd hurt him, Mac was happy to set up Isabella in her own house to live an independent life. He'd protect her from afar, watch over her as well as he could. He loved her enough to do that.

"I think we've spent plenty of time apart," he said.

"But how do I know our time together now won't be the same as it was before?" she asked, anguished. "With you coming and going without a word, you deciding when we'll be together and when I need a rest from you? You don't get to decide *everything*, Mac."

Mac spread his arms. "Look at me. I'm different now. Never drunk. Home for dinner, in my place for breakfast. No carousing with my friends. I am the model husband."

"Good heavens, Mac. You aren't a model anything."

"I want to be the man you want me to be: sober, dependable, reliable . . . God, all those boring adjectives."

"You think that is what I want?" Isabella asked. "I fell in love with the charming, unpredictable Mac all those years ago. If I wanted dependable and dull, I would have banished you and pursued the men my father had chosen for me."

"You are insanely difficult to please. You don't want the wild Mac, but you don't want the stay-at-home Mac, either? Is that what you are saying?"

"I want you to stop trying to be what you're not. I predict you'll become bored with your new role in a few months' time. You alternately obsess over something and then grow tired of it and forget all about it. Including me."

Mac regarded her in silence for a long moment. She colored under his gaze, but his anger had receded to hollowness. When he spoke, his voice was quiet. "You are a fool, Isabella Mackenzie."

"What?" She looked hurt.

"You have decided what kind of man I am, which makes it damned difficult to talk to you. You don't believe I can change, but I already have. You simply won't see it."

"I know you stopped drinking. I've noticed that improvement."

Mac laughed. "Stopped drinking? You make it sound

so effortless. I was sick and disgusting for an entire year. I hadn't realized how much I'd been using whiskey to blunt the pain of my own existence. I found myself facedown on a hotel room floor in Venice, hurting like hell, praying for the strength to *not* go in search of wine to ease the agony. I'd never truly prayed before. I was taken to chapel as a boy to mouth prayers, but this time I *prayed*. It was more like begging, actually. Quite an unusual experience for me."

Isabella listened, her lips parted. "Mac."

"I could tell you tales to make you blanch, my love, but I will spare you. The begging and praying didn't last one night. I did it for many, many nights, never ceasing. And then, just when I thought it was over, and I felt better, another night would come. My friends thought they'd 'help' me from time to time by holding me down and pouring whiskey down my throat. They ceased when I discovered the trick of spewing it back, all over their fine clothes. Eventually, my friends deserted me. Every last man of them."

Isabella's face was white. "They had no right to do that."

Mac shrugged. "They were wastrels and sycophants. Not a true friend among them. There is nothing like hardship to teach you who truly cares for you."

"Did you have no one at all? Oh, Mac."

"I did. I had Bellamy. He made sure I ate food and kept it down; he was the one who realized I could drink tea by the bucketful when water merely made me sick. I became quite the tea connoisseur, even beyond the haughty English who believe their knowledge of tea unsurpassed. An Assam tea brewed with jasmine is quite fine. You ought to try it."

Isabella's eyes were wet. "I'm glad Bellamy took care of you. I will tell him how grateful I am. He deserves a gift. What would he like, do you think?"

"I already gave him a large rise in wages," Mac said. "And I lavish constant praise on him. I worship Bellamy as a god, which, I assure you, embarrasses the hell out of him."

Isabella looked away. She was a regal, proud woman, and his wanting of her consumed every waking moment of his life. Staying away from her had been absolute hell, but when she'd left him, Mac had made himself let her, because she was right. If he'd gone back to her before withdrawal from drink had forcibly reformed him, he would have continued the pattern until he'd driven her so far away he could never have reached her again. Because he'd given her time to heal, he could now sit so close to her and drink in her scent.

Isabella looked out of the window for a long time, and when she finally turned to him, the rigid anger had faded from her eyes. "Whatever happened to your friend?" she asked. "The one you told me about at Lord Abercrombie's ball."

Mac went blank. "Friend?"

"The one who needs lessons in courting."

"Oh, that friend." He cleared his throat. "Yes, he is still anxious to learn courting techniques."

"We began practicing them once before. Perhaps we should start over again?"

"Is that what you wish to do?" Mac asked. "Start over?"

She nodded. "I think so."

Mac studied her in breathless silence. She looked back at him, her glittering green eyes so beautiful.

"In that case," he said in a light voice, "we should forget all about what happened last night in your bedchamber. That was far too scandalous for a courting couple."

She smiled a little. "Indeed. Quite improper. You must not mention last night to him."

"I never breathe a word about what goes on in my bedroom to my friends. It is none of their bloody business."

Mac lifted her gloved hand, pressed a light kiss to it, and moved himself back to the opposite seat. "A gentleman should never occupy the same seat as the lady in a conveyance. He should sit with his back to the coachman, giving her the forward-facing seat."

Isabella laughed. Damn, it was good to hear her laugh. "It will be amusing to watch *you* trying to be highly proper," she said.

Mac pinned her with a look, no more teasing, no more cajoling. "If that is what it takes, I will do it. I want to win you back, Isabella. No matter if it takes me one year or twenty, I'm a patient man. I will win your heart again, I swear it. Even if I have to be so highly proper my ancestors turn in their graves to see me change myself for a Sassenach."

Isabella smiled, but the look on her face told him she hadn't given in. But her quiet acceptance of his presence for the rest of the ride and her errands that followed made him know that she'd give him a chance. She wanted him to try, and she wanted him to succeed. That, at least, gave him heart.

~

The next morning, a bouquet of hothouse flowers arrived with a note for Isabella. Isabella touched the blossoms, noting that the bouquet was small and tasteful—yellow roses, violets, and baby's breath. No orchids or other exotics. The card was edged with gold and read, in Mac's handwriting:

> *I am most grateful, my lady, for the privilege of driving with you yesterday afternoon. Might you give me leave to walk in the park with you today, if the weather holds fine? I will call on you at three o'clock if that is convenient.*
>
> *Your most obedient servant,*
> *Roland F. Mackenzie*

Isabella smiled to herself. Mac was certainly playing the proper gentleman, especially using his real name. He hated being addressed as Roland Ferdinand Mackenzie, or Lord Roland, preferring the nickname that had been pinned to him at the age of two, when he couldn't pronounce any syllable of his long name but "Mac."

"A gentleman sending you flowers?" Mac asked in a mock gruff voice behind his breakfast newspaper. "Is he a proper sort of gentleman?"

"I believe so." Isabella sat down at her place, fingering the card, which she'd slipped into her pocket. "He has invited me to go walking with him this afternoon."

Mac folded down one corner of the paper, giving her a stern look. "And what have you decided?"

"I will accept. Going for a walk in a public place will be most proper. And agreeable."

"Be careful of his intentions. I've heard of this Lord Roland's bad reputation."

"I believe he's reformed," Isabella said. "So he tells me."

Mac tsk-tsked. "Be on your guard, my dear. Be on your guard. I believe he paints women—with their clothes *off*."

"Don't overplay it, Mac."

Mac grinned and raised the paper again. His smile could make a lady's good intentions fly out the window. Mac had slept in his own room last night, and Isabella had lain awake for a long while trying to banish her disappointment.

At three o'clock that afternoon, the doorbell rang, and Morton glided up from the back stairs to open it. Mac, dressed in a fine afternoon walking suit, complete with hat and walking stick, stood on the threshold. "I have come to call upon the lady of the house," he announced in grave tones.

Isabella stifled a laugh as she peered down from the

landing. Morton disliked games, and Mac had to more or less insist before Morton would show him into the drawing room.

Morton came out again and looked up at her, aggrieved. "My lady . . ."

"Thank you, Morton." Isabella gathered her skirts and glided down the stairs. "Indulge his lordship. He likes his bit of fun."

"Yes, my lady," Morton said mournfully and disappeared to the back of the house.

When Isabella entered the drawing room, Mac stood up, hat in hand. "My lady. I hope you are well."

"Indeed. I am in good health and spirits."

"I am pleased to hear it. Would you indulge me with your company in the park?"

"Why certainly, my lord. And thank you for the flowers. You were most kind."

Mac waved his hand dismissively. "It was nothing. I heard you liked yellow roses. I hope they suited."

"They suited me very well." Isabella heard Aimee's little voice in the hall, and she added, "Do you mind? Nanny Westlock says that Aimee needs to take some air, and I thought they could join us."

A startled look flashed through Mac's copper-colored eyes, but he covered it with another cool bow.

"Chaperoned by a nanny and a baby," he muttered. "Ah, well."

The weather was so fine that Hyde Park teemed with people. Mac dropped the pretense of being the proper suitor, tilted back his hat, and insisted on pushing the pram. Isabella strolled beside him, enjoying the sight of her broad-shouldered, kilted husband pushing a baby carriage. Miss Westlock dropped behind, a nanny indulging the master and mistress.

The Rotten Row flowed with horses and carriages, and the other paths carried families, walking couples, and nannies with children. Aimee sat up in her pram, holding onto the sides and looking about with interest. She was a robust child—hearty, Miss Westlock called her—and enjoyed peering at the world.

What Aimee felt about losing her mother, Isabella couldn't fathom. Perhaps the child was too young to understand what had happened, but all in all, she seemed to accept with her change in fortune. She was happy to bestow loving kisses on both Mac and Isabella, and though she made it clear that she preferred Mac, she was now content to be left alone with either Isabella or Nanny Westlock.

Isabella wondered whether Payne, her true father, would attempt to wrest Aimee back from them. Isabella didn't understand whatever strings Mr. Gordon had pulled to make the adoption legal, but he'd assured them that all would be well. Isabella still worried, though. Aimee did not need to be taken by a lunatic who set fires to houses and stalked women in parks.

"Mac, old thing!" A man's voice rang out and Isabella looked up to see four gentlemen bearing down on them.

She stifled a sigh. They were Mac's friends from Harrow and Cambridge, the boys who had worshipped Mac as their leader-in-crime during their school days. They were grown men now, but they'd collectively remained the wild tears who'd done anything to gain Mac's approval.

The one who walked in front, a short, rather slender young man with blond hair, had become Marquis of Dunstan at age twenty-two. His Christian name was Cadwallader, and they called him Cauliflower or Cauli for short. The others were Lord Charles Summerville, the Honorable Bertram Clark, and Lord Randolph Manning. None of these gentlemen had passed Isabella's father's rigorous screening as possible suitors for her, and it had been these four gentleman who'd originally wagered that Mac would never "crash" Lord Scranton's ball and dance with his virginal daughter.

"Do my eyes deceive me?" Lord Charles Summerville screwed a monocle into his left eye and peered through it. "Good Lord, it *is* Mac Mackenzie walking a baby. From where did you steal the damned thing? Paying off a wager, are you?"

"This is my daughter," Mac said coolly. "Miss Aimee Mackenzie. I've just adopted her. Pray watch your language in front of her as well as in front of my wife."

Summerville guffawed while Bertram Clark bowed to Isabella. "Ah, the lovely Lady Isabella. How delightful to see you again. You dazzle mine eyes, my lady."

Lord Randolph Manning gazed unsteadily at her. "I thought you well rid of this blackguard, Izzy. I'm devastated you've never sought solace in me. My door is always open, you know."

"Randy Randolph," Cauliflower chortled.

"Stubble it," Mac said. "Insult my wife again, Manning, and your eye will learn the exact texture of my gloved fist."

Manning blinked. "Good lord, what did *I* say?"

"Forgive my Lord Randolph," Bertram Clark said to Isabella. Mr. Clark had the best manners of the lot but also the reputation for being the most dissipate. "He's drunk, he's an idiot, and he swoons at your feet. We all do, as you know."

"It's quite all right," Isabella said. "I'm well used to his vulgar manners."

The four men burst out laughing. "As erudite as ever," Lord Charles said. "We've missed you, my lady. In truth, Mac, what *are* you doing with a baby?"

"I answered you. I adopted her."

Manning blinked his hazy eyes. "Dropped a by-blow, did you, Mac? Your lady wife is a most forgiving woman."

Cauliflower gaped, and Bertram Clark grabbed the back of Manning's collar. "That's it. Time to sober you up, old man." He dragged Manning off, Manning spluttering and continuing to ask what he'd said wrong.

"Cauli," Mac said in a quiet voice. Cauliflower, who was a foot shorter than Mac, turned red but gave Mac his attention. "Know this: Aimee is not my by-blow, and she will be raised as a proper young lady. Any other gossip is to be squelched. You know the truth, and I expect you to uphold it. You too, Charlie. Tell the others."

Cauliflower touched his forehead. "Right you are, chief. You can count on us. But by the bye—since wagers were mentioned—what about the one we made before you went to Paris? You know about the . . . ?" He trailed off, making a painting motion with his hand.

"The erotic pictures?" Mac finished. "Fear not, Isabella knows all. I keep nothing from my wife, as you know. I am working on them."

Charles shook his head. "Time's running out, Mac, old boy. I hope you know some merry tunes to sing with the temperance band."

"I've been told I have a nice baritone." Mac's words were light, but Isabella saw a muscle tighten in his jaw, his temper rising.

"We'll make certain every member of the club is out to watch you and cheer you on. It will cause quite a stir."

"I always enjoy making a stir. But I might come through with the paintings, you know."

Cauliflower made a point of pulling out his watch and studying it. "Very well. Not much time left, you know." He gave Mac a sorrowful look. "Don't let me down, old man. You've been my hero since I was ten years old."

"That was a long time ago," Mac said.

Cauli stuffed his watch back into his pocket, nodded to Isabella, and grabbed Charles by the arm. "Come on, then, Charlie. Let's have some champagne to celebrate our certain win."

Charles bowed to Isabella, somewhat unsteadily, and walked off with Cauli. Mac watched them go in unveiled disgust.

"To think I used to take pride in leading that gang of bullies."

"School makes one do odd things," Isabella agreed.

"Did you do odd things? At Miss Pringle's Special Home?"

"Select Academy for Young Ladies," she corrected coolly. "And yes. I was rather a tear."

"I think that's one reason I love you." Mac looked thoughtful. "I'd like to win that wager and rub their faces in it, before I give them all the cut direct. Would you still be willing?"

"To pose for you?" She glanced behind them, but Miss Westlock had maintained a discreet distance, pretending to study a guide to the park. "I think I might."

Isabella's skin tingled with the thought. Baring herself while Mac studied her with his warm eyes made her feel wanted and beloved. Her pulse quickened when she thought about what had happened the last time she'd attempted to pose for the paintings.

Mac bent his head and kissed her lips in full view of the entire park. Aimee looked on with great interest. "Good," Mac said into her skin. "I believe I feel inspired to paint today."

What absolute madness had persuaded Mac that painting Isabella in erotic poses was good for his health, he had no idea. He'd even fancied that his hand would be steadier now that they'd bedded each other. He must have been insane.

Bellamy helped Mac turn one of Isabella's large rooms

at the top of her house into a studio. There was light here from tall windows, and warmth, because Bellamy had installed a small parlor stove and stoked it with coal. Mac had no intention of letting Isabella catch cold.

She came upstairs fully dressed that afternoon, not wanting the servants to know that Mac was painting her unclothed. Let them believe he was doing a portrait of her, she said. Mac tried to be clinical as he tied his scarf over his hair and mixed paints, but when Isabella told him she needed him to help her undress, his sangfroid abandoned him.

Mac's palms sweated as he pulled off the bodice she'd unbuttoned and unlaced her corset. *Steady hands, not bloody likely.*

He used to undress her like this when they were married, kissing her as each piece of clothing fell away. Today, Mac let his lips graze her neck as the corset came off, then her shoulder as she unfastened her chemise.

Her skin smelled of roses. He pressed kisses to her glossy hair, inhaling her perfume. Isabella loosened her skirt, and Mac unbuckled the tapes that held her small bustle in place. He stepped against her after the cage came off, liking how her backside curved into his hip.

"I can't paint you," he said in her ear. "I want to love you."

"Perhaps painting instead will be a good exercise in restraint?"

"To hell with that."

Mac knew Isabella was as nervous as he was. Her skin flushed where he kissed it, and her bare breasts rose as he slid his hand around her waist.

"Come here," he said.

The chaise he'd chosen for her pose was not as accommodating as the one they'd used up in Scotland, a choice he'd made on purpose. He'd thought it would help him avoid temptation. Now he cursed himself. He was hard and ready and could think of nothing else but being inside her. Lessons in restraint be damned.

He pulled up his kilt, sat on a straight-backed chair, and pulled her down on top of him. Her breasts crushed against his bare chest, and she cried out softly as he pushed inside her.

The coupling was quick and hot. Too quick. Mac released before he wanted to, and he clung to her, wanting more.

Isabella smiled down at him. "I am certain I look ravished now."

She did. Mac hardened again at the sight of her—swollen-lipped, starry-eyed, face flushed. She had no idea how beautiful she truly was.

Mac made himself set up his easel while she arranged herself on the chaise. He forced himself to draw lines, to think of them as shapes and curves, not the legs, breasts, and hips of his delectable wife.

He was sweating profusely by the time he had a good sketch. "Damn stove," he growled.

"I think it's pleasant." Isabella swung her foot where it dangled from the chaise, her arm stretching languidly over her head. She might be sunning herself in a garden, except that she was naked and indoors.

"Too bloody hot." Mac wiped his forehead. "Shall we continue tomorrow?"

"That suits me. I'm rather stiff." Isabella put aside the sheet, which didn't cover her at all, and rose gracefully to her feet.

Mac was stiff himself, though not in the way she meant. He resolutely didn't look at her. Perhaps, just perhaps, he could contain himself until she left the room. He thought this until she asked, "Help me dress?"

It was another hour before they finally made it out of

the studio. Isabella had to scuttle down to her own room to change her clothes and redo her hair. This, Mac thought, as he watched her go, was going to kill him.

They settled into a routine—though *settled* was a bad word for it, in Mac's opinion. Each morning, they'd eat breakfast and read their correspondence, then Isabella and Mac would climb to the nursery to say good morning to Aimee and sit with her while she had her breakfast. Afterward, Nanny Westlock would begin Aimee's activities for the day, and Mac and Isabella would retire to the attic.

Mac worked on the paintings, and while he did so, he made sketches of Isabella's face for a portrait he wanted to complete later. They'd make love two or three times each sitting, neither of them able to keep their hands off the other. Perhaps the forbidden nature of what they did charged the air. After all, they were hiding from the rest of the household and making naughty pictures together.

After each painting session, they parted ways to write letters or take care of their own errands, although whenever Isabella needed to leave the house, Mac went with her. They'd run their errands together, he cheerfully carrying Isabella's parcels, she looking tolerantly bored as he settled accounts at the bank or spoke with Gordon about whatever business. No more mention was made of reversing their separation.

Mac didn't mind dawdling outside the ribbon shops or the elegant trinket stores in the Burlington Arcade while Isabella shopped. He was a man smitten with his beautiful wife, and he noted that smirks from passing gentlemen changed to looks of envy whenever Isabella emerged from a shop and took Mac's arm.

In the afternoon, they'd walk in the park or drive in the landau, depending on the weather or on what courtship activity Mac asked Isabella to do that day. They attended museum exhibits in bad weather, gardens and parks in good, or went sightseeing to the Tower or Madame Tussauds when the fit took them.

Payne had made himself scarce after accosting Isabella in the park, and Mac hoped against hope that the man had gone back to Sheffield and ceased his masquerade. Payne had never returned to the rooms he'd let, and Fellows had to admit that he'd reached a dead end.

Mac still wanted to kill him, but what he mostly wanted was the man out of their lives. Payne could fade into obscurity, and Mac could return to pursuing life with Isabella.

They'd ceased arguing about their separation, or about why Isabella had left him, or about the pain each of them had gone through. All of that was in the past. This was now, a new beginning. Aimee, of all people, had brought stability to their life, and Mac was going to enjoy it as much as he possibly could. He knew it would come crashing down, because everything in Mac's life crashed down sooner or later. But for now, he could admit to being happy.

By mid-October, he had finished four paintings of Isabella.

Isabella surveyed them critically as Mac varnished the last one. "They're very good," she said. "Vivid. I can believe this is a lady who enjoys her lover."

The first painting was of Isabella lolling back on the chaise. She dangled one leg from it, her foot brushing the floor; the other foot was propped up with her knee bent, fully exposing the goodness between her legs. She'd lifted one arm over her head, her breasts standing up in firm peaks.

The second painting showed her leaning over the back of the chaise, hips stuck out, head bowed, ready for her lover. In the third, she sat upright on the chaise, her hands cupping her breasts, nipples poking through her fingers. The fourth was her spread-eagled on a bed. Her right wrist and left foot were tethered to the posts with slackly tied ribbons; ribbons crumpled on the bed in the other two corners as though torn off in exuberant play. Mac and Isabella's coupling had been enthusiastic when he'd painted that one.

A jar of yellow roses appeared in each painting, either in full bloom, or drooping with petals falling. The famous Mackenzie yellow balanced the scarlet hues of the draperies and ribbons.

None of the paintings showed Isabella's face. Mac had painted her either in shadow or obscured by a fall of dark hair. No one viewing these pictures would realize that Mac had painted his wife.

Except Mac.

Mac tossed his brush into a glass jar filled with oil of turpentine. "They aren't bad."

Isabella gave him a look of surprise. "What are you talking about? They're gloriously beautiful. I thought you said you'd lost your ability to paint."

"I had." Mac wiped his brush on a rag, then stood the brush upright in a jar to dry.

"An inspiring subject, perhaps. A woman ripe for play."

"An inspiring model."

Isabella rolled her eyes. "Please don't pretend I'm your muse, Mac. You painted brilliantly before you ever met me."

Mac shrugged. "All I know is that when you left me, and I ceased to be a drunken sot, I couldn't paint a stroke. Here you are, and here's what I've done."

They were erotic paintings, yes, but not in the crass or crude way in which his friends thought of erotica. These were some of the most amazing things Mac had ever painted.

Drink might have been the thing that gave his paintings force before he met Isabella, but after meeting her . . . Mac had the right of it; she *had* become his muse. When he'd had neither drink nor Isabella, his talent had vanished. Now it had returned.

These paintings gave Mac giddy hope, excited him beyond happiness. *He could paint without having to be drunk.* He only needed to be intoxicated by Isabella.

Isabella studied the pictures. "Well, at least you'll be able to make the awful Randolph Manning eat his wager. You've won."

"No," Mac said in a quiet voice. "I've lost. I will find my friends and tell them I forfeit."

Chapter 18

The Scottish Lord and his Lady may be estranged, but the Lady's Buckinghamshire fetes show no sign of diminishing in extravagance. The wicked try to put about that the Lady has *admirers*, but this observer is pleased to remark that she seems to keep herself above suspicion.

—July 1879

Isabella stared at Mac, who kept his gaze on the paintings, a strange look in his eyes. He'd thrown a shirt over his sweating torso but left the red kerchief in his hair.

"What are you talking about?" she demanded. "These are perfect, exactly what they expected."

"Isabella, my sweet, the last thing I want is for Randolph Manning and the rest of my cronies to run their lascivious eyes over pictures of you."

"But they won't be. I mean, they will not know it is me. That was the point. You'll bring in Molly and paint her head on my body."

Mac shook his head. "No, I won't."

"We agreed. Molly always welcomes a job. You know she needs money for her little boy."

"We didn't agree." Mac wore his stubborn Scots look, which meant that neither God nor all his angels could move him when his mind was made up. "It was your idea for me to mix up heads and bodies. I never remember agreeing to it."

"You are the most exasperating man, Mac. What are you going to tell them? Why deliberately lose the wager?"

Mac tugged off his kerchief. "I will tell them that they were right, that I proved to be too much of a prude to paint the pictures."

"But you are not a prude. I'll not have them laughing at you."

Mac seated himself on the makeshift bed and leaned back on his elbows. While the bed looked lavish in the final picture, it was in reality a mattress with propped up posts draped in red material.

Mac's broad chest was damp within the V of the open shirt, his hair was a mess, and his bare legs were solid with muscle. The fact that this incredible man had singled out Isabella to be his lover and his wife still astonished her.

"Do you know why the pictures are good?" Mac asked.

"Because you are a brilliant painter?"

"Because I'm madly in love with the woman I painted. There's love in every brushstroke, every dab of paint. I couldn't paint when Molly posed because she's only a model to me, like a vase of flowers. You are real. I know what your flesh feels like under my hand. I know how slick your cleft is to my fingers, how your breath tastes in my mouth. I love every part of you. That is what I painted, and no one in the world will get to see these pictures but the two of us."

His words made Isabella warm and soften. "But you did so much work. Everyone at your club will ridicule you."

"I no longer care what those shallow profligates think of me. Where were they when I was suffering and thought I'd die of it? Bellamy was there, and Ian. Cam and Daniel. Even Hart came to help me. The gentlemen who always claimed to be my friends either tortured me or made themselves scarce." Mac gazed at the paintings and a smile played across his face. "Let them ridicule me. These pictures are for us, my wife. No one else."

"They'll make you join in with the Salvation Army's band," Isabella said unhappily.

Mac laughed as he hauled himself to his feet. "I've been practicing in my spare time. I clash a good cymbal."

"You don't own any cymbals."

"Cook's been letting me borrow her pot lids. I *want* to lose this wager, love. I've never been so happy to lose a wager in my life."

He came to her and kissed her, a slow Mac Mackenzie kiss, one that said he wanted to kiss her all night.

"Will you come with me, angel?" he asked. "I'll happily sing temperance tunes on a street corner if I know you're nearby."

Isabella smiled into his lips. "That is possibly one of the stranger requests a husband has made of his wife. Of course I'll come with you, Mac."

"Good. For now . . ."

The mattress was waiting. Isabella found herself laughing as she and Mac made good use of it.

One week later, on a chilly Wednesday evening, Mac stood with a five-member Salvation Army band at the end of Aldgate High Street where it widened into Whitechapel. He'd been practicing with them, and the female sergeant in charge was delighted that a twig of an aristocratic tree had joined their ranks.

A crowd had gathered by the time they started to play, consisting of a dozen of Mac's club cronies mixed with a score of street toughs, as well as men and women simply making their way home from a hard day's labor. Across the street from Mac, Isabella held Aimee, the two of them

surrounded by Bellamy, Miss Westlock, and two of the
strongest footmen to guard them.

The most rowdy were the Mayfair lords, who started
hooting and taunting as soon as Mac raised his cymbals.
The lady sergeant ignored them and cued her band. The
music blared, drowning out the lordlings.

> *All hail the Power of Jesus's name,*
> *Let angels prostrate fall. (Crash! Crash!)*
> *Bring forth the royal diadem*
> *And crown Him Lord of all! (Crash! Crash! Crash!*
>   *Crash!)*

Mac sang heartily; he clashed the cymbals as they'd
rehearsed, bellowing out the words. The sergeant encouraged the onlookers to join in, and soon half the street raised
their voices in song.

> *Bring forth the royal diadem*
> *And crown Him (Crash!) Lo-o-o-rd of all! (Crash!*
>   *Crash! Crash! Crash!)*

The hymn wound through six stanzas and finished to
much applause and a few jeers. The sergeant started her
appeal to the crowd, encouraging them to join the temperance movement, to throw off the shackles of drink and vice
and embrace Christ as their Savior.

Mac handed his cymbals to a fellow band member and
strolled the crowd, his tall hat held out for donations. It was
one of his best hats, made of brushed fur and lined with
silk. The cost of it could easily keep the lady sergeant and
her band fed for months.

Mac waved it under the noses of Cauli and Lord Randolph. "Come on then, gentleman, we've had the hymn and
the sermon. Time to pass the offering plate."

Randolph and Cauli grinned, thinking it a jest. "Good fun, Mackenzie," Cauli said.

Mac shoved the hat into Cauli's middle. "Dig deep, there's a good chap. Give your cash to the good sergeant instead of wasting it on gambling and drink."

Cauli blinked, dazed. "Dear God, they've got to him. He's joined the temperance movement."

"How the mighty have fallen," Randolph snorted.

"Thirty guineas?" Mac said in a loud voice. "Did you say you were giving thirty guineas? How very generous of you, my Lord Randolph Manning. Your ducal father will be proud. And you too, Cauli? The Marquis of Dunstan donates thirty guineas, ladies and gentleman."

The crowd applauded. Mac kept his hat pressed into Cauli's chest until Cauli sheepishly dropped a handful of notes into it. Randolph glowered, but he added his cash. Mac turned to his next friend.

"*Forty* guineas from you, the Honorable Bertram Clark?"

Bertram's eyes widened. "Forty? You must be joking."

"I never joke about charity. I am so moved by all this generous giving."

"Yes, I feel a movement coming on myself," Bertram muttered, but yanked out a wad of notes and dropped them into Mac's hat.

Mac moved to Charles Summerville, who quickly paid up without fuss. Mac swung the hat to the other aristocrats his friends had persuaded to accompany them. Some gave, grinning. Others snarled until Mac caught and held their gazes, and they meekly paid up.

Mac had known these men since the faraway days when they'd scrapped and fought at Harrow, establishing a hierarchy that had lasted into adulthood. Mac had been the leader of the troublemaking faction, a group that had fearlessly bullied older boys and tutors; sneaked out of school to drink, smoke, and lose their virginity; and scraped through with marks that barely let them finish. Though some of these men were or would become grand peers of the realm, and Mac was a third son, they still acknowledged him as their superior.

Mac finished his collection, deliberately not seeking out any of the poorer members of the crowd, and took the full hat back to the lady sergeant. Her eyes widened as she viewed its contents.

"My lord—thank you. And thank your friends. How kind they are."

Mac took up his cymbals again. "They are always happy to give to a good cause. In fact, I will make certain that they regularly support you."

"You are too good to us, my lord."

Mac didn't answer. "More music, sergeant?"

The sergeant brightened and led them off in a rousing rendition of a crowd favorite.

> *Sweeping through the gates of the new Jerusalem,*
>   *(Crash!)*
> *Washed in the blood of the Lamb! (Crash! Crash!*
>   *Crash!)*

Mac rolled back to Mayfair in his coach with Isabella seated next to him and Aimee in his lap. His arms hurt from all the cymbal banging, but he felt content and at peace.

And a little bit smug. The look on Randolph Manning's face when he'd been forced to cough up thirty guineas had been priceless. Randolph was notoriously cheap, always touching his friends for money although he had thousands upon thousands tucked away in his bank.

"What is funny?" Isabella asked.

Mac realized he'd chuckled out loud. "Thinking that my friends should know better than to wager with me."

She smiled, her face soft in the carriage's lantern light. "In other words, they thought you'd lost, but you really won?"

"Something like that." He didn't explain that the wager had let him win everything he'd ever wanted. The courting game had given Mac a place to start with Isabella, but if it hadn't been for the silly wager, he'd be a long way from the smile she now bestowed upon him. The wager had not only let him touch her and love her, but also to find the art that once more poured out of his fingers.

"You are a rogue." Isabella leaned her head on his shoulder. The straw of her hat scraped his chin, but he didn't mind. He had a warm, sleeping child on one arm, his wife on his other. What could be better?

He found out later, when Isabella waited for him at her bedroom door as he returned from carrying Aimee to the nursery. Mac decided he didn't give a damn how sore his arms might be as Isabella took his hand and led him inside.

Isabella was surprised the afternoon after Mac's bold debut with the Salvation Army to see her friend Ainsley Douglas stepping out of a coach at the front door, coming to call.

Isabella invited her in and had Morton bring tea. Ainsley had news, Isabella could tell, but neither said anything while Morton delivered the tea tray and three-tiered platter of cakes. Under ordinary circumstances Isabella liked the formality of taking tea, a comfortable ritual that gave even the shiest person words and actions with which to fill in awkward spaces. At the moment, however, she wished the ritual of pouring tea would drop to the bottom of the nearest well.

Ainsley set down her cup as soon as Morton had retreated and closed the pocket doors behind him. She leaned forward, a somber look in her eyes. "Isabella, I am so sorry. I came to warn you, before you read it in the newspapers."

Isabella jerked her cup, spilling a line of tea down her skirt. "Warn me of what? Has something happened to Louisa?" She thought of Payne and went cold.

"No, no, she is well." Ainsley said. She took Isabella's cup from her frozen fingers and set it on the table. "This is not about Louisa. Not directly."

Isabella had already read the morning newspapers from the *Pall Mall Gazette* to Mac's racing news and had seen nothing that might upset her personally. "What then? You have me nervous."

Ainsley took Isabella's hands in hers, her friendly gray eyes filled with concern. "My oldest brother Patrick—you know he is something in the City and knows everything that goes on there, usually before the rest of the world does. He got wind of the news this morning, and knowing we were great friends, he advised me to prepare you."

"Got wind of what? Ainsley, please tell me before I scream."

"I'm sorry; I'm trying to." Ainsley paused, her face drawn in sympathy. "It's your father, Isabella. He's ruined. Completely and utterly ruined. As of this morning, your family has been rendered penniless."

Mac had expected his friends to shun him after he'd embarrassed them over the Salvation Army wager, but typically, his antics had only raised him in their estimation. When he encountered Cauli outside Tattersalls in Knightsbridge that next afternoon, Cauli grabbed Mac's hand and wrung it with enthusiasm.

"You turned the tables on us but good, Mac old man."

Mac rescued his hand. "The Salvation Army was most pleased with your donation, the sergeant told me. She went on in adulation about you for hours. There was talk of putting up a plaque."

Cauli looked horrified. "God save me from being known as a philanthropist. Everyone in London will touch me for money."

"I was joking, Cauli."

Cauli sighed in relief. "Good, good. Very amusing. Ah, there's your brother Cameron. Is this a family reunion?"

Cameron was walking into the arcade with his usual long stride, a big man dressed in a greatcoat to ward off the chill in the October air.

"Cauliflower," Cameron greeted him when he stopped next to them. "Why don't you go find some other vegetables to play with?"

Cauli chortled. "Very good, very good. The fine Mackenzie wit. Well, I'll be off, so you can indulge in family warmth. Tallyho." He lifted his hat and wandered off toward the auction circle.

Cameron gave Cauli's retreating back a speculative look. "It's said he's the most erudite of the Dunstan line. Makes ye worry for the marquisate. I heard you were clashing cymbals over in Whitechapel last night, Mac. I never knew ye were so musical."

Mac shrugged. "A wager. When did you arrive?"

"Late train. I had Jockey Club business." He put his large hand on Mac's shoulder. "I need a word with ye, if ye don't mind."

Mac nodded, and they walked away together, Cam not speaking until they'd reached Mac's coach. Once inside, Cameron told Mac what had reached him from a friend of his in the City.

"Bloody hell," Mac exclaimed in shock. "How the *devil* did Scranton manage to ruin himself?"

Cam looked somber, the deep scar on his cheekbone shadowed in the closed carriage. "Bad investments, mostly. A railroad line that was never built, an invention of some gadget that never got past the drawing stage. Things of that sort. The last straw was a diamond mine in Africa. The fighting there is preventing anyone from getting to the mine, so he's been told. And it's doubtful there are any diamonds in it at all. Lord Scranton wasn't the cleverest when it came to his investments."

Mac imagined Isabella faced with the news, her worry for her family. "Damn, I knew I should have stayed home this afternoon, but I needed to settle an account. A brief errand, I thought. The bloody idiot."

"Many men trust the wrong advice," Cameron pointed out. "It sounded like a house of cards collapsing. A bottom card got yanked out, and everything else followed."

"Gambling with money meant to keep your wife and daughter in food and clothing is lunacy. I suppose when Scranton's creditors hear, they'll call in all their debts, if they haven't already. Damned bloodsuckers."

"Scranton's been sliding downhill for some time, Mac. Hart told me that years ago. The earl has had to sell off every piece of his estate that isn't entailed, and he's only leasing his house in London."

Mac stared at him. "Hart told you that? *Years* ago? Why didn't Hart bother to tell me? Why didn't you?"

Cameron shrugged, but Mac could tell that Cameron hadn't liked the decision. "Hart knew you'd feel obligated to let Isabella know, and he thought she didn't need more to worry her. I agree with him about that. Hart thought Scranton might turn around in the end, but the man's been damned unlucky."

"One day, Hart will have to stop deciding things for me."

"That will be an interesting day. I hope I'm there to see it."

The brothers were silent for the rest of the journey to North Audley Street, where Mac leapt out of the coach and hurried inside, followed closely by Cameron. Morton took their hats and coats and pointed to the closed drawing room door, a worried look in his eyes.

Mac shoved open the pocket doors, and Isabella jumped to her feet, her face paper white. Ainsley Douglas, who had been holding Isabella's hand, rose more slowly.

"Mac," Isabella said. He saw her struggle to retain her composure, not wanting to break down. "I'm afraid something rather dreadful has happened."

"I know." Mac went swiftly to her and took her ice-cold hands. "Whatever I can do, I will do. I promise you that."

"I'll leave you then," Ainsley said. "I am so very sorry to be the bearer of such bad news, Isabella."

Isabella turned to Ainsley, her eyes red with unshed tears. "I'm glad it came from you, my old friend. Thank you."

The two women hugged, and Ainsley kissed Isabella's cheek, tears in her own eyes.

As she moved to leave, Cameron stepped through the open door, and Ainsley stopped. The two froze in place for a tense moment, Cameron staring at her with narrowed eyes, Ainsley not quite meeting his gaze. Finally, Cameron gave Ainsley a cool nod. Ainsley flushed bright red, gave him a slight nod in return, and dodged past him out the door.

At any other time Mac would have been more curious about the encounter, but just then Isabella sank into him, her tears spilling from her eyes.

Cameron sat on the sofa in the very place Ainsley had occupied and pulled out his whiskey flask. "I was on my way to you with the news, Isabella, when I met Mac," he said. "I can poke around the City if you'd like and find out what happened. Hart has friends in moneyed places who can find out how up against it your father truly is."

Isabella shook her head. "It doesn't matter. I only want to make certain my mother is all right. She's never very good at managing in a crisis. And Louisa will be heartbroken. This will mean she'll have no debut ball."

"Not necessarily," Mac said. "Your father is lucky that his son-in-law is so rich and well connected. Hart knows the best financial wizards in the City—in all of England and Scotland, for that matter. I'll see what can be done to save your father from destitution, and your sister can go on with her plans for her coming-out."

"He'll not let you," she said sadly. "He'll never take a penny from a Mackenzie."

"We'll fix it so that he never knows. It sounds like an entertaining endeavor. I'll save him *and* keep his pride intact."

The small smile she gave him made Mac feel better. The expression Isabella had worn when he'd entered the room had reminded him strongly of the one he'd seen on her face the night he'd come home after her miscarriage. Mac hadn't been able to fix that tragedy, but he might be able to fix this one.

He got Isabella to agree to go upstairs and let Evans look after her, and then he and Cameron departed for the City to find out what they could.

~

Unfortunately, when Mac and Cameron met with Hart's man at the Exchange, he confirmed that Lord Scranton's situation was dire indeed. He'd not only been involved in bad investment schemes, but he'd borrowed heavily from banks and friends in order to do so. Now, those banks and friends were demanding to be repaid. In addition, it looked as though Lord Scranton had also been dipping his hands into funds from a syndicate he'd formed with some old school friends, and now he couldn't replace their money. He'd certainly dug himself in deep.

Mac did not want to report this awfulness to Isabella. He stayed away until late that night, trying to come up with ways to mitigate the damage. If he worked hard enough perhaps he wouldn't have to explain until things were slightly less awful.

He arrived home after Isabella had gone to bed, but he found her awake in the bed in his room, waiting for him. Mac held her, neither of them speaking, both of them worrying, until they fell asleep in exhaustion.

The next day, still more dire news reached Isabella. Inspector Fellows sent Mac a note to tell him that Earl Scranton was dead, having died of apoplexy in the night.

Chapter 19

"Mama." Isabella rushed across her mother's drawing room to the woman standing still as marble near the window. Lady Scranton turned at her footsteps, then with a sob, caught Isabella in her arms.

Mother and daughter held each other for a long moment, rocking and crying. Isabella sensed rather than heard Mac enter behind her, his presence filling the room like the sun after a long cold snap.

Lady Scranton disengaged from the hug and seized Isabella's hands. She was dressed from head to foot in black, her eyes swollen and red behind her veil. "Oh, my child, I thought I would never see you again."

"How could you not? Of course I would come to you, Mama. Of course you would see me again."

"I thought . . ." She trailed off on another sob. "I thought you would hate me."

"Never. Come and sit down, Mama. You need to rest."

Lady Scranton allowed herself to be led to a sofa. She glanced up as she sat, saw Mac, and gave a start. "Oh. Lord Roland. I didn't realize."

"Call me Mac." He seated himself on a chair, folding his arms on his knees. "I place myself at your service, madam. Anything you need or want done, you tell me, and I shall make it happen. Command me."

"That is kind, but . . ."

"Mother." Isabella sat at Lady Scranton's side, still holding her hand. "This is no time for politeness, and Mac isn't being polite. I know Papa was ruined. I know the creditors are busy taking everything. I know there isn't money even for a proper funeral."

Her mother's face crumpled. "I have a small widow's portion—so the solicitors tell me. In a trust."

"The creditors might find a way to take that too," Mac said in a gentle voice. "Do nothing until you know, and let me worry about your expenses."

"I can't. Isabella, your father would never have wished that I be on your charity."

Isabella rubbed her mother's hands, which were cold through her lace gloves. "Of course he never meant for you to be on anyone's charity. He lost his money trying to make a fortune *for* you. But we're family. It isn't charity at all. It's what families do."

Pride warred with desperation in Lady Scranton's eyes. Isabella saw that her mother did not want to be dependent on Mac, but also that Lady Scranton had been raised in a world in which she'd always been taken care of. A fortune wiped away with a stroke of a pen was not part of her understanding. Neither was a husband wrenched from her by a sudden illness. Isabella's mother's back was straight, her posture always perfect, but she trembled like a sapling in a storm.

"Isabella, I don't know what to do," she whispered.

"My dear lady," Mac said, rising. "You do not have to do anything. You sit and have a chat with Isabella, and I will rush about the City putting everything right. By this time tomorrow, all will be well."

Lady Scranton drew a shuddering breath as she looked up at him. "Why? Why would you do this for me? Lord Scranton refused to let your name even be mentioned in this house."

Smiling his most charming smile, Mac lifted Lady Scranton's limp hand in his. "I do it because I love and cherish your daughter." He leaned and kissed Isabella's cheek, letting his lips linger on her skin. "Stay with her until I return," he murmured.

He squeezed Lady Scranton's hand again, let himself out of the house, and was gone.

"What will he do?" Lady Scranton asked in trepidation.

"Exactly what he said he would," Isabella said, knowing the truth of her words. "You can put your trust in Mac, Mama. The man does drive me mad, but one thing he is very good at is taking care of people. He has proved that time and again."

Lady Scranton wiped her eyes on a black lace handkerchief that was nearly sodden. "I thought he would be cold and scornful. I thought he would mock us."

"He is not so unkind as that. He really is quite generous. His entire family is."

"We refused to acknowledge him or your marriage, or even let him speak to us about settlements," Lady Scranton said, sniffling. "We shut him out for stealing you from us. I thought he'd gloat about our ruin, laugh at us when we were forced to live in the gutter."

"Then you read Mac very wrong. He would never do such a thing. And you will not have to live in the gutter." Isabella took her mother's hands again. "Mama, what happened? With Papa, last night, I mean. Can you tell me?"

Lady Scranton looked not so much crushed in grief as very, very tired. "He called me into his study yesterday afternoon and told me he wanted me to take Louisa and go live in Italy, where I would be able to do well on very little. He wanted me to leave then and there, but of course I could not. I asked when he would be joining us, and he said he would not be able to for a long time. He'd stay behind and try to unravel the mess he'd made." A new tear trickled down her cheek. "He pressed me to pack and go at once, but it took too long—so many arrangements had to be made. I heard him downstairs in the night, but he never went up to his bedroom. I grew worried. In the small hours, I crept down again to his study and found him on the floor, his face all twisted. The room was a mess, papers everywhere, a table overturned where he'd fallen. The doctor said he'd had an apoplectic fit. He'd died instantly, apparently. Very little pain. That at least is a mercy."

Isabella put her arms around her mother. "Mama, I'm so sorry."

"God is punishing me, I think. For not having the courage to stand up to your father, for letting him banish you. I went along with it. I refused to see you or let Louisa see you. And now look at me." Fresh tears trickled down her face.

Isabella rocked her. "God isn't as cruel as that; you know that in your heart. Mac told me that Papa had started to lose money a long time ago, when I was still at Miss Pringle's. Everything seemed to go wrong year after year. It was not your fault."

Lady Scranton raised her head. "Then why didn't he tell me?"

"To spare you the worry, I imagine. He was struggling to get the money back so he wouldn't shame you."

Her mother shook her head. As Isabella held her close, she thought of things Mac had told her that she could never explain to her mother. It seemed that Lord Scranton had gone into considerable debt to give Isabella her coming-out ball, determined that it be the largest and most elegant of the Season. He'd pinned his hopes on pairing Isabella with one of three young men of fortune to whose families Lord Scranton owed a great deal of money. A marriage with one of them would not only wipe out that debt but let Lord Scranton climb out of the slough he'd gotten himself get into. Isabella had destroyed his hopes when she'd slipped away with Mac to marry him. The fathers of the other three gentlemen had been very angry and demanded that Lord Scranton repay them immediately.

Why did he not tell me? Isabella had asked Mac in indignation. *If I'd known I needed to marry to help him, I might not have let my head be turned by the first handsome gentleman who danced with me.*

Your father is proud and wanted to orchestrate all without anyone guessing. You were supposed to be dutiful without incentive. I'm afraid, love, that your father had no idea that you had any thoughts in your head at all.

But why did he object when I married you? You and Hart could have dug him out of debt and sent him and Mama off on a long holiday.

Mac had smiled. *And be beholden to Hart Mackenzie, the Scottish duke, the rest of his life? Never.*

Bloody fool, Isabella had muttered. This was before Bellamy had woken Mac in the wee hours and handed him the message from Inspector Fellows, who'd gone to investigate when he'd heard of the sudden death of Isabella's father. A natural death, Fellows had said. A sad one.

"I'm here now, Mama," Isabella said. "I won't leave you alone again."

Lady Scranton leaned into Isabella as another flood of tears escaped her.

Isabella stayed with her mother until Lady Scranton

declared she needed to lie down. Isabella helped her upstairs, delivering her to her redoubtable lady's maid. The maid whispered her gratitude to Isabella—Lady Scranton hadn't shut an eye since the earl's death, no matter how much the servants had tried to get her to sleep.

Isabella left Lady Scranton in her maid's capable hands and went down the painfully familiar hall to Louisa's room and tapped on the door. To a tired, "Yes, what is it?" Isabella entered.

Louisa rose from the chaise on which she'd been reclining and dropped the quilt that had covered her to it.

Isabella's breath caught. Louisa had filled out from the lanky colt Isabella remembered to a lady of soft curves, her eighteen-year-old face clear and strong. Louisa's eyes were as green as ever, and framed with rich, brown-red lashes. She wore black now, though without the veil her mother had donned, but Isabella's little sister had grown into such a lovely young woman. When she had her coming-out ball, she'd stun every gentleman senseless.

"Isabella." Louisa took a hesitant step forward. "They told me you were here, but Mama wanted me to stay in my room."

A sob wedged in Isabella's throat. Louisa started for her, slowly at first until she was running the last few steps to throw herself into Isabella's arms.

They ended up on the chaise, Isabella pressing her cheek to Louisa's wet face.

"Why did you not come that day in the park?" Louisa asked when they could speak again. "Mrs. Douglas planned so carefully, but you weren't there, and we dared not wait."

"I know." Isabella wiped her eyes, not wanting to lie, but she did not want to tell Louisa about Payne just then. "I had taken ill. It came on me suddenly."

"Mrs. Douglas said that. I was worried."

"Nothing I did not throw off quickly. But I was unhappy to miss the appointment."

"You are here now. It doesn't matter." Louisa clung to Isabella's hands, much as their mother had. "Isabella, what is to become of me?"

"Become of you? If you mean, where will you live, you and Mama are both welcome to stay with me. In fact, I think you should come home with me tonight."

"I don't mean that, although it's very kind of you." Louisa released Isabella's hands and stood up. Her dress was black taffeta with a three-tiered skirt—likely it had been an afternoon dress quickly dyed for mourning. Louisa's pale skin and red hair stood out against it like ice and flame. "It sounds so selfish with everything Papa did and what Mama is going through. But I can't help feeling as though I've walked off a cliff and still have not landed. Yesterday I was being fitted for my ball dresses; today I am not allowed to have any of them. I'll not have a Season; I'll not marry. I'm not clever enough to be a governess or anything like that, so I'll end up a ladies' companion with nothing to do all day but wind wool and brush dogs." Her hands fell with a thump against her skirts.

"Darling, of course you won't," Isabella said. "You'll live with me, and I'll take care of you. You'll have your ball and your Season, and any number of young men will want to marry you."

"Will they?" Louisa laughed, anger in her eyes. "I am not much of a catch now, am I? My father died a ruined man, and he cheated others, so many others. What respectable gentleman will want me? They'll be afraid my blood will taint their family."

Isabella wished she could tell Louisa she was wrong, but Isabella was well acquainted with aristocratic marriages. Breeding was very important to the upper classes, and any flaw in a young lady was considered insurmountable—unless the gentleman in question needed a large influx of cash and the lady came with a huge dowry. But Louisa without money would not hold that kind of attraction.

"You might not be a match for a gentleman wanting to make a brilliant social marriage," Isabella conceded. "But I wouldn't wish you to marry a gentleman who wants only your money or connections in any case. I want you to marry a man who loves you—who loves you so much it is of no matter to him what your father did. Papa's mistakes aren't your fault, and any man worthy of you will see only your beauty and sweetness. I urge you not to regret that you can't make a society marriage, and instead follow your heart."

"Like you did?" Louisa looked angrier. "You *left* us, Isabella. You ran away without a word to me. How could you?"

Isabella started at her sudden vehemence. "Louisa, I tried to send word. I wanted to see you, to explain myself, but Papa wouldn't hear of it. He blocked me at every turn, returned my letters to you in shreds. I didn't persist, because I did not want to make trouble for you."

"You could have found some way. But you were too busy being the grand Lady of Mount Street. Oh, yes, I read all the stories in the newspapers, every word of them. Perhaps it's lucky that I'll have no Season, because everyone remembers your scandalous elopement, and they'll speculate on whether I'll run off during my debut ball as well."

"Darling, it was a nine days' wonder, that is all. My true friends saw that I'd made a good match with a good man. I didn't marry Mac to cause a scandal. I married him because I fell in love with him."

"Then why did you leave him?" Louisa fixed her with an accusing glare. "If you loved him so much, and the marriage was so wonderful, why did you run away? Did you send word to *him* or simply disappear as you did from me?"

Isabella gasped, stung. "Louisa."

"I'm sorry, Isabella. I've been angry at you for so long. If you loved Lord Mac enough to turn your back on all of us, why did you turn your back on him as well?"

Isabella rose swiftly to her feet. "I did not turn my back on you. Papa turned his back on me. He refused me the house. He wouldn't let me speak to you or Mama. Never."

"You could have defied him. You could have found some way around him. Your husband is rich enough—you could have paid Papa's debts and let his pride go to the devil. You didn't come back because you didn't want to."

Tears streamed down Louisa's face. Isabella stared at her, aghast, hating the fact that her sister might be right. Isabella had been so angry at her father that she'd built a wall between her old life and her new. She wondered now if she could have worn down her father's defenses if she'd tried harder. But Isabella had been too hurt by Lord Scranton's fury, too defiant to reason with him. Isabella had loved Mac, still did, and she'd been angry that her parents had not rejoiced in her happiness. Lady Scranton not talking her father 'round had upset her too. And Louisa, caught in the middle, had only seen Isabella walking away from them.

"Louisa, I'm sorry," Isabella whispered. "I'm so sorry."

"Do you love Lord Mac?"

"Yes." Isabella's heart went into the word. "I love him very much."

"Then why?"

"Marriage is not simple, I'm sorry to say. There are so many facets to it, and every year brings something new. For the good and for the bad. I suppose that's why the marriage vows say *for better or for worse.*"

"But you love him?"

"I do."

Louisa moved to stand in front of Isabella. They were of the same height now, Isabella's funny little sister all grown up.

"I'm glad," Louisa said. "I'm glad that you found someone to love. Does he love you?"

Isabella nodded, the dratted tears welling in her eyes again. "Yes, he does. Rather a lot, I think."

"Then you were wrong to leave him. Why did you throw that away?"

"Because he didn't love me *enough*. It is difficult to explain. Mac loved me so intensely that he did maddening things for me and because of me. He'd disappear without a word for weeks, because he thought that would make me happy. He never thought to ask me what would make me happy, or what I needed from him. Mac did everything based on what *he* felt, never noticing what I felt."

"And that's why you left him?"

"In the end, yes."

Isabella remembered the dark days after she'd lost the baby, the despair she'd felt when Mac finally came home too drunk and crushed himself to comfort her. Everything between them had built and built into a wall of anger and hurt and sadness.

"One day I woke up and saw things clearly," Isabella said, half to herself. "I knew that Mac would never learn to love me without hurting me. I couldn't stay with him while he did the same things over and over again. I no longer had the strength to face him."

"Did you tell him? Give him a chance to try?"

"You didn't see the truth of us." Isabella sighed. "I don't know if you knew this, Louisa, but I was carrying a child, and I lost it. I needed a long time to recover after that ordeal, and Mac couldn't give that to me. He was hurting too, and he didn't know how to make everything all better. That drove him a little insane, I think."

She explained how the physical pain of the miscarriage had given way to months of grief, and then of tiredness. She'd no longer had the energy for the comet that was Mac Mackenzie.

"What about now?" Louisa asked. "I saw him arrive with you today, and my maid says he has been living in your house with you."

Isabella nodded. "Mac has changed. He is calmer—a bit. And he seems to think about things more." She laughed a little. "Usually. He still is impetuous and exasperating. It's part of what makes him so charming, I suppose."

"And you still love him?"

Louisa held her gaze, her look stern. Isabella realized at that moment that it would be Louisa who held the family together after this tragedy. Their mother was too worn down, too uncertain how to live without a cushion of money and security beneath her. Louisa would be the strong shoulder everyone leaned on.

Isabella's heart swelled as she thought of Mac, who was even now running all over London to make certain that Isabella's mother and sister wanted for nothing. Mac had no legal obligation to her family, and no emotional one to the people who had refused to speak to him after he'd married Isabella. He could have washed his hands of the Scrantons, claimed that Isabella's family deserved what they'd got.

But he didn't, and Isabella knew he never would. His compassion was as large as his heart, Mac, who'd decided to adopt a helpless little girl like Aimee so she wouldn't grow up in the gutter.

Even when Isabella had left him, Mac had made certain that Isabella continued to live as lavishly as she'd grown accustomed to. He hadn't punished her. He hadn't rushed into the arms of other women for consolation. He'd stopped drinking, stopped his all-night revels with his rakish friends, stopped wasting himself.

For her.

"I think I do," Isabella whispered to Louisa. "I do."

It was a heady feeling, this surge of love, and very, very frightening.

Chapter 20

It is said that the Scottish Lord has returned to the Continent to Paint, and rumor has it that his Lady has also taken a holiday there. They were seen in close proximity to each other in Paris, but each seemingly never noticed that the other was there.

—*June 1881*

Mac saw little of Isabella in the following weeks, because she was distracted with funeral arrangements and looking after her mother. But whenever they met in passing, Isabella would flash him a smile that set his heart throbbing. Other parts of his anatomy too.

He longed to stop her when she kissed his cheek on the way out of the breakfast room or rushed about packing up her mother's house to find out why she looked so pleased with him, but he also had much to do. He and Cameron spent most of their time with bankers and investment houses sorting out the tangle of Scranton's debts, buying them up or settling them outright.

Mac intended to take the debts he'd paid and make a show of ripping up the notes in front of Lady Scranton's face. He hoped to make the sad lady smile. And perhaps Isabella would seize Mac in an embrace of passionate gratitude and make some of his baser fantasies come true. Well, he could hope.

The fact that Cameron was just as willing to help warmed him. Cameron wasn't known for suffering fools gladly, but when Mac mentioned his gratitude, Cam said in surprise, "Isabella is family."

Hart, too, pulled stings from afar, and Ian himself came down, with Beth, of course, breaking the journey so not to tire her. The two of them stayed in Hart's town house, because Isabella's house now overflowed with her mother and sister, Aimee and Miss Westlock, and Mac. Beth and Ian spent most of their time at Isabella's nonetheless, and so did Cameron, which made finding time alone with Isabella damned difficult. But Mac, after three years of loneliness, couldn't help but like having the house full. Isabella, he noticed, never once suggested that Mac move into Hart's London mansion with Ian and Beth.

Mac kept a strict eye out for Payne, but the man seemed to have made himself scarce. Payne delivered no more paintings to Crane, nor did he stop to collect his money, and neither Mac nor Fellows nor the other policemen saw him lurking. Payne had never tried to find Aimee, which both relieved and disgusted Mac. What kind of man abandoned his own child? On the other hand, Mac had grown fond of Aimee and was happy enough that Payne wasn't trying to snatch her away.

Lord Scranton had a suitably grand funeral, and his family laid him to rest in his mausoleum in Kent. His heir, a distant cousin of Isabella's, took over the estate house, the only thing left of the earl's former holdings. The cousin, an affable middle-aged bachelor, was happy to let Lady Scranton and Louisa live there as long as they liked.

Lady Scranton liked the idea. She'd be on hand to advise on the running of the house she'd presided over for years, and she could organize village fetes and run the church's charity works to her heart's content.

Louisa was not so sanguine, but Isabella promised that Louisa would spend so much time at Kilmorgan and in Isabella's house in London that she'd be in no danger of moldering in the country. Also, it had been settled that Mac and Isabella would host Louisa's come-out ball, though their mother would be in the thick of the organization. Louisa would have her debut, not this spring, because the family would still be in mourning, but in the Season after that.

The afternoon after the funeral, which Hart and Daniel came down to attend, Ian planted himself in front of Mac and waited for Mac to notice him. This was Ian's way of letting Mac know he wanted a word.

Mac turned and walked with his brother across the sweeping lawn and down a lane lined with trees.

"Have you done it?" Ian asked.

Mac glanced at his brother, but Ian looked straight ahead. "Do you mean, is Isabella my wife again?"

"Yes."

"Do you think she is?"

"I don't know, which is why I am asking you."

Mac rubbed his upper lip, nervous for some reason. "You've been observing her for the last week. And me. You're a perceptive man. What do you think?"

"Do you share a bed?"

"Sometimes. Not as often as I'd like, but she's been a bit distracted, with her father ruining himself and dying and all."

Ian frowned, and Mac chastised himself. His brother took all words at face value.

"Yes, she has been distracted," Ian said. "You should be comforting her."

"I am. When she lets me."

Ian stopped walking, exasperated. "Are you man and wife again or not?"

"I am attempting to explain, brother mine, that I don't know. Sometimes I think so, but other times . . . I rushed her about revoking the separation, and I think that frightened her. I won't make that mistake again."

Ian didn't blink, and even though Ian didn't look directly at Mac, his stare was unnerving. "You are not trying hard enough."

"I am, Ian. I'm trying like the devil."

"You're not showing her your true self, because you fear looking like a fool."

This from a man who could not help but show his true self. Unable to master subtlety or lies, Ian said what was in the front of his mind, nothing more. This unnerved most people, but Beth managed to draw perfect sense from him.

"I did look like a fool," Mac said. "You missed my performance with the Salvation Army band. I was a master cymbal clasher."

"Isabella told me about that. But you did not let yourself be a fool. You make a joke of everything so people will laugh, so you will not have to face what you don't wish to."

"Stop it, Ian. This stark truth is killing me."

Ian ran his gaze up and down Mac's mourning suit. "You see? You are trying to joke again."

Mac lost his smile. "What do you want, Ian? For me to fall at her feet and show her what a pathetic wretch I've become? To expose every raw wound inside me?"

"Yes. Bare your soul. Hart told me what that metaphor meant a long time ago."

"But I don't think Isabella wants that. She wants funny and charming Mac, the Mac who makes her laugh and smile. Not mewling, pathetic Mac."

"Ask her," Ian said.

Mac heaved another sigh. "You're a hard man, Ian Mackenzie."

Ian didn't respond, which could mean that he didn't know what Mac meant, or that he didn't care. Both, probably.

The two of them continued their walk and ended up at the garden behind the house. Isabella stood with her sister and mother and Beth among the flower beds, with Beth holding Aimee. The ladies all wore black, but Isabella was regal and beautiful in it. She had one arm around her mother's waist, the other around Louisa's.

Mac's heart warmed. It had been a sad day, watching Isabella say good-bye to her father, but the fear and worry had left Lady Scranton's face. Isabella glanced up, saw Mac, and sent him a smile.

"There," Mac said to Ian in a low voice. "I'm sorry it took a tragedy to do it, but Isabella has been reunited with her family. Sins forgiven. Even if we are never truly man and wife again, seeing her as she is now, with her arms around the people she loves, is enough for me."

Ian looked at Mac in silence for a long time. "No, it isn't," he said.

He walked away from Mac and made for Beth and her welcoming smile.

~

Mac thought about Ian's words as they concluded their visit to Kent and returned to London. Louisa elected to stay with their mother and get her settled, not wanting to leave Lady Scranton alone too soon. Isabella had already asked them to travel with her when she went back to Kilmorgan for the Christmas season. Lady Scranton at first had been reluctant, but Mac had been at his most jovial and talked her into it. Isabella had given him a smile of gratitude for that too.

But Ian was right. Gratitude was not enough.

Exposing his soft underbelly was not something Mac was used to doing. Mac had thought he'd done it already, telling her about the terrible time he'd spent in Italy after he'd decided to give up drink. He realized now that he'd told her that to not only gain her sympathy, but prove that he took their marriage seriously. He hadn't actually showed her the entire wreck of a man that was Mac Mackenzie. Isabella might cheerfully grind her elegant, high-heeled boot into that wreck and walk away from him, but he had to take that chance.

Thinking about her slender ankles in those high-heeled boots did not help. Nor did thinking of her in nothing *but* the high-heeled boots.

He was visualizing this pleasant possibility while mixing paints in his studio one day when he heard Isabella walk in. He glanced up from his paint table, and his heart gave the excited twinge it always did when he saw her. She'd dressed today in a black gown trimmed with intricate loops of black braid, her red hair and green eyes startling color against this darkness.

"Mac," Isabella said abruptly. "Did you keep the letter I sent you?"

With effort Mac turned his attention back to his paints. "Letter?"

"The letter I sent you the night I left."

Ah. That letter. Mac kept kneading paint globs to hide his nervous start. "Why would you imagine I still have it?"

"I don't know whether you do. That is why I have to ask."

"You sound like Ian."

"Ian knows how to make people answer him."

Mac laid down his palette knife. "Touché. All right, then. Come with me."

He led her down the stairs to his bedroom. It still was

his bedroom; he hadn't slept with Isabella since the night her father died.

Mac opened the wardrobe and extracted the small box that Bellamy had saved from the half-burned house, knowing that Mac kept his most treasured keepsakes in it. He set the box on a console table and opened it. A well-creased letter lay on the bottom, worn with time and reading. Mac extracted it and held it out to Isabella.

"This appears to be it."

"Will you read it to me?" she asked.

His false cheerfulness died. "Why?"

"I'd like to remember what I wrote."

Why the hell should she want that? Was she demanding, like Ian, that he expose his soul? Perhaps, but Mac felt as closed-off from her as ever as he unfolded the paper.

The words she'd written had burned into his heart like fine lines etched into metal. Mac didn't truly need to read the letter, because he'd memorized every damned word of it. But he dutifully began.

"Dearest Mac."

Isabella shifted slightly, and Mac cleared his throat.

Dearest Mac,

I love you. I will always love you.

But I can live with you no longer. I've tried to be strong for you, for three years I have tried. I have failed. You tried to remake me in your image, dear Mac, and I tried to be what you wanted, but I no longer can. I am sorry.

I want to write that my heart is breaking, but it is not. It broke some time ago, and I have just now realized that I can leave my heartbreak behind and go on.

The decision to live without you was a painful one and not lightly made. I realize you can legally cause me much harm for taking this step, and I ask you, for the love we once shared, not to. It could be that I will not need to leave forever, but I know that I need time apart, alone, to heal.

You have explained that you sometimes leave me for my own good, so I will have a chance to recover from life with you. Now I am doing the same, leaving so that both of us have a chance to breathe, a chance to cool. Living with you is like being with a shooting star, one that burns so brightly that it scorches me. And I am watching the star burn out. In the end, Mac, I fear there will be nothing left of you.

I know you will be angry when you read this, because you can grow so angry! But when you stop being angry, you will realize that my decision is sound. Together, we are destroying each other. Apart, I can remember my love for you. But you are burning me. You have exhausted me, and I have nothing left to give.

Ian has agreed to bring this letter to you, and he will inform me of what steps you decide to take. I trust Ian to help us through. Please do not try to seek me yourself.

I love you, Mac. I will always love you.

Please be well.

Isabella

By the time he finished, Mac no longer looked at the letter but at her. Isabella turned away, lashes shielding her eyes. She moved to the window, a slender, graceful figure in soot black.

Outside on the street, carriages clattered by, coachmen whistled, and people called out to one another. Inside all was stillness. Mac glanced back at the letter, and saw the words he'd read over and over until he knew each by heart, each one stabbing him to the quick.

"Why did you keep it?" Isabella asked without looking at him.

Mac swallowed. "Who knows? I've tried to make myself burn it, but always I fold it up and put it back into the box."

Isabella turned and silently held out her hand for the paper. After a tense moment, Mac took it to her.

She unfolded it and skimmed the words. Her mouth tightened as she finished, and then in one short jerk, she tore the paper in half. Before Mac could protest, she moved swiftly to the stove and tossed the letter inside.

Mac was beside her, grabbing her wrist, but too late. "What are you doing?"

Isabella looked at him in surprise. "Why would you not want me to burn it?"

"Because that letter told me how you felt. Your true feelings, in black and white. I needed to know them."

"Those were my feelings *then*. They are not my feelings now."

The fire crackled as the last of the paper died away. Damn it, the letter had been his lifeline. It had been a reminder of why he'd pushed aside whiskey and wild living, why he'd chosen to reform.

"I read it for comfort," he said. "On the worst nights, when I was tempted to drink to ease the pain, I'd read it over again. And I'd tell you, in my head, that I was working to change—for you. That you didn't need to worry, I wouldn't let myself burn out. I would come back to you a new man."

"How on earth did that comfort you?"

"The letter kept me sober, love. I needed it to."

Was this the naked exposure? Foolish Mac, who'd used a hurtful letter as a prop to get him through the nights?

A part of him was crying out, the terrified boy who'd

been caught and beaten when his father had found his copy-books covered with drawings instead of lessons. Mac had been forbidden with threats of more beatings to indulge in art, but try as he might, Mac hadn't been able to stop.

The pictures had poured out of him—birds outside the window, the stream where he fished, his brothers, his mother, even his father. Mac had lived in the shadows of Hart and Cameron, both so much older, both tall, athletic, smart. But the art was his own.

The old duke had considered Mac's need to paint weak and unmanly. When Mac had started taking mistresses at age fifteen, his father had not hidden his relief. *I thought you'd be one of those unnaturals, boy. You stick with cunny and breasts and kill any man who tries to convince you otherwise.*

The old duke would have hated Mac now, his son so in love with a woman that he'd changed his whole life for her.

Women are like tar, his father had been fond of saying. *Useful in their own way, but they'll mire you fast if you're not careful. They entice with their bodies then bind you with their little tantrums and tears. Take them to your bed and enjoy them, marry the one with the right connections, but above all, keep them in their place.*

Isabella had never clung, never played games with tantrums and tears. She was a woman, not a girl, and could have brought his father to his knees with one scornful look.

I need that letter, the whimpering boy inside him cried.

Or did he? For one thing, every word of the damn thing was seared into his memory. For another, he'd done it: Mac had stopped living in a frenzy. He'd lived the wild life, he now knew, because he feared that he'd have to face his true self if he ever ceased drinking, painting, running, *always running away.*

"What are your feelings now?" Mac asked her.

Isabella kept her gaze averted. "I was harsh three years ago," she said. "I was tired and miserable and angry and afraid. I kicked you away because I couldn't face what I needed to while I was distracted with you."

"I *distracted* you, did I?" Mac wanted to laugh. "A kind word for it."

"You needed me to forgive you. You demanded it, and I no longer had the strength."

"I had no business demanding anything of you. I told you that before, remember? I humbly apologized, and I still do. I mean it."

"I know." Isabella finally looked at him, and he saw anxiety in her eyes, as though she worried that he wouldn't forgive *her*. "I did forgive you. I knew about everything you did after I left you. Ian reported to me—and when Ian makes a report, you can be sure I hear every detail."

They both smiled a little. Ian had the kind of mind that could remember a list of numbers three months after he'd seen it, or every word of a conversation from the previous week even when no one had thought him listening.

"So, where are we now?" Mac asked. "I'm a responsible teetotaler who's adopted a child, but you married a carousing, carefree, wild cad. Will you even like the Mac Mackenzie I've become?"

Isabella reached for his hand. "You . . . I don't know how to put this, but you're the *real* you now, I think. You've lost all the things you hid behind. As though you're naked and unafraid."

Mac squeezed her fingers. "I could be naked, if you like. It's warm enough in here."

"But there are things about the other Mac I still love," Isabella went on. "I love your humor, your ability to render things harmless by laughing at them. I love your charm. When you were playing with the band on the street corner, you rose to the occasion with aplomb and made your friends look like idiots for ridiculing people. I was so proud to be your wife that night."

Mac kissed her fingers. "You know, the sergeant said I was welcome to canvass with them any time. Then you can show me again how proud you are of me."

"And I love how you turn anything we talk of into a game of seduction."

"Now, that is good to know."

"It makes me feel wanted and loved." Isabella covered his paint-smeared hand with both of hers. "I'm willing to try to be your wife again."

Mac's heart thumped so hard he could barely breathe. Never mind the damn letter. Having Isabella herself was hundred times better. "What do you mean by that? Exactly. Be precise. Be as precise as Ian would be. I don't want to misunderstand. Misunderstanding would make me hope, and I can't live on false hope."

Isabella stilled his lips with her fingertips. "I mean that I'm willing to try to live as your wife, to see how we rub along. No more games. Just life."

"Try." Mac kissed her fingers before she lowered them. "Only try? Not—*yes, Mac, please reverse the separation and we'll live happily ever after*?"

"No hurrying. Living together as man and wife. If we both truly have changed, if we are able to settle down and trot along happily together, then we summon Mr. Gordon and have him attend to the legal matters."

While part of Mac rejoiced at her words, another part chafed in impatience. He wanted this done, finished, so that the gnawing in his belly could go away, and he wouldn't wake up in terror that she'd gone again.

Still another part of him felt a twinge of guilt. He'd started to show her his soft underbelly with the letter, but she'd cut him off before he could do much more. The letter was only part of it. She was wrong; he was still hiding, and she was praising him for it.

He gave her a wicked smile, the wretch inside him banished again. "You wish to live together as man and wife, eh? My deliciously scandalous lady." He grasped her hand and pulled her to him. "I'll agree to your terms. For now. Not exactly the dazzling romance I had in mind, but I'll take it."

"And, Mac?"

"Yes, angel?"

"I'd like to try for a baby."

Her words washed more hope through him. Isabella had been so terrified to conceive again after her miscarriage that they'd ceased sleeping in the same bed together. Mac had understood and wanted to give her time, but keeping away from each other had put even more strain on their already strained marriage.

"That sounds a fine idea," Mac's mouth said while his head rang with jubilation. "We've been doing quite a bit of trying already. Something may come of that."

Isabella shook her head. "I had my courses when we were in Kent."

"Mmm." Mac strove to suppress his sudden and acute disappointment. "Well, my sweet, we'll simply have to try harder." He touched a silken curl on her forehead. "And often. Much, much more often."

"May we today?"

"Certainly." Mac was fully erect behind his kilt, which she had to have felt even through her layers of skirts. "I know where a nice, soft bed is to be found. Across the room, in fact."

Isabella smiled, her eyes taking on a wicked sparkle. Mac tamped down his guilty feelings as he led her to his wide bed. She'd exposed a large part of her heart this time, but Mac's hurts would remain hidden until another day.

———

"I beg your pardon, my lady," Miss Westlock said as she walked into the breakfast room the next morning.

Isabella looked up from her letters and arched her brows in surprise. The usually tidy Miss Westlock's hair was mussed, her face ruddy, her collar askew. At the other end of the able, Mac lowered his newspaper.

"What happened?" he asked.

"As you know, my lord, it is my habit in the mornings to take a brisk walk in Hyde Park before Aimee rises."

"Yes," Mac said impatiently. Miss Westlock was a hardy sort, up before dawn, taking light meals and no drink, walking every day.

"Well, a peculiar thing happened this morning. A gentleman approached me along one of the walks, and for a moment, I thought it was your lordship."

Mac stiffened, and Isabella's pulse quickened. "Yes?" she prompted.

"When he reached me, I saw that, indeed, it was *not* your lordship. He looked most like you, but his eyes were different. His are most definitely brown, while yours, your lordship, are more like copper. He alarmed me, rather."

Isabella clenched her napkin so hard she felt her nails press her palms through the cloth. "What did he do?"

"He asked me at what time I took Aimee for her walk, and would I let him speak to her then? I asked him why, and he claimed he was her father. I of course had no way of knowing whether this was true, and I advised him to consult your lordship. When I said that, he became most incensed, declaring that *he* was your lordship, and that you were impersonating him."

Mac said nothing. Isabella saw his stare fix and a blood

vessel begin pulsing in his neck, and she recognized that Mac was very, very angry. He rarely grew truly enraged; yes, he liked to shout and could conduct blazing rows with her, but those didn't stem from true anger. Irritation, frustration, and exasperation, but not fury.

This was anger. Dangerous anger.

"What did you say to him?" Isabella asked Miss Westlock.

"I bade him good morning and started to walk away. He was obviously a madman, and I have learned that one does not engage a madman in conversation. And would you believe it? He seized my arm and tried to drag me away with him."

Isabella half rose in her chair. "Are you all right? We will summon the police."

"No, my lady, do not trouble yourself. I saw the wretch off with a few stout thumps of my umbrella. He hastened away. I doubt he wanted a constable to see him trying to accost a helpless woman."

No one looking at Miss Westlock, especially with her stout umbrella, would think of her as a helpless woman, but Isabella was too unnerved to smile.

"Did you see which direction he went?" she asked.

"Down Knightsbridge, but my lady, he could have gone anywhere after that. He might have hailed a hansom cab and be on the other side of the city by now."

"Damn him."

Mac's snarl made both women jump. He rose from his seat, resting his fists on the table, the rage in his eyes frightening to behold. "Damn the man. I've had enough of this." He kicked aside his chair and shouted for Bellamy.

"Mac," Isabella said in alarm. "Where are you going?"

"To see Fellows. I want Payne found, and I want him out of our lives."

Isabella leapt to her feet. "Perhaps you shouldn't . . ."

"I'm not afraid of him, Isabella. I'll fetch Fellows, and we'll hunt him."

"But if he's convinced himself that he's you, and you're him—or whatever he thinks—he'll be dangerous."

Mac gave her a feral smile. "Not half as dangerous as I am, my love."

Isabella wanted to tell him not to go, to stay with her, but her anger matched Mac's own. Payne had to be stopped. But the thought of the imposter trying to kill Mac terrified her.

Miss Westlock gave Mac an approving nod. "Her ladyship and I will hold down the fort, my lord, while you do battle. Between us all, we'll see him off."

Mac came to Isabella and gave her a hard kiss on the mouth. She tasted his rage and determination, and his strength. She loved all of it. Too soon, the pressure of his fingers disappeared, and she felt a cold draft blow through the room as Mac exited the front door.

Chapter 21

The family *Mackenzie* have descended on the capital, with the astonishing announcement that the youngest of them, Lord I—, has taken a wife. The artist Lord lately of Mount Street moved into a hotel for so brief a stay in Town, and his Lady, who had been sleeping at the same hotel, immediately changed her lodgings.

—*August 1881*

Mac didn't return. Rain came and went, and the day darkened, but Mac was not back by the time Morton tapped the gong to announce the evening meal. Isabella sat alone in the dining room, picked at her food, and sent most of the meal back untouched.

She paced the drawing room, watching the maid draw the curtains against the growing night. Isabella hated not knowing where Mac was and what he was doing. Were he and Fellows scouring London for Payne? Had they found him? Or had something happened to them? Inspector Fellows would surely send word to her if Mac had been hurt. Wouldn't he?

The clock ticked away slices of the night: eight, nine, ten, eleven. At midnight, Evans stood on the landing with her arms folded, her way of indicating that she thought her mistress should be in bed.

"Not until I hear word from Mac," Isabella said. "Not until then."

By three o'clock, Isabella's body drooped, though her thoughts still spun with agitation. When she found herself being supported by Evans, she succumbed and allowed herself to be put to bed.

She'd let herself sleep, she told herself. When she woke, Mac would be home. Or at least have sent a message.

It was strange, Isabella reflected as she curled up under the covers, that earlier in their marriage, when Mac had not turned up at home at his usual time, Isabella had never worried. She'd been annoyed, yes, but never seriously concerned. She'd known that he was simply out with his friends or had run off to Italy or some such place and that he or Bellamy would send word to her sometime.

Tonight was different. A dangerous man stalked them, and Isabella's worry kept her awake. Something new had begun between her and Mac, a deeper understanding, a deeper knowledge of each other. Their new relationship was fresh and fragile, and Isabella feared to lose it.

No, to be honest, she feared to lose Mac himself, no matter what was between them. She loved him. Losing him would put a hole in her life that nothing could ever fill.

Isabella rolled over into the pillow he'd slept on the night before, inhaling his lingering scent, and fell asleep, dreaming of his warm body on hers. She woke to find the sun high and Mac still gone.

TWELVE HOURS EARLIER

Lloyd Fellows allowed Mac to accompany him and his team of constables in the search for Payne. Fellows hadn't wanted to let Mac come with them—Mac knew the inspector would prefer it if Mac stayed the hell out of the way, but Mac couldn't. He simply could not sit at home waiting to hear that Fellows had lost track of Payne again. He wanted Payne caught, dealt with, and out of their lives, to know that Isabella was finally safe.

Mac's Highland ancestors would have gone after the beggar and run him through, then returned home and celebrated with much drinking, dancing, and bedding. Mac could forgo the drinking and dancing, but his blood was up, and he wanted to find the man. He'd deal with him and then spend three days bedding Isabella.

All through the afternoon, he moved with Fellows's constables through Chancery Lane and its environs, beginning with Payne's last known place of residence. Payne had never returned here, but he knew the area, and it was possible that he'd find someplace nearby to hide.

Mac made his way through Fleet Street and down through Temple Bar to the Strand. The traffic was thick, the thoroughfare jammed with carriages. Mac stepped on and off the road, around people, barricades, wagons, horses. He walked up Southampton Street, which had only a slightly lesser crush, to the wide market at Covent Garden.

They saw no sign of Payne. At least, Mac thought, he had plenty of people guarding Isabella, so even if Payne doubled back to North Audley Street, he'd never get near her. Bellamy might have a bad knee, but he knew how to fight dirty, and he was a dead shot. The man had also talked to his old chums, street toughs, most of them, and had them help him watch the house.

Mac and the constables joined up with the others, continuing to search until the sky was black. The rain poured down, and clocks all over the metropolis struck three. Fellows advised Mac to go home, giving him a look that said he was ready to haul Mac there himself.

Mac conceded and found a hansom cab. He wanted to tell Isabella what they'd discovered—nothing—and then decide what to do.

No, truth to tell, Mac wanted to shed his wet clothes and slide into bed next to Isabella, letting her warm him with her soft body. Damn Payne; Mac refused to let the man disrupt his life.

He sank into a half-doze as the hansom took him home, imagining how he'd kiss Isabella's skin and feel her fingers glide down his torso to the cock that hardened at the thought. Isabella's touch was skilled. She knew how to stroke him, how to glide her fingers around the tip and back down the shaft, slowly bringing Mac to the ready, but never letting it finish too quickly. Sweet, sweet woman.

A wash of chill rain filled the hansom, and Mac snapped his eyes open. A dark figure climbed into the cab and slammed the door.

Mac let out a roar and lunged for him, wanting nothing more than the feel of the man's throat under his hands. A cold ring touched his face, the end of a pistol barrel. Payne regarded Mac over the revolver, a Webley, Mac thought distractedly, the kind Hart liked. Payne's eyes were wide, dark, and full of fury that matched Mac's own.

Mac's heart thumped in rage. Payne would kill him. He didn't fear so much for himself or even for Isabella's safety—she was a sensible woman, and Hart, Cam, Ian, and Bellamy would protect her. What Mac feared was dying without seeing her again.

He wanted so much to see her again.

"I've got you," Payne said. His voice was scratchy and thin. "While you were hunting me, I hunted you."

"How bloody convenient for you," Mac growled.

The pistol dug harder into Mac's cheek. "You will stay the hell away from my wife," Payne said.

Mac's rage rose. "You touch Isabella, you son of a bitch, and I will kill you."

"You are in no position to make threats to me."

"I don't have to be. Even if you shoot me, you can be sure you'll never get away from Hart. He's a fucking obsessed bastard, and he's touchy about people harming his sisters-in-law. You will be praying to have me alive once Hart is on your trail."

Payne didn't look worried, which only proved how stupid the man was. Hart could be viciously vindictive, and he never gave up.

"Just tell me one thing," Mac said. "Why the hell do you want to be Mac Mackenzie?"

Payne's eyes flickered, and Mac expected any second to learn what a bullet felt like going through his skull.

"Mac has everything," Payne said. "Talent, friends, family."

"Samson Payne had that," Mac pointed out. "Family back in Sheffield. Talent. I've seen your work—it's bloody good. I don't know about friends. You'll have to tell me."

"Samson can't have art lessons. Samson can't leave home. Samson can't do anything but drudge all his life, while soft-handed lords have anything they want. I can do that. I can paint just like him. I'll do it so well that no one will be able to tell the difference, and then they'll think *he's* the fraud. The aristocrat's son stooping to steal the work of poor Samson Payne."

His singsong voice chilled Mac's blood. "You are all twisted up inside, aren't you? I would have given you the lessons, Payne. I would have helped you. It was yours for the asking."

"You would have seen how much better I was than you."

"Hell, scores of artists are better than I am. I paint what

I want and don't give a damn about contributing to the art world. That's why I give the bloody paintings to my friends, and they indulge me by hanging them on their walls."

Payne didn't appear to be listening. "Get out," he said.

Mac stilled, calculating the odds of smacking the gun away before Payne could shoot him. Pistol or no, Mac had no intention of diving out of this hansom cab and letting Payne finish the journey to North Audley Street and Isabella.

The pistol barrel was cold on his skin, Payne almost caressing him with it. Mac wondered why he didn't feel more fear, but maybe rage took care of that.

"If you shoot me, it will make a hell of a lot of noise," Mac said in a reasonable tone. "And people will have you."

"They will understand why I had to do it."

Miss Westlock is right; he's a complete madman. In Payne's mind, he would have shot the false Mac, and Isabella would welcome him into her arms for it.

The thought of Isabella waiting for Mac, perhaps in that dressing gown that clung to her body like water, made the berserker in him roar to the surface. Mac knocked his elbow into Payne and ducked as the pistol exploded in his ear. He fought through the ringing in his head, trying to knock Payne away. The hansom spun sideways as the horses bolted at the sound, the driver's shouts dim in Mac's deadened hearing.

Mac had no way of knowing what had happened to the damn pistol, but the mad Highlander in him didn't care. Killing the man with his bare hands would be so much more satisfying.

Payne slithered from Mac's grasp. As the hansom rocked, the door flew open, and Payne scrambled to the pavement.

"No ye don't, ye bloody bastard." Mac leapt after him.

He yanked at Payne's coat, but Payne gave a mighty twist, plunged in front of a cart, and darted into a narrow passage on the other side of the street.

Mac went right after him. Rain poured down, blotting out all light. Mac had no idea where they were, but the streets were rubbish-strewn and narrow, and Payne ran through them with the ease of familiarity. Mac ran fast, faster, pounding through puddles and filth, rain pouring into his face.

Payne kept darting through the maze of passages, the man surprisingly swift on his feet. They crossed a wider street filled with carriages, too damned many for this time of night.

Payne put on a burst of speed, but Mac had plenty of energy to keep up with him. After Payne died, *then* Mac could rest.

Payne charged into another narrow lane, and Mac sprinted behind him. This passage was dark and noisome, with the skittering of rats to go with it.

Rats in a hole, Mac thought grimly. Payne kept good company.

He reached the end of the passage, a blank wall with no doors. And no Payne.

Damn the man, he'd doubled back. Mac turned to run after him.

A light flashed, followed by a horrible noise that penetrated even his deafened ears. After two steps, Mac's feet no longer worked. His knees buckled against his will, and the pavement rushed up to meet him.

What the hell? What the hell? Mac put his hands on the cold ground, trying to push himself up, but his breath was gone. A large wet patch stained his side—he must have fallen into a puddle. He'd let Payne face Bellamy for that. The former pugilist enraged about Mac's clothes was a fearsome sight.

Payne's footsteps echoed as the man walked down the passage to Mac. Mac smelled the acrid stench of a pistol that had just been fired. He opened his mouth to shout, but his lungs wouldn't work. For some reason, he could barely breathe.

And then pain came. Terrible, blossoming pain, spreading from his side up into his arm and down his leg. *Damn it to hell.*

Payne, silhouetted by the brighter street beyond the passage, holstered his pistol, scooped Mac up by his armpits, and began to drag him away.

***

"I don't know where he is," Inspector Fellows repeated in irritation. "We hadn't found Payne by three, and Lord Mac said he'd go home to tell you. He got into a hansom cab, and that was the last I saw of him."

Isabella rubbed her hands and paced the drawing room. She'd barely been able to stay still while Evans dressed her, but she reasoned she couldn't rush downstairs in her dressing gown. She was a proper Englishwoman, an earl's daughter, and an aristocrat's wife. She could not appear in undress in front of visitors. Both Fellows and Cameron had answered her frantic summons, arriving very quickly after her messages.

"He never came home," she said in a bleak voice. "Morton and Bellamy were looking out for him especially."

She did not want to voice the thought that Mac could be dead. The world would cease to turn if that happened. As fear welled up in her, Isabella knew that she loved Mac with all her heart, and she did not care whether he wanted to live with her forever, or run back to Paris to paint, or stay out all night with his friends, or spend all day in bed with her. She simply wanted Mac home, whole and safe and sound.

"We are looking," Fellows said.

Isabella clenched her hands. "Look harder. I don't care if every man in Scotland Yard must be out on the streets searching for him. I want him found. I *need* him found."

"*I'll* find him," Cameron said. "I'll make damn sure."

"I'm coming with you," Isabella said. As the two men exchanged a glance, she swung from them in irritation and called to Evans to fetch her coat.

Cameron stepped in front of her. "Isabella."

"Don't 'Isabella' me, Cameron Mackenzie. I am coming with you."

Cameron's scarred cheek twitched, and his eyes, more golden than Mac's, regarded her steadily. "Yes," he said. "I suppose you are."

~~~

Mac's first thought upon waking was surprise to be alive. His second was terrible need to see Isabella.

He peeled open his eyes, wincing when bright gaslight stabbed through them. He lay on a floor, and though he felt the prickle of a thick woolen carpet, the flat surface was hard. His side hurt like hell. He made the mistake of moving and groaned out loud when pain raked through him.

Mac let his head drop back, trying to calm his breathing. He needed to think, to figure out where he was, to decide how to get away.

The smell here was stuffy and wrong, like a house too long shut up. As his eyes adjusted to the light, he saw that the colors of the room were garish, the walls done in bright pinks and reds and covered with gold-framed paintings his eyes were too blurred to make out. Money had gone into making this room, but his artist's soul cringed at the gaudiness. Cost without taste. A bloody crime.

His vision began to clear, and Mac saw the pictures.
Hell.

They were Mac's. At least some of them were—originals he'd done years and years ago. Many were paintings done in Mac's style, but he knew he hadn't painted them. There were pictures of Kilmorgan, of the house in Buckinghamshire, various views of Paris and Florence, Rome and Venice, of Cam's horses, of the Mackenzie dogs.

Two whole walls held nothing but Isabella.

Cold seared Mac's stomach. Every painting portrayed Isabella nude. Isabella sitting on a straight-backed chair with her legs spread, Isabella reclining on a sofa, Isabella stepping out of a bath, lying on a rug, standing outside naked with one hand on the branch of a tree.

She'd never posed for these, Mac knew she hadn't. Mac knew she *wouldn't.* Likely Payne had drawn a model, probably Mirabelle, Aimee's mother, then had painted in Isabella's head, the opposite of what Isabella had asked Mac to do with the erotic pictures.

Mac wanted to be sick, and at the same time his rage rose so swiftly that his entire body pulsed with it.

"You're a dead man." Mac drew in as much air as he could and shouted it. "Do you hear me? You're a dead man!"

The door swung open. Mac couldn't screw his head around to see who'd entered, but he heard a man's tread move toward him. Booted feet stopped at Mac's side, and Mac stared up at Payne.

Now that he had light, Mac saw that the man did resemble him, at least superficially. Payne's eyes were brown and set deeply into his face; his hair had been brushed the way Mac wore his, but it fought a widow's peak. His cheeks were more hollow, and Mac suspected that what Fellows had suggested was true: that he filled them out with cotton wool when he needed to. He hadn't at the moment, and the hollow cheeks gave his mouth a drawn look.

He wore a full dress kilt of Mackenzie plaid, formal

coat, and polished boots. Seen at a distance or in the dark, or by someone who did not know Mac well, Payne could easily pass for him.

"You have it wrong," Payne said coldly. "It is I who will kill you."

Mac laughed. It came out feeble and hoarse. "Then why haven't you already?"

"Because I need her to come to me."

Mac's blood chilled as he understood what Payne had done. He hadn't planned to shoot Mac in the hansom at all—he'd wanted Mac to chase him through the back streets of London to this place. Leading Mac as a fox led the hounds. Except the fox was in his hole now, ready to annihilate the hound foolish enough to follow him down it.

"She'll never come here," Mac said. His head spun with dizziness; it took so much damn effort to speak.

Payne went down on one knee next to him. "She will come here to watch you die. I alerted a constable that I'd found Payne, and he ran off with the news. She will be safe with me, where she belongs, with her husband who will take care of her."

"Like hell she will."

"Isabella has been trying to get away from you for some time. I thought she'd managed it when she left you three years ago, but no, you kept turning up. Following her about, insinuating yourself on her when she made it clear she didn't want you. You should die for that."

Fear bit him when he realized Payne had been watching her for that long. And none of them had known. *He* hadn't known. He hadn't watched out for her well enough. "Isabella is the only thing I care about," Mac croaked. "Hell, why am I arguing with you? You're a madman."

"You don't care for her. You love yourself too much and care nothing about what she wants, what she needs. That is how I know you are not the true Mac, her true husband.

I cherish Isabella. I will keep her and protect her, dote on her. I will worship her as she deserves."

"If you think Isabella wants to be put on a pedestal, you don't know her very well. She likes her independence."

Payne shook his head. "She wants to be cared for, and I will live to care for her. Not to prove to my father that I can make something of myself, not to prove to Hart that I'm not a wastrel. For her. Even my art isn't as important as she is."

Dear God, it was humiliating to hear truths coming out of Payne's mouth. Yes, Mac had tried desperately for years to make his father proud, even when he told himself he cared nothing for it. He'd gone on trying to prove himself to his father even after the man was dead.

He'd even been trying to prove himself to Hart, and to Cam, and to Ian, he realized. His three brothers had turned their obsessions into practical living, while Mac had devoted himself to art for its own sake, as he'd explained to Payne in the hansom. For its own sake? He wondered now. Or had he decided not to try to exhibit or sell his paintings because he feared he'd be a failure?

Isabella had never once thought Mac inadequate.

"I do love her," Mac said, his anger stilling to a point of calm.

"Then why didn't you stay with her? Why did you keep running away, leaving her vulnerable to every man with designs on her? This is how I know I am the real Mac Mackenzie. Because I would never have done those things to Isabella. I'd have treated her like an angel. You never understood what you had in her."

Damn, the man was mesmerizing. Mac needed to concentrate.

"She'll never come to you," Mac said. "She'll know the difference."

Payne rose swiftly to his feet, cocking the revolver. *Well done, enraging the madman with the gun.*

"She will come. She will come, and she will stay with me."

Isabella, be sensible, don't come. Let me rot.

Payne walked away, his Mackenzie plaid swirling around his knees. Mac's vision began to cloud, and despair washed over him.

He would never see Isabella again. He'd never see her bend over him, her red hair falling to tickle his face, never see her green eyes flash in anger, never smell the attar of roses that clung to her skin. He'd never again touch the petal-soft smoothness of her, never cup the firm perfection of her breast.

His senses drifted, and he was dancing with her again at Lord Abercrombie's ball, when she'd been dressed in the blue satin ball gown with yellow roses in her hair. The beauty of her cut like a knife. She'd talked to him in a voice smooth like fine wine, and he'd drunk her in.

Bare your soul, Ian had advised.

Mac hadn't done it yet. He'd let her love him again, but he'd not surrendered the entirety of himself to her. He knew that, and the knowledge beat at him.

I dragged her off and married her, because if I hadn't simply taken her, if I'd given her the choice, she never would have chosen me.

But Mac had changed. He'd given up everything but moving doggedly through life. For her.

For her? The nagging thing inside asked. *Or so that she'd feel sorry for you and acknowledge your martyrdom?*

Hell and damn, he couldn't even win an argument with himself.

Isabella, please, I need to see you one more time.

He'd loved the determined and naïve debutante he'd met

that first night. He'd loved the young woman she'd become, bold enough to fall into step with Mac's life, putting up with his dissipated friends and his skin-baring models. Mac had loved showing off how well his proper young wife took Mac's scandalous life in stride, and he'd never realized just how strong Isabella had been to do it. Nothing in her upbringing or education at her select academy could have prepared her for someone like Mac, not even the redoubtable Miss Pringle. And yet, she'd done it.

Mac had loved the woman she'd become: admired by society, able to stand on her own and look her neighbors in the face, notwithstanding that her family disowned her and her marriage fell apart. The world hadn't blamed Isabella; they'd blamed Mac.

Perceptive of them.

I want to love you, Isabella. Not as Mac the scandalous, or the reformed Mac, but as myself. The Mac I truly am.

The one who loves you.

I love you, Isabella.

And he'd never have the chance to tell her.

Chapter 22

Delicious rumor puts the Scottish Lord having moved in with his Lady in North Audley Street. The Lord's Mount Street house was sadly burned, but observers say the Lady welcomed him with open arms. They have been seen about Town together in a most friendly fashion.

—September 1881

Time ceased to have meaning. The room gently spun around him, the women who were not Isabella staring down at him in their garish, erotic glory. The artist in Mac whispered that the pictures were quite well done—Payne was exactly the sort of man Mac would have taken under his wing once upon a time, and helped build his career.

No chance of that now, Mac thought dryly.

Darkness came and went, though there was no change in the level of gaslight. The fading was his own vision sliding in and out. Mac had no more feeling in his legs and feet. Payne was going to let him die here.

Mac heard his own voice issue from between his cracked lips.

In bonny town, where I was born.
There was a fair maid dwellin'.

Made every youth cry, "well-away!"
Her name was Iiiis-a-bella.

The last time he'd sung that, Isabella had slammed open the door of the bathroom and fixed him with an outraged stare. His skin had prickled as her gaze had roved his body spread in her bathtub, and he'd had the absurd fear that she'd not be impressed by what she saw.

Will she still want me? he'd wondered. *Will I still be the man whose body she likes to admire? To touch?* He hadn't been timid with a woman since age fifteen, but Mac had worried that Isabella would sneer at him and turn away.

Her name was Iiiis-a-bella.

"Mac?"

I'm here, love. Come to bed, my sweet, I'm cold.

"Mac? Oh, Mac."

Mac forced his eyes open, wishing the blackness would clear. He felt a silken touch on his skin, smelled the faint odor of roses. Her beautiful face hovered above his, eyes burning beneath red curls.

"Isabella," he whispered. "Love you."

"You're bleeding. Mac, what happened?"

The world went black for a moment, and when it became light again, he felt a towel or blanket or something being pressed hard into his side. It hurt like hell, but that was good, because the pain meant that he was still alive.

Awareness cut through the fog. Then fear. "No," he croaked. "Isabella. Run. Go!"

"Don't be stupid. Cam's here. And Inspector Fellows."

"Payne?"

"They're looking for him. Mac, don't fall asleep. Keep looking at me."

"My pleasure." It hurt to smile, but his beautiful wife was by his side, her scent overriding the terrible coppery smell of blood. "I need to bare my soul, my love. Will you let me bare my soul to you?"

She leaned closer. "Hush, darling. We'll take you home, and everything will be all right."

"No, it won't. I've been lying to you. I haven't bared my soul."

Her hot tears fell on his face. "Mac, don't die. Please."

"I'll do my damnedest."

Mac heard his words come out a slurred mumble. Isabella wouldn't be able to understand him. He had to make her understand him.

"I can't lose you." Isabella stroked his hair, her touch so dear to him. "I don't want to live without you, Mac. I never was a whole person until I met you."

Whole. That's what Isabella had made *him*. She'd been the best part of him, and when Mac had lost her, he'd had nothing left of himself. That was what Ian had been trying to tell him.

Mac reached for her hand, relief flooding him when she took it. "Need you, love."

"Don't leave me." Isabella's voice was becoming desperate.

"Isabella."

Mac blinked, because the word hadn't come from him. Rage flooded him again as a shadow fell over them, cast by the tall form of Payne.

"Run," Mac tried to say. "Get away."

Instead, his beautiful lady rose to her feet to confront him. "You shot him. Damn you." She struck out with her fists, and Payne suddenly found himself having to fend off a hundred and twenty pounds of enraged female. Mac was torn between panic and laughter. Isabella was strong, he had cause to know.

But not strong enough. She got one shout out of her

mouth before Payne clapped a hand over it and lifted her from her feet. Isabella fought, her eyes wild.

All of Mac's rage focused on one single point. He heard the cries of his ancestors ringing in his head, urging him to take his enemy, to kill him. If he'd had a claymore in his hand, Mac would have sliced off the bloody Sassenach's head with it.

As it was, he had to make do. The wild strength let him haul himself to his feet. He was cold, his vision blurred, but Mac would perform this one last act to save the woman he loved. If he died of the deed, so be it.

Snarling, he threw himself at Payne. Payne had to release Isabella, who stumbled back and wasted no time screaming at the top of her lungs.

Payne brought his pistol around and pointed it at her.

No! Mac grabbed the man's arm, striking him on the hand so that his grip went slack. Payne fought hard, seizing the pistol again even as he dropped it, shoving the barrel into Mac's ribs. Isabella shouted something, running at the pair of them as they grappled.

The pistol's barrel scraped away from Mac's body, but now it pointed at Isabella. Mac wrenched himself into her, sending Isabella to the floor as the pistol went off. A second roar followed.

Mac expected oblivion. Or excruciating pain. Maybe one first then the other.

Instead, Payne crumpled on the floor, a stunned look on his face. Blood spouted from a wound in the exact center of his forehead.

What the hell?

He saw through a haze of smoke the cold eyes of Inspector Fellows over the barrel of another Webley. Behind him was his brother Cameron, a hulking brute of a man, also with pistol in hand. Cameron's eyes reflected the rage Mac felt.

A family affair. Nice shooting, Inspector.

Isabella was on the carpet, her black skirts spread around her, eyes wide with fear. Mac rocked on his weak legs, Payne's pistol somehow still in his hand. He dropped it.

"Mac!" Isabella scrambled to her feet, her arms coming around him even as Mac crumpled.

He turned on her a look of fury. "What th' bloody hell were ye playing at, woman?" he roared. "When a man has a pistol, ye run t'other way. That could be you shot daed on the floor, not him."

"Mac, shut up." Tears were streaming down her face. "Cease talking and stay alive for me. Please."

Mac sank into the warmth of her body, even as Cameron's strong arm supported him on his other side.

"Anything for you, Isabella, love," Mac said. "Anything at all. You just ask me."

"I love you, Mac."

Mac turned his head and kissed her smooth cheek. Did anything smell better than this woman, so warm and sweet? "I love you, my Isabella." He sighed. "I do believe I will lose consciousness now."

The last thing he remembered was Isabella's lips in his hair, her soft voice saying over and over that she loved him.

THREE WEEKS LATER

Isabella sat in Mac's studio in her black dress with her hands in her lap. A bowl of yellow hothouse roses rested on a table next to her, a mix of rosebuds, full-blown flowers, and those that had already started dropping petals.

Mac was half-hidden behind his large easel, his painting boots and strong legs showing below the canvas, his formidable frown and red kerchief above it. He held the palette against his bare, tight arm, and scowled at the canvas as he slapped on paint. He still wore a bandage on his side where the bullet had barreled through his flesh, but he was healing well. A strong constitution, he'd said with a shrug. That was Mac, careless about the most important things.

Isabella's limbs had grown at bit stiff with the sitting, but she knew better than to move. Mac might be focusing on one crook of her finger, and if she shifted, it would break his concentration. A petal fell from a flower, and she silently admonished it.

Mac lowered his brush and stepped back. He studied the painting for a long time, so long, frozen in place, that worry gnawed at her. She jumped up, damn the pose.

"Mac, what is it? Is it the pain?" She knew he hadn't quite finished healing, no matter how robust he pretended to be.

Mac didn't answer, his gaze fixed on the painting. Isabella glanced at it in curiosity, but she could see nothing wrong with it. It was a Mac Mackenzie painting, muted browns and blacks highlighted with brilliant tones of red and yellow. Isabella sat a bit primly, her coppery curls piled high on her head, one ringlet drooping down her cheek. A little smile hovered about her mouth, and her eyes sparkled with good humor. The painting wasn't finished, but already it glowed with life.

"It's lovely," she said. "What is the matter? Do you not like it?"

Mac turned to her, a strange look in his eyes. "Not like it? It's bloody wonderful. It's the best thing I've ever done."

Isabella made her voice light. "What, even more than the erotic pictures?"

"Those were different. *This* . . ." Mac pointed at the painting with the handle of his brush. "This is beauty."

"I'm pleased that your high opinion of yourself has returned."

Mac dropped the brush and caught her shoulders, never mind that he smeared yellow paint on her black gabardine. He studied her intently, the strange look still in his eyes.

"My love, Ian told me right after your father died that I needed to bare my soul to you. Well, here it is, the good and the bad of it." He pointed to the portrait. "That's my soul right there, crying out for you."

Isabella looked at it again. The woman who was herself through and through smiled out at Mac.

"I don't understand. It's just a picture of me."

"Just a picture." Mac laughed, but tears wet his eyes. "It *is* just a picture. Of you. Painted by me, with love in every stroke." He drew a breath. "That's what I didn't understand before. This is why my talent went away and now has come bursting back."

He looked so joyous that Isabella wanted to kiss him, but she still didn't understand. "Explain?"

"I can't, love. I always thought my ability came from astonishing luck, or a drunken stupor, or lust for you. When I painted the erotic pictures, I assumed they came out well because I wanted you so much."

She shot him a sly look. "But you discovered you didn't want me so much?"

"No, I want you all the damn time." His fingers went to the nape of her neck, caressing, warming, loosening her.

"You were explaining."

He smiled. "It wasn't the lack of drink that took away my ability, love; it was my own bitterness. I know that now. Once I sobered up I couldn't shut out my anger at you for leaving me, and at myself for causing it. I buried my love, because it hurt me too damn much to feel it. And my paintings were awful. When I decided to let myself love you—just *love* you, what you are, no matter what you thought of me, it came flooding back." Mac drew another shaking breath. "I think I can paint anything now."

Isabella's heart squeezed with sudden happiness, but she said, "There's a flaw in your reasoning."

"Can't be. It's what I feel."

She shook her head. "You painted beautifully before you ever met me. I've seen your paintings from that time. They are excellent. Don't pretend they're not."

"I think then I was in love with life itself. I was young, out from under my father's fist, finally free of him. I could do anything I pleased. But then I met you, and my world came crashing down."

Isabella wished she could fix this moment in time, with Mac's body hard against hers, his eyes filled with naked emotion.

"Why did we make ourselves so unhappy?" she asked, half to herself.

"You were an innocent, and I was a debauched rake. I think it was inevitable that it wouldn't work."

Isabella slid her hands across his bare shoulders. His skin was warm and firm, muscles solid beneath it. "You make yourself out to be such a bad man, but you're not. You took care of me from the night you met me, and you've never stopped. You take care of everyone you love."

Mac looked affronted. "I *am* a debauched rake, my darling. I've spent years cultivating my disreputable reputation. Remember how I taught you to take whiskey neat and sit on my lap and kiss me in front of my friends?" He deflated, the humor leaving him. "I wanted to make you bad like me, because I knew I'd never be good enough for you."

"You were always good enough for me," Isabella said, her heart in every word.

"Sweetheart, you wound me. A rake has his pride." Mac slid her hands from him and held them in his. "I'm busy baring my soul to you, Isabella. Let me continue."

"If you wish."

Mac took a deep breath, closed his eyes, and sank to his knees. The movement hurt him, she could tell from the way his grip tightened on her hands.

"Look at me." Mac spread his arms, still holding her hands so that their arms moved out to the sides together. "What do you see?"

Her blood heated. "A very handsome man I happen to be married to."

"A wasted man. I am nothing. I can make pictures come out of my hands when I'm not feeling sorry for myself. That is all there is, what you see here at your feet."

"No . . ."

Mac's voice went hard. "All there is, Isabella. Everything else—the joker, the wild bohemian, even the debauched rake—is what I've pasted on to keep the world from over-running me. But it's all fake. I use that façade to keep you from seeing and despising me."

She smiled. "If I believed that, I never would have married you."

"I didn't give you much bloody choice, did I? You were right to leave me, because I took what you gave me and threw it carelessly away. And now here I am, charging in and telling you that you'll take me back, whether you like it or not."

Mac released her, letting his hands fall to his sides. His eyes held undisguised fear and love, and a pain she'd never seen before. "But this time, it is your choice," he said. "If you don't want me back, I'll go. I'll take care of you as I did before, without obligation, without you having to bother with me and my obsession for you."

Obsession. Isabella had seen the paintings in Payne's hideaway in the rookery in Marylebone, the pictures of herself that had made her ill to look upon. They were destroyed now, but they'd been painted from obsession.

Her gaze slid to the painting Mac had just finished, and beyond that to the stack of the nude paintings he'd turned to the wall so that no servant who chanced up here would see them.

Mac had painted all of those pictures of her from love. Payne had painted from crazed jealousy and a strange need. There was a difference, and it was plain to see from the picture that now rested on Mac's easel.

Mac loved Isabella, truly loved *her*.

It was obvious in everything he did.

"Mac," she said in a quiet voice. "Being with you has always been my choice."

Mac looked up at her with such stark astonishment that her eyes brimmed with tears. "No, I forced the choice upon you," he said.

She smiled, feeling her mouth shake. "No. You never did. I chose."

Isabella touched Mac's face, loving the hardness of his jaw, the rough of his whiskers.

"Bloody hell," he whispered.

"Poor Mac. You are on your knees for nothing."

A sudden, rakish smile split his face. "Not for nothing, my sweet. I've decided to do it properly this time."

He *was* decadent, which made Isabella adore him. He was also half-naked with a gypsy scarf on his head, which made her crave him. She suddenly wanted more than anything to fall against him and have the pair of them land in a happy tangle on the floor.

"Do what properly?" she made herself ask.

"Court you. I'm supposed to be the model gentleman courting a lady, remember? Spilling out my heart in my studio is not the way."

"I like it," Isabella said. "It's perfect."

Mac's eyes darkened. "Do not tempt me to ravish you until I've done this properly. I've never done anything properly with you."

"Very well, if you must."

"Isabella Mackenzie." Mac took her hands again, still on his knees. "There is something important I would like to ask you."

Isabella's heart beat swiftly. "Yes?"

"I've asked some friends to help me. Will you walk with me over to the window?"

"As you wish."

It was difficult to be calm while he was being so mysterious. He rose with some difficulty, and Isabella pretended she didn't notice the soft grunt as he got to his feet. She followed him across the room to the window, whose curtains had been pulled back to let in the light.

Mac flung open the window, and early November air poured into the room. He leaned out and shouted, "Now!"

A band struck up a tune. Isabella peered around Mac and saw the little Salvation Army band, directed by the lady sergeant, pumping away enthusiastically. Next to it stood Cam and Daniel and Mac's club friends.

They were holding something. At Mac's bellow, they unrolled and held up a banner that read: "Will You Marry Me?—Again."

Isabella burst into tears. She turned around to find Mac next to her on one knee, something clutched in his hand.

"The first time I had no engagement ring," he was saying. "I made you wear one of my rings, remember? It was so big you had to hold it on." Mac opened his hand, which contained a thin gold ring encrusted with sapphires and one large diamond. "Marry me, Isabella Mackenzie. Make me the happiest man in the world."

"Yes," Isabella whispered, and then she turned and shouted it out of the window. "Yes!"

The crowd below cheered. Daniel whooped and punched the air, and Cam was laughing as he dropped the banner, drew out his flask of whiskey, and toasted them.

Mac got to his feet and crushed Isabella against him. "Thank you, my love."

"I love you," Isabella said, her heart in every word.

He nuzzled her. "Now, about that baby we were trying to conceive."

Isabella went hot with excitement. She'd kept the secret for a week now, wanting to make certain Mac was fully healed before she sprang the news on him. "I don't think it will be necessary to try any longer."

Mac jerked back, a frown on his face. "I don't under—" He stopped, not smiling, not angry, just still. "What exactly do you mean?"

"I mean what you suppose I mean."

The tears that flooded Mac's eyes were echoed by her own. "Oh, God." Mac clasped her face between his hands and pressed a hard kiss to her lips.

He released her, turned back to the window, and shouted out of it, "I'm going to be a father!"

Daniel started dancing around, using the banner like a matador's cape. Bertram Clark cupped his hands around his mouth. "Quick work, old man!"

Mac slammed down the window. He pointedly snapped the curtains across it, shutting off the view, though Isabella could still hear the happy sounds of the brass band.

Mac scooped her to him in strong, strong arms. "I love you, Isabella Mackenzie. You are my life."

She simply looked at him, beyond words.

They never made it to the bedroom. The paint-smeared gown and Mac's kilt came off, and he slipped the ring onto her finger as he kissed her on their way down to the floor.

Epilogue

Lord Roland F. Mackenzie and his wife announce the birth of a daughter, Eileen Louisa Mackenzie, in the small hours of the twenty-second of July, Anno Domini Eighteen Eighty-Two.

Mac slathered paint on the canvas, ignoring the screams echoing around him. His entire being was transfixed by the green and black shadows of the valley that stretched all the way to the loch in the distance.

Nearby, his wife, younger brother and sister-in-law, nephews, and two children fished, watched fishing, or ran about screaming. At least, Aimee ran about. Ian's little boy and Mac's little girl were old enough only to lie in their baskets waving their fists. All three were screaming, however.

Ian was in the painting, standing in a stream in a kilt and loose shirt, his fishing pole steady. Beth and Isabella were the picture's foreground, two ladies sitting on a picnic blanket, heads together. The two babies' baskets lay next to them. Daniel headed after Aimee, making her squeal in delight as he chased her. Dogs milled about, all five of them, loping from the ladies to Ian to Daniel and Aimee to Mac, and then starting all over again.

Mac painted with vigor, trying to capture the exact moment of shadow before the ever-changing Scottish sky turned the picture into something new. At last he gave a sigh of satisfaction, threw down the brush, and stretched his arms.

"Gracious, it's about time you finished," his lovely red-haired wife said. She'd left off her mourning black for her father about the same time their baby had been safely delivered. Today Isabella wore a gown the color of the summer sky, while Beth sat next to her in bright pink. Two flowers on a Scottish meadow. "I'm famished."

"We waited for luncheon for you," Beth said. She started setting out plates and cups that the cook at Kilmorgan had tucked into a very large picnic basket. "Ian, time for lunch!" she called.

Ian kept on fishing without turning around.

"I'll fetch him," Mac said. He swept up his daughter, Eileen Louisa, and gave her a sound kiss. The little girl stopped screaming and blinked at him.

Mac tucked Eileen into the crook of his arm and waded out to Ian. The stream was shallow here, burbling over rocks and forming deep pools where fish liked to hide.

"The ladies want their lunch," Mac said to him.

Ian didn't turn. His attention was fixed on the swirling water, watching the pattern the eddies made.

"Ian."

Ian pulled his attention away from the water and focused on Mac. Exactly on Mac, looking into Mac's eyes. Ian had become much better at that in the last year.

"The ladies want their lunch," Ian repeated in the exact

tone Mac had used. "Good. I'm hungry. You took a long time painting."

Mac shrugged. "I wanted to get it right."

Ian hauled in his line. He gazed a moment at Eileen before reaching out and carefully chucking her under the chin. He'd been learning how to do that too. Eileen kicked her feet and let out a burble of approval.

"You and Isabella have been happy?" Ian asked Mac as they started back.

"Since we've been married again, you mean?" Gordon had been ecstatic to reverse their separation, and Mac had made a festival of it at Kilmorgan, with guests and flowers and all the trimmings.

Ian frowned, waiting patiently for Mac to answer the question.

"Very well, my wise little brother," Mac said. "Yes. We are reconciled. We are happy. Ecstatically happy, especially of late."

He put his heart in every word. Throughout the past year, Mac had alternately worried himself to death over Isabella and been extremely excited about the coming baby. He'd nearly smothered Isabella with his protectiveness, he knew from her exasperated looks, but he was damned if he would let her go through losing another child. And he would never leave her alone again.

The day of Eileen's birth had been the most joyous of Mac's life. He'd entered Isabella's bedchamber to find his wife propped up in bed holding Eileen, smiling her triumph. Mac had wanted to paint her like that, a new, deeply happy mother with her babe in her arms, her red braid snaking over her shoulder like a rope of flame.

Isabella had been aghast, sure she looked a mess. To Mac, she'd never been more beautiful. Mac had taken up little Eileen and kissed her tiny forehead, thanking God for her and his wonderful wife.

"In fact," Mac went on, barely able to contain his delight. "Isabella told me this morning that child number two will be with us sometime next year."

He couldn't keep the wide smile off his face. He and Isabella had celebrated the happiness of that announcement quite thoroughly.

"I am supposed to say congratulations, aren't I?" Ian said, breaking Mac's thoughts. "Then, you are to say congratulations to me."

Mac raised his brows. "Oh really, old chap? You too?"

Ian nodded. "Beth also will have a child."

Mac laughed uproariously and clapped Ian on the shoulder. "Our timing is impeccable, brother."

"It's only odds," Ian said without changing expression. "We each enjoy going to bed with our wives, and we do it as often as we can. The probability of another conception, given the time since our first children were born, is high."

"Thank you for that analysis."

"You're welcome," Ian said in all seriousness, although Mac swore he saw a gleam of humor in his brother's eyes.

"What about you, Ian?" Mac asked. "I spilled my heart to you. Your turn. Are you happy?"

For answer, Ian shifted his gaze to Beth. At that moment, both ladies laughed. Isabella threw back her head, exposing her white throat, her red lips wide with her smile.

Likely the two ladies were making fun of their men. Not that Mac minded.

Beth lost her hat and screeched as one of the dogs gleefully grabbed it in his mouth and ran away. She leapt up and chased him.

Ian gave Mac a grin, his eyes lighting with more joy than Mac had ever seen in them. "Yes," Ian said. "I am happy." He turned and ran to help rescue Beth's hat.

Mac walked over to the blanket, bouncing Eileen in his

arms, and dropped next to Isabella, who was still laughing. "What is funny, my darling?"

"Highlanders and their legs."

Mac studied his sun-browned legs stretching out from his kilt. "What's wrong with our legs?"

"Nothing at all, Mac dear. Beth is thinking of writing an article on Scotsmen."

Mac watched Beth running after the dog, her skirts in her hands, Ian cutting the chase short by grabbing the dog's collar. Beside Mac, Ian's son dozed off in his basket.

"Really, what is wrong with our legs?" Mac repeated.

"Nothing at all." Isabella sent him a smoldering look. "I like to think of them wrapped around mine."

Mac covered Eileen's ears. "Really, my dear, you are unseemly."

"I'd like to be even more unseemly. Next time, perhaps we should picnic on our own."

"I could arrange that."

"I find it odd that being with child makes me so randy," Isabella said thoughtfully.

Mac wanted to laugh at her choice of words, but he heated under her smile. She was so beautiful sitting here with him, the sun on her brilliant hair, her green eyes like emeralds in shadow.

"I'll not argue with you," Mac said.

"Good." Isabella gave him a wicked wink and reached for Eileen. "Perhaps we can make a start while everyone is chasing the dogs."

Mac looked over at Ian, who was trying to persuade the dog to give up the hat. Daniel had caught Aimee and was tossing her in the air. Beth stood back and watched Ian, hands on hips, a loving smile on her face.

Mac wrapped one arm around Isabella and caught her lips with his. Between them, Eileen made happy noises.

"I love you, Mac Mackenzie," Isabella murmured.

"I love you, Lady Isabella."

"We had a scandalous marriage before," she said, eyes sparkling. "Perhaps we can make this one even more scandalous?"

Mac smiled into the next kiss, his entire being rejoicing. He breathed in the scent of her, warm from the sunshine, and the powdery sweetness of Eileen.

"My wicked little debutante," he said in a low voice. "We'll be as naughty as you like. All of society will swoon to behold our decadent ways."

Isabella slanted him a sinful smile. "I'm looking forward to it," she said.

Turn the page for a preview of the next
historical romance by Jennifer Ashley

The Many Sins of
Lord Cameron

Coming soon from Berkley Sensation!

Chapter 1

I saw Mrs. Chase slide that letter into Lord Cameron's pocket, I know I did. She did it almost under my nose. Bloody woman.

Ainsley Douglas sank to her knees in her ball dress and thrust her arms deep into Lord Cameron Mackenzie's armoire.

Why did it have to be Cameron Mackenzie, of all people? Did Mrs. Chase know? Ainsley's heart thrummed before she calmed it down. No, Phyllida Chase could not know. No one did. Cameron could not have told her, because it would have come 'round to Ainsley again with breathtaking speed, society gossip being what it was. Therefore, it stood to reason that Cameron had kept the tale to himself.

Ainsley felt only marginally better. The queen's letter hadn't been in the pockets of any of the coats in the dressing room. In the armoire, Ainsley found shirts neatly folded, collars stacked in collar boxes, cravats carefully separated with tissue paper. Rich cambric and silk and softest lawn met her fingers, costly fabrics for a rich man.

She pawed hastily through the garments, but nowhere did she find the letter tucked carelessly into a pocket or fallen between the shirts on the shelf. The valet had likely gone through his master's pockets and taken away any stray paper to return it to Lord Cameron or put it somewhere for safekeeping. Or Cameron had already found it and returned it to Phyllida, or perhaps he'd thought it female silliness and burned it. Ainsley prayed fast and hard that he had simply burned it.

Not that such a thing would completely solve Ainsley's dilemma. Phyllida, blast the woman, had more of the letters stashed away in her house in Edinburgh. Ainsley's assignment: Retrieve them at all costs.

The immediate cost was to her dove-gray ball dress, the first new gown she'd had in years that wasn't mourning black. Not to mention the cost to her knees, her back, and her sanity.

Sanity was further disturbed by the sound of the door opening behind her.

Ainsley froze. She backed out of the wardrobe and turned around, fully expecting Cameron's rather frightening Romany valet to be glaring down at her. Instead, the door blocked whoever had pushed it open, giving Ainsley a few more seconds to panic.

Hide. Where? The door to the dressing room lay across the length of the chamber, the armoire behind her too full for a young woman in a ball dress. Under the bed? No, she'd never dash across the carpet and wriggle beneath it in time.

The window with its full seat was two steps away. Ainsley dove for it, stuffed her skirts beneath her, and jerked the curtains closed. Just in time. Through the crack in the drapes, she saw Lord Cameron himself back into the room with Phyllida Chase, former maid of honor to the queen, hanging around his neck.

The sudden burn in Ainsley's heart took her by surprise. She'd known weeks ago that Phyllida had stuck her claws into Cameron Mackenzie—Isabella, his sister-in-law and Ainsley's great friend, had told her. Why should Ainsley mind if Phyllida pursued him? She was the sort of woman he preferred: lovely, experienced, uninterested in her husband. Likewise Cameron was the sort Phyllida liked: rich, handsome, not looking for a deep attachment. They suited each other well. What business was it of Ainsley's?

A lump formed in her throat as Lord Cameron shut the door with one hand and slid the other to the small of Phyllida's back. He scooped her to him, leaned down, and took her mouth in a leisurely kiss.

The lump in Ainsley's throat tightened. There was desire in that kiss, unashamed, unmistakable desire. Once, Ainsley had felt it. She remembered rippling heat softening her body, the point of fire of his kiss. It had been so long ago, but she remembered the imprint of his mouth on her lips, her skin, his hands so skilled. With effort, she banished the memories. She'd successfully managed to for six years; she could do it now.

Phyllida melted into Cameron with a hungry noise, and Ainsley rolled her eyes. She knew full well that *Mr.* Chase was still in the garden, following Isabella as she led the house party on a ramble through the gardens, the paths lit by paper lanterns under the midnight sky. Ainsley knew this because she'd slipped away from the party as they moved from ballroom to gardens, so that she could search Cameron's room.

They couldn't have let her search in peace, could they? No, the bothersome Phyllida could not stay away from her

Mackenzie male and had dragged him up here for a liaison. Selfish cow.

Cameron's coat slid to the floor. His waistcoat and shirt outlined the hard muscles of a man used to riding and training horses. He moved with ease for such a big man, comfortable with his large and strong body. He rode with the same kind of grace, and the horses under him responded to his slightest touch. The deep scar on his cheekbone made some ladies say his handsomeness was ruined, but Ainsley disagreed. The scar had never unnerved her, but his tallness had taken Ainsley's breath away when Isabella had introduced her six years ago, as had the way his gloved hand swallowed her smaller one. Cameron hadn't looked much interested in an old school friend of his sister-in-law's, but later . . . *Oh, that later.*

At the moment, his golden gaze was reserved for the slim, dark-haired beauty of Phyllida Chase. Ainsley happened to know that Phyllida kept her hair black with the help of a little dye, but she'd never say so. She would never be that petty. If she and Isabella had a good giggle over it, what harm was there in that?

Cameron's waistcoat came off, followed by his cravat and collar, giving Ainsley a fine view of his bare, damp throat.

She looked away, an ache in her chest. She wondered how long she would have to wait before attempting to slip away—surely once they were on the bed they'd be too engrossed in each other to notice her crawling for the door. She drew a breath, becoming more unhappy by the minute.

When she summoned the nerve to peek back through the drape, Phyllida's bodice was open, revealing a pretty corset over plump curves. Lord Cameron bent to kiss the bosom that welled over the corset cover, and Phyllida groaned in pleasure.

The vision came to Ainsley of Lord Cameron pressing his lips to *her* bosom. Hot breath burned her skin, hands traveled down her back to her buttocks. And then a kiss. A deep, hard kiss that awoke every single desire Ainsley had strived to suppress. She remembered the exact pressure of the kiss, the shape and taste of his mouth, the rough of his fingertips on her skin. She also remembered the icicle in her heart when he'd looked at her, and through her, the next day. Her own fault. She'd been young and allowed herself to be duped, and she'd compounded the problem by insulting him.

Phyllida's hand was under Cameron's kilt now. He moved to let her play, and the plaid inched upward. Cameron's strong thighs came into view, and Ainsley saw with shock that scars marked him from the back of his knees to the curve of his buttocks.

She couldn't stop the gasp that issued from her lips. They were deep, knotted gashes, old wounds that had long since closed. Good heavens, she hadn't seen *that*.

"Darling, did you hear something?" Phyllida asked.

"No." Cameron had a deep voice, that one word gravelly.

"I'm certain I heard a noise. Would you be a love and check that window?"

"Damn the window. It's probably one of the dogs."

"Darling, *please*." Her pouting tone was done to perfection. Cameron growled something, and then Ainsley heard his heavy tread.

Her heart pounded. There were two windows in the bedchamber, one on either side of it. The odds were one-to-one that Lord Cameron would go to the other window. Even bet, Ainsley's youngest brother Steven would say. Either Cameron would jerk back the curtain and reveal her or he would not. Steven didn't like even bets. Not enough variables to be interesting, he'd say.

That was because Steven wasn't sitting on a window seat waiting to be revealed to Lord Cameron and the woman who was blackmailing the Queen of England.

Lord Cameron's broad brown hands grasped the edges of the drapes in front of Ainsley and parted them a few inches.

He stopped. His golden gaze locked with hers, strong face stilling in anger.

Ainsley gazed back at him, the first time she'd met his eyes in six years. Now he looked at her fully, like a lion on a veld eyeing a gazelle. The gazelle in her wanted to run, run, run. The defiant tomboy from Miss Pringle's Academy, now a lofty lady-in-waiting, stared back at him in defiance.

Silence stretched between them. His large body blocked her from the room behind him, but he could easily betray her. Cameron owed her nothing, and once upon a time, she had rejected him under awkward and humiliating circumstances. That is, any other man would have been humiliated and furious; Cameron had simply dismissed her, uncaring. Later when he'd learned about the intrigue, he'd been ice-cold, and looking down at her now, he knew good and well she was here because of another intrigue. He could betray Ainsley now, hand her to Phyllida, be done with her and think it served her right.

Behind Cameron, Phyllida said, "What is it, darling? I saw you jump."

"Nothing," he said in a gruff voice. "A mouse."

"Oh, do kill it. I can't bear mice."

Cameron let his gaze tangle with Ainsley's while she struggled to breathe in her too-tight lacings. "I'll let it live," he said. "For now." Cameron jerked the curtains closed, shutting Ainsley back into her glass and velvet tent. "We should go down."

"Oh, why? We've just arrived."

"I saw too many people coming back into the house,

including your husband. We'll go down separately. I don't want to embarrass Beth and Isabella."

"Oh, very well." Phyllida didn't seem much put out, but then, she likely assumed she could hole up with Lord Cameron any time she wanted and enjoy his sinful touch.

For one moment, Ainsley experienced deep, bone-wrenching envy.

The two fell silent, no doubt restoring clothing, and then Phyllida said, "I'll speak with you later, darling."

Ainsley heard the door open, more muffled conversation, and then the door closed, and all was silent. She waited a few more heart-pounding minutes to make certain they'd gone before she flung back the draperies and scrambled out. She was across the room and reaching for the door handle when she heard a throat clear behind her.

Slowly, Ainsley turned around. Lord Cameron Mackenzie stood in the middle of the room in shirtsleeves and kilt, his golden gaze once more pinning her in place. He held up a key in his broad fingers.

"So tell me, Mrs. Douglas," he said in a deceptively soft voice, "what the devil are you doing in my bedchamber—this time?"

NEW FROM NATIONAL BESTSELLING AUTHOR

ALLYSON JAMES

Stormwalker

"*Stormwalker* boasts a colorful cast of characters,
a cool setting, and a twisty mystery!
A fresh new take on paranormal romance!"

—Emma Holly

Janet Begay is a Stormwalker, capable of wielding the raw elemental power of nature, a power that threatens to overwhelm her. Only her lover, Mick, is able to calm the storm within her—even as their passion reaches unimaginable heights of ecstasy.

But when an Arizona police chief's daughter is taken by a paranormal evil, they find themselves venturing where no human can survive alone—and only together can they overcome the greatest danger they've ever faced.

penguin.com

Enter the rich world of
historical romance
with Berkley Books.

Lynn Kurland

Patricia Potter

Betina Krahn

Jodi Thomas

Anne Gracie

Love is timeless.
penguin.com

M9G0907

Penguin Group (USA) Online

What will you be reading tomorrow?

Patricia Cornwell, Nora Roberts, Catherine Coulter,
Ken Follett, John Sandford, Clive Cussler,
Tom Clancy, Laurell K. Hamilton, Charlaine Harris,
J. R. Ward, W.E.B. Griffin, William Gibson,
Robin Cook, Brian Jacques, Stephen King,
Dean Koontz, Eric Jerome Dickey, Terry McMillan,
Sue Monk Kidd, Amy Tan, Jayne Ann Krentz,
Daniel Silva, Kate Jacobs...

You'll find them all at
penguin.com

*Read excerpts and newsletters,
find tour schedules and reading group guides,
and enter contests.*

Subscribe to Penguin Group (USA) newsletters
and get an exclusive inside look
at exciting new titles and the authors you love
long before everyone else does.

PENGUIN GROUP (USA)
penguin.com